SHADOW HOUSE

SHADOW HOUSE

MICHAEL ALLEGRETTO

Carroll & Graf Publishers, Inc.
New York

First Carroll & Graf edition June 1994

Allegretto, Michael.
    Shadow house / Michael Allegretto. — 1st Carroll & Graf ed.
        p.   cm.
    ISBN 0-7867-0070-X : $19.95 ($26.95 Can.)
    1. Man-woman relationships—Colorado—Fiction. 2. Women
detectives—Colorado—Fiction. 3. Mountain life—Colorado—Fiction.
I. Title.
    PS3551.L385S5   1994
813'.54—dc20   94-4671
                                                                   CIP

12-20-94

Carroll & Graf Publishers, Inc.
260 Fifth Avenue
New York, NY 10001

Manufactured in the United States of America

This is for Linda.

SHADOW HOUSE

1

Annie Honeycut blew into her hands and rubbed them together. The midnight air was colder than she expected. It had been months since she had been in the mountains at night, and she had forgotten how chilly it could get, even after a warm day. She zipped up her jacket, looped the camera strap over her shoulder, then shoved her hands in her jeans pockets.

Her car looked abandoned, parked alone before the inn. She briefly considered driving—it was at least a mile to her destination, a cold, dark mile. But she had already been thrown off the mansion's grounds twice that day, and her old yellow Mustang stood out like a warning sign.

So she hunched her shoulders and walked past her car, heading through the shadows toward the west end of town.

The sky was clear, filled with icy stars. A gibbous moon had just cleared the mountaintop to her left, adding to the pale illumination from the street lamps. There was no movement in the street or the shadowy yards. Tiny, tidy Victorian houses stood mutely behind their wrought-iron fences, staring at Annie with shaded windows. The only sound, save for the scuffle of her rubber soles on the uneven walk, was the occasional faint growl of a semitruck climbing the highway, far up the mountainside to her right.

Cold air began to work its way through her jacket, making her quicken her pace.

By the time she reached Main Street she was shivering. Her fingers and toes ached from the cold. She hurried across the wide, empty street, feeling exposed and vulnerable. Alpine Street tilted upward before her, lit by the moon.

She trudged up the hill toward the Owen mansion.

Only the upper story of the great house was visible, pale and insubstantial, rising like a specter behind the solid black hedge. The cupola capped the house like a head. It stared down at her with dark window-eyes.

Annie hesitated at the gateway in the hedge, shivering. She fought off a sense of dread, then passed through.

Moonlight painted the grounds white and black, smearing shadows from every tree and bush. The house was silent and still. The front porch yawned like a giant black maw. Annie half expected to see Karl the handyman emerge from it, pallid and stiff-legged as a corpse.

Moving away from the porch, she walked around to the side of the house, stepping only on the moonlit grass, avoiding the pitch-black shadows as carefully as if they were mine shafts. Now she stood at the base of the trellis, thick with vegetation. Her gaze followed it up to the roofline. It looked higher than it had during the day—impossibly high. And the distance from the top of the trellis to the cupola window, a modest-looking reach this afternoon, now appeared vast. There was something about the house that seemed more dangerous than any rock face she had ever ascended.

She began to have second thoughts.

Why climb up there and risk breaking her neck? She already had enough pictures of the house to fulfill her contract. What could possibly be gained? A shot inside the cupola, that's all, which as far as she knew had nothing to do with the long-ago murders in the house. A picture of a room. Terrific. And maybe not even that—the film in her camera was very sensitive, but it required *some* light. And a flash would be useless, merely reflected back by the window glass.

She fixed her gaze on the distant painted windows. From where she stood, they looked perfectly blank. But earlier that day she had studied them through a telephoto lens and found peepholes scratched in the paint. More, she had seen movement behind the holes. Someone was in the cupola.

Chills raced through her body like startled mice. She could sense someone up there now, watching her. Waiting for her.

Stop it, she told herself.

She refused to run away scared. If someone was up there— asleep—so much the better. She wanted an interior shot, and even a poorly lit picture of someone in bed, or even an *empty* bed, would be better than nothing at all.

Come on, do it. Ten more minutes, that's all it will take.

She pushed through the bushes to the trellis. Then she looped the camera strap over her head so that it crossed her chest like a bandolier. She started to climb, blindly working her hands and feet through the vegetation, seeking purchase on the wire trellis. The vines felt cold and alien to her touch. Leaves rustled about her, living things, pawing her face, clutching her clothing. For one horrifying moment she imagined them moving beneath her like serpents, and she nearly let go.

By the time she had climbed above the first-floor windows, she was in pain. The openings in the wire trellis were narrower than her feet, forcing her to rest her weight on her toes, causing cramps in the arches of her feet and her calf muscles. Her hands ached, and the cold wire bit painfully into her fingers.

She climbed on.

When she glanced to her right, she could see the town beyond the bordering hedge, a patchwork of pale light and shadow under the misshapen moon.

She continued to climb, finally pulling herself level with the second-story windows. Then she glanced down—a mistake. The ground seemed impossibly far below, as if she were peering into an abyss. Vertigo nearly overwhelmed her. She had climbed rock faces much higher than this. What was wrong with her? She squeezed her eyes closed and tried to ignore the height. And the pain. The fiery cramps that had begun in her fingers and toes now spread along her arms and legs.

Part of her mind screamed, *Don't be so damn stupid what the hell is the matter with you go back down.*

She climbed upward.

At last she reached the roofline.

She raised her head above the top of the trellis and breathed in cold night air, feeling as if she had just surfaced from deep under water. The roof was pitched steeply above her, much too steep to climb. To her left was the cupola, a squat, four-sided tower. The edge of its south-facing window was an arm's length away.

She held the trellis with one hand, then lifted the camera to free the strap from her shoulder. The camera slipped. She grabbed it awkwardly, accidentally hitting the shutter release.

The shutter's click was as loud as a gunshot, loud enough to wake everyone in the house, everyone on the adjacent street, everyone in *town.*

She froze, like a convict caught going over the wall. She held her breath and waited for lights and sirens. But the house remained dark and silent.

She got a grip on the camera, then leaned to her left, away from the trellis, terribly aware of the void below. At first she couldn't find the peephole. She leaned out farther, stretching until her face was near the window. And there it was—a silver-dollar-size opening scratched in the paint, so near the edge that it had been hidden by the window frame.

She leaned as far as she could, straining her right arm from fingers to shoulder, gripping the trellis with her fingertips and toes. Now she could peer in through the hole.

The interior of the cupola was a small, square room. It was barren, eerily lit by a spear of moonlight. There were four windows, one in each wall, but no door. In the center of the floor was a rectangular hole that gaped as black as a pit. And as Annie watched, trying to ignore the flames of pain in her arms and legs, something began to emerge from the hole.

It rose from the opening, as if the house were spewing forth a gigantic larva. The thing was enormous and rounded and white. It turned toward Annie, a pale naked creature, twisted and grotesque. It stared at her with an eye the size of a hen's egg.

Annie screamed and jerked away, dropping her camera, losing her foothold.

She fell.

She grabbed wildly at the trellis, snatching leaves, snapping vines, sliding, falling, dragging vines with her, fingers desperately clawing at the vegetation, seeking the wire trellis beneath. She half slid, half crashed down the side of the house until her foot caught in the wire, jolting her to a brief stop, instant relief, then immediate terror as her feeble handhold was broken and her body angled outward, pivoting away from the trellis, pulling her foot free from the wire. She fell to the lawn.

She landed on her back, slamming the breath from her lungs.

There was no pain. Only terror. That *thing* in the cupola was clambering down the stairs right now, scrambling for the front door, coming to get her.

She rolled onto her side, gasping for air, and instinctively reached for the camera. Gone. Now she remembered dropping it. Probably in the bushes.

Forget the camera. Run!

She rose to her hands and knees, fighting to regain her breath. Fear clawed at her. She had to get away. She had to tell people what was in the cupola, tell anyone who'd listen, tell *everyone.* But mostly she had to get away.

She staggered to her feet, praying that her legs could carry her across the grounds and through the gateway in the hedge. If she could make it out to the street, then . . .

Suddenly, she heard the thing behind her, moving swiftly through the shadows.

She turned to face it, strangling on a scream.

2

Nora Honeycut woke up Saturday morning feeling that something was wrong.

She rose quickly, disturbing her two cats, curled up at the foot of her bed. Wearing only her nightgown she padded barefoot through the small house, looking for the problem. But everything seemed in order. No doors or windows open. Oven off and furnace on. No flood of rusty water from the aging water heater. Still, the feeling persisted.

She knelt on the small rose-colored sofa and parted the front drapes with the back of her hand. Her two-year-old Volkswagen Rabbit was still at the curb where she had parked it last night after work. Not that she really expected it to be missing—auto theft was rare in Cedar Falls. But something sure felt wrong. And if it wasn't the cats or the house or the car, then what?

A bad dream, she thought and shrugged it off.

She started the coffee, then let out the cats, who had finally strolled into the kitchen.

As usual, Gypsy went out eagerly. She was a large gray shorthair who had wandered into the yard last year and hadn't yet decided to move on. Although Nora had no idea where Gypsy spent her days, she knew the big cat would return this evening.

Henry, on the other hand, took his time creeping out—sniffing

Nora's shoe, sniffing the doorstep, sniffing the air, and finally hustling out onto the back porch. She had gotten him years ago as a kitten, and he liked the comforts of home. He'd be scratching on the door in ten minutes, she knew, and he'd spend the rest of the day inside.

Nora took a quick shower, then toweled off in front of the mirror, leaning forward like a scout on the lookout for the enemies: wrinkles and gray hairs. She had a few of the former (*laugh lines,* she told herself), and as yet none of the latter. But as she pulled a brush through her neck-length black hair, she knew it was only a matter of time before the black would be streaked with gray. Not that thirty-six was over the hill.

It's not exactly adolescence, either, kiddo.

She examined herself in the mirror. Her stomach was still flat, her breasts were firm, and her thighs had not yet decided to take over the rest of her body. Of course, for the past few years, she had spent her lunch hours on Mondays, Wednesdays, and Fridays dancing up a sweat at a health club. Hey, a girl needs all the help she can get.

Nora put on pantyhose, a muted green skirt, an off-white blouse, a green-and-brown sweater, and soft, brown leather shoes with rubber soles—her work clothes.

After she let Henry in she filled four small bowls with food and water, two for Henry on the kitchen floor, and two for Gypsy outside on the back porch, just as she did every day. Then she fixed her usual breakfast—juice, cereal and milk, toast and coffee.

She slipped on a coat and locked the door on her way out.

It was a chilly, bright morning, the last Saturday in September. The giant maples and oaks that flanked the front walk were changing, showing off red and yellow and brown. A car drove by and honked, a neighbor from down the street. Nora waved.

She unlatched the gate and stepped through. There was no fence, merely a waist-high chain-link gate supported by a pair of metal posts that spanned the walk. The gate had been in place when she bought the house four years ago. As far as she knew, there had never been a fence. But she had left the gate standing—first as a joke, then as a conversation piece, and finally as tradition. Or maybe superstition. She never walked around it.

The drive to work was spectacular. Mature trees overhung the residential streets with brilliant displays of yellow and red. Flower beds and planters were bright with colors, and the lawns made a crisp green background.

Nora parked in the small lot beside Sunshine Florists and unlocked the heavy glass door. Entering the shop felt like pulling on an old, comfortable coat. She left the CLOSED sign turned out, but the door unlocked. The shop didn't officially open for another half hour, but if any customers wandered in this early, she wasn't about to turn them away.

The first things she checked were the glass-fronted coolers, one on either side of the shop. Temperature and humidity were both okay, and all the stock looked and smelled fresh.

In the back room she noticed a stack of mail on the work table. It had been delivered late yesterday, and she had been too busy to bother with it. She sorted through it now, mostly bills and advertisements. There were three envelopes, though, that looked as if they might contain checks, and she opened these first. She had a number of high-volume regular customers, churches and funeral parlors, to whom she extended a line of credit. Gratefully, they usually paid on time.

Nora smiled and thought, *My bosses.*

She remembered how she had felt when she first purchased the shop six years ago, that finally she'd be running a business her way and not taking orders from anyone. But, in effect, she now took orders from *hundreds* of bosses, her customers, each one telling her what to do, demanding to be pleased, and usually but not always paying her promptly. Still, the sense of accomplishment, of being in business for herself, made any hassles connected with it seem minor.

In a way, she had her ex-husband to thank for it. If he hadn't been such a bastard, she'd probably still be married to him, still working as an accountant.

She had graduated from Iowa State University with a master's degree in accounting and a B.S. in business administration, and she took the first job offered to her—junior member of an accounting firm in Des Moines. A year later she married Zachary Holt, her supervisor.

She knew going in that it was chancy to marry someone you worked with, let alone someone you worked *for*. But she was prepared to deal with that. What she hadn't counted on was his being an alcoholic.

After three years of drunken rages and physical abuse, she left him and moved back to Cedar Falls. The day after her divorce was final she changed her name from Holt back to Honeycut.

Jobs were scarce in Cedar Falls, but she felt comfortable there. Safe. Her parents were supportive of her and glad (despite the circumstances) that she had moved home. She was the only one of their three children available to them, so to speak. Annie was away at college in Colorado. And Robert was dead.

Nora found work as a bookkeeper in a nursery, and she began to learn the flower business.

She rarely dated. Not that she wasn't asked out. But Zachary Holt had put her off men. That is, getting involved with men. It would take time to get over her "three years in hell," as she came to think of her failed marriage.

After two years with the nursery, she found out about a small flower shop for sale. The married couple that owned the place were in their late sixties and ready to retire. In fact, in recent years, they had slacked off and let their business dwindle. Still, Nora saw potential. She had been considering going into business for herself, possibly as an accountant, but this seemed like a perfect opportunity. She obtained a small business loan—plus a modest loan from her parents—and she became the proud owner of Sunshine Florists.

Fortunately for her, Hattie Armbruster came with the shop.

Hattie had worked there for more than twenty years. Nora immediately promoted her to manager. And Hattie began to teach Nora the thousand and one details she knew about the business.

During the next few years, the business flourished, and Nora settled in. As a child she had dreamed of traveling to far-off places and doing exciting things. But those were only dreams. This was reality. And not so bad, really.

Besides, her dreams were being fulfilled—vicariously, at least—through her baby sister Annie.

She smiled, thinking of Annie, wondering how she was doing. It had been awhile since she had talked to her and—

The bell jangled over the front door. Hattie bustled in, a short, compact, pink-cheeked woman in her fifties, with iron-gray hair cut in a Peter Pan style.

"Good morning," she said, beaming. "Isn't it a wonderful day? The trees are positively brilliant! Makes you wonder why anyone would want to live anywhere else but Iowa."

Nora grinned. "You're probably right."

They spent the next half hour going over the orders for the following week. On Monday there was a funeral for which seven large floral arrangements had been ordered. Nora and Hattie would get started on them today. And Central High's homecoming was next Saturday, so they would be busy all week making corsages. They agreed that this was a job for Tara and Laurie.

The two young woman walked in together at nine. Nora put them to work, under Hattie's supervision, and she began to assemble one of the funeral wreaths.

Just before four her father called.

Nora could tell by his voice, by the way he said her name, that something was wrong, that something terrible had happened. Before he could say another word, she asked quickly, "Is Mom all right?"

"It's . . . Annie."

"Annie?" *Oh God please no.*

"Honey, your sister is dead."

"Oh, Dad, no. Oh my God. How did . . . what happened?"

"She was killed in a fall in Colorado," he said. "It was an accident. Please, honey, come home. Your mother needs you."

3

Nora left Hattie in charge of the shop and drove to her parents' house. The fall-colored trees, which should have glowed in the afternoon sun, looked dull and lifeless. Dead.

Annie is dead.

The words sounded unreal in Nora's mind. She clutched the steering wheel as she drove, dry-eyed, too dazed to cry. She recalled the ominous feeling she had early that morning. And was it merely a coincidence that she had been arranging a funeral display when her father called? Perhaps she had sensed Annie's death. For despite the difference in their ages, they had always shared a special bond, almost like twins.

Nora remembered when Annie had come into the world, a "happy surprise." Nora was ten, Robert was twelve, and their parents hadn't planned on another addition to the family. Of course, Annie immediately became the little princess of the house. They all had to work hard not to spoil her. She was quick and bright, and her presence seemed to magnify the love and cheerfulness that already existed in the family.

Annie loved her parents, but she adored Nora. And she absolutely worshipped Robert. She constantly tried to tag along after her big brother. He called her a "pest," but he often caved in, giving her a ride on his bike or letting her carry his baseball mitt to practice.

Annie was six when Robert was killed in a car accident.

Everyone in the family was devastated. Annie most of all. She changed. Before, she had been filled with an inner joy, but now she seethed with rage. She was moody and quick to anger. She disobeyed her parents and her teachers, adopting the attitude that she might as well do whatever she *felt* like doing, because at any moment death could come.

Nora was the only one able to stay close to Annie. She never chastised her little sister for the trouble she got into. It was more than understanding and forgiveness. It was an acceptance, almost a sanction. Because Nora, too, was enraged at the unfairness of the world to take away her only brother, and she felt that something must be done, some action must be taken to strike back.

And so she let Annie do it, because she could not.

Nora was sixteen at the time, and the sudden end of her brother's existence frightened her terribly. Life was fragile. You had to be careful.

She became overly cautious and apprehensive, withdrawn. She hid in books, studying harder than ever. She excelled in school, but her social life deteriorated. Her parents urged her to get out of the house more often, to have fun. She tried. But whenever she went out with friends, to a movie or bowling, she took Annie with her.

Meanwhile, Annie struggled through lower and middle grades, doing well in the few subjects that interested her and failing the rest. Despite her sparkling intelligence, she barely made it through high school. By then, Nora had graduated from college, married, and was nearing divorce. Although the two sisters were geographically separated during those years, they remained close, carrying on frequent phone conversations and exchanging lengthy letters.

By the time Nora left her husband and moved back to Cedar Falls, Annie was away at college in Colorado.

Two years later, while Nora was settling in to her comfortable, safe life operating the flower shop, Annie dropped out of college and began working as a free-lance photographer. She traveled throughout the states and abroad, taking assignments wherever she could find them, the more exotic the better, occasionally returning to Iowa, usually during the holidays.

She and Nora remained in constant contact. Nora shared her excitement, embraced it, as if she were going along for the ride.

But now Annie was dead.

Nora refused to think how that would eventually affect her. And worse, how it would affect her parents.

She steered into their driveway, painfully aware that she was the last one, their only child.

Her father let her in. She could see that he had been crying— his eyes, normally bright behind his spectacles, were unfocused and rimmed in red. And he seemed to have shrunk within his cardigan sweater and slacks. Nora put a word to his appearance: defeated.

She kissed his cheek. "Are you okay?"

He nodded sadly. "You're mother, though . . ."

"Where is she?"

"Baking."

Nora followed him through the living room, which seemed smaller than when she had visited last week, as if the walls had been pushed inward, shoving everything closer together—her father's reading chair, the overstuffed sofa with lace doilies on the arms, the fragile-legged tables, the lamps with pleated shades. Even the framed reproductions on the walls seemed crowded together.

The kitchen felt warm, perhaps too warm. Her mother was trimming the doughy crust from a pie.

"Oh, hi, honey," she said, with an agonizing smile. "I'm glad you're here. I'm just putting a pie in the oven. You like pumpkin, don't you?"

Pumpkin pie had been Annie's favorite. "Sure, Mom." Nora watched her mother slide the pie dish into the oven. Her skin looked as delicate and frail as old linen, and her white hair was as wispy as a cloud. She looked too old, Nora decided, much

older than her sixty-two years, as if she had aged a decade in
a day.

"You'll stay for dinner, won't you?"

Nora stepped toward her. "Mom . . ." Wanting to hold her, to
comfort her, to be comforted.

"I was going to bake a ham." There was a dazed look in her
eyes. "Is ham all right with you?"

Nora choked back a sob. She touched her mother's shoulder,
then hugged her lightly and kissed her forehead. "Sure, Mom,"
she said quietly. "That would be fine. Can I help you with—"

"No no no, you visit with your father. I'll join you in a little
while."

Nora hesitated, aware of the pleading in her mother's face.
Then she left her alone and sat with her father on the couch.

"She hasn't accepted it yet," he said softly. "She hasn't even
cried. I think she's in shock."

"Do you want me to call the doctor?"

"I . . . don't know. Should we?"

He looked worried and unsure of himself in a way he had
never been before. Nora felt sick to her stomach. *Annie oh Annie
why did you have to die?*

"Let's wait," she said. "She's dealing with it the best way
she can."

Her father nodded and gave her hand a squeeze.

"Dad, how did you find out?"

He heaved a sigh. "We got a call from a Sheriff Parmeter in
Idaho Springs, Colorado. He said the accident happened in a
small mountain town near there. Lewiston."

"In a town?" Nora had assumed that Annie had fallen while
rock climbing. Her sister had been an experienced climber, although she often pushed herself to the limit, usually to gain a
dramatic viewpoint for a photograph.

"She fell off a house," her father said.

"What?"

"The sheriff said she was climbing the trellis on the side of
the house and she slipped and fell and . . ." His voice caught,

and he looked quickly away. "The fall broke her neck. At least
. . . she died quickly."

Nora was frowning. "Why was she climbing on a house?"

"Apparently to take pictures. They found her camera nearby."

"God, I can't believe it." Some of Nora's grief had turned to
bewilderment. Annie could go up a rock face without a rope.
Nora had seen her pictures. "Was anyone with her?"

"I don't think so." He gave her a pained look. "To tell you
the truth, when the sheriff said Annie was dead my mind went
blank. He gave me some more details, I'm sure, but I was in a
daze. I told him I'd call him back. I have to make arrangements
to . . . to bring Annie home."

"Why don't you let me do that."

"No, I . . ." He shook his head.

"Really, Dad, let me help. I want to do it."

He nodded and spoke barely above a whisper, "Thank you. I
wrote down his number. I'll get it."

He left her alone on the couch. She could hear him talking
to her mother in the kitchen, their voices a low murmur. Her
eyes moved about the room and fell on a photograph on the end
table. It had been taken two years ago, when she was thirty-four
and Annie was twenty-four. They were smiling at the camera,
the sun in their faces, their parents' snow-covered yard in the
background. Except for their blue eyes, they hardly looked like
sisters. Annie—blond, perky, and bright. Nora—taller, dark
hair, serene.

Her father returned with a lined sheet of notepaper.

"If you'd rather not, I can—"

"No," she said "I want to talk to the sheriff."

Mostly, she wanted to know how her sister, an experienced
rock climber, could fall to her death in somebody's yard.

4

Nora's mother broke down while she was setting the table—she had set four places. She wept and moaned and clung to her husband and her last living child.

Nora was thankful. Holding in the grief was more painful than expressing it. She knew because that's what *she* was doing, trying to maintain an outward air of calm resignation, while inside she was crumbling, like a sand castle awash in the rising tide. But she had to be strong for her parents. Or at least appear so. She had to take care of them.

Eventually her mother's sobbing subsided, and she sat with her father in the living room. Nora used the kitchen phone to call Sheriff Parmeter in Idaho Springs. She asked about Annie.

"We have her at a funeral parlor here in town," he said. He gave Nora the name and suggested that she have a mortuary in Cedar Falls contact them and work out the arrangements for transportation. His tone was respectful, but matter-of-fact, as if he'd had similar conversations before. He explained how they had verified Annie's identity through the fingerprint files at the motor vehicle department. Then they had contacted the manager of her apartment building, who gave them her father's phone number.

"Can you tell me what happened?" Nora asked. "I mean, exactly how did she die?"

"As I explained to your father, your sister was climbing up the side of a house in Lewistown late last night and she apparently lost her balance and fell."

"She was climbing in the dark?"

"Apparently so. The caretaker of the house discovered her body early this morning. He notified the Lewiston chief of police, who called me immediately. I had the town doctor examine her, and he estimated she had been dead between three and six hours. Which meant she fell sometime after midnight."

"Then no one was with her at the time?"

"No."

"My father said you found her camera nearby."

"Yes. Apparently she was climbing up there to take pictures."

"Pictures of what?"

"I have no idea."

Nora felt disquieted, as if something were wrong. *Annie's dead, that's what's wrong.*

Parmeter said, "If you like, I can have her things shipped with the body—her camera and a few possessions we found at the inn where she was staying."

Nora wanted to press him for more details about the circumstances of Annie's death. But it seemed pointless. She said, "Yes, that would be fine. Thanks for all your help."

"If there's anything else you need, let me know. And you have my sympathy."

Nora phoned Hattie and asked her to close up the shop.

Hattie said, "I'm sorry for you, Nora. And for your parents."

"I know. Thank you."

Hattie sucked in her breath, trying not to cry. "I miss her already."

"So do I."

Nora stayed with her parents until early evening, all talk of dinner forgotten. When she got home Gypsy was lying in the twilight on the front stoop, and Henry was waiting for her inside. They followed her through the house, circling her, bumping her ankles.

She was stiff and tense, and her head hurt. She was at once
hungry and mildly nauseated. She opened the refrigerator, then
the cupboards, trying to decide what to eat, or even if she should.
It was a moment before she felt her shoulders heaving and her
body trembling, and a moment longer before she realized she
was crying.

She didn't know how long she stood sobbing at the kitchen
counter, but by the time she had stopped, the room was dark
and the cats were gone.

That night she dreamed of an unfamiliar house.

She stood at the end of a long, dark hallway. Annie hovered
at the other end, dressed in a white, diaphanous gown, beckoning
to her, calling her name, pleading for her to come. Nora desperately wanted to be at her sister's side, but she was terrified to
move. There was something between them, something unseen
in the dark, lying in wait. *Please help me*, Annie begged. Her
words chilled Nora to the bone. And then the shadows in the
hallway took shape, and something began to emerge, something
enormous, rising up between her and Annie, something hideous.

She awoke with her heart pounding.

Late Sunday afternoon, while the shadows lengthened and
most of their friends and neighbors settled down to dinner, Nora
and her parents stood on the tarmac of the Waterloo airport and
watched baggage handlers unload a simple wooden coffin from
a Great Lakes airliner, set it on a gurney, and roll it into the
rear maw of a hearse. Nora followed the hearse in a mini-funeral
procession along the five miles from the airport to the mortuary
in Cedar Falls.

While her parents met with the funeral director, Nora sat in
an outer room. She had Annie's green nylon overnight bag before
her. Besides the clothes Annie was wearing, this was the only
thing that had been shipped with the body. It held a change of
underwear, a nightshirt, a sweater, her purse, her makeup bag
. . . and her camera.

Nora noticed that the counter was on 2—one frame had been exposed.

Annie's last photograph, she thought.

On Monday morning Nora worked alone in the shop, with the front door locked and a CLOSED sign in the window. She couldn't remember if Annie had a preference in flowers, but she knew her favorite color was yellow. She made a large funeral display with every yellow rose that she had in the cooler—four and a half dozen.

That afternoon, she remembered the film in Annie's camera. She knew that if the photo was any good at all—or even if it wasn't—her parents would want a print. She dropped off the film canister at a custom photo lab, and requested two eight-by-ten prints, one for herself.

The funeral was held on Tuesday morning at her parents' church. Every pew was filled. The minister, an elderly man with rosy cheeks and a bald pate, spoke kindly of Annie, although Nora knew that her sister hadn't attended church since she was a teenager. Of course, neither had Nora. The minister's words sounded hollow to her, even though she knew him to be a man of sincerity and compassion. She found herself feeling sorry for him, which seemed to her utterly absurd.

But then, Annie being dead was absurd. She was indestructible, full of vigor and vitality. She should have outlived them all.

There was a long funeral procession to the cemetery, followed by a brief ceremony. Wind-scattered leaves danced about the tombstones. In the distance Nora saw a workman smoking a cigarette, leaning against a backhoe, waiting for everyone to leave.

Scores of mourners stopped by her parents' house. Her mother and a few close friends stayed in the kitchen and dished up coldcuts and cakes.

Nora reopened her shop on Wednesday. She and Hattie and the part-time girls were swamped, trying to catch up on orders.

Nora found it difficult to concentrate on the work, though. She was preoccupied with the coming weekend. Annie's affairs in Denver had to be tended to, and she had promised her parents that she would take care of everything.

She phoned the airlines that night and charged a round-trip plane ticket, scheduled to leave Saturday afternoon, October second—Great Lakes Airlines from Waterloo to Chicago, then United Airlines to Denver.

On Saturday morning, Nora packed a garment bag and a carry-on. Her next-door neighbors Mike and Linda had agreed to watch her house and feed her cats while she was away, and Linda had offered to drive her to the airport in Waterloo.

On the way out of town Nora remembered Annie's film.

She asked Linda to swing by the photo lab. When she opened the manila envelope and drew out the prints she felt both anticipation and sadness—for this was the last photograph Annie would ever take.

But the photo was a disappointment, an out-of-focus, black-and-white shot of God-knows-what, little more than a conglomeration of blotches of varying shades of gray. It was impossible to tell what the photo represented. Although in the lower left-hand corner there was a grouping of smudges that somewhat resembled a human form.

5

W illy, heavy and misshapen, climbed the stairs into the cupola.

It was a small, square, empty room with a wooden floor and sloping walls that rose to a high, tiny ceiling. There was a window in each wall, tall and narrow, the glass rounded at the top. The glass panes were covered with thick brown paint.

Cold daylight lanced through the tiny eye-holes that he had scratched in the panes.

Willy shuffled across the floor, humpbacked, hunched over, using his massive right arm as a crutch. His fingers were curled like an ape's, and his knuckles were thick with calluses. He shivered in the chill air and used his withered left arm to pull his robe about him like a cape. It was the only garment that fit his pale, grotesque form.

He stopped at the first window, as he always did, day after day, year after year, and turned his overly large right eye, his good one to the tiny peephole.

He peered down at the mountain valley and the town that it held—Lewiston—a long, slender wedge of steeply roofed houses, false-front stores, and tree-lined streets.

He studied the people, locals and strangers. His eyesight was astounding. He could recognize individuals as they emerged from their homes and walked the streets. And he could pick out the faces of strangers through the windshields of their vehicles as they entered the town.

The strangers he examined most carefully.

He searched for the One.

Willy shuffled to the window on his left. Few houses could be seen from there, for the town ended abruptly at the foot of a mountain. It rose like a green-and-brown wall, etched across the middle by the thin line of the highway. Willy examined every building, then crossed the floor to the opposite window. Few houses here, too. Still, he studied each one—yards, porches, windows. The One could be hiding anywhere.

Willy heard sounds below him in the great house.

He shuffled past the rear window and its view—a steep mountain face, very near, and a twisting road that was infrequently traveled.

More sounds from below.

Willy started down the stairs from the cupola.

It was time for his feeding.

6

Nora hated to admit it, but flying made her nervous.

She wasn't bothered by the roaring takeoff, which seemed almost like an amusement park ride. It was the hours-long, droning flight, where passengers relaxed with magazines or meals and flight attendants smiled pleasantly, all of them seemingly unaware that they were hurtling along at six hundred miles an hour, thirty thousand feet above solid ground, enclosed in nothing but a thin-skinned metal tube. Logic told her that it was safer to fly than to drive, but she also knew that if anything should go wrong up there, she'd be completely powerless to save herself. In effect, she was putting her life in other people's hands.

Whenever she flew, which was infrequently, she thought of the old joke about a man terrified of flying. His psychiatrist tells him, "There's no use worrying about dying in an airplane crash, because whether you fly or not, when it's your time to go, it's your time to go."

The man responds, "Yes, but what if it's the *pilot's* time to go?"

When the plane banked for its final descent, Nora got a sweeping view of the Denver suburban sprawl, a flat sea of rooftops and trees, partially obscured by a thin brown cloud. Only the tops of the clustered downtown buildings shined clearly through. To the west, the city spread to the foot of the Rocky Mountains. The mountains in which Annie had died.

Nora walked for what seemed like a mile to claim her baggage; then she took a taxi to Annie's apartment.

She had been to Denver once before, years ago, before Annie was born. Her parents took her and Robert on a road trip, driving across the plains of Nebraska and eastern Colorado, through Denver, and into the mountains. It was a great adventure for her, and she loved it. The mountains were so alien, so different from anything she had experienced. They had seemed mysterious and primeval. Eternal.

She stared out now at the passing houses and trees, bright in the afternoon sun. She could occasionally glimpse the tops of the taller downtown buildings, which she was certain had not been there during her childhood visit. The mountains, though, were not in sight.

"Which direction is west?" she asked the cabbie.

"Straight ahead."

She leaned forward, trying to peer through the windshield.

"If you're looking for the mountains," he said, "forget it."

"Why?"

"Too much smog."

Annie's apartment was in an unassuming, three-story brown brick building on Logan Street, near the downtown area. It was an older part of the city, where mature, yellow-leaved elms were crowded on all sides by brick and asphalt and concrete. Nora paid the cabdriver, then carried her bags up the concrete steps and through the front entrance. She stood in the small vestibule, sorting through Annie's keys. On second thought, she buzzed for the manager.

He was a middle-aged, paunchy man, and he was still saddened by Annie's death.

"I was shocked when I heard," he said, as he carried Nora's

bag up the stairs. There was no elevator. "The police told me they would notify her family. I've been keeping her mail."

When they reached the third-floor landing, Nora's heart was pounding, and she was short of breath. She smiled weakly at the manager. "I thought I was in better condition."

"It's the altitude. Takes a few days to get used to it."

He unlocked the door and set Nora's bags inside.

"When your sister moved in," he said, "she paid an extra month's rent and a security deposit. We can work out the refund whenever you vacate the apartment. The furniture came with the place, but everything else is hers. Yours, I mean. I, ah, I'm really sorry about Annie. She was a nice girl. You have my sympathy."

She had heard that phrase a hundred times during the past week, and although she knew that people were being kind and that they truly wished her well, she had to fight off cynicism. What good was sympathy? Would it bring back Annie?

"Thank you," she said, and closed the door after him.

The small living room contained a sofa bed, a stuffed chair, and a pair of end tables and lamps, a TV set, and a bookcase. There were few personal touches, few decorations—a print on the wall, a couple of plants sorely in need of water by the window. It looked as if Annie had recently moved in, when in fact she had lived here well over a year. But Nora knew that Annie had never been a homebody. This was a place to stay when she was in town, a place to store her clothes.

Nora carried her bags through the living room, around the end of the kitchen counter that served as a room divider, and into the bedroom.

There was a more intimate feeling here than in the living room. A stuffed bear nestled in the pillows at the head of the bed. More stuffed animals congregated on the floor in the corner and on the room's only chair. A skirt and sweater were laid out on the foot of the bed, as if Annie had planned to wear them next.

Nora laid her bags on the bed. She felt like an intruder. She unpacked and hung up her clothes in the closet, gently pushing

Annie's things aside to make room. During the next few days she knew she'd have to sort through everything—but she wasn't prepared to start yet. It was too depressing, too final. She'd work her way up to it. First she'd need to get boxes and packing tape. And she needed to get Annie's car.

The phone hung on the kitchen wall above an answering machine, its red light blinking madly. Nora asked the long-distance operator for the number of the Lewiston police department.

A man answered, "Chief Fellows."

Nora introduced herself as Annie Honeycut's sister, thanked the chief for his sympathy, then said, "I want to pick up Annie's car."

"Yes, ma'am. We've got it locked up safe and sound. Come up anytime."

"I'd like to do it tomorrow. That is, if I can get a bus ride."

"Well, the bus runs every day, but I'm afraid it doesn't stop in Lewiston."

"Oh."

"Tell you what, though. You take it to Idaho Springs, and I'll meet you there."

"Thank you. You're very kind."

"No problem. See you tomorrow."

After she hung up, she stared at the light blinking on Annie's machine. Six messages. She hesitated, then pushed the playback button. It was a practical matter—she *had* to listen to Annie's calls in order to deal with all her affairs. Still, she felt as if she were eavesdropping.

"Hi, it's me." A man's voice. "Just checked in the hotel. Seattle seems nice, but conventions are always a pain in the ass. Talk to you later. Love you."

There were four more messages from the same man, telling Annie he was sorry he kept missing her, saying he'd see her "next week" when he got back to Denver.

Annie's boyfriend, she thought, *and he doesn't know she's dead.*

There was one other message. "Hello, Annie, this is Susan with Premier. We need to talk about your remaining photos. The publication date of Brickman's book has been pushed up, so we're in a bit of a rush. Call me at two one two . . ."

Nora wrote down the area code and number. She dialed it at once, and when there was no answer, she jotted down a reminder to call back Monday. She didn't know how Annie's death would affect the "publication date," and frankly, she wasn't too concerned. That was a business problem that would be dealt with by others.

The male caller, though, was a different matter. From his tone, Nora could tell that he and Annie were more than just casual friends. She dreaded that he'd call while she was there. *Sorry, Annie's not here. She's dead.*

A knock on the door—the apartment manager with a bundle of mail.

Nora sat at the kitchen counter and sorted through it, most of it junk. There were three bills: telephone, utilities, and a custom photo lab—all of which she opened and set aside. And there was a greeting card, addressed to Annie in a firm hand. There was no return address, but it was postmarked SEATTLE, WA.

She hesitated, then slit open the card.

It showed a pair of cartoon bears, hugging, with a suitcase beside them on the ground. Inside was printed, "I miss you already." It was signed "Thomas."

No doubt this was the man who had left the messages. Annie's latest love. Nora wondered idly how long they had been together. It had been some months since she and Annie had discussed each others' lovelife (not that Nora had much to discuss), and Annie had been "between relationships," as she liked to describe it. Obviously, she had met Thomas since then.

Nora had always envied Annie's ability to get close to people so quickly. Annie was braver than she, stronger, more willing to take risks. If she met a man that she liked, she was ready to jump into a relationship with both feet.

Nora was the opposite. She would test the waters of a possible relationship carefully, holding back, analyzing, examining at length. The problem was, she usually took so much time that before she got her feet wet the water had turned cool. She knew a lot of it had to do with her first marriage. She would *not* get into another situation like that—being yelled at, being hit.

Of course, she knew that not all men were like her ex-husband, in fact most of them weren't. Probably. The point was you could never know for certain until you immersed yourself in a relationship. You had to take the plunge. Since her divorce, she hadn't been willing to do that. She had been content to go out occasionally with a few male acquaintances, never letting things get too serious. Sometimes a blind date. Rarely sex. And truly, she hadn't felt the need for a meaningful relationship. Or perhaps she hadn't allowed herself to feel the need. In any case, she had been content to have her business and her few friends and her parents.

And Annie.

Nora tossed the junk mail in the paper sack that served as a wastebasket under the sink. Then she checked the refrigerator and cupboards for food. There wasn't much. She made a sandwich with stale bread and lunch meat near its expiration date. She sniffed the lone carton of milk, poured it down the drain, then heated water for tea.

After she ate, she browsed through the apartment, mentally cataloguing items, trying to divide them into three categories: things she'd ship home, things she'd take home in Annie's car, and things she'd give to Goodwill.

Then she came across Annie's portfolios stacked beside the bookcase in the living room. She spent the rest of the evening looking at photographs—mountain scenes, cityscapes, exotic places with palm trees and curious-looking animals. All the places Annie had visited in her short lifetime. All the places that Nora would probably never see. And the people Annie had met—children, elderly couples, cowboys, businessmen, dancers, waitresses, construction workers—all of them captured by Annie's camera at a telling moment of joy, triumph, anger, tragedy.

Nora slept that night on the couch. The idea of sleeping in Annie's bed seemed too intrusive.

She dreamed again of the unfamiliar house and the dark hall-way. Annie stood at the far end, dressed in white, beckoning to her. Nora felt deathly afraid, but she started forward, wanting to be with her sister. Then something intervened, rising up from the shadows in the hallway. Something horrible.

7

At noon on Sunday Nora took a taxi downtown to the bus depot, then boarded a Greyhound bound for Idaho Springs and points west. The bus carried her out of the suburban sprawl via Sixth Avenue. A few miles later it swung up and around the ramp onto I-70 and headed into the foothills.

The day was crisp and sunny, the sky a hard blue above the steep hills. Most of the slopes were thick with evergreen trees, but a few were rocky and barren. That is, mostly barren. Nora spotted scraggly vegetation sprouting from the very rocks, like alien plant life that had no need for soil.

The bus topped a rise in the road, and Nora was presented with a sweeping view of gray, misty peaks. The mountains looked impossibly rugged and uninviting, and she knew that Lewiston lay within them. Then the bus dipped down between slopes, and the high peaks were obliterated by nearby hills.

Nora began to feel a pressure in her ears. She knew the bus had been steadily climbing, gaining altitude, even though the highway rose and fell. She tried to guess how much higher she had climbed since leaving the mile-high elevation of Denver. Two thousand feet? Maybe three. She swallowed once, and her ears popped, relieving the pressure.

The bus raced toward a sheer mountain face, then plunged into a long, lighted tunnel. When it emerged from the other end, the hills had become mountains. Nora began to see small clusters of aspens, flaunting their yellow leaves amid the sober pines. And there were occasional barren spots high up on the mountainsides, fan-shaped mounds of sickly yellow and brown— mine tailings, century-old reminders of the long dead boomtown days of silver and gold.

The bus left the highway and entered Idaho Springs.

The town was a few miles long, but quite narrow, shaped by the deep mountain valley. Nora saw a number of brick buildings and Victorian homes, all dating from the last century. But there were also many newer structures: ranch-style houses, restaurants, service stations, a high school, a supermarket—all apparently de- signed for the working-class residents rather than for tourists.

The bus stopped in front of a café on the main street. Nora climbed out, the only passenger to disembark.

The air was noticeably cooler here than in Denver, making Nora wish she had worn pants and a sweater instead of a skirt and blouse. At least she had a coat. She slipped it on as the bus growled away in a fog of exhaust. Then she looked around for the bus depot. Cars were parked bumper to bumper along the street, and a few pedestrians passed her by on the sidewalk. She was about to ask someone for directions when she heard:

"Excuse me, Miss Honeycut?"

The large man standing in the café's doorway was in his mid- forties, Nora guessed, and more than a few pounds overweight. He was decked out in spotless khaki pants and shirt and pointed- toed cowboy boots. A wide black belt was slung under his ample gut, and his weathered, white Stetson hat was tipped back far enough to show his pale forehead. There was a gold-plated star over his heart and a pearl-handled Western-style revolver on his hip. A brass plate on his pocket identified him as R. FELLOWS—CHIEF OF POLICE.

"Yes?"

"Chief Fellows," he said, smiling, touching two fingers to his hat brim.

Nora sensed a casual confidence in him, as if he were a kindly uncle meeting his out-of-town niece. She relaxed for the first time since leaving Cedar Falls.

"Thank you for coming," she said. She glanced around. "I was looking for the bus depot."

"It's the café," he said with a grin. Then he held out his arm like an usher. "If you'll come this way. My car's right down the street."

He held her hand to help her step up into a dark blue four-wheel-drive vehicle that rested on fat, oversize tires. She saw a light bar on the roof and a gold star on the door above the words LEWISTON POLICE. Fellows gunned the engine, then chauffeured Nora out of town on I-70, heading deeper into the mountains.

After he had melded with the thin flow of highway traffic he said, "I know I said this before, but I truly mean it. You have my deepest sympathy."

"Thank you."

"Your sister's death was a terrible tragedy. Everyone in Lewiston felt it."

Nora was mildly surprised. "Was Annie well known in your town?"

"Well, no, that's not what I meant." Fellows explained that Lewiston was a small, quiet place, no more than two hundred souls, an old mining town, better preserved than most, a place for tourists to browse or skiers to stop on their way to or from the slopes. "Not much ever happens there," he said. "It's always a shock when someone dies."

"I see." Nora was still troubled by the details of Annie's death. She said, "Sheriff Parmeter told me that Annie fell while climbing up the side of a house to—"

"The Owen mansion, that's correct."

"—To shoot photographs."

"Apparently so, yes."

"At night."

Fellows nodded, driving with one hand.

"That seems odd, don't you think?"

"Not really," he said. "For some reason your sister was dead set on taking close-up pictures of the Owen mansion, and I think she was there at night so nobody would spot her. You see, she'd been warned off the grounds twice that day."

Nora stared at him. "Warned off? Sheriff Parmeter never told me that."

Fellows shrugged. "He probably didn't think it was important. And really, it had nothing to do with what happened later."

"Who gave her the warning?" Nora was disquieted by this news.

"Well, sometime around noon that day she knocked on the front door and asked Karl if she could photograph the house, inside and out."

"And Karl is . . . ?"

"Karl Gant, the caretaker. He's lived there with Miss Owen for years. Anyhow, he told your sister that the house and grounds were private property and if she wanted pictures she'd have to take them from the street. According to Karl, she became insistent, didn't want to take no for an answer, so he shut the door in her face."

Nora winced inwardly. She could imagine how Annie would have reacted to *that*.

"Well, a few minutes later Karl looked out the window, and there she was, standing in the yard, pointing her camera at the house. He probably overreacted, but he went storming out of the house, yelling at her to go away. Which she did."

"Is that all he did? Yell, I mean."

"Yes."

"You're certain?"

He glanced at her, then returned his eyes to the road. "I've known Karl Gant for years, and I know that he wouldn't hurt anybody. If he says he shouted at her and that's all, then that's all he did. You can believe it."

"I'm sorry," Nora said. "I wasn't trying to accuse him of anything."

Fellows nodded and said, "Anyway, a few hours after that, Karl came into town to pick up Miss Owen's medicine at the pharmacy. He stopped me on the street, and he was telling me the whole story, when he spots your sister's car going up the road toward the house. I'm telling you, he about threw a fit. I told him to settle down, I'd handle it. When I got to the mansion I found the car parked in front, so I started searching the grounds. Guess where I found her? Climbing the trellis up the side of the house. I could hardly believe it. I wouldn't have thought it possible for someone to crawl up that thing."

"Annie was an experienced climber," she said. "I have pictures of her . . ." Her voice trailed off, and she felt moisture push up from the bottom of her eyes. *That's all I have left,* she thought, *pictures.* She shook her head and looked away. "I'm sorry, I . . . It's still hard for me to believe that she's gone."

Fellows nodded.

"Please," she said, "finish what you were saying."

"Well, there's not much more to tell. When I came into the yard, she was about halfway up the trellis. She seemed embarrassed as hell that I'd caught her. After she climbed down, I asked her what she thought she was doing. She said she was trying to photograph a flower blossom on the trellis. Of course, I knew that was bullsh—, er, a fib."

"What do you suppose she wanted to photograph?"

"Beats me. But there weren't any flowers on the trellis."

"Do you think she was trying to get onto the roof for some reason?"

"It's possible. In any case, she shouldn't have been there. So I put a little scare into her, said she was trespassing and that I could take her to jail, fine her, and so on. She seemed truly sorry, so I let her go. I figured that would be the end of it." He shook his head sadly. "In a way, I feel responsible for her death."

"What do you mean?"

"Maybe I should have arrested her. If I had, she might still be alive."

Nora wondered if that were true. Annie had always been stubborn. It would take more than a slap on the wrist and a fine to keep her from doing something she set her mind to it.

What had she been so determined to photograph?

Fellows slowed the vehicle, and Nora saw the exit sign for Lewiston. She had dreaded this moment from the beginning— visiting the town where her little sister had died. The vehicle glided down the ramp, passing from bright sunlight into deep mountain shadow.

And suddenly, Nora's mouth was dry and her palms were sweaty. Her heart hammered in her chest. She felt overpowered by a premonition that something horrible lay just ahead.

Something deadly.

8

Victorian-era homes lined the streets of Lewiston. They were meticulously restored, displaying a variety of architectural styles. Gothic revival. Italianate. Queen Anne. French. The houses were fronted by tiny elegant lawns, brilliant clusters of mountain flowers, and spiked iron fences. Flagstone sidewalks, buckled in places by the roots of huge old elms, flanked either side of the narrow street.

Fellows drove slowly along Alpine Street. "We've got your sister's car over at Gunther's garage. Normally there's a charge for storage, but in this case—"

"Could I see where she died?" Nora asked suddenly. The words seemed to jump from her mouth.

Fellows glanced at her. "Of course. If you like."

She nodded, staring straight ahead. A sense of dread still enveloped her. But she felt an almost irresistible urge to visit the site of Annie's death. As if it were her duty. As if Annie wanted it.

Fellows stopped at the intersection of Alpine and Main Street. Obviously, this was the town's commercial center—a few blocks of century-old two-story brick buildings with large windows on the ground floor and tall, narrow windows upstairs. Nora saw signs for an art gallery, a clothing boutique, a silversmith. They all seemed to be open, which surprised her, since this was Sunday. But she guessed that the main source of income for the town was tourists. And, in fact, there were dozens of people strolling about the sidewalks, peering in windows.

"You can see the Owen mansion from here," Fellows said.

In the distance a cupola rose from the rooflines and treetops, looking out over the town like a watchtower.

Fellows eased the vehicle up Alpine Street, which rose gradually to meet the mountain half a dozen blocks away. The upper story of the house came into view above a towering evergreen hedge. The house's pale yellow paint and brown and white trim contrasted sharply with the dark mountainside behind it. Enormous blue-green pine trees stood beside the house in attendance.

Just before Alpine became a snaking road up the mountain, Fellows turned left on Silver and drove halfway down the block-long dead-end street. The Owen house was the only residence there. In effect, the last building in town. The mountain behind it rose up like a great protective wall.

Fellows steered off the weathered and broken asphalt pavement and parked on the dirt shoulder.

From there the house was completely hidden behind the massive hedge, which Nora assumed encircled the property. She saw a narrow break in it, a gateway.

Nora climbed out of the vehicle. No houses occupied the opposite side of the street, for the embankment dropped steeply
away. This afforded her an excellent view of the town, long and
narrow, defined by the valley. She could see tiny figures moving
along the streets below. It was very quiet, just a faint shushing,
like wind in the trees. But there was no breeze. The sound came
from cars and trucks on the highway, far to her left and high
above the town, heading toward the Continental Divide.

"This way," Fellows said.

He ushered her through the gateway in the hedge. They entered
the grounds—an acre or more of thick lawn, overgrown bushes, and
stately evergreen trees—and Nora got her first close-up view of the
perfectly restored house. It was a mixture of styles: French mansard
roof with Queen Anne–patterned shingles, Italianate windows, and
Greek Revival pediments. And the cupola, rising above it all.

Nora stared up at the cupola's dark windows . . . then she
realized that the glass was coated with dark brown paint. So, too,
were the windows along the house's upper story. She felt a chill
and pulled her coat close about her.

She turned to Fellows. "Why—"

"Around here," he said.

She took a last look at the painted windows, then followed him
around to the south side of the house. The yard was enormous, a
sea of ankle-deep grass with islands of giant pines and dense
bushes. All of it was bordered by the high, impenetrable hedge
and buried in deep mountain shadow.

"That's where she was climbing," Fellows said, pointing.

A three-foot-wide, vine-covered trellis clung to the side of the
house, rising from behind waist-high evergreen bushes and ascending to the roofline, about twenty-five feet overhead. A section near the top of the trellis was partially clear of vegetation,
exposing the heavy-gauge wire beneath.

Nora realized with a shock why the wire was visible. The vines
had been violently yanked free, and they hung down like greenish-
brown entrails.

"Apparently she fell from up there," Fellows said.

Nora tried to imagine what it must have felt like to tumble

down from that height. Suddenly she felt dizzy. She turned her back on the house, staring out at the grounds, fighting off nausea, blocking out the image of Annie plunging to her death.

"Karl found her right about there," Fellows said, but Nora wouldn't look. "The doctor and I got here a few minutes later and checked for vital signs, but she was already cold." He cleared his throat. "Sorry. I didn't mean to be so blunt."

"It'a all right," Nora said. She still had her back to the house, and she was staring across the sprawling yard. In an odd way, it seemed familiar—the placement of bushes and trees and the bordering hedge. It was as if she had been here before. But of course, that was impossible.

She turned toward Fellows and saw him looking up at the cupola. The corner of his lower lip was tucked between his teeth, giving him a fearful expression. Nora guessed that he, too, was imagining Annie's terrible fall. He caught her watching him, and his worried look vanished.

"I'd like to leave now," she said.

As they made their way toward the front yard, Nora was surprised to see a man standing near the corner of the house, watching them. He was in his sixties, she guessed, about six and a half feet tall—or he would be, if he weren't slouched over with age. Despite his years, he appeared formidable, with wide shoulders and large, powerful hands. His navy-blue cardigan sweater looked hand-knitted, and it hung on him like a drape. The toes of black, lace-up shoes poked out beneath his baggy, charcoal slacks.

"Howdy, Karl," Fellows said. "This here is Nora Honeycut. It was her sister who had the accident last week."

Karl looked briefly startled. Then he nodded, not quite meeting Nora's gaze. "I'm sorry for your loss," he mumbled. His eyes shifted from Fellows to the ground to the curtained window at his side. He was obviously nervous, anxious for them to leave.

"We were just on our way out," Fellows told him, then led Nora to the gateway in the hedge.

She stopped for a last look at the house. Karl was still standing in the yard. He was staring up at the cupola. Then he seemed to sense Nora watching him, and he turned to face her. She was too far away to clearly see his face, but she thought she read two emotions there—anger and fear. He turned away and strode toward the front porch.

Fellows was waiting, holding open the car door.

Nora asked, "Why are the windows painted?"

"The windows?"

"Yes. The ones on the second story and the cupola. They're covered with paint."

"Oh, that. Miss Owen closed off the top half of the house years ago. It costs quite a lot to heat a place that size during the winter, and there's only the two of them—Miss Owen and Karl."

"But why did they paint the windows?"

Fellows shrugged. "I really don't know."

9

They drove to Ed Gunther's garage, a few blocks off Main Street. It was a small, squat, brown-brick building fronted by a concrete apron and a pair of gasoline pumps. A yard adjoined it, surrounded by a tall, wooden fence. Before Fellows even stopped the vehicle the garage bay door rolled noisily up. A man came out wearing an olive-drab jumpsuit, a bright orange baseball cap, and a grizzled beard. He wiped his hands on a rag, hardly glancing at Nora and Fellows, and walked to the fence. He unlocked a padlock the size of his fist and swung open the gate.

Fellows drove in behind him.

The yard was a tightly packed cemetery for dead autos. Some of the rusting carcasses had been chopped apart, their fenders, bumpers, and windshields stacked in separate piles, like donor organs awaiting recipients. Annie's old yellow Mustang, battered as it was, looked fresh and alive compared to its surroundings.

When Fellows climbed out of the police vehicle, Gunther told him, "I gassed her up, like you told me, Chief. That'll be eleven dollars and—"

"Don't worry, Ed." He turned to Nora. "If there's anything I can do for you, you let me know."

"Thank you. I appreciate your help."

There was a faint odor inside the Mustang that reminded Nora of Annie. A cologne she had worn, perhaps. Or maybe she just imagined it.

The car wouldn't start at first, but after Nora pumped the gas pedal, the engine roared awake. There was a layer of dust covering the windshield, so she flipped on the wipers and worked the washer. No liquid squirted out, but the wipers cleared off a pair of reasonably clean fan-shaped openings. She backed slowly out of the yard into the street.

As she drove away she glanced in the rearview mirror.

Fellows and Gunther were standing by the open gate, staring after her.

Nora felt uneasy on the drive back to Denver. And it wasn't simply because of the car—although that was certainly part of it. She was accustomed to driving her Volkswagen, compact and tight-turning, and although Annie's Mustang wasn't the biggest car on the road, it certainly felt that way. The hood seemed to stretch before her for a city block. And the power was much more than she was used to, the engine growling at idle, roaring when she touched the gas pedal, and springing forward when she eased off the clutch.

But the car wasn't the main reason for her unease. She couldn't shake the feeling that she had been to the Owen house before. Not the house, exactly—the grounds. She wondered if she had visited a similar location in the past. Although nothing came to mind.

When Nora got to the city she drove around looking for a supermarket. She needed groceries for a day or two and cardboard boxes for packing Annie's things. The checkout clerk told her she could have all the boxes she could haul away from the rear of the store.

In the alley behind the building Nora unlocked the trunk, ready to fill it with boxes. But the small space was crammed with Annie's photo equipment—camera bags, a tripod, lights and light stands, and coils of extension cords. She relocked the trunk and jammed as many boxes as would fit in the back seat. Did Annie always haul around that much photo gear, she wondered, or had she packed it only for her trip to Lewiston?

Nora pulled out of the alley and realized she had only a vague idea of where she was in the city and not a clue how to get to Annie's apartment. She went back inside and asked the clerk for directions.

She trudged up two flights of stairs, a bag of groceries in one hand, a few empty boxes in the other. She was breathing hard from the climb—but not so hard as yesterday.

As she unlocked the door, the phone began ringing. She dropped the boxes inside, then hurried through to the kitchen, set the grocery sack on the counter, and answered the phone with a breathless, "Hello?"

"Hi, Annie, it's Susan."

"I'm sorry, I—"

"I hope you don't mind me calling you on a Sunday, but I'm anxious to hear about the remaining photos. We're right on deadline and unless—"

"Excuse me," Nora said. "I'm Annie's sister."

"Oh, I'm sorry. Here I am babbling on without even listening. My name is Susan Scheer, Annie's editor in New York. Is Annie there?"

"Annie is . . ." She still wasn't used to delivering the news. Maybe she never would be. "Annie died last week."

"She died? Dear God, what happened?"

"It was an accident. She fell from a house in the mountains west of Denver. Apparently, she was trying to take photographs."

"What?" the woman whispered, shocked. "Not the Owen mansion in Lewiston."

"Well, yes, how did you . . ."

"Annie was there on an assignment for us. Oh, my dear God."

Nora felt a flicker of anger. "My sister was climbing to the roof of that house in the dead of night," she said, accusation in her voice. "Are you the one who told her to go up there?"

"Good Lord, no." The woman sounded horrified. "We would never ask her to do anything like that. We always left the details of the shots entirely up to Annie. All we gave her was the location and a brief history of the site, so she could create whatever mood was called for."

"What mood did you want from the Owen house?" Nora still wanted to know why Annie was climbing the trellis.

"Eerie, spooky, something like that. I should explain. We're publishing a book on infamous locales in the rocky Mountains, sites of—my God, this sounds so gruesome now—sites of murders, massacres, gunfights, all sorts of violent deaths and, well, you probably don't want to hear about it."

"Please. I do."

"Well, the text is being written by a western historian, and we contracted with Annie to photograph the sites—old houses and buildings, ghost towns, failed mines, deserted Indian camps, abandoned pioneer settlements, whatever, mostly in Wyoming, Colorado, and New Mexico. It has turned into a rush job, so Annie was sending us the photos as she produced them. And I must say, they're quite good. She had to work with some bland-looking sites, and she made them appear stunning, even frightening, by using a variety of camera angles, unusual lighting, and so on. The Owen house was her last assignment. Oh, God. I'm sorry. I didn't mean it to sound that way."

"That's all right." Nora was thinking that Annie wouldn't have needed camera tricks for the Owen place—it already looked forbidding. "Why is the mansion in your book?"

"There were two murders there." She added hastily, "None of them recent. One occurred before the turn of the century, and the other about sixty years ago. The killers and the victims all were members of the Owen family."

"I see." This troubled Nora, although she couldn't explain why. Annie's death had been an accident, not murder. Everyone knew that. Still, it seemed like such a terrible coincidence that Annie had died at a murder site.

"Annie may have taken pictures of the house," Nora said. "I haven't yet looked through all her things. I just found her camera gear in the trunk of her car."

"Please don't worry about pictures. We can get by without them if we have to."

"Okay, but if I find anything, I'll send it to you."

Susan gave her the address in New York. She paused. "There's, ah, another matter I suppose we could deal with now. Annie has money coming to her. How would you like us to handle that?"

Nora asked her to make the check out to the estate of Annie Honeycut and mail it to her parents' address.

"Of course. And . . . I'm terribly sorry about Annie. You have my sympathies."

Outside, Nora searched through the camera bags in the trunk of Annie's car. She found dozens of unopened little yellow boxes of film and two small plastic canisters of exposed film. She hoped they contained photos of the Owen house—not for the sake of Annie's editor, but for her own. Perhaps she could find the reason why Annie had been on the trellis.

What difference does it make? she thought. *Annie's dead and nothing will bring her back.*

Still, she had to know.

She hauled the rest of the cardboard boxes upstairs, then looked through the bills she had opened yesterday. There it was: F-STOP—CUSTOM PHOTO LAB. The address was on the bill. She found a city map in the Yellow Pages, located the street, and tore the map from the book. Then she locked up the apartment and headed out.

10

The photo lab was in a modest brick building in a mostly residential neighborhood not far from Annie's apartment. Nora parked in front, went up the short walk, and turned the knob. Locked. She cupped her hands to the sides of her face and peered through the front window.

There was a man standing at the customer counter with his back to her. She rapped on the glass. He turned to face her— a young black man wearing rimless glasses, blue jeans, and a rugby shirt. She pointed to the front door. He shook his head and mouthed the words, "We're closed."

Of course, she thought, *it's Sunday.*

She had been so preoccupied she had forgotten. She turned and walked toward the car, wondering whether to search for an open lab today or simply return here tomorrow.

Then the front door opened behind her. The young man leaned out and asked, "Is Annie with you?"

Nora did a double take. She had never seen this man before in her life. How did—

He nodded toward the street. "Isn't that Annie Honeycut's car?"

"Oh. Oh, yes," Nora said. She went up the walk. "I'm Annie's sister. I brought some of her film to be developed, and I forgot today was Sunday."

43

"Hey, if it's a rush job for Annie, I'll do it right now. Come on in." He held out his hand. "Pleased to meet you, by the way. My name is Daniel."

Nora shook his hand and went inside. The place smelled faintly of chemicals. Except for the counter, there was little in the room—a couple of metal chairs, a table laden with photo magazines, a rack of brochures and booklets, a light table near the back doorway . . . and dozens of enlarged black-and-white photos tacked to the walls.

Daniel took the film canisters from Nora. "How is Annie? I haven't seen her for awhile."

There was no nice way to phrase it, no subtle way to lead in, no way to change the fact. Still, she'd never get used to saying it. "Annie is dead."

Daniel was shocked—he had done some work for Annie less than two weeks ago. Nora told him how Annie had died while photographing a mansion in Lewiston.

Daniel shook his head. "I still can't believe she's gone." He stared down at the film canisters in his hand. "Her last photos."

Her last except for one, Nora thought.

"This will take me an hour or so," Daniel said. "You can come back, or you're welcome to wait here."

"I'll wait."

An hour and a half later Daniel emerged from the back room with a pair of contact sheets and an envelope containing the negatives. Nora set aside her magazine and joined Daniel at the counter.

"Spooky-looking place," he said.

All the frames on both eight-by-ten sheets, a total of seventy-two exposures, featured the Owen house. The first few shots had been taken from the end of the block and showed only the cupola rising above the massive hedge. The next half dozen photos revealed the front of the mansion. Obviously, they had been taken from the grounds. Annie must have snapped them before Karl ran her off. The remainder of the frames on the first contact sheet and all the frames on the second had been taken from a high vantage point, as if Annie had climbed the mountain behind the property. There were wide-angle shots of the house and the town beyond, narrowly focused shots of the grounds and the house, and at least two dozen extreme close-ups of the cupola. That is, the painted windows of the cupola.

Apparently Annie had found them intriguing, although Nora couldn't see why. These prints, though, were too small to make out details.

"Do you have a magnifying glass?"

Daniel handed her a small, powerful loupe. Nora used it to closely examine the shots of the cupola's windows. Featureless. What had Annie seen there?

"If you like, I can make blowups."

Nora put down the magnifier. There was nothing more to see. "Thanks, but that won't be necessary. How much do I owe you for these?"

He held up his hand. "No charge. Think of it as a favor for Annie. For you."

"Thank you."

Daniel hesitated. "You know, Annie was a terrific person. And a hell of a photographer. We rent darkrooms here, and she frequently used them. She said she never lived in one place long enough to set up her own. And lots of times she asked me to develop and print her work, because, she said, I was better at it than she was." He smiled. "That wasn't true, though. She just didn't have the patience to stand still for an hour." His smile remained, but his eyes became sad. "I'm going to miss her."

Nora heated a can of minestrone for dinner. It wasn't yet six, but she was famished. And exhausted. She felt as if she had been driving all day. While she ate, she studied the contact sheets—seventy-two tiny pictures of the Owen mansion, nearly two dozen of them of the cupola.

What had caught Annie's eye?

Whatever it was hadn't shown up in the photos. Perhaps it didn't matter. She would mail the contact sheets and the negatives to Annie's editor in the morning. She wondered if she should also send the other photo, Annie's last. Despite its poor quality, the editor might want it.

Nora frowned, recalling that photograph.

She hadn't looked at it since yesterday morning on her ride to the Waterloo airport. *God, it seemed like days ago.* The print had appeared to be a collection of meaningless gray blotches, nothing more. But there was something about it, that is, her memory of it, that had changed.

Her flight bag was on the closet shelf in the bedroom. She took it down and got out the manila envelope containing the two identical prints—one for her, one for her parents, she remembered. She pulled one out. It still looked like a jumble of blotches in varying shades of gray. But the longer she studied the photo, the more it seemed to make sense. Then she rotated the print until the corners were pointed up and down and side to side—and it became clear.

A picture of the grounds beside the Owen mansion.

There were bushes and trees, a portion of the bordering hedge, even the town beyond, all captured by Annie's wide-angle lens.

Nora wasn't surprised that she hadn't understood the photo earlier, especially since she was unfamiliar with the scene. The picture was terribly out of focus—the street lights beyond the hedge were fuzzy globs of light, and the moonlight and shadows made the lawn look as hard and flat as concrete. Also, the viewpoint was odd—high up, looking down. And the angle was askew, tilting everything to the side.

She must've taken it from the top of the trellis, Nora thought, *and it's tilted because . . .*

Her blood froze. It struck her that Annie had tripped the shutter release as she fell from the trellis. She could almost hear her sister's scream emanating from the photo.

Nora knew she would never send this print to Annie's editor. She'd sooner destroy it than risk sensationalism. See the Amazing Photo! Taken during the Plunge of Death!

Staring at the print now, she had a revelation. This morning the grounds on the Owen mansion had looked familiar to her, and this picture was the reason. As blurred as it was, it exactly depicted the trees, the bushes, and the surrounding hedge. The image must have been stuck in her subconscious.

Although there was something that didn't fit.

She looked closer. She had noticed it yesterday when she first saw the photograph, but at the time it had been merely another portion of the overall confusion of blotches. Now it almost leapt at her from the corner of the print. An odd shape within the shadow of the hedge. A lighter area of gray, smooth and symmetrical. A human shape. Or nearly human—short and squat with an overly large head.

She frowned, trying to recall the grounds as she had seen them—majestic trees, heavy bushes, the towering hedge. Had there been a statue? A birdbath? Anything at all to account for this evenly proportioned shape?

No.

A chill crawled up her neck. *Is that a person?*

She frowned at the print. The symmetrical collection of gray blotches was near one corner of the photograph. It didn't take much imagination to see a torso, arms, and legs. The head, though, was much too large. Of course, that might be a result of the severe camera angle and the lack of focus. Whatever the case, the longer Nora stared at the gray splotch, the more it looked to her like a human being.

And if it was a person—a man—then he had been on the grounds when Annie fell. He had been right *there.*

Nora felt her throat constrict. *Now wait a minute. Think it through.*

Annie had gone to Lewiston to photograph the Owen mansion. She took a few shots from the street and a few more from inside the hedge, before Karl the caretaker kicked her out. She went back later, and Chief Fellows ran her off. Then she either climbed or drove up the mountain behind the house and used a telephoto lens to shoot nearly two rolls of film, much of it of the cupola's painted windows. She had become so obsessed with the cupola that she climbed up the trellis later that night for a close-up shot.

Then she fell.

Karl had found her body in the morning, hours later. He immediately summoned Chief Fellows, the town doctor, and Sheriff Parameter.

Then who is the man in the photo? Nora thought. *If he saw Annie fall—and he must have—why didn't he call the ambulance or the town doctor? Why didn't he do something? And why hasn't he come forward yet? He was a witness. He could at least tell the police what happened.*

Unless . . .

Unless he was responsible for Annie's death. The thought horrified her.

No, that can't be. Her death was an accident. Besides, why would anyone want to harm her? All she did was photograph the house. She climbed the trellis and accidentally fell. No one else was there. This shape on the photo is just a meaningless gray blotch.

She studied the photo again, trying to be objective, not allowing her imagination to see something that wasn't there. The distant town. The hedge. Trees and shadows. A squat, symmetrical shape.

Her stomach was as tight as a fist.

Without question, the shape was a man.

Later that night she phoned Cedar Falls to check on her cats—both fine, according to Linda. Then she called her parents. Her mother tried to speak cheerfully, but there was a deep sadness underlying her voice. It pierced Nora's heart like an icepick.

"How is the packing going?"

"Slower than I'd expected," Nora said. She had yet to pack a single item.

"Is there a problem?"

Someone was present when Annie died. "No, nothing like that. It will just take me a day or two more."

"Well, you let us know before you start driving back," she said, as if she could be there to watch over her little girl, her last living child.

"I will, Mom."

Nora sat on the couch for a long time, staring at flickering images on TV, seeing nothing, thinking of her parents, her brother, dead, her sister. Dead. She didn't realize she was crying until she felt warm drops run down her cheek and drip off her chin onto her hands, folded in her lap.

In the bathroom she splashed cold water on her face. Her knees were trembling. She patted her skin dry and stared at herself in the mirror above the sink. A stranger stared back, haggard and downcast, hair in disarray, mascara smudged.

She ran water for a bath, then changed her mind and pulled up the lever, sending water through the shower head. She stripped, leaving her clothes in a pile on the bathroom floor, then stepped into the tub, pulled the shower curtain closed, and stood under the hot needle-spray. Steam filled the room, and hot water pounded her body. But there was a cold knot inside her that the heat could not reach. She tried to empty her mind— or at least to fill it with familiar, safe thoughts: her house, her cats, the shop. But other images appeared. Annie's grave. The photographs of the cupola. The man-shape.

She shampooed her hair, digging her fingers into her scalp, massaging vigorously, trying to rub out the mental pictures.

She could not.

She wrapped up her hair like a turban with one of Annie's pale yellow bath towels, then dried herself with another towel and padded barefoot and naked to the bedroom. She hadn't thought to pack a robe and slippers, but Annie's fit her well enough.

She studied the photograph one last time. Everything in it seemed so clear now. The south grounds of the Owen house, taken from high up, and the gray and white town in the distance beyond the black wall of the hedge. Here were trees, and there bushes and shadows. Near the corner of the print a symmetrical shape, short and squat. Obviously a man. That is, if one discounted the overly large head.

Nora slept in Annie's bed, not willing to face another night on the lumpy, angular couch. She detected Annie's scent in the sheets and pillowcases. She could almost imagine her sister there with her. She fell asleep, comforted.

Her dreams, though, were disturbing.

Again she stood in a long, dark hallway. Annie was clad in white and floating at the far end, beckoning to her. Nora wanted to go forward, but fear kept her back. She sensed something hideous in the shadows before her. It moved in the dark, making a rustling sound.

Then the thing emerged.

Oddly, it was composed of gray and white blotches.

11

On Monday morning Nora phoned Hattie at the shop. They discussed a few orders that had just come in—a retirement banquet, a wedding. Nora said she'd try to be back in Cedar Falls by Wednesday. Hattie told her not to worry, everything was under control.

Perhaps in Cedar Falls, she thought, *but not here.*

She slid a copy of Annie's last photograph into her purse, locked the apartment, and walked downstairs to the Mustang. It started with a roar.

Before yesterday afternoon, Annie's death had been a source of immense grief and depression. But as upsetting as it was, it was something Nora could deal with, something she could eventually manage, even overcome. What she felt now, though, was more than grief. Ever since she had deciphered the photo, her insides had been twisted into knots.

Someone was there when Annie died. Someone saw it happen.

Nora had been over it in her head a hundred times, trying to understand why this man had chosen to remain silent. The only reason she could come up with, the only plausible explanation, was that he was afraid to have his presence revealed. And although there was no proof of intentional violence, a single word kept drifting in and out of Nora's mind.

Murder.

Nora knew she was pushing her speculations to a morbid extreme, that there was no *real* reason for her to believe that someone had murdered Annie. Still, she couldn't ignore the photograph. That was definitely a matter for the police.

The question was *which* police.

Nora had first considered taking the photograph to Chief Fellows. But Lewiston was a small town. The person in Annie's picture might be someone Fellows knew well, perhaps even a friend. If so, she wondered if Fellows could put friendship aside and uphold the law. Possibly. But even if he could be trusted, did he have the experience and the equipment to conduct a thorough criminal investigation? She doubted it.

Which left Sheriff Stanley Parmeter.

Nora jockeyed her way through the morning rush-hour traffic. When she finally reached the interstate she gave the Mustang its rein. It carried her eagerly into the mountains.

The morning was crisp and clear, but clouds were forming between the peaks ahead. By the time she made the turnoff into Idaho Springs the sky was overcast and gray.

Nora stopped at a service station, asked directions, then drove into the center of town. She parked near the courthouse, a two-story red brick building, which, according to the sign, had been erected as a public school a hundred yards ago. Another sign pointed the way around the side of the building to the sheriff's office.

The receptionist relayed Nora's request over the intercom, then directed her into an adjoining room.

Nora had spoken with Sheriff Parmeter on the phone a little over a week ago, discussing the disposition of Annie's body. She had formed a mental image of him by the sound of his voice—small and soft-spoken.

It didn't fit him.

He was in his mid-fifties, Nora guessed, tall and raw-boned, with a spotless khaki uniform and a callused handshake. His hair was thin, brushed straight back from a high forehead, giving prominence to his aquiline nose. He appraised Nora with cool blue eyes, and asked her to be seated in one of the straight-back wooden chairs before his desk.

"What can I do for you, Ms. Honeycut?"

His voice still doesn't fit him, she thought, *not even in person.* She said, "I've come to Colorado to settle my sister's affairs."

"That's always very trying. Can I be of some help?"

"I hope so. I . . ." Nora stopped, unsure. When she left the apartment she was certain that a mystery surrounded Annie's death and that justice must be done. Now, though, she felt as if she had just awakened from a dream, one whose convoluted logic had dissipated in the harsh morning light of reality. Of *course* Annie's death had been an accident. There was no reason to think otherwise. She had let her imagination run wild. She should apologize to Parmeter for wasting his time and get out of there right now.

Still, there was the photograph. . . .

"I have some new information about the death of my sister."

"Oh?"

"Maybe her death wasn't an accident."

"What do you mean?" Parmeter's eyes narrowed, giving him an intense look that was almost frightening.

Nora withdrew the photo and laid it on his desk. Parmeter lifted it carefully by the edges, as if it were still wet from the developing tray. He studied the print for a few moments, then raise his eyes to Nora.

"What am I looking at here?"

"Annie took that picture from the trellis of the house on the night she died. See there," she said, leaning over to point. "In the shadow of the hedge, that's a man standing there."

Parmeter laid down the print. "Where did you get this?"

"From the film in her camera. One frame had been exposed, and I had it developed. The point is, supposedly no one knew about her death until Karl Gant found her in the morning. But someone was in the yard when she fell. Right there." She tapped the glossy print.

Parmeter looked down at the photograph without touching it. Then he raised his eyebrows and shook his head. "I'll be honest with you, Ms. Honeycut, I'm damned if I can see a man in that picture."

"But right *there*. Look. His arms, his legs."

He squinted at the photo. He slowly shook his head. "I don't know. I suppose those gray blotches look *sort of* like a person. That is, if you ignore the size of what would have to be the head. And, of course, if that's what your mind was set on seeing."

He had spoken gently and without sarcasm. Still, Nora thought, *He's being kind to a screwball.*

Parmeter seemed to sense her embarrassment. He said, "Okay, for the sake of argument, let's say that is a man." He spread his hands, so what.

"Then he was there when Annie died," Nora said, "and he still hasn't come forward. Maybe because ... he killed her."

"Whoa, now." Parmeter sat back in his chair. "You're getting way ahead of yourself. First off, there was no sign of foul play at the scene of your sister's death. All the evidence shows that she fell from the trellis. And second, Doc Newby examined her and determined that the fall broke her neck. It's apparent even in the pictures."

"What pictures?"

He hesitated, and then he said soberly, "It's standard procedure to photograph the scene and the body."

"I want to see them," Nora blurted.

Again Parmeter hesitated. "I don't think that would be a good idea."

"I want to see those pictures." Her voice was tight, higher-pitched than usual, not her own. In truth, she didn't want to look at Annie in death. But she felt she must. Was it her duty? Or did she think Annie would do it if their situations were reversed?

"I have a right to see them," she said. "Annie was my sister."

"Yes, you have the right," Parmeter said slowly. "But those photos may not be how you want to remember your sister."

Nora held his gaze, but said nothing. Her fists were clenched tightly in her lap.

Parmeter sighed. "All right." He rose from the desk and walked to the rear of the room, out of Nora's sight. She kept her eyes focused on a faint cigarette burn on the edge of his desk. She heard him close a metal file cabinet, and a moment later he reached around her and placed a stack of eight-by-ten color photos before her on the desk.

"Do you want to examine them in private?" he asked quietly.

Nora shook her head. Parmeter sat down behind his desk. Nora leaned forward, letting her eyes fall on the first photo.

Annie lay sprawled on her back, her faded blue jeans and red ski parka in sharp contrast to the deep green lawn. One leg was bent awkwardly beneath her. The other one was stiff and straight, slightly off the ground. The heel of her white athletic shoe was caught in the evergreen bushes beside the house. Her head was twisted at an impossible angle, and her blond hair was splayed about as if she were under water. Her eyes and mouth were open, giving her a look of alarm.

Nora flipped through the dozen or so photos, which were blurred now by the moisture in her eyes. Annie's body was pictured from several angles, and a few shots had been taken from a distance to show the side of the house and the trellis.

Nora turned over the last photo and wiped her eyes with the back of her hand.

"I want you to understand that we don't take any death lightly," Parmeter said. "Even when it's obviously an accident. My deputies and I and the police in Lewiston made a thorough investigation of the scene."

"You didn't perform an autopsy," Nora said. She made it a statement, not an accusation.

"That's correct. But if there had been anything even remotely suspicious, I would've called in the Colorado Bureau of Investigation and transported your sister's body to Denver where a forensic specialist could do a postmortem." He paused. "In fact, if anything suspicious ever comes to light, we can *still* order an autopsy."

Nora looked at him.

"Although," he said, "exhuming a body can be more than a little traumatic for the surviving relatives. You and your parents. It's something to consider. Because frankly, I don't see anything here"—he tapped the photo that Annie had taken—"to warrant an autopsy."

"So you won't do *anything*?"

"What would you have me do?"

Nora opened her mouth, then closed it. She stared down at Annie's photo. Last night the images on the print had been obvious to her, but now they were merely fuzzy gray splotches.

Parmeter said, "Let's look at this from another angle." Nora thought he meant the photograph, but he said, "Did your sister know anyone in Lewiston?"

"No."

"Or have any enemies there?"

"Of course not, but—"

"Then why would anyone in town want to murder her?"

"Maybe . . ." She bit her lip.

"Let's hear it."

Nora met Parmeter's gaze. "Annie was being paid by a New York publisher to photograph that house. She was persistent about doing her job, maybe even obsessed. That's why she was climbing the trellis that night. But earlier in the day she had been run off the property, once by Karl and once by Chief Fellows."

"How do you know that?"

"Fellows told me. I was in Lewiston yesterday to get Annie's car, and I had Fellows show me where she died. Karl was there, in the yard. They both seemed, I don't know, nervous about something. They kept glancing at the house."

"Are you suggesting that someone murdered your sister, and Chief Fellows and Karl Gant are hiding him in the Owen house?"

"I . . . don't know." Nora shook her head and looked away. She felt like a fool. She stood abruptly, picking up the photo. "I'm sorry I wasted your time."

"Hold on a minute." Parmeter rose from his chair. "I can sympathize with you. Your sister's death was a terrible tragedy, and you want to be sure that no detail goes unexamined. May I have that, please." He took the photo from her. "I'll tell you what. I'll drive up to Lewiston today and talk to everyone involved, see if there's anything we may have overlooked."

"What if they're all in it together?" Nora said, and immediately regretted it.

Parmeter gave her a faint smile, not quite condescending. "If so, I'll find that out, too. In any case, I'll give you a call. Okay?"

Nora nodded good-bye and walked out, tight-lipped, feeling her anger stir. She guessed what Parmeter must think of her— a grief-stricken, paranoid woman who was letting her anguish affect her judgment.

What truly angered her, though, was the possibility that he might be right.

12

Willy licked the inside of the small glass jar until it gleamed in the dim light.

He set it on the tray with the others, then pawed through them to make certain he hadn't missed any. One left. He picked it up clumsily with his clublike right hand and sniffed. Banana. One of his favorites. Licking a dollop of purée from the jar, he recalled the last time he had eaten a *real* banana. Years ago.

Back then, Miss Owen and Karl would feed him. They would cut his food into small pieces and place it in his misshapen mouth. Often they stayed with him for awhile after he had eaten. He enjoyed their company.

But for the past few years Miss Owen had been too weak to climb the stairs. And since he wasn't allowed on the main floor, he rarely saw her. Occasionally Karl would carry her up, but it was a hardship for both of them.

Of course, he saw Karl frequently. Three times a day the tall old man would bring up a tray laden with open jars and leave it on the table in his room.

Karl apologized for feeding him this way, but lately Miss Owen had required more of his attention. This left little time for him to prepare Willy's meals and hand-feed him. The jars were an expediency. Willy didn't mind. Although he wished Karl could eat with him, just for the company.

He licked another dollop from the jar, savoring it.

And then an image came to mind, unbidden. A face in the window. The woman who had climbed the trellis. It had been many days ago, but the memory was vivid.

The first thing he had heard was a rustling sound outside the house. *On* the house. He had felt a surge of panic. Were they coming for him? Was it finally happening, just as they all had feared?

Then his fear gave way to anger—someone was invading their house. And then rage—was it the *One?* He clambered up to the cupola to look out his spy-holes. And he came face to face with the woman. She *saw* him

She must not be allowed to tell.

Later, Karl had calmed down and told him that everything was being taken care of. No one would know. There was nothing to worry about.

He was worried, though. Perhaps the woman had not acted on her own. What if she had been sent by the hated One?

Willy shut his eyes and pictured the One's face, every line distinct, every pore and hair burned into his mind. Hatred washed through him like effluvium from a sewer.

He closed his huge fist, shattering the jar, piercing his hand with shards of glass.

His roar echoed in the room.

Then he heard Karl hurrying up the stairs.

13

When Chief Roy Fellows returned from lunch, a sheriff's car was parked in front of the building.

The daily special from Mary's Café (meat loaf and macaroni salad) began to coagulate into an uncomfortable lump in his stomach. There were a dozen reason why the county sheriff might be in town, but Fellows had an uneasy feeling that it had to do with the Honeycut girl.

Stay calm, he told himself and walked into his office.

Sheriff Stanley Parmeter and Griff had their heads together over something on Griff's desk.

"I can't tell *what* it is," Griff said. He was Lewiston's lone patrolman and Fellows's only assistant, young and eager. He had a military haircut and weight lifter's arms, which stretched the fabric of his uniform to the tearing point.

"I'd like to take this over to the house," Parmeter said. Then he looked up and saw Fellows. "Howdy, Roy. Come here and take a look at this."

Fellows stepped between the two men and stared down at the photographic print on the desk. "What've you got?"

"Nora Honeycut brought this to me this morning," Parmeter said. "It was the only exposed print in her sister's camera, the one she had with her when she fell. It looks like it was taken from the top of the trellis."

"Oh?" Fellows's stomach muscles tightened around his cold, lumpy lunch. He and Karl and Doc Newby had been too preoccupied after the girl's death to think of searching the grounds for her camera. Parmeter had found it in the bushes. Thankfully, the sheriff hadn't considered developing the film—and really, there had been no reason to. Still, Fellows had wanted to destroy the film, just to be safe. But Parmeter had taken the camera with him and shipped it to Iowa with the body. And now, here was the developed film, come back to haunt him.

"Let me see that," Fellows said. He picked up the photo, expecting the worst. But it was a hodgepodge of grays and whites. "What the hell's it supposed to be?" he asked, masking his relief with a frown.

"According to Miss Honeycut," Parmeter said, pointing, "this is the town, this is a hedge, trees here and here, and this right here is a person."

Fellows's frown deepened. The harder he looked, the more the blotches seemed to take on a near-human form. Incredibly, poor focus and all, it resembled Willy. "Doesn't look like much of anything," he said.

"I agree, Chief," Griff put in

"I thought we might go up to the house and compare the picture with the yard, see how it fits."

"Sure thing, Stan," Fellows said with forced nonchalance. "I'll drive."

When the two men were seated in the police vehicle Fellows asked, "How do we know this picture came from the girl's camera?"

"Ms. Honeycut swore to it," Parmeter said.

"Hmm. And did she also swear it was taken on the night her sister fell?"

"Yes. Why, do you doubt her?"

"No reason to. Only . . ."

"What?"

"Nora Honeycut struck me as the excitable type, if you know what I mean. Ready to jump to conclusions."

"I suppose that's possible."

Fellows nodded and started the engine. "You bet it is."

They drove to the Owen mansion. The pale yellow paint reminded Fellows of old bones bleaching in the sun, and the windows were as dark and sunken as eye sockets in a skull. Fellows led Parmeter through the gateway in the hedge. The sky was overcast, but somehow the grounds looked shadowy. And it was cooler here than in town, making Fellows shiver. Or perhaps the chills came from knowing that Willy was watching them. He forced himself not to look up at the cupola. He fought to remain calm.

"I'd better tell Karl what we're doing," he said. "We don't want to upset Miss Owen."

Parmeter waited in the yard, and Fellows mounted the porch, his boot heels making hollow sounds. He rang the bell. A moment later Karl answered. Fellows told him in a low voice, "The sheriff's here to look around the grounds."

Karl's gaunt face registered alarm. He peered past Fellows and whispered hoarsely, "Why? What's wrong?"

"That damn girl's camera, that's what's wrong. She snapped a picture when she was on the trellis."

"A picture of *Willy*?"

"Keep your voice down. And take it easy, the picture's not that clear."

"But what if he wants to search the house?"

"He won't."

"But—"

"Just relax and stay inside," Fellows snapped.

Karl hesitated, then withdrew into the murky hall and closed the door. Fellows rejoined Parmeter in the yard.

"Miss Owen is sleeping, so we'll have to be quiet."

Parmeter nodded.

They walked around to the side of the house and stood near the bushes at the base of the trellis. Fellows's thoughts tumbled back to the morning a week and a half ago. A bead of sweat trickled down his side.

Karl had found the body early in the morning and phoned him in a panic. It had taken him only five minutes to get to the house. The old man was standing some distance from the dead girl, wringing his hands and glancing nervously about, as if he expected the townspeople to show up at any moment with torches and a lynching rope. In the dawn light Fellows could see that the girl's position was all wrong. Obviously, she hadn't died from a fall.

"What are we going to do?" Karl moaned. "What if there is an investigation."

"There won't be. Go in the house and call Doc Newby. Then call the sheriff."

After Karl had left, Fellows quickly rearranged the girl's arms and legs, even hooking one of her feet in the bushes.

Now he watched Parmeter's eyes move up the trellis. Large clumps of vines had been ripped away to expose the wire beneath, like the ribs of a wounded beast. He followed Parmeter's gaze along the roofline to the cupola. He held his breath.

"Have those windows always been painted over?" Parmeter asked.

"As far as I know."

Parmeter continued to stare up at the coupla's windows. Finally he lowered his eyes, turned his back on the house, and faced the yard. He held up the photograph, comparing it to the scene before him. Then he crossed the grounds and squatted down before the towering hedge, examining the grass.

Like an Indian, Fellows mused, *searching for signs of game.*

He walked over to him. "Find anything?"

"Not really." Parmeter stood up. "I was just trying to determine where *that* might be." He put his finger on the photograph, indicating the humanoid-shaped collection of blotches. I still can't decide if that's a person."

"Well, whatever it is, it would be right about where we're standing."

"I think so, too."

Fellows said casually, "My guess is her camera picked up a shadow from those tree limbs overhead. Or maybe moonlight reflected from the windows." He winced, thinking he may have said too much.

Parmeter pursed his lips and looked back toward the house, studying the upper floor and the cupola.

"And you know, even if it *was* a person," Fellows said with forced composure, "one thing's for sure. He or she didn't push Annie Honeycut off that trellis."

Parmeter nodded. "No question about that." He continued to stare at the windows. "Why do you suppose they're painted? The windows, I mean."

"To keep the sun out."

Parmeter looked at him

Fellows shrugged. "At least, that's what Karl told me. Miss Owen had him close off the top floor years ago."

Parmeter nodded. "Well, I guess I'm finished here."

Fellows led him across the grounds and through the gateway in the hedge. As they were climbing in the car, Fellows inadvertently glanced up at the cupola.

He could sense Willy watching.

14

When the phone rang at six thirty that evening Nora was tired and hungry.

After her brief visit with the sheriff in Idaho Springs, she had driven back to the apartment and spent the rest of the day sorting through Annie's clothes—pants, shirts, blouses, sweaters, skirts and dresses, shorts, halter tops, jackets, coats, ski apparel, shoes.... At first, she thought she'd ship most of it to her parents. But now she realized she'd only be burdening them with the ordeal of giving it away. So she had packed a dozen cardboard boxes, sealed them with tape, and labeled them GOODWILL.

There were several sweaters she decided to keep for herself. Although she was a full size larger than Annie, her sister had liked to wear her clothes baggy, and most everything would fit her. She also set aside Annie's silk scarves for her mother. And her mother would certainly want all of Annie's gold and silver jewelry, not that there was much, mostly rings and earrings.

Now she put down the roll of tape, brushed a strand of hair from her face with the back of her hand, and answered the phone. It was Sheriff Parmeter.

"I would have called earlier, but I was in court until six."

"That's all right," Nora said. She had been waiting anxiously all afternoon. "Did you go to Lewiston?"

"Yes."

He told her that he had interviewed Chief Fellows, Officer Griff Clayton, Dr. Everett Newby, and Karl Gant. He had also reread the reports, compared Annie's photograph to the grounds of the Owen house, and reexamined the photos of the scene and the body. In all, he had found nothing suspicious, nothing to indicate that Annie's death had been anything more than a tragic accident.

Nora had expected this, but she was far from satisfied.

"What about the man in Annie's photo?" she asked flatly. Her copy of the photograph lay before her on the kitchen counter. The man-shaped image near the hedge practically jumped out at her.

"I'm inclined to believe it's a shadow, not a person."

"It *is* a person." She heard the anger and frustration in her voice.

Parmeter said calmly, "Well, even if it is, that doesn't change the fact that your sister fell from the trellis and broke her neck. She wasn't pushed."

Nora couldn't argue with that. It seemed improbable that somebody had climbed up after Annie and thrown her off the trellis. And there were no windows near enough for anyone to reach out and push her. But if someone had been on the grounds and seen her fall, why hadn't they come forward?

"What if . . . what if she didn't die from the fall? What if whoever was in the yard killed her *after* she fell?"

"There's no evidence of that."

"How can you be so certain? There was no autopsy."

Parmeter sighed. "Doc Newby is more than qualified to make that judgment. He says your sister's neck was broken in the fall, and there were no other marks on her body."

"You can't just leave it at that."

"Yes, Ms. Honeycut, I can. I will."

"No," she said loudly, surprising herself. A tiny voice in her head nagged her to not let this go, not yet. "This morning you mentioned the Colorado Bureau of Investigation. Why don't you call them in? Perhaps they're more experienced to investigate this."

"As I explained before, there's no reason for me to contact them."

"Then what if *I* did?"

Parmeter sighed again. "Of course, that's up to you. But they rarely respond to inquiries by the public."

"So you're saying that *sometimes*—"

"Ms. Honeycut, the first thing they would do is call me, and I'd give them every bit of information I've given you. And all of it points to the fact that your sister's death was an accident."

Nora said nothing.

Parmeter continued, his tone gentle, "It's not uncommon in this type of situation for friends or family of the deceased to want a detailed investigation. When the death of their loved one is sudden and unexpected, they refuse to believe that the cause could be insignificant. But the sad fact is that's often the case."

He paused, as if waiting for Nora to respond. When she did not, he said, "I'm truly sorry for your loss. If I can be of further assistance, please call."

Nora hung up.

She felt torn apart inside. Part of her wanted to believe that Parmeter was right, that Annie's death had been simply an accident, something she must accept and live with. But another part insisted that there was more to it.

Is it only the photo?

She studied the black-and-white print on the kitchen counter. Maybe Parmeter was right about that, too—the gray splotches might be shadows, not a man. And even if it was a person, that didn't necessarily mean Annie's death was anything more than an accident.

But it wasn't just the photo, she realized now. And, in fact, she had mentioned it to Parmeter—Chief Fellows and Karl Gant had both been uneasy at the Owen house.

Nora frowned, thinking back, trying to remember exactly how Karl had acted when she had seen him on the grounds. He had appeared unnerved by her presence, as if he could hardly wait for her to leave. Understandable, perhaps, given that her sister had died in his yard. But then she had caught him staring at the cupola. And when he turned toward her his face had registered fear and anger. The anger, perhaps, she could understand—she had been intruding on his privacy.

But what was he afraid of?

Then there was Chief Fellows. She had seen him glancing nervously at the upper story. There had been a brief flicker of fear in his eyes, almost too brief to notice. But she had seen it.

And why were the windows painted?

Goose bumps rose on her arms.

There's something in that house that frightens them, she thought.

She wondered if it was connected to Annie's death. She felt certain that it was. Which meant that Fellows and Karl knew more than they were telling. In effect, they were covering up. This thought sickened her. And it outraged her, as well. She had to *do* something. At the very least she had to convince Parmeter to look deeper, to turn the town upside down if necessary to find the truth. And if *he* wouldn't do it, then maybe she—

A knock on the door.

Nora wiped her hands on her jeans and pulled open the door, realizing at once that she should have used the security chain, or at least looked through the peephole. After all, Denver was a city, maybe not as large and dangerous as New York or Miami, but neither was it as safe as Cedar Falls.

However, the man standing in the hallway did not appear threatening. He was of medium height and build, around forty, Nora guessed, pleasant-looking, with dark hair going gray and laugh lines at the corners of his eyes. He wore a herringbone sports coat and dark brown slacks, and his tie was casually pulled loose from his collar.

He smiled and said, "Hi, is Annie home?"

"No, she's . . I'm sorry, no."

"Oh? I saw her car outside and I thought . . . well, anyway, when she gets back, would you tell her Thomas stopped by? I just got into town and—"

Nora stiffened. "Thomas? Are you the one who left the phone messages?"

He gave her an odd look. "Messages? Well, yes."

Nora stepped back, pulling the door wider, gripping the doorknob so hard it hurt her fingers. She said, "I'm Annie's sister. Perhaps you had better come in."

15

Thomas walked in, then stopped short when he saw the floor cluttered with cardboard boxes.

"What's going on here?"

Nora closed the door and said quietly. "There's no easy way to tell you this. Annie is dead."

"What?" He gave her a tentative grin and glanced about the apartment as if he expected to see Annie peeking around a corner, laughing in her hand. "Is this a joke?" he asked, but his face was beginning to register pain.

"It happened just over a week ago," Nora said softly. "She died in a fall. I'm sorry you had to find out this way."

"My God, I can't believe it." He pressed his fingers to his forehead. "Annie, dead."

Nora watched him, feeling his grief.

After a moment he let his arm fall to his side. "I've been out of town on business, and every time I called I figured I was just missing her. How did she . . . what happened?"

Nora hesitated, then gave him what she considered to be the "official" story of Annie's death, suppressing the urge to blurt out her suspicions.

Thomas was shaking his head. "God, it's just unbelievable. Annie, of all people. I mean, she was so young and alive and—" He stopped abruptly, embarrassed. "Jesus, what am I saying, as if you wouldn't know. She was your sister. You must be devastated."

"Yes, it has been difficult. Especially for my ｟   ｠nts."

"I'm so sorry for you. If there's anything I can do . . ." He paused. "I should introduce myself. Thomas Whitney."

He extended his hand, and Nora shook it.

"Nora Honeycut."

"I know," he said, giving her a half smile. "Annie talked about you."

Nora was suddenly aware of her unkempt appearance—faded jeans, baggy sweat shirt, and beat-up athletic shoes, clothes she had brought specifically for the chore of packing. She brushed a hand halfheartedly through her hair. "I've been packing up Annie's things and . . . oh . . . it just occurred to me. I haven't looked through all of it yet—does anything here belong to you?"

Thomas shook his head no.

"I was going to give most of it to Goodwill, but if you know anyone, perhaps some of Annie's friends. . . ?

"She never mentioned any girlfriends. Of course, I haven't known her for too long." He glanced at the boxes. "I should leave. I can see you're busy."

"No," she said quickly. "What I mean is, I was ready to take a break. Would you like some coffee?" She wasn't sure why, but she didn't want him to leave. Perhaps he represented a connection with Annie, and she was reluctant to let go. Or maybe she just needed someone to talk to.

"Sure," he said. "Coffee sounds fine."

They sat at the kitchen table, a pair of steaming mugs between them—his, white with a cartoon drawing of a penguin; hers, solid yellow.

"I met Annie only a few months ago," Thomas said, "but I felt as if I had known her for years."

"She could have that effect on people. I think it's because she didn't hold anything back."

Thomas sipped his coffee. "Of course, I'd be kidding myself to think our relationship would have lasted." He gave her a weak smile. "Too many differences. Age, for one. I mean, I didn't feel as if I were robbing the cradle, although some of my colleagues accused me of it."

Nora could see why. There had to be at least fifteen years separating them—not exactly a May-December relationship, but close. Over the years she had met a few of Annie's boyfriends, and they had all been near to her age. *In other words,* she thought, *young.* She wondered if Annie's dating Thomas meant that she was changing her goals, seeking someone more mature. And what about Thomas? What was his motive for dating a girl so young? Midlife crisis?

Stop it. You're acting like an overprotective older sister.

"How did you and Annie meet?"

"On a flight here from New York. I had been there on business, and Annie was returning from Bermuda. We were seated together by chance, and before we even got out of the Eastern time zone I found myself telling her all about my work as an architect, my marriage, my kids, my divorce. She was about the easiest person to talk to I had ever met. She gave me her number, and a few days later I called and asked her to dinner. She said, 'Okay, but I pick the place.' " He grinned. "We ate at some greasy little taco joint on South Broadway. My stomach didn't get straightened out for two days."

Nora laughed. It was the first time she had done so in a week and a half, and it was a relief, as if she had opened a fist clenched for so long she had forgotten it was a hand.

"She liked to take chances," Nora said. "With food, with . . . whatever."

"I got that impression. Some of her assignments sounded pretty dicey."

Nora looked down and said softly, "More so than she knew."

"You mean Lewiston."

"Yes. I . . ." She met his eyes, then looked away. She felt him staring at her.

"Is something wrong?"

She fidgeted with her cup, trying to decide whether to confide in him. She had met him barely twenty minutes ago, knew nothing at all about him. Except that he and Annie had dated for several months. No doubt Annie had loved him, trusted him. The question was could she trust Annie's judgment.

"I could be all wrong about this," she said. She got the photograph and set it before him on the table. "The police found Annie's camera near her body, and only one frame had been exposed. I had it developed in Cedar Falls, and I didn't recognize what it was until I visited the grounds of the Owen house. It's apparent that Annie took this picture from the top of the trellis, perhaps accidentally, when she fell." Nora pointed to the print. "This is the town in the distance. This is part of a hedge that surrounds the grounds, and these are trees and bushes. And this right *here* was not on the grounds when I was there yesterday. I think it's a man."

Thomas picked up the photo, frowning.

"If it is a man," Nora said, "then he saw her fall. Now according to the town doctor, Annie died sometime between midnight and three in the morning, and yet her body wasn't 'discovered' until six. So if someone was there and saw it happen, saw the 'accident,' then why didn't he call an ambulance or the police? Why would he remain silent?"

Thomas looked up at her.

"Unless her death wasn't an accident," Nora said.

"Not an accident?" Thomas held her gaze for a moment, then stared down at the photo. "Have you shown this to the police?"

Nora went back to her chair and sat down. "The sheriff in Idaho Springs. I was there today."

"And?"

"He sees shadows, not a man."

Thomas studied the print. "Well, it is pretty fuzzy."

"It's not just the photo that's wrong," Nora said evenly. "It's the people in Lewiston. Two of them, at least." She described her impressions of Chief Fellows and Karl Gant. "I think they're hiding something, maybe even covering up the circumstances of Annie's death."

Thomas laid the print carefully on the table. "That's a very serious charge."

Nora said nothing. She had hoped to convince him. She needed to convince *someone.*

It was a moment before Thomas spoke. "What should we do?"

She was gratified by "we." His question, though, was troubling. What *should* they do? Or more correctly—what should she do? Deep down, though, she knew. She had known ever since Sheriff Parmeter's phone call. She just hadn't verbalized it, hadn't faced up to it. Until now.

"I'm going back to Lewiston," she said, "and try to find the truth."

"I see." Thomas picked up his coffee mug, then immediately set it down. "Maybe I should go with you."

"No."

"Look, if you're right about Annie's death, it may not be safe for you to—"

"I can take care of myself," she said, more loudly than she had intended. A minute ago she had wanted his support. Now she was determined to act alone. Was she trying to prove that she could be as brave as Annie?

Thomas drew back, a bit bewildered. "I'm sorry. I didn't mean to imply anything. I'm only offering to help."

"I know." She felt contrite. "I appreciate your concern, but I feel this is something I have to do on my own."

"Of course. I understand." He checked his watch. "I should be going."

At the front door he said, "Will you call me if anything turns up?"

"Yes."

He jotted his home phone on the back of a business card. "Call me anytime. Even if you just want to talk."

"Thank you."

"And . . ." He smiled. "Now don't take offense . . . be careful in Lewiston, okay?"

She smiled back. "Okay."

She locked the door behind him. Then she phoned her parents and told them she'd be staying in Denver longer than expected—some minor problems with the apartment and the landlord, nothing to worry about.

Later, she lay in Annie's bed, wishing that Annie were there to help her. It was illogical, of course—if Annie were there, she'd be alive, and Nora wouldn't *need* any help. Still, she longed for her sister. Annie had been brave, perhaps even fearless. And Nora was afraid. Partly because of what she'd have to do, but mostly because of what she might find.

She wished she had Annie's courage.

16

On Tuesday morning Nora phoned Hattie at the shop. There were problems.

At least Hattie perceived them as such. First of all, Kirk Usterhaus was making a nuisance of himself again. He had phoned the shop twice yesterday, insisting to speak to Nora, and he had come in this morning just to make sure that Hattie had told him the truth about Nora being out of town and that she wasn't simply ducking his calls.

Nora had talked to Usterhaus in the past, and her answer to him had always been *no*.

He wanted to buy the shop. He owned several flower stores in Cedar Falls and Waterloo (successful stores, Nora had to admit), and he wanted to add hers to his chain. He coveted her business for two reasons—a prime location and a solid clientele. His offers were generous, but Nora always declined. Owning the shop was her life, her safety. And even though it sometimes felt more like a burden than a business, she didn't dare let go.

She told Hattie to give Usterhaus the boot if he bothered her again.

The second problem was more immediate. One of the part-time girls was arguing with Hattie and not following her directions.

"I think you should have a word with her," Hattie said. "Can you call back later when she comes in?"

"No, Hattie, you're going to have to deal with her yourself. There are . . . other things I have to do today."

Nora locked the apartment and drove to the F-STOP photo lab. She asked Daniel to blow up one corner of Annie's last negative. The shop was quite busy, and he told her it would be a few hours before he could get to it. She told him she'd pick it up that afternoon.

Then she drove toward Lewiston.

Along the way she tried to formulate a plan, or at least a proce-dure. But there was nothing in her past to guide her, no experience to follow. All she had to go on were Annie's photograph and her impressions of Chief Fellows and Karl Gant. She thought about the image in the photo—a short, squat person with an overly large head. It certainly wasn't Fellows or Karl, but she'd bet it was some-one they knew. If only she could get one of them to talk.

Nora smiled wryly at the image of herself trying to break down Fellows under questioning. The tough old cop was hardly likely to be shaken or tricked into opening up. But Karl might be a different story. He was an old man, and he might show some weakness. If she confronted him and pushed for the truth, maybe she'd learn something.

That is, if she could maintain her nerve.

✿   ✿   ✿

The town had changed.

In only two days the color had faded from everything—the trees, the houses, even the people. All of them looked flat and dead. And the air was thinner, almost impossible to breathe, as if the oxygen had been sucked up into the high, pale blue sky. Even the sounds were different—from the hollow voices in the street to the deadened rumble of the Mustang, idling at the intersection of Main and Alpine.

Of course, she knew it was she who had changed, not Lewiston. The secrets of Annie's death hung before her like a thin black mist.

She nosed the car through the intersection and up Alpine Street toward the Owen house. The cupola rose above the treetops, watching her, waiting. She approached Silver Street and started to turn left toward the house. Then her nerve seemed to rise up on startled wings and fly from her body. She drove straight ahead, cursing her cowardice.

The road curved sharply to the left and began to ascend the face of the mountain. It was too narrow to turn around and too steep to safely back down, so Nora drove on, looking for a wide spot in the road, shifting into low gear to negotiate the steep, tight turns.

A rusted roadside sign informed her that the mountain pass was fifteen miles away. She hoped she wouldn't have to go that far—she was not accustomed to driving mountain roads, and the drop-off at the edge looked lethal.

But after a mile or so on the odometer and a vertical climb of several hundred feet, she saw a wide, flat dirt expanse that stretched beyond the next hairpin curve. She pulled onto the shoulder and shut off the engine.

She sat there for a time, trying to gather her courage. What was she afraid of? All she planned to do was talk to Karl. But it was more than that—she was going to have to confront him. To get in his face, as Annie would have said. And confrontation was something she had always avoided. She had never been a fighter. She had always strived to get along, to avoid conflict, to take the safe, quiet route.

Get yourself together, she thought. *You can do this.*

She climbed out of the car to stretch her legs. The mountain shadow was deep and the air was chilly, making her glad she had worn a turtleneck under her sweater. She stepped cautiously to the edge of the rocky embankment.

The town lay below her in miniature, like a Christmas display in a department store window—tiny old-fashioned houses, perfect models of cars and people, and delicate little fake trees. The only thing missing was the flocked snow.

The Owen house was clearly visible. It was higher than the rest of the town, but several hundred feet lower than the ledge where Nora stood, and several hundred yards away. Even from that distance the house looked enormous, much longer than it was wide. The brown line of a driveway was visible, running from the rear of the house and across the mottled green grounds to Alpine Street. There was a shiny black car parked in back.

It suddenly occurred to her that this was where Annie had taken the pictures on the contact sheets—the elevated view of the town, the shots of the grounds, the close-ups of the painted cupola windows.

She felt giddy from the height, and she took a step back from the edge.

Then she saw a tiny figure emerge from the back door of the house and either kneel or crouch down beside the car. Was it Karl? She couldn't tell for sure. And she couldn't see what he was doing. She wished she had binoculars.

Then she remembered Annie's gear in the trunk of the Mustang. She pulled the keys from the ignition, unlocked the trunk, and sorted through the camera bags. She found a lens the size of a megaphone and attached it to a camera body. But the lens was so heavy that it was impossible to hold steady—the scenery jumped and jiggled.

She dragged a tripod from the trunk, fumbled with the clamp, and finally got the camera attached. Setting up a few feet from the ledge, trying to ignore the sheer drop before her, she aimed down at the grounds and twisted the focusing ring.

An evergreen bush leapt up before her eye. Amazed by the

power of the lens, she swung it slowly, panning across shrubbery and lawn, searching for Karl, finding the car. But Karl was no longer there. She turned the camera to the house and began methodically examining each window along the ground floor. They all wore heavy curtains.

A car came down the road behind her, and Nora suddenly straightened up, feeling guilty, as if she had been caught committing a crime.

But the car continued down the mountain road, the occupants barely giving her a glance.

Nora put her eye to the camera and began studying the upper-floor windows—each one smoothly coated with paint. Then she angled the lens toward the cupola. Two windows were visible to her, rear and side, both painted over. Nora wondered why Annie had taken two dozen pictures of the cupola windows. What had she found that was so interesting? There was nothing there.

Except . . .

She squinted into the camera, concentrating on the side window. Near the corner of one pane was a dark spot, no larger than a silver dollar. As she watched, the dark spot changed— light, dark, light, dark. It took her a moment to understand what she was looking at. The spot must be a hole scratched in the paint, and someone was moving behind it.

A peephole?

Nora shivered. She stared at the spot until her neck and back ached from bending over the camera. The spot remained black. She began to wonder if she had only imagined seeing movement. She swung the camera a bit and examined the rear window. There was a black spot there, too, perfectly round. She studied it for a few minutes. No sign of movement, no change of color. Perhaps it wasn't an opening at all, merely a dirty spot on the paint.

She straightened up and rubbed her back. There was nothing to be gained up there, she knew. She had been stalling. It was time to do what had to be done.

She loaded the gear in the trunk. Then she eased the Mustang downhill toward the Owen house.

17

Nora parked before the towering hedge. As she stepped through the gateway, a rogue cloud move before the sun, throwing the house and grounds into shadow. She had a strong sensation that she was being watched.

She followed the stone walk to the house, her eyes on the windows. They stared back sightlessly. She mounted the front steps and crossed the porch, floorboards groaning underfoot. The front door featured a leaded glass window, covered on the inside by a lacy white curtain. There was a brass lever set below the window. Nora hesitated, then gave it a twist.

The ball made a jarring sound.

A moment later she heard a board creak beyond the door. She sucked in her breath, expecting the door to fly open. But nothing happened. She felt certain, though, that someone was standing behind the door, listening, waiting for her to go away.

She rang the bell, and then again, determined not to leave until she had confronted Karl—although she was beginning to wonder if it would be wise to incite the old man to anger. He was, after all, a very *large* old man, with hands that looked as if they could crush bones.

The front door latch clicked.

Nora stepped back, squared her shoulders, and lifted her chin, trying to display more resolution than she felt.

The door slowly swung inward.

And there in the murky entryway stood not Karl, but a small, frail old woman. She wore a black dress with tiny white dots, long sleeves, and a high collar. Her gray hair was done up in a bun, and her soft brown eyes looked watery and slightly magnified behind gold-rimmed spectacles. Her face was pale, except for spots of color on her cheeks and lips. There was a cameo brooch at her throat.

Nora had the impression the woman was dressed up for going out. Maybe it was the heavy smell of her perfume.

"Yes?" Her voice was clear and high-pitched, almost childlike. Something about it put a shiver down Nora's spine.

"I'm sorry to disturb you. Miss Owen, isn't it?"

"Yes?"

"Is . . . ah . . . is Karl here?"

"Karl is out back washing the car."

"I see. Well, could you—"

"He *always* washes the car before I go into town. It's bank day, you know. And Mr. McOllough at the bank always comments on how clean and shiny my car is."

"I see." Nora wondered if Miss Owen might be senile. Still, she had been in the house the night Annie died. Perhaps she saw or heard something. "I'm sorry to disturb you. My name is Nora Honeycut. Annie Honeycut is . . . was my sister."

"Who?"

"The young woman who . . . had the accident last week."

"Accident?" For a moment she looked puzzled. Then she nodded. "Oh, yes. Karl told me about her. Snooping around the house he said. Trespassing. Still and all, I hope she recovered."

"Recovered?"

"Yes. They took her to the hospital in Idaho Springs. Is she still there?"

Nora hesitated, then told her, "Annie Honeycut is dead."

"Oh, my." Miss Owen put her fingers to her brooch.

"Were you home that night?"

"Oh, dear. Dead, you say?"

Nora nodded, forcing away the image of Annie, twisted and broken on the ground. "Were you at home the night she fell?"

"Home? Yes, of course."

"Did you see or hear anything unusual?"

"Unusual? What do you mean?"

"Did you hear voices outside late at night?"

"No, I'm quite a sound sleeper." She smiled wanly. "A blessing at my age, you know."

"What time did you—"

A gaunt figure loomed behind Miss Owen.

"The car is ready, ma'am."

"Oh, good." She turned her back as if Nora were not there and said, "Let's be off."

Karl glowered over Miss Owen's head. "I'll just speak to this woman for a moment," he said. "Then we can leave."

"Who? Oh, yes, very well." She disappeared into the dimly lit house.

Karl stepped outside and pulled the door half closed behind him. He wore dark trousers, spattered with wet spots, and a white shirt with the sleeves rolled up to his elbows. The muscles in his forearms were corded beneath his pale, splotchy, old-man's skin.

"What do you want?" His tone was menacing.

Nora's resolution began to fail. Her mouth felt dry, making it difficult to speak calmly. "I want to talk to you about my sister's death."

"She fell. It was an accident."

"There's more to it than that. Someone was there that night."

"No one—"

"I have a *photograph*."

Karl glared at her, saying nothing. But a tic had appeared in his right eye.

He's holding something back, Nora thought.

"Someone was there, Karl. There's no use lying about it. And I think you know who it was."

There was no mistaking the fear in his eyes. She had gained an advantage, and she pressed on.

"Chief Fellows knows who it was, too, doesn't he? You're both protecting him."

"We are protecting no one."

"Who was it, Karl?"

He shook his head no.

"What did he see that night, Karl?" she said, her anger building. "Or was he the one who hurt my sister?"

"Go away from here." He turned to enter the house.

Nora grabbed his arm and shouted, *"Damn it, Karl, what did he do?"*

Karl jerked free, pulling her off balance. She stumbled into him, her face so close that she could smell the musty odor of his clothes. Quickly she pushed away. His arm felt as hard and unyielding as a statue.

He narrowed his eyes and raised his chin, and he seemed to look down on her from a great height. "She should not have come back here," he said coldly. "We *told* her to stay away. We warned her that she'd be in danger if—"

He stopped abruptly, clenching his jaws.

Nora felt the wind go out of her, and she could barely speak. "You *knew* she was in danger?"

Karl glared at her and said nothing.

Nora felt sick to her stomach. When she spoke, it was barely a whisper. "Someone killed Annie."

"She fell. It was an accident."

Nora could see he was lying. She choked back the bile rising in her throat. "You bastard. You *know* what happened. When the sheriff finds out—"

Karl held up his hand, palm forward. It looked large enough to envelop her head.

"You had better leave here now," he said.

He pushed open the door behind him and backed into the house, his gaze fixed on her. And then she read something in his face that surprised her. Pity.

"Get out of town before something happens," he said. "Something bad."

He gently closed the door.

18

Nora sat in the car, hunched forward, gripping the wheel, her forehead pressed to the backs of her hands. She felt physically ill. Her breathing was rapid and shallow. Annie murdered. The phrase snarled in her mind like a rabid animal, crouched in the shadows. She had searched for it, all the while hoping it didn't exist.

Even now she tried not to believe. But how could she doubt it? She had seen the truth in Karl's face, heard it in his denial, heard him practically admit it. *We warned her that she'd be in danger.* They knew she would die if she came back.

"Oh, my God," Nora moaned. "They killed you, Annie. They killed you."

Gradually she became aware of a warmth within her—a small, bright flame of anger. She pushed back from the wheel, her fingers still wrapped around it in a death grip.

Think, damn it. You've got to do something.

Karl had told her what to do, a not-so-subtle warning. Get out of town before something happens. Something bad.

Like what happened to Annie, she thought.

Her first impulse was to go to Sheriff Parmeter again. But he had already seen Annie's last photograph and reinterviewed everyone in town, and he remained convinced that her death was an accident. What could she tell him that he didn't already know?

Yes, sheriff, I talked to Karl Gant and I could see by his eyes that Annie was murdered.

Ridiculous. If only there were some piece of evidence, something she could show to Parmeter and say, "Look at this. This proves Annie was murdered." But there was nothing to show him. And no one to back up her claims.

She frowned, wondering if that were true.

Was there anyone who could verify her suspicions, someone who knew the truth and who Parmeter would listen to? Certainly not Karl—he might squirm while he lied, but he would lie. And obviously not Chief Fellows. If Fellows knew the truth—and Nora was certain that he did—then he had been covering up a murder. In effect, he was an accomplice after the fact and not likely to admit it.

Nora ground her teeth at the memory of Fellows—polite, sympathetic, just a good old boy, a small-town cop. She was both enraged and sickened by the idea that a policeman, a man sworn to uphold the law, would abet Annie's killer.

I'll get you, too, you son of a bitch. Then she grinned without humor. *Oh, right, Nora Honeycut, righteous avenger.*

She looked at herself in the rearview mirror. Her mascara was smudged, giving her a look that would frighten away small children. She wiped it off with a tissue from her purse and tried to clear her thoughts.

Besides the man who had killed Annie (There, she had said it without the slightest hesitation. It was a *fact.*) there were four other men who had viewed Annie's body at the scene. Sheriff Parmeter. Chief Fellows. Karl Gant. And the town doctor. What was his name? Parmeter and Fellows had both mentioned him.

Newby, she thought. *Doc Newby.*

She started the car, made a tight U-turn, and drove into town, pushing Karl's warning from her mind and looking for someone to direct her to the good doctor. She stopped at the Main Street intersection and looked right and left. The courthouse and police station were half a block to her right. She turned left, searching for a place to park. Cars lined the curb, bumper to bumper, so at the next street she turned left again and pulled into an empty slot.

On her side of the street there was a bookstore, a bakery, and a shop featuring Indian jewelry.

Nora entered the bookstore—it seemed like the right place to get information. There were a few customers browsing within the tightly packed maze of book-laden tables and shelves.

"Good morning."

The woman who had greeted her was in her sixties, with soft gray hair and an open smile. She wore a peach-and-white sweater, a long skirt, and brown leather boots. She had been arranging a display rack, and she held a packet of postcards in one hand. "May I help you find something?"

"Actually, I'm looking for the town doctor."

"He's not far from here. Go down Main Street to Prospect and turn right. It's about three more blocks, a big white house on the left. You can't miss it."

"Is that his residence?"

"His residence and the clinic."

"Thank you." She hesitated. "Pardon me for asking—how well do you know him?"

"Doc Newby? Very well. He was in Lewiston when I moved here, let's see, twenty-seven years ago."

"I take it he's well-respected in town."

"Oh yes, he's a very good doctor. I'd say we're lucky to have him."

"Does he have a family?"

She shook her head. "His wife passed away some fifteen years ago, the poor woman." Her mouth turned down at the corners. "That was a bad time for everyone in town."

"How do you mean?"

She looked down for a moment at the cards in her hand before she spoke. "Well, you see, Doc took her death very hard. He started drinking. It got so bad that a lot of the townspeople were afraid to see him professionally, afraid he might make a mistake, prescribe the wrong medicine, that sort of thing. And to complicate matters he had a young son, a real wild child, who Doc more or less let run loose. At least for awhile." She smiled and shook her head. "I don't know why I'm telling you all this. That was a long time ago. Besides, Doc is a fine man."

The house was a compact, two-story, box Italianate structure, as white as an iceberg. Nora went up the flagstone walk to the dark-paneled front door. There was a hand-lettered sign beside the doorbell: EVERETT J. NEWBY, M.D.—CLINIC HOURS 9–4.

Nora wasn't sure whether to ring or just walk in. She tried the doorknob. Unlocked.

She opened the door, jangling an overhead bell, and entered a small, empty foyer. There were doors to the right and left and a stairway dead ahead. The hardwood floor gleamed dully under a high overhead light globe. A sign by the right-hand door proclaimed WAITING ROOM. Nora peeked inside. The easy chair and the couch were both unoccupied.

She heard a murmur of voices from the other doorway. She stepped through into a small, carpeted office. There was a heavy, antique desk, a pair of straight-back visitor's chairs, and a faint odor of disinfectant. A ceiling-high bookcase filled one wall. The wall behind the desk held half a dozen framed documents, all with official-looking seals. There was an open doorway in the rear corner of the room.

Voices drifted in. A moment later a woman stepped through the doorway. She was thirty-ish, wearing beige pants and a russet suede jacket with fringe on the sleeves. There was a prescription slip clutched in her right hand. She looked surprised to see Nora. Her surprise turned to mild embarrassment when a small, white-haired man came out right behind her and said, "You get that ointment today, and it'll clear up your rash in no time."

"Thank you, Doctor," she said and hurried out.

Doc Newby turned to Nora. He wore a charcoal-gray cardigan sweater with patches at the elbows. Nora guessed that the patches were more for utility than style, since Newby's slacks were baggy at the knees and his shoes worn at the heels.

He gave her a scolding frown. "I'd prefer that you didn't barge in here. That's why we have a waiting room."

"I'm sorry, I—"

He waved his hand. "Never mind. What seems to be the problem?"

"I'm not ill. I just want to talk to you. My name is Nora Honeycut. Annie Honeycut's sister."

His eyes narrowed briefly behind his bifocals.

Nora said, "Can you spare a few minutes?"

"Unless there's someone in the waiting room."

"There isn't."

Newby motioned Nora into a visitor's chair, then sat behind his desk.

"What can I do for you, Miss Honeycut?"

"Perhaps you can answer some questions about my sister's death."

Newby shifted in his seat. "Sheriff Parmeter was here yesterday, and I went over everything with him."

"About how Annie died."

"Yes."

"How the fall broke her neck."

Again Newby shifted in his seat. "Yes."

"Please don't take this the wrong way, but how can you be certain her neck was broken by a fall from the trellis and not some other way?"

Newby folded his hands on the desktop, fingers interlocked. "Because I *examined* her. It was evident from the position of her body and the condition of her vertebrae."

"But you didn't perform an autopsy."

"No. There was no need."

"And you're certain that's how her neck was broken. By the fall."

"Yes."

"Certain beyond a doubt."

Newby held Nora's eyes with a steady gaze that flickered for only a split second. "Yes, beyond a doubt."

Before that moment Nora had considered three possibilities.

One, Newby was competent and his examination had found nothing suspicious. Two, Newby was incompetent. Or three, Newby knew that the fall hadn't killed Annie, and he was keeping his mouth shut.

Nora felt her anger return, sidling up to her like a newfound friend. "You know more than you're telling."

"I beg your pardon." He puffed out his small chest, trying to look indignant, looking ridiculous.

"Annie's death was no accident," Nora said flatly.

Some of the color drained from Newby's face. "What are you saying?"

"I think you and Chief Fellows and Karl Gant are covering up."

"No."

"Annie was murdered, wasn't she?" Hysteria had crept into Nora's voice. "Who did it? Who killed my—"

"No one."

"You're *lying!*"

Newby stood up so suddenly that he nearly knocked over his chair.

"Why did they kill her?" Nora shouted.

Newby winced and drew back. "I think you'd better leave, Miss Honeycut." His voice was strained.

"You *bastard!* You know—"

"Please." There was a wild look in his eyes, as if he might bolt from the room.

Nora had the insane urge to grab the old man by the lapels and throttle him until he told the truth. She stood slowly, glaring at him. "I'm going to find out what happened," she said with contempt. "No matter what it takes."

"Please." Newby's voice was pathetic.

Nora gave him a final look of disgust and walked out.

19

Chief Roy Fellows was searching the town for Nora Honeycut's yellow Mustang when he saw it pull away from the clinic. His stomach already had been roiling, but now it felt as if someone had poured in battery acid.

The trouble—gastric and otherwise—had started yesterday when Sheriff Parmeter came to town. Fellows had guessed correctly that the reason for the visit was the Honeycut woman. But he hadn't been certain if Parmeter was there because he was suspicious or just curiosity. Big difference. Fellows could satisfy the man's curiosity. *Yes, Sheriff, I caught her climbing that trellis once before. Oh, this photograph? I don't know, it looks like shadows to me.*

But if Parmeter were suspicious, then Fellows had to be very careful indeed. Casual, but not too casual—someone in town had died. Concerned, but not too concerned—it had been an accident, after all, the girl's own fault. He had to act just right, and he had to act as if he weren't acting. Tough to do in any case. Especially with the juices boiling in your gut.

He kept reminding himself that there was no way for Parmeter to know about Willy. In fact, there was nothing at all for him to find. The girl's body was six feet under, and the death site was cleaned up. There was nothing. Except that goddamn photograph.

The figure in the shadows seemed to leap from the eight-by-ten glossy, at least to Fellows. It was uncanny how it resembled Willy, even in the dark. Thank God the girl hadn't used a flash. Because really, if you didn't *know* it was someone standing there, you could easily believe it was just another shadow.

After Parmeter had left town, Fellows had tried to smother the fire in the stomach with drugstore medicine. He drank enough of it that afternoon to paint the hull of a battleship solid pink. That evening he had switched to Budweiser and Jim Beam, thinking and drinking and trying to figure out if there was anything at all that Parmeter might turn up—besides the photograph.

He had drunk himself to sleep and had awakened this morning with a team of Clydesdales clip-clopping in his head.

He hated to admit it, but at forty-eight he was too old to do battle with Bud and Jim and not feel it the next day. He had dragged himself into the office, with the small consolation that the coals stoking his stomach-caldron were down to a low smolder.

Until Karl phoned.

The old man was so upset he was raving. Fellows could hardly understand him, and his pounding hangover didn't help any. He had to tell him to slow down and start over before he understood what he was saying: "Nora Honeycut just left the house. She knows her sister's death was no accident. She'll ruin us all."

Fellows talked to Karl long enough to determine that Nora probably didn't *know*, but she sure as hell *suspected*. He told Karl to relax, he'd handle it.

Then he had gone looking for the woman—that is, for her beat-up yellow Mustang.

And now he saw it pulling away from Doc Newby's place.

The fire in his belly flared up, threatening to consume his reason, or at least his restraint. As he parked in front of the doctor's bright white house, he tried to ignore the fire and the dull throbbing in his head. He had to know what Nora Honeycut had said to Newby. And more important, what Newby had said to her.

He found the doctor behind his desk, elbows on the blotter,

fingertips pressed to his forehead—so lost in thought that he hadn't even heard Fellows come in.

"So," Fellows said, making Newby's head snap up, eyes wide. "Where do you keep the aspirin?"

"You startled me."

"I'm serious, Doc. My head's killing me."

He lowered his bulk into one of the visitor's chairs and waited for Newby to bring him three tablets and a glass of water from the back room. Fellows swallowed the medicine, then wiped his hand on his pants leg and set the empty glass on the desk.

"Did you and Nora Honeycut have a nice chat?"

"How did you. . . ? You saw her leave."

Fellows grunted.

"She knows about her sister," Newby said gravely.

"What did you tell her?"

"Nothing."

"Then that's exactly what she knows—nothing."

Newby shook his head, then pushed up his glasses and pinched the bridge of his nose. "This is bad, Roy. That girl . . ." He dropped his hand and let his glasses fall back into place. But he kept his eyes lowered, not meeting Fellows's gaze, staring at a spot on the blotter. "We both know it wasn't the fall that killed her. Willy—"

"How do you know? You're not a pathologist."

"I'm a *doctor,* damn it!" His face flushed and his eyes blazed at Fellows. "I know about broken *bones!*"

Fellows winced, raising a hand. "Doc, please, my head."

Newby breathed heavily through his nose. Gradually the redness drained from his face, leaving behind a blush, high on his cheeks.

Fellows said, "It doesn't matter how she died. All—"

"It doesn't *matter?*"

"All that matters," Fellows continued evenly, "is that she's gone for good, and now her dumb-ass sister is trying to stir up trouble. I'll just get rid of her, that's all."

"What do you mean?" Newby looked horrified.

"Relax, Doc. I mean I'll run her out of town. The thing for you to do is stay calm and keep your mouth shut."

"Calmly cover up a murder," Newby said with sarcasm.

Fellows leaned forward, set his elbow on the desk, and made a fist with one finger extended, like a gun barrel. He sighted over it at Newby's face. "You're involved in this as much as anybody. Maybe more. Don't forget about that little occurrence a few years ago. *Doctor.* You want to talk about cover-ups?"

He let the question hang in the air between them. Newby chewed the inside of his cheek and looked away.

Fellows grunted. "All right, then." He pushed himself to his feet. "Did Miss Honeycut say where she was going?"

Newby shook his head, still facing away from Fellows.

"Cheer up," Fellows said. "Things could be worse."

Newby gave him a pained look. "What?"

"The girl saw Willy. What if she had gotten away from him and started screaming her head off? Then we'd *all* be screwed."

Newby said nothing.

Fellows said, "Have a nice day, Doc."

He went outside, climbed in the police vehicle, and gunned the engine. Then he went looking for Nora Honeycut.

20

When Nora left Doc Newby's clinic she was shaking so badly she could hardly drive.

She was both sickened and enraged. Newby not only had confirmed her suspicions about Annie's death, he also had shown himself to be part of the cover-up, part of what now looked like a conspiracy. She had never felt such anger. In fact, she had come dangerously close to physically assaulting Newby, a small, old man. The urge had been so unlike anything she had ever experienced, so alien to her, it seemed as if she had been temporarily possessed.

By Annie?

She parked near Main Street and sat with her hands trembling in her lap. She needed something to calm herself down—a pill, a drink.

She walked to the restaurant on the corner.

The courtyard was rimmed with colorful flowers and a low white picket fence. There were half a dozen round metal tables, several of them occupied, all of them floating in pools of too-cool shade beneath striped umbrellas. Nora sat on the south side of a table, alone in the sun. Tourists strolled past, gazing idly at her and the other diners as if they were part of the scenery.

Half a dozen blocks away the cupola rose above rooftops and trees. It looked ominous to Nora. Evil.

"Would you like a menu?" the waitress asked, startling her.

"Ah, no." Nora suddenly felt self-conscious, as if the other customers and even the people strolling past the courtyard were glancing at her, waiting to see what she would do, what she would say. "Just hot chocolate, please."

When it came, Nora blew steam from the surface and sipped the rich, dark liquid. Some of the tension began to melt from her neck and shoulders.

She replayed her conversations with Doc Newby and Karl Gant, running them through her mind as if they were on videotape, slowing the speed there, tightening the focus there. Had she misinterpreted what she had seen and heard? Was she wrong to assume that Annie had been murdered?

No.

There was no mistaking Newby's fear. Nor Karl's—she had read it in his eyes. Fellows, too. She was scratching at the truth, and it scared the hell out of them. Or was there something else they feared?

Nora stared at the distant cupola. Its blank windows seemed to mock her.

"Would you like more hot chocolate?"

Nora nodded absently, her eyes on the roof of the Owen house.

When the waitress returned, she set down the cup and saucer and said, "It's really something, isn't it?"

"What?" Nora turned to face her, and she seemed to see her for the first time—a middle-aged woman with dark blond hair twisted in a French braid. She wore a full skirt, a peasant blouse with little flowers embroidered around the neckline, white athletic shoes, and a name tag that read CELIA.

"The Owen mansion," Celia said. "It's probably the most photographed house in Lewiston."

"It is?" Annie had been run off the grounds, not once but twice. "I heard they were touchy about people coming inside the yard, much less inside the house."

"Oh, no, no, that's private property. I mean lots of tourists take pictures from the street."

"I see." She hesitated. "Do you know the owner?"

"Miss Owen? I guess everybody around here does, not that I've ever spoken to her except to say hello. It was her grand-daddy who built that house. They say he practically owned Lewiston back then. Miss Owen is still the richest person in town. Heck, the *only* rich person."

"And how does Karl Gant fit in?"

"He's Miss Owen's butler, chauffeur, gardener, and handyman all rolled into one. Been with her for years. In fact, I believe he worked for Miss Owen's parents." She gave Nora a sly grin. "There was a time that folks in town thought it was scandalous that those two lived under the same roof, not being married and all. 'Course, now they're too old for anyone to care what they do."

"I met them the other day," Nora said carefully. "They seemed . . . odd."

"Oh, they are that."

Nora recalled what Annie's editor had told her about the house. "Is it true someone was murdered in there?"

Celia glanced at the other diners, then she winked at Nora and lowered her voice. "More than one person. But that's not something the visitors' bureau likes to put in its brochures."

"What happened?"

"Oh, it was a long time ago. Miss Owen's granddaddy suppos-edly suffocated his wife in her own bed. And then, about sixty years ago, Miss Owen's mother killed her husband—that is, Miss Owen's daddy." She smiled. "Some folks in town say the house is haunted by their ghosts."

"Haunted?"

"It's just talk. Mostly kids, you know, making up scary stories, claiming they've seen strange lights or whatever, daring each other to run up and ring the doorbell, and so on. Of course, the house does have sort of a bad reputation. More recent deaths, I mean."

Nora's stomach tightened. Annie was already part of the house's notoriety.

"Just the other week a young woman died there," Celia continued. "She was climbing on the roof for some stupid reason, and she fell off. Broke her neck."

Nora choked back the cold lump in her throat. "You said 'death's.'"

"Oh, we had a real bad one about five years ago. A young woman, a girl, really, was raped and strangled on the grounds beside the house. Some drifter did it, according to the police. But the man got away and was never caught, and there were some people in town, mostly kids, you understand, who claimed that she was murdered by the ghost of Miss Owen's daddy. They say he came right out of the house and killed her." Celia sighed. "Of course, that kind of talk only made things worse for the poor girl's mother. She practically became a recluse. Sort of like Miss Owen."

Nora wondered if there could be a connection between the girl's death and Annie's.

"What's the woman's name?"

"Betty Connor."

"Does she live in Lewiston?"

"Her place is six or seven miles up the mountain pass road, the one that goes behind the Owen House." Then Celia looked reproachful. "But Betty's not fond of visitors, much less strangers. I doubt she'll want to talk to you, if that's what you're thinking."

"Listen to me," Nora said evenly. "The young woman who died at the Owen house last week was my sister."

Celia took a step back, shocked. "Dear Lord. Oh, I am sorry."

"It's important that I talk to Betty Connor. Now please, how do I find her."

Celia hesitated. "I . . . suppose I'm not the one to say no. As I said, you take the pass road until—"

A horn honked.

It was one short beep, just enough to make Celia, Nora, and

the few other diners look toward the street. A Lewiston police vehicle idled at the curb. Chief Fellows leaned over the passenger seat and looked through the side window directly at Nora. He crooked his finger, come here.

"Does he mean you?" Celia asked, her voice wary.

"I'm afraid so."

21

When Nora was twelve years old she broke her mother's favorite vase.

Actually, Annie broke it, but Annie was only a child, barely two, and Nora was supposed to have been watching her while her mother was next door visiting a neighbor and her father was coaching Robert's baseball team.

Nora had quickly inspected Annie for cuts. Pieces of the vase lay about them on the hardwood floor, a jagged jigsaw puzzle that moments before had been a glorious bird of paradise. After Nora had determined that her bawling baby sister was unhurt, she collected the broken pieces in a paper sack. Then she took Annie upstairs and hid the sack under her bed.

She was in a panic. Her father had bought the vase for her mother years ago. What would he do when he found out she had been watching TV instead of watching Annie? She prayed that they wouldn't notice right away that it was gone. Maybe she could use her allowance money to buy another one, replace it before they even missed it.

Then she heard her father and Robert return home. And a few minutes later—she couldn't believe he had already discovered it!—her father called her downstairs. He was standing at the bottom of the stairs, wearing a frown and holding a piece of the vase that had somehow escaped her attention. She was frightened. He had never struck her, of course, and he rarely ever raised his voice to her. But she had never seen him so angry. It was her fault, and she was afraid to guess what he might do.

That's how she felt now, leaving the courtya. nd going out to Chief Fellows's car.

His face was flushed with anger. It wasn't hard to guess why. He must have already spoken to Karl or Newby, and one or both of them had told him about her accusations. She hadn't wanted to confront Fellows. She had hoped to move around town behind his back, find what she wanted, and sneak out, unseen by him.

Of course, Lewiston was too small for that. And Fellows was not dull-witted, not in the least.

As Nora approached his vehicle she tried to act calm. But she was so tense she nearly stumbled off the curb.

The passenger-side window slid down. "Get in," Fellows said. It wasn't a request.

Nora climbed in and shut the door. What first struck her was the faint stink of stale booze, an odor she had become all too familiar with during her marriage.

Fellows's presence seemed to fill the vehicle, and Nora could only focus on small details: the half-moon sweat stains under the arms of his khaki shirt, a fine red net of broken capillaries high on his cheeks, tiny white scars on the back of his left hand where it rested on the dashboard. The hand itself was bunched in a fist, pale and speckled, like a small, swollen, fleshy animal. There was little about him to remind her of the kindly policeman who had met her in Idaho Springs two days ago.

"Karl Gant phoned me this morning," Fellows said, measuring his words. His bloodshot eyes bored into Nora's face like lasers.

"And I just left Doc Newby. Both of them are pretty upset by what you've been saying. I could hardly believe my ears, so I wanted to hear it from you."

"You heard correctly." Her voice sounded amazingly firm.

Fellows pushed back his hat with his index finger and let one corner of his mouth curl up. "You actually think someone killed your sister?" He clucked his tongue and shook his head. "Lady, you are so off base you're out of the ballpark. Why would anyone want to hurt that little girl? Answer me that."

"I don't know," she said, "but I think it has something to do with the Owen house."

Fellows leaned toward her until his face was barely a foot away. Nora could smell his sour breath. "What's that house got to do with anything? There's nothing there but an old lady and her chauffeur."

He was challenging her, she knew, daring her to disagree. She had an almost unbearable urge to call him a liar, to shout in his face, to *punch* his face. She drew back, startled by the thought, afraid she might really do it.

This is Annie, she thought, *Annie's memory egging me on.*

What she truly wanted was to get out and walk. She felt trapped in the car with Fellows. She put her hand on the door handle. Then she realized that was exactly what he wanted her to do—run.

Nora held perfectly still, not moving a muscle, not even blinking, meeting his stare.

Fellows held her gaze a moment longer. His disgust for her seemed to ooze from his pores like sweat. Then he sat back and put his hands on the steering wheel. He stared out the windshield at something far away, perhaps beyond his sight. "I told your sister not to go climbing on that house," he said. "And she did it anyway. Stupid." He swiveled his head toward her. "She fell and broke her neck and that's all there is to it."

Nora said nothing.

Fellows pursed his lips. "You know something, Miss Honeycut? I don't give a good goddamn *what* you believe, just so long as you keep it to yourself. But if you cause any more trouble in this town, I'll come down on you like an avalanche. And no, that's not a threat. It's a guarantee." He pushed in the clutch and shifted into gear. "Now I suggest you finish eating your lunch, then get the hell out of Lewiston." A grin appeared on his face. "Damn, I'm starting to sound like an old western movie."

Nora got out and shut the door.

At once the vehicle jerked backward a foot and a half, and the side-view mirror caught Nora square in the shoulder. She cried out as she was knocked to the side, nearly off her feet. She regained her balance and put her hand to her arm. It felt as if it had been struck by a baseball bat.

Thank God it didn't hit me in the head.

She looked toward Fellows, expecting to see him jumping out of the vehicle and rushing to her side. But he remained planted firmly in the driver's seat. He stared at her through the passenger window.

"You all right?" he asked casually.

"Yes, I think so, I—"

He clucked his tongue and shook his head. "You had better hurry on out of town, Miss Honeycut. Accidents can happen."

He drove slowly away.

Nora stared after him, not quite believing what had just happened. Fellows had intentionally struck her with the mirror.

A notion darted through her mind, one that she believed she had exorcised forever: *I deserved that.*

During her marriage that thought had plagued her. Her ex-husband had not only been abusive, but he had laid the blame on her. Like a fool, she had accepted it. At least, for awhile. She had been too ashamed, and perhaps too frightened, to tell anyone about it, to *do* anything. Finally, though, she had regained her sense of self, and the anger had come—anger at him and anger at herself for putting up with him.

That son of a bitch, she thought.

She would *not* let Fellows get away with this. She'd go to Sheriff Parmeter right now and press charges.

She looked around quickly for witnesses, anyone who could back up her story. Otherwise, she knew, it would be her word against Fellows's. But tourists strolled by on Main Street, oblivious to what had just occurred. When Nora looked toward the restaurant she saw Celia staring at her, eyes wide with fright.

Nora walked into the courtyard, rubbing her shoulder. It throbbed painfully.

Celia was no longer in sight. Nora sat at her table and waited. Eventually, Celia emerged from the restaurant, carrying a tray of food. She set the plates before two young couples at a nearby table, then started to go back inside. Nora called to her.

Celia hesitated, then walked over. "More hot chocolate?"

"You saw what happened, didn't you?"

"What do you mean?"

"Come on, Celia, you were looking right at me." Nora tried hard to keep the anger from her voice. "Chief Fellows slammed into me with the side mirror of his car."

Celia was shaking her head. "I . . . I didn't see anything."

"Listen, damn it—"

"Please. I have to get back to work." She turned to leave.

Nora grabbed her arm.

Celia stopped, not attempting to pull away. "Please," she said.

"Are you afraid of Fellows? Is that it?"

"Just leave me out of it." There was a sad look on her face.

Nora held her arm a moment longer, then let go. Celia hurried away. Nora left some money on the table and walked out. When she reached the edge of the courtyard, she glanced back.

Celia and another waitress were talking with their heads together, watching her.

22

Nora drove carefully as the road switched back and forth up the mountain. The ground dropped steeply away—first to her right, then her left. She passed the dirt shoulder where she had parked this morning. Far below lay the town, a collection of dollhouses. Overlooking them was the Owen mansion. The shadow of the mountain was draped over it like a funeral veil.

Nora believed that the secret behind Annie's death lay within the mansion. She had said as much to Fellows. And he convinced her she was right by issuing her a subtle threat and a blatant physical blow.

Her shoulder ached terribly. The pain should have served—was *meant* to serve—to frighten her away. But it was having the opposite effect. She was more determined than ever to find the truth.

The road twisted and climbed up the mountain, until it finally took Nora around to the other side.

The curves in the road became much gentler, the rise more subtle. Nora passed a small lake with a parking area and picnic tables. And every half mile or so there was a packed-dirt driveway leading to a house or cabin set back among the pines. At the mouth of each driveway stood a mailbox on a post.

She wished Celia had given her more specific directions before Fellows had arrived and frightened her into silence. All she could do now was read mailboxes and hope she didn't miss the one she was looking for.

The Gilroys. The Meads. The Johnsons.

Connor.

Nora turned into the long, narrow, rutted driveway. The cabin lay among towering pines. It was a simple, split-log, one-story structure with a steeply pitched roof and a sheet-metal chimney flue. There was no front porch, merely two steps leading up to the door, with a window on either side.

The curtains parted and a face appeared in one window.

Nora parked twenty feet from the cabin and climbed out, rubbing her right shoulder. It was a smoldering ache, but it flared into pain whenever she moved it suddenly.

As she approached the cabin, the front door opened.

The woman standing behind the screen door was in her early forties, Nora guessed, wearing a bulky green sweater and blue jeans. Her auburn hair was streaked with gray. She wore no makeup to mask the lines around her eyes and mouth. She held her right hand away from her body, out of sight behind the doorjamb, apparently resting on a cane.

"What is it you want?" There was no friendliness in her voice.

"Are you Betty Connor?"

"Who wants to know?"

Nora came forward, saying, "My name is Nora Honeycut and I—"

"Keep your distance." The woman brought her right hand to her side. It rested not on a cane, but on the barrel of a lever-action rifle.

Nora stopped abruptly. She knew something about guns, particularly that they made her nervous. Her father had owned a few rifles and shotguns, and he used to take her brother hunting. Nora had been sickened at the sight of the dead pheasants that they had brought home. Guns meant violence and death. She was unnerved by the casual manner in which Betty Connor held the rifle, as if she were quite familiar with its use.

Nora said. "I hope I'm not intruding. I'd like to have a word with you. A friend of yours told me where you lived. Celia."

"Celia who?"

"I don't know her last name. She's a waitress at the restaurant on Main and Alpine."

Betty Connor nodded, as if Nora had just passed a test.

"Celia told me that you and I have something in common," Nora said.

"And what might that be?"

"We've each lost a loved one on the grounds of the Owen mansion."

The woman frowned but said nothing.

"Annie Honeycut was my sister," Nora said.

"The girl who fell?"

She nodded. "The official story is that she broke her neck in the fall. But I think there's more to it than that." She was hesitant about declaring her suspicions. For all she knew, Betty Connor and Chief Fellows might be the best of friends. But what did she have to lose? "I think Chief Fellows is hiding something," she said. "Lying about how my sister died. Doc Newby and Karl Gant, too. They all want me to stop asking questions and leave town. Now I don't know if there's a connection between my sister's death and your daughter's, but I'd like to talk to you about it."

Betty Connor did not speak, did not move.

"If I've come at a bad time . . ."

"No," she said, unlatching the screen door. "Please come in."

The small living room was a shrine to Betty Connor's dead daughter. Framed photographs of the girl covered the wall behind the faded couch and filled the end table in the corner. There was a low, chipped, walnut coffee table wedged between the couch and the overstuffed chair. It held a single photo in a silver frame: a pretty teenage girl in a turtleneck sweater, her face tilted up, a light smile touching her lips, a distant look in her eyes.

"Please sit down." She motioned Nora toward the couch.

Before Nora sat, she quickly scanned the photos on the wall.

They showed the girl as an infant, a child, an adolescent, wearing dresses or shorts or jeans. Always alone. There were no pictures of the girl's parents.

Betty Connor sat in the room's only chair. Nora noted with relief that she had left her rifle leaning against the wall by the front door. She wasn't sure where to begin, so she nodded at the photo on the coffee table.

"Your daughter was beautiful."

The woman smiled wistfully. "Bonnie was a lovely child. Prettiest girl in town. Although she had a mind of her own. That offended some folks. Too wild, they said. And maybe she was."

The girl in the photos didn't look wild to Nora—she looked like a prom queen. She said, "Mrs. Connor, I—"

"Please call me Betty."

"Betty. I, ah, know it must be painful to talk about your daughter's death, but—"

"I'm over the pain," she said quickly.

Nora nodded. *You'll never be over it.* "Can you tell me how she died?"

"She didn't just *die*, you know. She was murdered."

Nora said quietly, "Yes, I know."

"Do you also know that the man who did it got away?" There was venom in her voice, and her hands were clenched in fists on her knees. Given the opportunity, she'd empty her rifle into the murderer's chest, Nora had no doubt of that.

She said gently, "Can you tell me what happened back then?"

Slowly the fire went out of Betty's eyes. She relaxed her hands and rubbed the palms on her knees. "Yes, of course," she said in a small voice. "What would you like to know?"

"Everything about it."

23

Betty Connor explained that five years ago her daughter Bonnie had been seventeen years old and so pretty that all the boys in Lewiston and Idaho Springs (where she had just finished her junior year in high school) followed her around with their tongues hanging out. Of course, this made the other girls jealous. They spread rumors that the real reason the boys drooled over Bonnie was because she was "easy," that she "did it" with practically any boy who'd ask.

True, Bonnie had plenty of dates, and it was a rare night that she stayed home with her mother.

On her last night alive, a warm Friday in mid-July, she had a date with Cole Newby, Doc Newby's son. He was a few years older than Bonnie, a good-looking boy—tall, blond, blue-eyed, and very popular among the young ladies in town.

Cole's sights, though, were set on Bonnie Connor.

Although most girls would have killed to be in her shoes, Bonnie toyed with Cole, teasing him, leading him on. But she refused to "go all the way" with him.

On that Friday night Cole drove Bonnie to Denver to a beer party thrown by one of his fellow construction workers. Bonnie and Cole both had a good time. They stayed until midnight, when the apartment manager called the police because of the noise, and the party broke up.

During the drive back to Lewiston things turned sour between Cole and Bonnie. He accused her of flirting with half the guys at the party, and she said he drank too much. By the time they arrived in town they weren't speaking. And Cole had become so sick from drinking that he had to stop at his house before he could drive Bonnie up the mountain.

The moment he stopped the car, Bonnie jumped out and told him she'd had enough, that she would walk home. Cole told her she could go to hell, and he went inside.

His father's Friday-night poker game was just breaking up.

For the previous few years Doc Newby had hosted the game in his clinic's waiting room. The regular players included Cecil McOllough, manager of the Lewiston National Bank & Trust; Michael Berardi, a third-generation town grocer; Bill Kneisel, serving his fourth term as mayor; and police chief Roy Fellows.

Cole stopped for a minutes to say hello to his father's friends, then he went upstairs to bed.

About twenty minutes later Karl Gant phoned, asking desperately for Chief Fellows. He said he had just witnessed a murder.

The poker players raced to the Owen residence and found the body of Bonnie Connor—beaten, raped, and strangled. There was a piece of checkered material, apparently from a shirt pocket, clutched in her hand. Karl was trembling so badly he could hardly speak. He had seen the murderer flee, a man around thirty, short and stocky with long dark hair and a beard and wearing a long-sleeved checkered shirt and dark pants. The man had driven off in a green two-door sedan. Chief Fellows had spotted a similar car earlier in the day—a stranger passing through town. A drifter.

Fellows immediately called the county sheriff and the highway patrol, and an all-points bulletin was issued. But the man was never found.

Despite Karl Gant's description of the killer, the sheriff's investigators interrogated Cole Newby at length. They also questioned all the poker players and everyone who had attended the beer party in Denver. They even obtained a warrant to search the Newby house for a shirt matching the cloth swatch found in Bonnie's hand. No such shirt was ever found. The sheriff explained that he didn't seriously suspect Cole, but he was simply covering every base. Obviously the boy was innocent.

"But he killed her," Betty said to Nora.

"What?" Nora shook her head. "You told me he was upstairs in his father's house at the time. There were witnesses."

"Cole Newby should've brought Bonnie home, like he was *supposed* to," she snapped. "If he had, she'd be alive today. She wouldn't have been attacked by some low-life drifter and ..." She shook her head and looked down at her hands. When she spoke, her voice was barely audible. "Cole killed my little baby just as sure as if he had strangled her."

Nora could feel her grief. Or perhaps she was confusing it with her own. After all, there were definite similarities between the deaths of Bonnie and Annie. Both had died violently on the grounds of the Owen mansion. And shortly after each death the same men had been present: Karl, Newby, and Fellows.

Of course, Karl lived there. And the town doctor and chief of police would attend *any* unnatural death. So maybe it was just a coincidence. She wondered about the other men who had been at the scene of Bonnie's murder.

"Do all the poker players still live in town?"

Betty raised her head and blinked, as if she had just come out of a dream. "Excuse me, what?"

"The poker players. I mean besides Doc Newby and Chief Fellows. Are they still around?"

"Yes, they all live in town. But from what I hear they don't play anymore."

"Why not?"

"I don't know."

"What about Cole Newby? Does he still live with his father?"

"No. He was real upset by Bonnie's death, as well he should be. He felt responsible, and according to his father he was too ashamed to stay in town. He joined the army or the navy, I forget which, and I haven't seen him since." She sighed wearily and stared at the silver-framed picture of Bonnie. "It's just as well," she whispered.

Nora sensed that she was drifting away. "What can you tell me about the Owen house?"

"An evil place," she said absently, not looking at her.

"Do you mean the stories about it being haunted?"

Betty eyed her. "There are no such things as ghosts," she said evenly. "But there is evil. And sometimes it can *focus* itself. Like in the Owen house. Look what it did to your sister. And my daughter. And it goes way back. Miss Owen's grandfather murdered his wife in there, or so they say, and her mother murdered her father in their bedroom. You can look *that* up in the history books."

Nora pictured the Owen house, miles away, brooding. Waiting. A worm of fear wriggled in her brain.

"Does anyone live there besides Miss Owen and Karl?"

Betty shook her head no. "No one else has stayed in that house since Miss Owen's mother passed away, forty or fifty years ago. Of course, that was before my time."

"Who else could I talk to about that?"

Betty started to shake her head, then stopped. "Well, if anyone would know, it would be Meg Andrew. She and Miss Owen grew up together. 'Course, I'm not even sure she's still alive. Last I heard she was in a nursing home in Denver." Her eyes had returned to the silver-framed photo and her face had gone slack.

"Which nursing home?"

Betty shrugged, barely there anymore. "Maybe she's dead," she said quietly. "People die."

24

Nora left Betty Connor's house wishing there was something she could do for her. Obviously Betty still grieved for her daughter, five years after the girl's death. That was understandable. The problem was that Betty had become isolated. She had withdrawn not only into her tiny house, but into her own mind. She'd cut herself off from the world. And the longer she remained withdrawn, the nearer she came to madness.

In some ways, Nora had to admit, she was like Betty.

After her brother Robert's death, she had become withdrawn, afraid to take chances. And the more she hid from the world, the more she grew to fear it. She attended college, but one close to home. Then she let Zachary Holt—big, blustery, confident Zachary—take her as his wife, promising to protect her. But no one was there to protect her from Zachary. And after her divorce, when she invested in the flower shop, her friends saw it as a bold move, an adventure. But Nora knew the truth: the business was a security blanket, something to cling to, something to crawl under. It was the perfect excuse for not getting involved with men (*I'm sorry, I'd love to go out next Saturday, but I've got too much work to do*). And it was the ultimate reason for never leaving Cedar Falls, not even for a few days (*I have to mind the store*).

In fact, now that she thought about it, her time in Denver and Lewiston has been the longest she has spent away from home since college. And it was because of Annie.

She had to grin at that. Annie had often tried to drag her away from her shop, away from their hometown—all to no avail. Until now. In death she had succeeded.

Nora steered around the last few hairpin curves and came off the mountain. She had been trying to drive mostly with one hand, because every time she flexed her right arm, her wounded shoulder flared with pain. She drove past the Owen mansion, its upper story and cupola peering blindly over the towering hedge, windows blanked with paint.

She felt apprehensive as she approached Main Street. The longer she stayed in Lewiston, the greater the chance of again crossing paths with Chief Fellows. And as much as she hated him for his lies and his threats and his physical assault on her, she feared him, too. He held real power in Lewiston, the power of the law. This was his territory. He had the authority to arrest her for even a minor infraction, whether actual or invented. She dreaded to think what he might do to her in the secrecy of his jail, out of sight of the townspeople.

Of course, the only way to completely avoid him was to leave town and never come back, to accept the "official" version of Annie's death.

Not very damn likely, she thought.

She turned left on Main Street, scanned the storefront signs, and parked before Berardi's grocery store.

Betty Connor had told her that six men were present shortly after her daughter's murder. She had confronted three of them already—Chief Fellows, Doc Newby, and Karl Gant. Of the remaining three, the town mayor seemed the least likely to be of help, since he and Fellows were certainly associates if not good friends. Which left the grocer and the banker. She had no idea what they could tell her about the Owen house in general or Bonnie Connor's death in particular—or if any of it had to do with Annie. But it was either talk to them or do nothing.

The first thing she noticed when she entered the store were

the aromas. Garden-smell of misted vegetables and fruit. Dark, rich odor of ground coffee beans. Faint scent of fresh bread sifting in from the bakery next door. Even the old hardwood floorboards and shelves added an underlying, natural fragrance.

All of it seemed so natural, normal. Safe.

There appeared to be only one person working, and Nora assumed he was Berardi. Like the store itself, he was small, compact, and efficient-looking.

By Nora's estimate he was around forty, an inch shorter than she, and thick through the chest and shoulders. His face was round and shiny, and his short black hair was curly on top. He wore dark slacks, a blue workshirt with the sleeves rolled up to the elbows, and a white apron that was draped over his small paunch and hung to his knees. At the moment, he was ringing up an order on a massive brass cash register.

The customer, an elderly woman in a print dress, handed Berardi a mesh-knit bag. He put her items inside, thanked her by her first name, and walked her to the door.

He came back smiling. "Afternoon. Can I help you?"

"Are you Michael Berardi?"

"Yes, ma'am."

Nora introduced herself as the sister of the woman who had fallen to her death last week at the Owen mansion. After accepting Berardi's condolences, she explained that she had just left Betty Connor and they had discussed a possible connection between the deaths of her daughter and Annie. She decided not to mention Betty's idea of the connection—the evil nature of the mansion.

Berardi's eyebrows came together and the corners of his mouth turned down. "How can you tie the two? One was a murder, the other an accident."

"Maybe an accident."

Berardi's frown deepened. "I haven't heard anything about that. And I spoke to Roy Fellows only yesterday."

"Chief Fellows . . . believes it was an accident," Nora said carefully, not wanting to alienate Berardi. "And he may be right.

But Annie was my sister, and I feel duty-bound to her and to my parents to be certain. I hope you can understand."

Berardi folded his arms across his chest and studied Nora's face for a moment. Her shoulder was throbbing, but she resisted the urge to rub it. Finally the grocer nodded and said, "What would you like to know?"

Nora said, "Betty told me that on the night her daughter was murdered you were playing poker at Doc newby's house."

"That's true. Me and Doc, Roy Fellows, Cecil McOllough from over at the bank, and our mayor, Bill Kneisel."

"Were you there when Cole Newby came home?"

"No. The game had broken up, and Bill and I had already left. There was just Doc, Roy, and Cecil. In fact, I didn't hear about Bonnie until the next day."

"I see."

"I was shocked when I heard. So was everyone in town. This was the sort of thing that happened in Denver, not in Lewiston. We were outraged and a little scared. A lot of people up here own guns, and everyone kept them loaded and handy for the next few months."

"How did people feel toward Cole Newby?"

"I for one was sympathetic. I think most people were. Everyone knew the boy felt awful about what had happened. He blamed himself because he hadn't driven Bonnie home. But nobody held that against him."

"Betty said the sheriff was suspicious of Cole."

"I wouldn't say 'suspicious.' He questioned the boy, sure. But Karl Gant *saw* the murderer, and the man didn't look anything at all like Cole Newby. Besides, it *had* to be a stranger who did it because—"

A customer walked in, a young woman with a small child in tow. She and Berardi exchanged hellos, then Berardi excused himself from Nora and went off to assist the woman.

Nora's gaze drifted out through the hand-lettered front window. Tourists and townies walked by. They were easy to tell apart—the tourists looked aimless. Her mind settled on Karl Gant. He had discovered Annie's body, and he alone had seen

Bonnie Connor's killer. She wondered why suspicion hadn't fallen on him for the deaths. She wondered if—

A Lewiston police vehicle cruised slowly past the store. Quickly, Nora stepped back, out of sight. Then she realized that Annie's yellow Mustang was parked out front, bright as a neon sign. But the police car continued down the street without stopping.

"Something the matter?"

Nora turned to face Berardi, her heart pounding. "Ah, no, not at all. You were saying that Bonnie's murderer had to be a stranger. Why?"

Berardi looked uncomfortable. "I don't like to tell tales about the dead . . . but that young girl was more than a little promiscuous. I think she'd had sex with every boy in town over the age of fourteen. Some men, too."

"What are you getting at?"

Berardi shifted his feet. "Well, the girl was *raped* before she was killed. And as far as I know, she never said no to any male in town."

"Are you saying that a local man wouldn't have *had* to rape her? That she would have simply consented?"

"Well . . ."

Nora despised Berardi's reasoning, but she saw no point in arguing. She changed the subject.

"Do you still play poker?"

Berardi shook his head. "Not with Fellows or McOllough or Doc. Sometimes I'll play with Bill Kneisel and a few other men in town, but nothing on a regular basis. It's not like it used to be."

"Why did the other three stop playing?" The same three, Nora noted, who were present when Cole Newby came home that night.

"Well, we *all* stopped for awhile, mostly because Doc wouldn't play and his place was the best available site. He took Bonnie's death real hard. After all, he had helped with her birth, and his own son was indirectly involved in her death. He stopped socializing. For a long time he hardly talked to anyone, unless it was professionally."

"What about Fellows and McOllough?"

"As for McOllough, he always was a snob. Richest person in town, you know, except for Miss Owen. After Bonnie's death, I never even saw him unless I had business with the bank."

"And Fellows? Why did he quit?"

Berardi frowned. "I'm not sure. I guess he just lost interest. And then he acquired some land, and that had him preoccupied for awhile."

"Land?"

"His uncle died and left him a spread up in Montana. For a while he was going up there every chance he got. In fact, the city council warned him about spending too much time away from the job. They threatened to fire him. He still visits his place now and then, but not like before. He told me he'll retire in a few years and move there."

"You say he got this land right after Bonnie Connor was murdered?"

"I wouldn't say 'right after.' A year or so later, I suppose."

A man with a cane entered the store.

"You'll have to excuse me," Berardi said.

He turned, and Nora touched his arm, stopping him. "Is McOllough still at the bank?"

"Yes."

"One other question. Where can I find Meg Andrew?"

Berardi gave her an odd look. "Isn't she dead?"

25

Willy watched the woman park the yellow car and go into the store where Karl bought food. He knew who she was—the sister of the dead woman who had seen him.

He had been watching her for two days.

Yesterday she had been to the house with Chief Fellows, snooping about the grounds. He had felt unsettled by her presence, as if she were aware of his existence, as if her dead sister were *communicating* with her, telling her about him.

She had come to the house again this morning, exchanging angry words with Karl. The old man felt threatened, Willy knew. His fear hung about him like fog, even after the woman was gone.

Willy had watched her drive away. With his magnificent eye he had tracked her yellow car through the streets of Lewiston, losing it for a time in the trees. For a long while he had waited for it to appear on the distant highway ramp that led out of town. It had not.

Later, though, he had seen it return to Main Street, and later still it had come up the hill toward the house. He had watched it anxiously, sensing Karl's fear below him in the house. If the woman came here again and managed to get inside . . .

But she had driven past the house and disappeared over the mountain.

Sometime later she had returned.

Willy was disquieted. This woman was like an evil wind, gusting through the town, rattling windows and stirring up trouble.

He shifted his feet and moved his great eye closer to the peephole. The yellow car was still parked in front of the store. The woman had been inside for a long time. Why didn't she just leave town? How much longer—

There! She was coming out. Now perhaps she would leave.

But she didn't go to her car. Instead, she walked down the street and entered another building.

Willy had no idea what she was doing. But he sensed danger. For her and for himself.

Perhaps for everyone.

26

When Chief Fellows called in at headquarters, Griff told him, "Cecil McOllough phoned for you. Twice."

Fellows felt a lump of charcoal ignite in his stomach. McOllough wouldn't have phoned unless there was a problem. And he'd had enough problems already today, what with the Honeycut woman trying to shake something loose from Karl and Doc Newby. He handled her, sure, although maybe a bit too roughly. But his ire had been up, and it had been all he could do to stop from *really* laying into her.

It had taken him hours to calm down. Thankfully there had been some routine police work he could jump into. Nothing like a reported assault to take your mind off your troubles.

Little Timmy Johnson, age five, had been bitten on the hand by Gretchen, age three and a half. Gretchen was Ed Gunther's Doberman pincer. When Fellows had arrived at Doc Newby's place, Timmy and his mother were both in hysterics, and Timmy's father Sherm was ready to take his twelve-gauge over to Ed Gunther's and do in Gretchen—and Ed, too, if he got in the way.

While Newby dressed Timmy Johnson's wound, Fellows got a look at the boy's hand. Not that bad—a small gash and no broken bones. He talked to Timmy in private for a few minutes to hear his side of the story; then he drove Sherm Johnson over to Gunther's to examine Gretchen. He found Ed apologetic and Gretchen playful. She wagged her tail and dropped a stick on the ground on her side of the fence, daring Fellows to reach for it. There was a break in the fence right there, just wide enough to reach through. Apparently Timmy Johnson had reached, and Gretchen had snatched the stick and Timmy's hand at the same time.

Fellows made sure Gretchen's rabies shot was up-to-date. And he made damn sure that Sherm accepted Ed's heartfelt apology. He told Ed to fix his fence and pay the doctor bill, and he told Sherm to tell his kid to stop grabbing sticks from strange dogs. Case closed. He drove Sherm back to the clinic and called in his location, feeling better than he had all morning.

That's when Griff told him about McOllough.

"Is there trouble at the bank?" Fellows asked, figuring that Griff wouldn't know what real trouble was.

"No, I asked him that. He said he just needs to talk to you about something. Over."

"Okay, I'm sure it's nothing." *Like hell*, he thought. "I'll swing by the bank on my way in. Out."

He drove to Main Street and parked before the Lewiston

National Bank & Trust. Inside it looked the way a bank should, as far as Fellows was concerned—high, white plaster ceilings with ornate light fixtures suspended by brass chains; old, dark wood counters and wainscotting; thick, floral-patterned carpet underfoot. Quiet and cool. Almost like a church. Better, really, because the riches promised here were more immediate.

There were two customers, one at each cage. Fellows waited for a free teller to announce his presence to Cecil McOllough. Then he saw the bank manager emerge from his office at the rear and wave him on back.

McOllough wore his usual blue suit, vest, white shirt, and striped tie. He was a short, wiry man in his mid-fifties, bald on top and still trying to hide it—Fellows noted with amusement—by plastering a few long strands of hair over his scalp. McOllough shut the door behind Fellows and motioned him into one of the visitor's chairs before his massive antique desk. He sat beside Fellows, not behind the desk, so he could speak more quietly.

"I had a visitor a few hours ago," McOllough said in a hushed tone. His voice was high-pitched, and it had always reminded Fellows of a girl he once dated.

"Who?"

"Nora Honeycut."

"*What?*" Fellows couldn't believe it. "What time was this?"

"Around one thirty. I phoned you earlier, but Griff said you were out on a call."

And here I was afraid I had been too rough on her, Fellows thought. *Looks like I wasn't rough enough.*

"What the hell did she want?"

McOllough shushed him, waving his hand palm downward, glancing at the door. "Not so loud, someone might—"

"All right, all right," Fellows said impatiently. But in a low voice, ceding to McOllough's wishes. This officious little bastard always irritated the hell out of him, even when there wasn't a problem. He supposed the feeling was mutual. It didn't matter, though—they were business partners, not friends.

"She was asking me all sorts of questions. She knows something, Roy. She could cause us a lot of trouble."

"What questions?"

"About the Owen house. Who else might live there, why all the windows are painted, all sorts of things."

"What did you tell her?" Fellows's tone was menacing.

"Nothing, I swear to God, nothing at all."

Fellows eyed him for a moment. "What else did she ask you?"

"About our poker games, and—"

"Poker . . . ?"

"—and Bonnie Connor."

"What?"

"Shhh." McOllough glanced nervously at the door.

"All *right*," Fellows said irritably, straining to keep his voice low. "Just tell me."

McOllough explained how Nora Honeycut had asked to see him, ostensibly on bank business, but once they entered his office, she told him she was the sister of Annie Honeycut and that she was suspicious about the way Annie had died. She believed there might be a connection between Annie's death and the death of Bonnie Connor. She wanted details about that night five years ago.

"What did you tell her?"

"As little as possible," McOllough said. "But she seemed to know a lot already—about Bonnie, the poker game, who was there, and how we all stopped playing. I half expected her to say something about Willy."

"Willy?"

McOllough held up the palms of his small, pink hands, as if he might try to push Fellows away. "She didn't, though. I'm just saying I thought that would be next."

Fellows eased back in his chair, pushed his hat brim up with his index finger, and shook his head. "She's fishing. She doesn't know anything that can hurt us."

"She knows about your land."

Fellows narrowed his eyes and spoke in a mean whisper. "What did you tell her about that?"

"Nothing," McOllough said quickly. "But she knew when you

got it and how the city council reprimanded you for being away from the job. Michael Berardi told her."

Fellows worked the muscles at the points of his jaw. *Honeycut, you meddling bitch.*

"What are we going to do?" McOllough had spoken tentatively, as if he were afraid of what Fellows might say.

"Whatever's necessary. What else did Miss Honeycut say about me?"

McOllough shook his head. "She just asked a lot of questions, mostly about your land—where it was, how much acreage, and so on. I told her I didn't have any details."

"Is that all?"

"Yes. Well . . ."

"What?"

"She asked about Meg Andrew, and I told her the name of the nursing home where she lives." He added defensively, "I wanted to give her *something*, just to get her out of here."

Fellows frowned. "What the hell does she want with old lady Andrew?"

"I didn't ask." McOllough wet his lips with a quick tongue. "Look, Roy, what did you mean a minute ago about doing 'whatever's necessary'?"

"What do you suppose?"

McOllough's face turned bone white.

Fellows said, "Maybe we could lock her in a room with Willy and see what develops."

McOllough said nothing.

Fellows grinned at the small man's uneasiness. "Don't worry about Miss Honeycut. I'll handle her. If she ever comes here again, call me immediately." He hoisted himself out of his chair.

"Wait." McOllough stepped around to the business side of the desk. He unlocked a drawer and withdrew a thick, white envelope. "Today was payday," he said.

Fellows took the envelope without a word. He tucked it inside his shirt and walked out.

27

Chief Fellows spent the next half hour searching Lewiston for Nora and her yellow Mustang. But apparently she had left town. In a way, Fellows was glad. Another confrontation with her today could be bad news—for both of them.

He drove to the stationhouse and found Griff studying a catalogue of police equipment. The open pages showed a variety of black leather gloves with small, cunningly placed pouches filled with lead powder. He looked up, eager for news.

"Did you speak to Mr. McOllough, Chief?"

"Sure did." Fellows poured himself a cup of coffee, then sat behind his desk and pushed around some papers, trying to look busy so Griff wouldn't bother him. He had to figure out what to do about Nora Honeycut. He had a nagging feeling that she would return.

"What was the problem?"

He glanced up. Griff was staring at him, eyebrows raised, begging for details.

Fellows sighed and told him the first lie that popped into his head. "Oh, it was a catastrophe, all right. McOllough says old man Wannamaker's cats are planting their poop in his wife's flower garden, and he wants me to do something about it."

Griff smiled. "What did you tell him?"

"I asked him if he wanted me to shoot the cats or just arrest them."

Griff laughed.

Fellows sipped his coffee. Hot and bitter. He wondered if he should have been more aboveboard with Griff. Maybe it was time he brought the boy up to speed. "You remember Nora Honeycut, don't you?"

Griff paused for a moment, mentally shifting gears. "Sure. She was in town Sunday, right? To pick up her sister's car."

Fellows nodded. "Well, she's back, and she's trying to stir up trouble."

Griff closed his catalogue and sat up straight. "What sort of trouble?" He looked focused now—no longer a big, naïve kid in a uniform, but a cop.

Fellows was pleased. In the eighteen years since he had been appointed chief he had gone through half a dozen officers, and Griff was by far the best. He was reliable, honest, not too smart, and strong as a draft horse. Most of all, he did what Fellows told him without hesitation or complaint. Griff was someone he could count on. Not that he could tell the kid *everything*, certainly not about Willy and the Owen house.

"Miss Honeycut's been talking to a few folks in town, trying to raise doubts about her sister's death. She claims the girl was murdered, or some such bullshit, and that the whole town is covering it up."

Griff shook his head in disbelief. "Why is she saying that?"

"Because she's fucking nuts, that's why. If she shows up here again and you see her, detain her and call me. We'll put the fear of God into her. We don't need her kind in Lewiston."

"Gotcha, Chief."

Fellows stood and drank the rest of his coffee. "I'm going to find out who all she's been talking to and smooth any ruffled feathers." He knew of at least one such person—besides Karl, Newby, and McOllough. He hoped there weren't any more.

"What do you want me to do?"

"Nothing. Unless Miss Honeycut shows up."

✿   ✿   ✿

Fellows found Michael Berardi dusting cans on a shelf near the rear of his store. He was thankful there were no customers— some people in this town had ears the size of satellite dishes.

"Slow day?"

Berardi lowered his feather duster and gave Fellows a neutral smile. "At the moment. What can I do for you, Chief?"

Too busy for small talk, Fellows thought dryly. He and Berardi had played poker together for years, but they had never been close friends. It wasn't just because of their different life-styles— Fellows being a bachelor and Berardi having a wife and four kids. There was a more fundamental difference. Fellows knew what Berardi thought of him: crude and narrow-minded, maybe even a bigot. And Fellows considered Berardi a wimp. After all, the grocer didn't hunt, didn't even *own* a gun, for chrissake.

"I understand Nora Honeycut was in here earlier today, and it wasn't to buy vegetables."

Berardi nodded soberly. "That's top-notch police work, Chief."

Fellows frowned at him. "This isn't funny. Miss Honeycut is a troublemaker."

"Oh?" Berardi gave him an innocent look. "She seemed like a nice lady to me. A little high-strung, perhaps. But who could blame her? Her sister's been dead for less than two weeks."

"That doesn't give her the right to spread lies around town. She's been telling people her sister's death was no accident."

"She does seem to have doubts."

"They're not doubts, they're delusions." Fellows spread his hands and spoke with gentle concern. "Now, maybe Miss Honeycut has always been a little off base, or maybe, as you say, it was her sister's tragic death that pushed her over the edge. Either way, the woman is emotionally and mentally distressed. I don't want *her* problems to become *our* problems."

Berardi gave him a half smile. "Thanks for your concern, Chief."

Fellows hooked his thumbs in his gun belt and said, "Why did she pick you to talk to."

"She had been up to see Betty Connor, asking about Bonnie's

death. Betty told her about it, about that night, the poker game, and so on. My name came up, of course. So did yours."

"So I hear. And Miss Honeycut asked you about me, right?"

Berardi nodded.

"And you found it necessary to tell her about my land and the city council's reprimand."

Berardi shrugged. "It's no secret."

"It should be from her. She's an outsider, and it's none of her damn business what goes on in this town."

"Except that her sister died here."

Fellows narrowed his eyes at Berardi. "You and I both know her death was an accident. And—"

A man and two small boys had entered the store. Berardi waved to them. "If you'll excuse me, Chief."

Fellows stood where he was, blocking the aisle. "Listen, I don't want there to be any doubt in your mind about the death of Annie Honeycut. Sheriff Parmeter and I have looked at it from every possible angle—and then we looked at it again solely for the benefit of the sister. You understand? That girl's death was an accident, and that's all there was to it."

Berardi cocked his head and gave Fellows a questioning look. "No one besides her is doubting you, Chief."

Fellows stepped aside and let the grocer past, wondering if he had pushed a little too hard.

He walked out. Behind him he heard Berardi and the customer laughing. He sat in the police vehicle and considered driving over the mountain and talking to Betty Connor, find out what she told Nora Honeycut.

A waste of time, he thought. *Betty would burn down her house before she'd let me inside.*

Ironic, he knew, considering that they had once been lovers, years ago. It had started a few years after Betty's deadbeat husband abandoned her and four-year-old Bonnie. Betty invited Fellows to Sunday dinner, and after little Bonnie was tucked in bed, they finished the bottle of Chianti he had brought and made love between her perfumed sheets.

It hadn't been what you would call a torrid romance—more

like a dinner and a quickie once a week or so. Betty, though, was looking for a commitment. Fellows wasn't sure what he wanted, but it wasn't the responsibility of a family. Eventually the affair ended.

Still, they had remained friends. Betty even came to him when Bonnie was in junior high and constantly getting in trouble. Fellows had spoken to the girl, trying to sound like a father instead of a cop, not really pulling it off.

He crossed paths with Bonnie a number of times over the years—usually finding her drunk and disorderly with older boys. She was turning into a slut. Still, out of resp. ^or Betty, he always let her off with a warning. Not that he hadn't slapped the shit out of more than one of her "boyfriends."

When Bonnie was murdered, Betty snapped. She screamed for justice, and it never came. She hated Cole Newby, even threatened his life. After the boy left town, Betty looked around for someone else to be a target for her hate.

Me, Fellows thought, starting the car.

And why not? After all, he was the law in town. He was the one paid to protect the citizenry and apprehend the miscreants. And he had failed. More, in Betty's mind, he had failed as Bonnie's substitute father. If he had done a better job counseling her, she wouldn't have gone out with the likes of Cole Newby. She wouldn't have been walking at night near the grounds of the Owen house.

Fellows pulled away from the curb and thought back to the night he and the others had discovered Bonnie's corpse. The night they had discovered Willy. They had made a commitment to one another, a pact. It was for the good of all, they reasoned. Now, though, there was no turning back. Willy's existence had to remain a secret or they were all finished.

And really, he hadn't been too difficult to hide.

But then Annie Honeycut had blundered on the scene. The stupid woman. She had gotten right in Willy's face, and that had been the end of her. And now her sister was hanging around, asking questions, poking her nose where it didn't belong.

Fellows didn't think Nora Honeycut knew anything that

could hurt them. Not yet, anyway. But if she were allowed to continue, she might stumble onto something. He couldn't afford to let that happen. The question was what should he do? He had already given her a strong message, and she had chosen to ignore it.

He smiled grimly and thought about the suggestion he had made to McOllough. Lock her in a room with Willy.

Not a bad idea. Except that another "accidental" death would bring Sheriff Parmeter back here in a minute. And this time he might dig a little too deep.

No, an accident for Nora Honeycut was out of the question. At least in Lewiston.

But what about in Denver? Fellows mused. *Maybe I should find out where she's staying and pay her a surprise visit.*

28

Nora drove out of the mountains, aware of how much her thinking had changed in a single day. This morning she'd had only a vague suspicion about Annie's death. Now she was convinced that her sister had been murdered.

It seemed unbelievable, and it left her feeling sick and horrified. And enraged. Not simply at the killer, the person in the photograph, short and squat, with a deformed head. But she was incensed with the men who knew the truth and were covering it up: Chief Fellows, Karl Gant, and Doc Newby. And she was angry with Sheriff Parmeter for not believing her.

However, why should Parmeter believe her? What did she have to show him? A fuzzy photograph, open to interpretation. Her own impressions of several citizens of Lewiston. A bruised shoulder.

She rubbed her arm now, wincing, thinking that if she could hand Parmeter some evidence, even a *reason* why someone would want Annie dead, then maybe he'd listen to her.

The reason, she felt certain, lay within the Owen house. The problem was finding it—although, Betty Connor may have provided her with a source of information: Meg Andrew. The woman had been a childhood friend of Miss Owen and a long-time resident of Lewiston. If there were secrets about the Owen mansion, she might know them.

Assuming she's alive, Nora thought.

But any search for Meg Andrew would have to wait until tomorrow. Nora was exhausted, physically and mentally, and her head was throbbing.

She searched for aspirin at Annie's apartment. She was certain she had brought a bottle, but she couldn't find it in her carry-on bag, her garment bag, or her purse. And the medicine chest was empty, of course, because she had already boxed up most of Annie's things.

She used a kitchen knife to slit the tape on a cardboard box, then dug through cosmetics, cologne, deodorant, hand lotion, face cream, contact lens cleaner, finally unearthing a half-filled bottle of pain reliever.

She shook out two capsules, hesitated, shook out two more, and washed them down with a glass of water.

In the bathroom she pulled her sweater up over her head, grimacing from the pain in her shoulder. When she saw her arm in the mirror, her stomach turned. A livid, reddish-purple bruise spread from her shoulder halfway to her elbow. The skin was unbroken, but it was raised and tender to the touch.

She pictured Fellows sitting in his car, a smug look on his face.

"You bastard," she muttered.

She started to put her sweater back on, then winced from the pain and set it aside. She raised the shower curtain from the tub and set the plug. After the water was running at the right temperature, she undressed in the bedroom, padded naked back to the bath, then eased down into the tub, letting the hot water slide up to her chin like a blanket.

She closed her eyes and let the bath envelop her.

Later, she awoke with a start. The water was tepid. She drained the tub, closed the curtain, and showered, staying under the hot spray until the room was heavy with steam.

After she had dried herself and wrapped her hair in a towel, she wiped steam from the mirror and examined her wounded arm. The bruise didn't look quite as bad as before. Or perhaps there was just less contrast with her skin color, pink now from the hot shower. But at least the sight of it didn't turn her stomach.

She sorted through her things to get dressed. Everything she had brought—three changes of clothes, including what she wore on the plane—looked limp and wrinkled.

Nora sighed, retrieved the kitchen knife, and began cutting open the boxes lined up in the living room, thankful that she hadn't yet called Goodwill. She dug through Annie's things, trying to find something that would fit, finally settling for a pair of yellow sweatpants and a white pullover, long-sleeved cotton shirt.

She started to pull on the pants. Suddenly, a feeling of despair rose up within her, as if it had been waiting to catch her off guard. She felt helpless against it . . . and foolish, standing naked, miles from home, light years from her comfortable, normal life. She clutched Annie's pants to her chest, fighting back the tears, knowing that if she let them come they would drown her.

Annie oh Annie why did you have to die?

When Nora awoke the next morning, her right arm was stiff and sore. The bruise was darker than before, purple with a greenish tinge around the edges. She tried to work the stiffness out while she dressed in her own beige skirt and Annie's white blouse and chocolate-colored sweater.

After breakfast she phoned the Crest Manor nursing home and asked for directions. Then she spent twenty minutes with Hattie discussing a few problems at the shop. The woman was beginning to sound frazzled. She wanted to know when Nora would be back.

"I'm not sure," Nora told her. "I have to straighten out a few things."

She locked the apartment and set out in Annie's Mustang.

Her first stop was the photo lab. Daniel had the blowup she had requested yesterday—an enlargement of one corner of Annie's last photo. She had hoped it would give her a better look at the person on the grounds. But if anything, it was less distinct than the original. The large-headed, squat figure was even more abstract than before, a blown-up conglomeration of grayish blotches.

Nora shoved the photo in her purse, rechecked the directions she had jotted down, and went to see Meg Andrew.

The nursing home was in Wheat Ridge, a small suburb on Denver's western edge. Nora thought that the aging building looked more like a center for detention than for geriatric care. She wondered how long Meg Andrew had lived there. Not too long, she hoped. She prayed the woman would be amenable to visitors and at least semi-lucid.

The news was a bit worse. The woman Nora had spoken to earlier had been mistaken—Meg Andrew was not there. At least for now. The receptionist told her that Miss Andrew had been in the hospital for nearly a week, and she wasn't expected back until tomorrow.

Nora sat in the car, all dressed up and nowhere to go. She considered visiting Meg Andrew anyway, but the idea of firing questions at an old woman in a hospital bed didn't appeal to her.

But perhaps she could prepare herself for tomorrow's interview. At least she could find out enough about the Owen mansion to ask intelligent questions.

What had Betty Connor said?

You can look it up in the history books.

Nora spent the rest of the day in the Western History Department of the main branch of the Denver public library and at the Western Heritage Center across the street. She pored through books, old newspapers, and even some personal journals, their pages frail with age and veined with flowing, faded script.

She found a surprising amount of historical data about Lewiston. Much of it, though, was useless to her. However, she did come across some interesting details about the fortunes of the Owen family. And, more important, their misfortunes. It seemed that every calamity that befell the Owenses had occurred in their Lewiston mansion. As if the house itself were cursed.

She left the library at five, her eyes watery from strain.

She felt famished, too hungry for the meager fare at the apartment and too tired to stand in line at a grocery store. So she stopped at a drive-through for a box of fried chicken and a container of coleslaw. To make it a bit more palatable she picked up a bottle of Chardonnay at the liquor store.

Nora trudged up the two flights of stairs, the aroma of food wafting about her, making her stomach growl. She walked with her head down, sorting through her keys, and so she was nearly abreast of Annie's apartment before she saw that the door was ajar.

She froze. Hadn't she locked it on her way out this morning? *Yes, definitely.*

Then someone had broken in. In fact, they might still be inside. She had a sudden, wild notion that whoever was in there wasn't simply a burglar. It was Chief Fellows or Karl Gant, come here to make certain she never bothered them again.

Get away, she thought. *Right now. Run downstairs and get the manager.*

Before she could move, the door swung open.

29

Thomas Whitney stood in the doorway with a startled expression. Otherwise, he looked much the same as he had two days ago—sports coat and slacks, necktie pulled loose.

Nora felt immediate relief. But it lasted only a moment. She took a step backward. "What are you doing here?"

"God, you scared me. I didn't know you were out here."

"Answer me," she demanded, more unsettled than angry. "What are you doing here? How did you get in?"

Thomas came into the hallway. Color had risen to his face. "I'm really sorry. I know how this must look to you, but . . . you see, I found a few of Annie's things at my apartment. Her jacket and a pair of earrings." He waved vaguely inside toward the coffee table. "I brought them here on my way home from work, and when you didn't answer the door, I took them down to the manager. He lent me his key and said I could leave them inside." Thomas held up a key with an attached tag. "I only got here a few minutes ago. I apologize. I should have known better than to walk in uninvited. I'm really sorry. I'll just . . . ah . . . well, good-bye." He started toward the stairs, obviously embarrassed.

"Wait." She had spoken impulsively, not wanting him to leave. He was the nearest thing she had to a friend in this city. And perhaps she didn't want to be alone, not after having received such a fright—even if he was the one who had frightened her. "I appreciate your bringing Annie's things."

He nodded, uneasy. "I should have left them downstairs with the manager, instead of coming up here and—"

"It's all right. Really."

They stared at each other for an awkward moment.

Nora said, "Why, ah, why don't you come in for awhile and we can talk. About Annie."

"Well . . ."

"You can stay for dinner, if you like."

"Oh, no, I don't want to impose, especially after—"

"Hey, it's no imposition. Cheap wine and take-out chicken."

"Home cooking," Thomas said with a smile. "Sounds terrific."

Nora put plates and napkins on the table. Thomas twisted the corkscrew and pulled out the cork with a pop. He said, "By the way, I spoke with the sheriff in Idaho Springs yesterday."

Nora turned to him, the box of chicken in her hand. "You talked to Parmeter?"

He nodded. "After what you told me the other day, your misgivings about Annie's death, I mean, I couldn't rest until I knew more. So I called him. He said he had gone to Lewiston and checked things out." Thomas shrugged. "At least we know for sure it was an accident."

"It was *not* an accident," she said. She plunked down the box for emphasis.

Thomas spoke gently. "Well, I know what you think about the photograph Annie took. But Parmeter said—"

"It's not just the photograph, damn it. It's the people in that town." She folded her arms and took a deep breath. "I'm sorry if I sound angry. It's . . ." She shook her head and looked away.

"What is it? Tell me." He touched her arm, then withdrew his hand. "Please. I want to know."

"All right. But let's have some wine."

They sat at the table, the bottle between them. Nora swirled the wine in her glass, clinking a pair of ice cubes.

"I spent most of yesterday in Lewiston," she said, "and I'm convinced that some people up there are hiding the truth about

Annie's death." She related her conversations with Karl Gant and Doc Newby and how they had both appeared unnerved by her questions, how they seemed unable to hide their fear. And she told him about her run-in with Chief Fellows, his nervousness, his threats. "He gave me a little something to remember him by," she said. She pushed up the sleeve of her sweater, wincing as the fabric brushed over the bruise.

Thomas leaned forward and stared in disbelief. "Holy shit. Fellows did that to you?" There was anger in his voice.

Nora described the incident.

"Have you talked about this to Sheriff Parmeter?"

Nora shook her head. "It would be pointless—my word against Fellows's, and he'd either deny it or say it was an accident." She smiled wryly and gently pulled down her sleeve. "Another Lewiston accident."

Thomas set his jaw and stared at his fist wrapped around the stem of the glass. "That son of a bitch," he said under his breath.

"My sentiments exactly."

He looked up at her. "What are you going to do?"

"I don't know for sure," she said. "The main thing is I have to find something concrete, something I can show Parmeter to convince him to investigate Annie's death. I want him to really dig into things, tear that town apart if he has to." She sipped her wine. She was relaxed now, completely at ease with Thomas. She could see why Annie had been attracted to him. He was kind, intelligent, someone she could talk to.

Then she felt a pang of guilt. Here she was enjoying the company of her dead sister's lover.

It's not like that, she told herself . . . or Annie. *Not like that at all.*

She took a drink of wine and said, "I found out some things today that might help. At the library, of all places. Not enough to take to Parmeter, but it's a start. The history of the Owen family. And their house." She paused. "That place is bad news."

"What do you mean?"

"It's a long story." She smiled. "How about we zap the chicken in the microwave first. I'm starving."

While they ate, Nora explained that Miss Chastity Owen was

the last living member of the Owen family, and that her grandfather Christian had built the mansion.

"He was a violent, greedy man," she said.

She told him that in 1864, when Christian Owen was twenty years old, he moved from St. Louis to Lewiston and went to work for a man named McNulty, who ran a general store. A year later McNulty was found murdered, his head caved in with a miner's pick. His body was discovered on a hill at the edge of town. Coincidentally, the future site of the Owen mansion. Christian Owen was suspected of the murder, but there were no witnesses, no evidence, and no arrest. A few months later he married McNulty's widow and took over operation of the store.

During those days, the mountains around Lewiston were pockmarked with silver mines and crawling with miners who dreamed of striking the mother lode. The town's population swelled to three thousand—prospectors, vagabonds, con men, whores, whiskey drummers, merchants, and even a few God-fearing families.

Christian grubstaked dozens of miners for a share of their future finds. With a little luck and more than a little deception he eventually became the sole owner of two of the largest silver mines in the state.

The money poured in. Christian spent lavishly, importing European craftsmen to Lewiston to build a fine hotel, an opera house, and a magnificent mansion for him and his wife. But he also invested in railroads and steel back East, knowing the flow of silver couldn't last forever.

By the time he was thirty-five, he was the wealthiest and most powerful man in the region. He had everything he wanted. Except an heir.

Christian grew to hate his barren wife. What good was an empire with no son to inherit it? He derided the poor woman in public, until she was too humiliated to show her face at the opera, parties, or even in the shops in town. She confined herself to the prison of their great house, alone, except for the servants.

Christian began spending more time in the town's saloons and houses of ill repute. He fancied himself a ladies' man, and to prove it he slept with every young whore in Lewiston.

Then he met Sabrina.

She was a new arrival in town, a strange, beautiful woman, with olive complexion, raven hair, and dark eyes. No one knew where she came from. The townspeople believed she was either a gypsy or a half-breed. One thing was certain—she cast a spell over Christian. He became obsessed with her. He dressed her in silk and jewels and strutted about the town with her clinging to his arm.

Then, quite suddenly, Christian's wife died. The cause was unknown, but it was thought to be a failed heart . . . or a pillow pressed to her face. Two weeks after his wife's death, Christian married Sabrina.

"What does any of this have to do with Annie?" Thomas asked.

"There's a pattern of murder connected with that house. It's as if the building itself is . . . evil. Let me tell you the rest."

30

"After Christian Owen married Sabrina," Nora said, "all of their house servants quit."

The servants had said they could feel the presence of Christian's first wife. A few of them claimed to have seen her ghost staring out the windows of the cupola. Most of the citizens of Lewiston discounted these stories as foolishness. Some, though, believed. Christian was forced to hire new servants from out of town.

Eight months after their marriage, Sabrina gave birth to a boy—Lucas. Christian proudly showed off his son to Lewiston society and showered the child with affection. He set up a sizable trust fund to secure his son's future.

Sabrina, though, turned away from her son and refused to be confined to the role of mother. She was too wild and passionate to sit home and rock the cradle. She became a frequent visitor to the town's saloons—and the beds of other men.

Then, just before Lucas's first birthday, Sabrina disappeared without a trace. Some townsfolk said she had grown tired of Lewiston, packed up, and moved out. But others believed Christian had murdered her and buried her body in the cellar of the great house. They wondered aloud about the spirits of Christian's two dead wives, now under the same roof—and what horror these two might spawn.

Christian didn't remarry, but hired nannies to help raise his son.

The women quit, one after another. A few left saying the house was haunted. But most of them got out because little Lucas Owen was a terror. He was dark, like his mother—skin, hair, eyes, and (some said) soul. He seemed to enjoy inflicting pain, whether it was biting a playmate or strangling a kitten. Twice he was caught trying to set fire to the house.

When Lucas was ten, he killed another boy, a child of three, by crushing his head with a rock. Christian defended his son against the outcries of the townspeople, swearing that the death had been an accident. But soon after the incident he enrolled Lucas in a military academy back East. A year later the boy ran away from the academy and was not seen again for years.

Christian lived alone now in the great house. He aged rapidly.

When the silver market crashed just before the turn of the century, the mines closed down, the population of Lewiston dwindled to two hundred souls, and the town nearly died. Christian hung on to much of his wealth through his investments. He pumped just enough into the town to keep it alive.

Then unexpectedly, Lucas returned to Lewiston. He was

twenty-one years old, an imposing figure—tall, broad-shouldered, and darkly handsome. He had come to claim his fortune.

But there were obstacles. His father had seen to that.

Christian had carefully constructed his financial empire to keep the power of liquidation forever out of the hands of his heirs, granting them access only to dividends and interest from a trust fund. The income from this fund was substantial, more than enough to satiate even a greedy man, even Lucas. There was, however, one iron-clad provision: to receive income the heir must reside in Lewiston.

Lucas was enraged. He had planned to take   share of the fortune abroad, to sail to Europe and live a life of glorious debauchery. He railed at his father, even threatened him. But Christian, now old and frail, would not be cowed. He loved Lewiston, and he would not see the town abandoned. So Lucas had to choose between two disagreeable alternatives   leave town as a pauper or stay as a prince.

He stayed.

A few months later Christian Owed died. A stomach ailment. Some believed he had been poisoned.

Lucas hired lawyers to find a loophole in the trust, one that would allow him to receive his income and still live away from Lewiston. They were successful. Lucas married a local woman, Emily Booker, who nine months later gave birth to a daughter, Chastity, and while his family resided in the mansion in Lewiston, Lucas lived abroad. He returned once each year to pad his money belt. Sometimes he'd stay for as long as a month—if there happened to be any fresh young maidens in town, waiting to be deflowered.

Then, when his daughter was fifteen years old, Lucas tried to molest her in her own bedroom. His wife intervened by blowing off the back of his head with a single shot from a Winchester rifle.

Emily Booker Owen was never tried for the murder of her husband. She shut herself up in the great house and rarely ventured into town. Her daughter Chastity also became a recluse. And the rumors spread that the Owen house was haunted, now that the vile spirit of Lucas Owen had joined those of his parents, Christian and Sabrina. Figures were seen wandering the grounds at night, and faces appeared in the cupola windows.

"That's everything I learned," Nora said.

Thomas slowly shook his head. "I still don't see what any of this has to do with Annie's death."

"There's something in that house that—"

"I don't believe in ghosts," Thomas said.

"Neither do I."

"Or in evil houses."

Nora wasn't so certain about that, but she said nothing.

Thomas said, "If Annie was murdered, then—"

"She was."

"If so, then a living, breathing person did it. Not a spirit."

"Of course. But whoever did it had a reason. And I think the reason lies within the Owen mansion, maybe something from its past."

Thomas looked doubtful. "I'm not trying to be obstinate, but I still don't see the connection between murders that occurred sixty or a hundred years ago and Annie's death."

"The house itself is the connection. And the people who live there. Miss Owen's mother was a murderer, her father was a murderer, her grandfather—"

"Are you implying that Miss Owen killed Annie?"

"No. No, of course not. But she's a strange woman. Karl's strange, too. I get the feeling—I don't know how to say it—it's as if the house *influences* them. Even Doc Newby and Chief Fellows seem frightened by it. And something else I haven't mentioned—a young girl was murdered on the grounds five years ago." She described the death of Bonnie Connor. "Now, maybe all those murders are a coincidence. But I don't think so." She pictured the mansion, isolated from the town, standing above it like a fortress. She felt a chill. "Just the sight of the house is enough to make you think it's hiding some terrible secrets." she said. "Especially the painted windows."

"The what?"

Nora poured herself another glass of wine. "The windows on the second story and the cupola are painted over."

"Why, for God's sake?"

"I've asked about that. Apparently, Miss Owen and Karl closed off half of the house because there was too much upkeep for them to handle and it was too expensive to heat in the winter."

"How long have the windows been painted?" Thomas asked pointedly.

"At least twenty years. Why?"

He shook his head. "I guess I was thinking it might be significant if it had been done after Annie's death. Or after Bonnie Connor's murder. As if Miss Owen and Karl were trying to hide something in there."

"I wonder," she said. "It might be interesting to know exactly when they were painted." She sipped her wine. "In any event, I intend to keep digging until I find something to take to Sheriff Parmeter."

"So you're going back to Lewiston."

"Not yet. Betty Connor gave me the name of a woman who grew up with Miss Owen, someone who might be able to help. Meg Andrew. I plan on seeing her tomorrow."

"Let me go with you."

Nora hesitated. Thus far, her search for the truth had been intensely personal. And why not? Annie was her only sister. But there was more to it than that. Ever since she had arrived in Colorado, she had felt Annie's presence. It was almost as if her dead sister had not yet "gone over to the other side," as her mother would have phrased it. As if Annie were hanging around, standing behind her, watching her, encouraging her.

When she had gone to Lewiston to confront Karl and the others, she had been completely out of her element, nervous and frightened every step of the way. But she had found strength in Annie, as if she weren't proceeding alone. In an odd way she felt closer to Annie now than she ever had. Would she lose that feeling if Thomas were along? Would she lose Annie?

Annie is dead, she told herself. *And Thomas is . . . here. And I can use all the help I can get.*

"Yes, I'd like you to come with me," she said.

"Thanks, I appreciate it. I really need to do this, to do *something* for Annie. For you, too."

"What do you mean?"

"I want to help. Annie's death was a shock to me, and I can only guess at the pain you must feel. I'm not the kind of person who can walk away from something like that." He shook his head. "Jesus, that must sound self-righteous as hell, but all I mean is—"

"You don't have to explain," Nora said. "I understand."

They finished dinner in relative silence, as if there was no more to say. Nora told Thomas she would pick him up the following morning at eight. He wrote out directions for her, and she walked him to the door.

"See you tomorrow," she said.

"Yes. And I . . ." He hesitated. There was something in his eyes she hadn't seen before. Tenderness. He cleared his throat and said, "Yes, well, see you in the morning."

Much later, Nora had the nightmare.

Once again she stood at the end of a long, dark hall. Annie was at the other end, dressed in white, hovering above the floor, calling to her. *Help me, Nora, please help me.* But Nora was too frightened to move. She knew something was in the hallway, hiding in the shadows. Waiting for her. Annie cried out. *Please, Nora!* Nora forced herself to move forward. And then slowly the shadows coalesced. They took shape. And life. The thing rose up, unearthly. It came toward her.

Nora sat up abruptly, heart hammering in her chest.

She took a few deep breaths and told herself it was only a dream. Then she got out of bed and walked through the apartment, switching on every light, pushing away the shadows. She sat on the couch with her feet tucked beneath her, hugging her knees, feeling like a little girl afraid of the dark.

It was a long time before she returned to the bedroom.

And longer still before she slept.

31

Willy thrashed in his sleep.

Someone was trying to get into the house. Willy could hear him on the floor below, scratching at the front door, clawing at it, ripping it to splinters.

The hated one.

The One broke through the door and entered the house. Willy could sense his murderous greed. He had returned to claim his fortune, and he would kill anyone who tried to stop him.

Suddenly, to Willy's horror, Miss Owen emerged from her room. She stood in the hallway, blocking the path of the One, demanding that he leave her house. But he came forward and attacked her, threw her to the floor. She cried out for Willy. Then her cries were cut off as the One fell on her and began to strangle her.

Willy awoke with a gasp.

He lay naked on his bed, feverish, breathing rapidly. His sheet was soaked with sweat. Images burned at the edge of his mind. What he had seen had been more than a dream.

He rose from the bed and shuffled across the room, hunched over, his naked body as ponderous as a giant white slug. He moved along the second-floor hall toward the head of the stairs, pulling himself forward with his oversized, heavily muscled right arm, as thick as a third leg.

He stood at the top of the stairwell and stared down into blackness. He held his breath and listened. The only sound was his heart thumping in his massive chest.

Was someone down there?

He could sense Miss Owen and Karl, asleep in their beds. But were they alone? Was there another, deadly presence?

Willy started to take the first step, and then stopped. It was forbidden. Miss Owen and Karl had demanded that he never venture downstairs. He always obeyed—nearly always—for he knew they wanted what was best for him. And the few times that he disobeyed had resulted in near disaster.

But if the One were really down there . . .

Willy felt rage rise within him like a beast with a will of its own. It urged him on, forcing him to descend the dark staircase.

He stepped off the bottom riser into a long, murky hallway that stretched away to his right and left. He stayed in the shadows, listening for the slightest sound.

Nothing.

He peered down the hallway, turning his large eye first toward the rear of the house, then the front.

There! Was that a person?

Hovering above the floor was a form wrapped in a pale, milk-white gown. Insubstantial, ghostly. A woman?

As Willy stared, the figure began to resolve itself. It was not a person or a spirit, but merely the leaded glass window in the front door with moonlight sifting through the lacy curtain.

Willy should have felt relieved. But he did not. He knew that the dream and the sensations that had brought him downstairs were real.

The One was coming.

32

On Thursday morning Nora watched the local news before she got dressed. The temperature was expected to reach the high fifties under partly cloudy skies. Cool weather, if she were in Iowa. And there she would have worn a sweater and brought a coat. But she had learned that in Denver's dry air, fifty-eight degrees felt to her like sixty-eight. She dressed in a skirt, a silk blouse, and a blazer.

After she finished her toast and rinsed out her coffee cup in the sink, she drove to Thomas's apartment.

She felt apprehensive, and she tried to explain it away as nervousness about interviewing Meg Andrew—an old woman, possibly senile, and perhaps her last hope at learning more about the Owen mansion. But it was more than that. It was Thomas.

She felt attracted to him.

True, they had been together only twice, each time in Annie's apartment and certainly under stressful conditions—but the feeling was there. It was easy to explain. After all, he was a good-looking man, caring and sensitive. Also, he was about her age, and like her, divorced, living alone. She had seen something in his eyes last night, something that had come and gone quickly, as if he had forced it away—a tender look that had nothing to do with pity or sorrow. Affection.

For the first time in years she became aware of a place inside her, a warm and wonderful place that she had kept locked up for too long. Without meaning to, she had opened it. Or perhaps Thomas had.

But this was wrong. The circumstances were untenable. Thomas had been seeing Annie, sleeping with her, and she had been dead for less than two weeks. It would be unthinkable to allow anything to develop between them. Still, as she parked in front of his apartment, she had to fight off the morbid feeling that they were "going out." And more, that they had been introduced to each other by Annie.

Thomas was waiting in the building's vestibule. He waved as he came out. They exchanged good-mornings, and Nora steered the Mustang into traffic.

"Thanks again for letting me come with you."

"I'm glad you want to." Then she added quickly, "What I mean is, it makes it easier if someone else is along."

"Sometimes it does. Although you've done well enough on your own—going to Lewiston and confronting Karl and the others."

She smiled. "If you want to know the truth, I was scared to death. Confrontation is not my strong suit."

"You don't expect that sort of trouble from Meg Andrew, do you?"

"I don't know what to expect."

But Meg Andrew was not at the nursing home. The receptionist told them that the doctor had decided to keep her in the hospital for one more day.

"Now what?" Thomas said as they walked out to the car.

It was cool in the shade of the building, but as they stepped into the sunlit parking lot, the sun felt warm on Nora's back. She took off her blazer and laid it in the backseat.

"There's not much we can do until tomorrow," she said.

"Unless we visit her in the hospital."

"I'd rather wait until she comes home."

"You're probably right." He paused. "What would you think about driving up to Lewiston?"

She turned to him. "Now?"

"Unless you have other plans. I've already taken the day off work, and, well, I want to see where Annie ... where it happened."

Nora pictured the grounds of the Owen mansion, the cupola, the painted windows—and she had a sudden premonition that something waited for her inside the house. Fragments of a dream rustled through her mind, like pieces torn from a photograph, chased by a cold wind. She clutched at them, catching a few partial images. A dark hallway. A woman in white. A hideous thing in the shadows.

"If you'd rather not go," Thomas said, "that's okay. But I think I'll drive up there on my own. I promise I'll keep a low profile."

"No." Nora swept the dream fragments from her mind. "No, we'll go together. I'll show you where Annie died."

They headed west out of the metro area on Sixth Avenue, then followed I–70 into the mountains. As they gained altitude the sky became overcast and the air grew noticeably cooler. Nora closed the Mustang's vents. They sped past vast armies of pine trees, standing at attention. In the distance, rising above the trees, were magnificent peaks, gray and commanding and immortal.

Thomas said, "I keep thinking about your parents. This must be devastating to them."

"It is. And doubly so because Annie was the second of their children to die young."

"I didn't know that."

"Our brother Robert was killed in a car accident when he was seventeen. His death was ... I don't know how to describe it. It changed all of us, perhaps Annie most of all. She adored him. He was strong, athletic, smart, good looking. A hero. Someone who would live forever—at least in the eyes of a six-year-old girl. Maybe in the eyes of us all."

"You say Annie changed. How so?"

Nora smiled wryly. "Before Robert's death, she was a real

sweetie, always eager to please. But after the accident, she acted as if she didn't care what people thought of her. She became reckless, threw caution to the wind—at home, in school, on the playground. She took on every challenge, every dare. Had anyone climbed to the top of the biggest elm tree in the park? No? Annie would try it. Had anyone stood up to the classroom bully? No? Look out, here comes Annie."

Thomas laughed.

"She went out of her way to take chances," Nora said. "She pushed herself to the limit. It used to scare the hell out of my poor parents."

"What about you?"

"I guess she scared me, too."

"No, I mean, how did Robert's death affect you?"

Nora sighed. "I was unbelievably depressed. And frightened. If death could so easily take Robert, who was strong and quick-witted and able, how could *I* ever feel secure. I felt weak and helpless, and I . . . withdrew. It took me years to get over his death." She paused. "Maybe I'm still not over it."

They rode in silence for a time.

Thomas said, "Have you told your parents about Annie's last photograph and—"

"Good God, no," Nora said. "They don't know anything about this. I can't imagine how they'd react if they thought her death was anything more than an accident. As far as they know, I'm here to sort out Annie's things, pay off her bills, and so on. They'd prefer it if I were home, tending to my own business."

"A flower shop, right?"

She glanced at him.

"Annie told me," he said. "She was really proud of you for owning your own business. She envied you."

"She did?" It was Nora who envied *her*. "For what?"

"Let's see, how did she put it—for establishing something last-ing, a solid business. For being stable."

Nora smiled. "Oh, it's stable, all right. Like an anchor. Some-times I wish I could just . . ." She shook her head. "I don't know. Pull it up and let it go."

"You mean sell it?"

"I've had offers."

"What would you do if you sold?"

Nora shrugged, steering with both hands. "I've tried to imagine it, but I can't. Running that shop is about the only thing I've done since I left college. Maybe I'm too involved with it to ever let go."

"Owning a business—you could do worse."

"Sure, I know. It's just that sometimes I feel as if I'm missing something."

"What?"

She shrugged again. "Life."

Nora saw the exit sign ahead and in the distance the roof-peaks of the Victorian houses. She slowed, then turned down the off-ramp.

Thomas said, "I wonder if it will look the same."

"What's that?"

"The town. I haven't been here for years."

"You never told me you had been to Lewiston before." Nora wasn't sure why, but that bothered her.

"Sure, lots of times."

She waited for him to explain further, but he said nothing.

33

The town was waiting for them under gray skies. A chill mountain breeze swept down the valley, and the few tourists on the sidewalks hurried along from shop to shop with coats buttoned, collars up, and chins tucked down.

Nora steered the Mustang through town. She kept a wary eye out for Chief Fellows, although she had no idea what she'd do if she spotted him. Certainly not speed away. Whatever happened would be up to Fellows. Besides, what could he do so long as she broke no laws? Still, it was comforting to have Thomas there.

"There's the house," she said.

The cupola rose ominously above rooflines and treetops, staring over the town with blank windows. Thomas leaned forward, his expression grim.

"It looks . . . hateful," he said. "Or maybe it's because I know what happened there."

"Maybe."

They crossed Main and continued up the hill to Silver Street. Nora turned left and parked before the towering hedge that surrounded the grounds. When they climbed out, the chill air penetrated Nora's clothes as quickly as if she had been doused with ice water. She put on her blazer, wishing she had brought a coat. She stood for a moment with her back to the hedge and looked out over the valley. It held the town like a crucible. The only sound was the hiss of the wind hastening down the steep mountain slopes and pushing through the pines.

"Ready?" Thomas said.

Nora crossed her arms and shivered, then turned to face the opening in the hedge. "I guess."

"What's wrong?"

"I don't know. I just have a bad feeling about this place."

"You don't have to go in there. Why don't you wait in the car while I—"

"No," she said. "I'm all right. Besides, there's something I want to see."

She led Thomas through the gateway. When he got his first full view of the house, he whispered, *"Jesus."*

Nora understood his reaction. There was something hostile about the mansion. It seemed more like an entity than an edifice, belligerent, designed to repulse visitors, to warn them away.

She studied the structure for a moment, trying to pin down exactly what created such a sense of malevolence. Perhaps the mélange of architectural styles—not exactly strident, but not quite blending smoothly together. Or the front porch, which gaped like the maw of a gigantic beast. Or the painted windows. Certainly those.

Or that my sister died here.

She started toward the side of the house.

"Shouldn't we ask first?" Thomas had spoken as quietly as if they were in a cemetery.

Nora turned and whispered, "If Karl sees us he'll call the cops. Let's just take a look, then leave."

Thomas hesitated, scowling at the cavernous front porch. He nodded. "Okay."

Nora led him across the lawn and around the corner of the building. She pointed to the top of the trellis. Vines hung down like strips of hide, withered and brown, dead.

"She fell from up there."

Thomas's eyes moved to the roofline, then down to the bushes and the lawn. "Is that where . . . they found her?"

Nora nodded, staring at the lawn, remembering the photographs that Sheriff Parmeter had shown her of Annie's blanket-draped body. She imagined what it must have been like when the photos were taken, Fellows and the others standing around her sister like gravediggers. She found herself scrutinizing the grass, morbidly looking for the indentation of Annie's body. Of course, there was nothing.

She turned away from the house and opened her purse. She withdrew Annie's last photograph, then held it up, comparing the image of the yard with the yard itself. Thomas stood beside her. Nora tapped the corner of the print. The blurred, squat figure seemed to crouch beneath her finger.

"He was standing over there, wouldn't you say?"

Thomas looked from the photo to the yard. "I think so. Near that tree."

They walked across the lawn, away from the house. Nora felt exposed and vulnerable. While Thomas scanned the ground, she nervously watched the house and the gateway, fully expecting Karl or Chief Fellows to come bearing down on them. Then she saw movement to her left.

"*Come here,*" she whispered urgently, tugging at Thomas's arm, pulling him with her behind a thick juniper tree. She pointed toward the rear of the house.

The back end of the old black Cadillac jutted out behind the building. And Karl was there, leaning over the trunk, laying something inside. He walked away, out of sight. A minute later Nora heard the slap of a screen door, and then Karl reappeared carrying a tall stack of cardboard boxes. Each box was about two feet square and three or four inches high. When Karl set them in the trunk, Nora heard the dull chink of glass. Again Karl stepped out of sight. A minute later he returned with another tall stack of boxes.

Nora could see that all the boxes were marked with the same blue logo, but she couldn't make out exactly what it was.

Karl laid the boxes in the trunk with the others, slammed the trunk lid, then stepped out of view. The car rocked on its springs, and the engine started.

"Come on," Nora said, heading across the yard.

"What?" Thomas hurried to catch up.

"Let's find out where he's going."

34

As they hustled through the gateway in the hedge, they saw the shiny black Cadillac glide down Alpine Street. Thomas barely got his door closed before Nora jerked the Mustang in a tight U-turn.

"Why are we doing this?" Thomas asked, obviously perplexed.

"I want to find out what's in those boxes."

"Why? What difference does it make?"

"Maybe none," Nora said. "I'm just curious. Besides, it might give us some idea of what goes on in that house."

Nora stayed a few blocks behind the Cadillac as it stopped at the intersection at Main Street, then continued across. Karl drove at a maddeningly slow pace, straight through town. He steered onto the interstate heading east. There was a moderate amount of traffic, and since Karl drove at a sedate forty-five miles an hour, every vehicle on the highway passed him by. Nora was forced to hang back and endure tailgaters and angry looks.

"Now *I'm* curious," Thomas said. "Where do you suppose he's taking them?"

"Maybe Idaho Springs."

But Karl passed the exits to Idaho Springs and continued eastward.

They followed him down out of the mountains, leaving behind the overcast sky. The city spread before them under a hazy patchwork of blue and white.

Karl left the interstate on C-470 and drove south along the western edge of the metro area. After a few miles he headed east into the city on U.S.-285, which eventually transformed itself into Hampden Avenue. He turned south again on Federal, a wide boulevard that led them through an older, less populated suburb of Denver. There was enough traffic for Nora to stay safely within half a block of the Cadillac. A mile later they turned off Federal and headed down a two-lane blacktop into an area of warehouses and weedy fields. The Platte River lay ahead.

Suddenly the Cadillac slowed and turned right onto a hard-packed dirt driveway. Nora stopped and read the sign near the entrance—MUNICIPAL LANDFILL.

The black car halted at a small shack a few hundred feet from the street. Nora saw Karl hand money to a man inside the shack, then drive into the dump.

"Big mystery," Thomas said. "He's throwing out the trash."

Nora chewed her lip. "But why drive fifty miles to do it?"

Thomas frowned, staring at the distant veil of dust that had enveloped the Cadillac.

"Maybe we should go in."

"He might spot us," Nora said.

"So what? At least we'd find out what's in the boxes."

Nora hesitated. "All right." She pulled into the driveway. As she approached the shack, a man leaned out the window. She stopped beside him.

"Whatcha got?" he wanted to know. He was around fifty, wearing a dirty baseball cap and three-days' growth of beard. One of his front teeth was missing.

"We, ah, just want to drive in," Nora said. "How much is it?"

"Not till I know whatcha got. We don't allow no flammables."

"We don't have anything like that. Can't we just go in?"

"No, by God, not till I see what you've got in that trunk." He came out of the shack."

"We don't have time for this," Thomas said.

The man leaned down beside Nora's window. "Let me have your keys."

"I, ah, I'm sorry," she said, then stomped on the gas and popped the clutch. The Mustang jumped forward, tires spinning in the dirt, enveloping the shack-man in a cloud of dust. He ran after them, waving his arms.

Nora drove for a hundred yards along a dirt path. Then she was forced to pull far to the side when a dump truck lumbered by the other way, wrapping them in a dusty cloak. She waited impatiently for the dust to settle and the visibility to return. She started forward. And suddenly a black car appeared out of the dust, heading toward the entrance. Karl.

"Damn it, we're too late," Nora said. "He already unloaded the boxes."

"We could go in there and try to find them."

"That could take days."

Nora wheeled the Mustang in a U-turn and followed the Cadillac past the shack. The man was back inside, talking on the phone, waving his arm in agitation. He gaped at them as they drove past.

Karl turned east onto the asphalt road, and Nora followed.

"Now what?"

"I don't know," she said. "We might as well see where he's going."

Karl crossed the river, then went north on Santa Fe Drive, busy with commercial traffic. A quarter of a mile later he turned off Santa Fe and entered an immense parking lot surrounding a Pace Warehouse store. He steered the Cadillac down the crowded lanes and pulled into an empty slot.

Nora parked a few rows away. She watched Karl leave his car, cross the lot, and enter the store.

"So now he's going shopping," Thomas said.

"What do they sell here?"

"Practically everything. Food, furniture, clothing, automobile tires, liquor, you name it. But you have to be a member to get in."

They waited.

Twenty minutes later Karl emerged from the store pushing a large flatbed truck laden with boxes. Nora thought that they looked like the ones he had loaded in his trunk in Lewiston and, presumably, disposed of at the dump—similar in size, shape, and blue logo. Karl opened the trunk of the Cadillac and began stacking the boxes inside.

"He doesn't know me." Thomas opened his door. "I'll just go over there and see what he's got."

Nora watched him walk between cars and pass within a few feet of Karl. He looked like a child beside the giant chauffeur. She saw Thomas hesitate, staring down, then move on. He made a wide circle and returned to the car.

Nora raised her eyebrows. "So?"

"You won't believe this."

"What?"

"Baby food."

"*What?*"

"At least a dozen cases. What are they doing up there, running a nursery?"

Nora frowned and shook her head. "I don't get it." She watched Karl slam the trunk. He pushed the flatbed toward the store's entrance.

"You said Miss Owen was senile," Thomas said. "Maybe she dines on the stuff."

Nora frowned, trying to come up with another, more logical explanation. She could not.

"Okay, let's say you're right," she said. "Then why does Karl drive all the way to Denver to get it? He could buy baby food in Lewiston. Or in Idaho Springs."

"It's probably a lot cheaper here."

Nora exhaled audibly. "Come on, Miss Owen is the richest woman in Lewiston. Why have Karl drive a hundred miles round trip to save a couple of bucks? Besides, he probably burned up that much in gasoline."

Thomas spread his hands, searching for an answer. "So maybe Karl's embarrassed for her. He doesn't want anyone in town to know about her eating habits."

"It's possible . . ."

They watched Karl return to the Cadillac, get in, and drive slowly from the parking lot.

Nora started the engine. "Of course, we're assuming he's taking the boxes home."

"Where else would he take them?"

"We're going to find out."

They followed the Cadillac back to Lewiston. Nora stayed well behind. She stopped at the intersection of Main Street and watched the black car continue up the hill and turn into the driveway behind the Owen house.

"*Bon appétit,* Miss Owen," Thomas said.

"I wonder."

Nora turned right on Main Street and parked near Berardi's grocery store. Thomas followed her inside. The short, stocky grocer was flicking a feather duster over shelves of cans. Nora greeted him and introduced him to Thomas.

She said, "This may sound like it's coming from left field, but does Miss Owen buy her groceries here?"

"Sure. That is, Karl does. Occasionally, Miss Owen will come in with him."

"*All* their groceries?" Nora asked.

Berardi looked at her, then at Thomas. "Why do you ask?"

"Just curious," Thomas said.

Berardi scowled at them for a moment, then shrugged. "Yes, I believe all their groceries. Karl comes in every Friday and buys what I'd say is a week's supply for two people. Elderly people."

"Do you sell baby food?" Nora asked.

Berardi blinked. "Baby food? Sure."

"Does Karl ever buy any?"

"*Karl?*" Berardi nearly burst out laughing. "Why the hell would Karl want *baby* food?"

"That's what I'd like to know," Nora said.

35

They sat in the Mustang.

"So who's the baby food for?" Nora said.

"I don't know, but I'm so hungry I could eat some of it right now."

Nora checked her watch—two fifteen. She was so focused on Karl that she had forgotten about lunch.

"I saw a restaurant with a courtyard back at the intersection," Thomas said.

The last time Nora had been in there Celia the waitress had shunned her, and Chief Fellows had slammed a side-view mirror into her shoulder. It still hurt.

"Let's go somewhere else," she said.

They found a restaurant on the north side of town, a small white frame building with a blue-shingled peaked roof. It was deserted inside, but aromas hung sweetly in the air. They wondered if the place was closed. Then a waitress appeared from the back wearing a white blouse, a blue skirt, and a friendly smile. She gave them their pick of the nine empty tables. After they had seated themselves by the front window, Nora ordered a club sandwich and iced tea, and Thomas got the day's special—pot roast, mashed potatoes, and vegetables.

The waitress left them, and Thomas said, "Maybe Miss Owen and Karl supplement their diet with baby food."

"Are you serious?"

He arched his eyebrows. "What else would they do with it?"

Nora just shook her head.

"Maybe they feed it to their cats," he suggested.

"Did you see any cats around there?"

"No, but I'm saying if they *have* cats . . ."

"I don't know." Nora was unconvinced. "Whatever they're doing with it, they're taking great pains to hide the fact—driving all the way to the city to buy it and paying to dispose of the empties at the dump."

"What do you think is going on?"

"There's only one way to find out."

"What?"

"Go in the house."

Thomas glanced toward the kitchen, where the waitress had disappeared. He spoke in a low voice: "Are you saying *break in?*"

"Well, no. What I had in mind was talking our way past the senile Miss Owen."

"And what about Karl?"

"We do it when he's not around."

"But how will we know when he . . ." A grin spread across his face. "When he's at Berardi's store buying groceries, right? On Friday."

"Exactly. And tomorrow's Friday."

Their food arrived. Thomas ate in silence, obviously famished. Nora chewed a bite of her sandwich, then sipped her iced tea. She recalled something that Thomas had said when they arrived in town, something that had troubled her for no apparent reason.

"You told me you had been here quite a few times in the past. To Lewiston, I mean."

Thomas nodded, chewing.

"When was the last time?"

He gave her a brief frown. "Years ago. Why?"

"I don't know. I guess I was afraid that you might *know* some of these people and that . . . God, this sounds so paranoid . . . that you were keeping it from me."

He smiled and shook his head. "Not at all. And it's been at least ten years."

Nora felt relieved—and a bit contrite.

Thomas said, "My wife and I used to take the kids skiing. Lewiston was a good place to stop for a toddy on the drive back to Denver. I haven't been here since the divorce."

Nora was glad to change the subject. "Do you and your children still ski?"

"I don't. They do."

"Are they in Denver?"

He pursed his lips and shook his head. "They live in Salt Lake City with their mother and her brand-new hubby. She took them and about half my income."

"You sound bitter."

"Do I? I don't mean to. It's just that sometimes your life takes directions you didn't expect, and there doesn't seem to be much you can do about it."

"Tell me."

"You were married?"

"Briefly," Nora said. "He drank. Which, I suppose, is okay for some people, but the more he'd drink, the meaner he'd get. My only regret is that it took me three years to summon the courage to kick him out."

"You did it, though. Some people never get that far."

"I suppose you're right."

"Are you seeing anyone now?" Then he added quickly, "I'm sorry, that sounds like I'm prying."

"It's okay. The answer is yes and no. I have a few male friends that I see now and then—for dinner and a movie. But there's no one . . . serious."

Thomas nodded, smiling faintly. "I wonder what Annie would think of us being together."

Nora said quickly, "What do you mean?"

"God, I don't mean it that way, not *together* together. I mean investigating, or whatever it is we're doing."

Nora hesitated. "I've thought about that myself. I know she'd be surprised at me. I've always taken the cautious route, the path of least resistance. This is more like something *she* would do. And no doubt she'd be better at it than I am."

"Why do you say that?"

"She's braver, I guess. She was."

"Don't sell yourself short," Thomas said. "You've shown courage, too."

Nora scoffed. "Hardly."

"Hey, you faced up to Fellows and Newby and Karl, and you were scared to death. You said so yourself. That took guts."

Nora didn't see it that way. The real test would come tomorrow. She knew what had to be done, and it frightened her.

She said, "Tomorrow when we go to the Owen house . . ."

"Yes?"

"What if Miss Owen just slams the door in our faces?"

"We'll deal with that if and when it happens."

"Yes, well, even if she lets us in, she's not likely to allow us to wander through her house, searching for . . . whatever."

Thomas chewed his lip. "Well, we'll think of something."

Nora took a long breath and let it out. "I know what Annie would do. I mean if she were me."

Thomas looked at her, waiting.

Nora said, "She'd have you distract Miss Owen at the front door, while she sneaked in the back."

He frowned. "I don't think even Annie would do that."

"I do."

"Wait a minute. Are you saying, *you* want to sneak in the back door?"

"It's not that I want to. But it might be our best chance."

"Best chance?" He exhaled audibly. "You know, breaking and entering is a criminal offense. And if that's not enough for you, there's a law in this state called 'make my day.' It gives a home owner the right to shoot an intruder, no questions asked."

"Are you trying to talk me out of this?"

"You're damn right."

"And what about Annie? Do we just forget about her?"

Thomas opened his mouth, then closed it.

"I'm going in that house tomorrow," Nora said with more confidence that she felt. "One way or the other."

36

It was nearly midnight when the doorbell rang, and Doc Newby was drunk.

He had been drinking a lot more since the Honeycut girl's death. What had once been a pre-dinner drink had now become two or three stiff vodkas. And instead of drinking a few glasses of wine with his meal, he'd usually finish the bottle. Or else he'd just stick to vodka and skip dinner altogether. He would drink until he couldn't keep his eyes open, trying to sort things out, trying not to remember, then stumble to bed. Sometimes he'd wake up in the morning still in his easy chair, the TV tuned to a murmur.

He rattled the ice in his glass, took the last swallow, and clicked off the TV. He pushed out of his chair and walked unsteadily downstairs to the front door, hoping this call wasn't too serious—at the moment he didn't trust his medical abilities.

The porch light was always on, and so when he opened the door the man standing there was fully illuminated.

He was in his early twenties with shaggy brown hair and a full beard. The collar on his blue denim jacket was turned up, his jeans were faded and worn, and his work boots were down at the heel. He took a final drag on his cigarette and flipped it toward the dark street in a long, orange spiraling arc.

Recognition was dawning in Newby's foggy brain as the young man said, "Well, Pop, aren't you going to ask me in?"

"Cole."

"The one and only."

"I hardly knew you with that beard."

"What did I do, wake you up?" Cole stepped forward, forcing Newby to stand aside, sniffing the air as he passed by. "Or interrupt your drinking is more like it." He sauntered along the hallway toward the stairs, leaning into the waiting room, then the office. "Place looks about the same. You got anything to eat? I've been living on drive-through burgers for four days, and I spent my last couple of bucks on gas in Denver." He climbed the stairs without waiting for his father.

Newby slowly closed the door. He stood for a moment with his back to the house, leaning on the doorknob for support. Then he turned and went upstairs.

Cole was squatting before the open refrigerator, setting food behind him on the kitchen table—a loaf of bread, sliced ham, a head of lettuce, a jar of mustard. There was an uncapped bottle of beer in his left hand. He shut the refrigerator and took a swig.

"So, Pop, how've you been?" He sat at the table and began making a sandwich. "Long time no see, right?"

"Five years to be exact." Newby pulled a chair away from the table and sat, his hands in his lap. "What are you doing here?"

"Hey, come on, is that any way to greet your only son?" He grinned wide enough for Newby to see a molar missing, upper left.

"The last letter I got from you was almost four years ago," Newby said with contempt. "You were in Pensacola, and you were shipping out the following week."

"Yeah, well." Cole's grin faded, and he opened the jar of mustard. "The navy and I had a parting of the ways."

"Meaning what?"

Cole spread his hands—a slice of bread in one, a yellow-smeared knife in the other. "It means I got busted by the Florida cops for selling cocaine, and the navy gave me a dishonorable discharge, and I spent twenty-two months in a federal lock-up."

He held Newby's eyes, then pointed at the ham with the knife. "You want a sandwich?"

"You still haven't answered my question."

"What question is that, Pop?"

"What are you doing here?"

Cole grinned again. "Maybe I'm thinking about moving back in with you, looking up my old friends, becoming a solid citizen of Lewiston."

Newby looked down at the table and shook his head. "No, you can't."

"Why not?" Cole's eyes widened in mock innocence.

Newby clenched his jaws and said nothing.

"Well?"

"Because of what happened five years ago!" Newby shouted, banging his small fist on the table. He glared as his son, his breath whistling through his nostrils, his lips pressed together in a thin white line. After a moment he said angrily, "Because of Bonnie Connor and Willy and the rest of it, *that's* why you can't stay here. There are people in town who haven't forgotten what happened. And a lot of others who don't know but would be quick to suspect."

Cole sat back in his chair and smiled easily. "Well, Pop, *you're* still living here, and it hasn't seemed to bother you any. Same with Fellows and McOllough over at the bank. That is, I assume they're still in town."

"Of course they're here," Newby said. "Neither one can trust the other with the mon—" He stopped abruptly and looked away.

Cole narrowed his eyes. "With the what? The money?"

Newby chewed the inside of his lip and said nothing.

Cole leaned forward. "You were about to say 'with the money.' What money?"

Newby would not meet his son's gaze. He put his hands on the table to push himself out of his chair. "I'm going to bed."

Cole reached out, quick as a snake, and grabbed him by the forearm, keeping him from standing.

Newby winced. "Let go."

"Tell me what you were going to say."

"You're hurting me, and I'm telling you to let go. I'm your father and—"

Cole barked a laugh. "You're a weak old man, and I could snap your arm like a stick." He tightened his grip, and Newby's mouth opened in pain. Cole held on a moment longer, then released him.

Newby pulled his arm to his chest and rubbed it. The skin on his forearm was striped with red finger marks.

"Look what you did," Newby said, his voice pained.

Cole waved his hand. "Sorry, Pop."

"Why don't you just leave."

"I aim to," Cole said. He drained the rest of his beer and set down the bottle with a small, sharp rap. "I was just passing through this piss-ass town on my way to California, and I thought I'd drop in and say hi to my old Pop. Oh yeah, and maybe borrow a dollar or two."

Newby put on a resigned expression, but said nothing.

Cole stood and retrieved another bottle of beer from the refrigerator. He twisted off the cap and tossed it in the sink. "But before I go anywhere, you and I need to talk."

He sat back down, picked up his sandwich, and took an enormous bite. He chewed a few times, then shifted the wad to his cheek and spoke around it.

"Now let's hear all about this money that Fellows and McOllough don't trust each other with."

37

The alarm woke Nora at 5 A.M. She had set it that early because she had no idea what time Karl did his grocery shopping, and she wanted to be in Lewiston before the store opened.

She washed quickly, then examined the bruise on her arm. It wasn't as sore as it had been, but it was as ugly as ever—reddish-purple tinged in yellowish green. She cursed Chief Fellows under her breath and began digging through the boxes in the living room for clothes. She felt like a scavenger, or the first person to arrive at a garage sale, desperate to find what she wanted before anyone else showed up. She dressed in Annie's slacks, a long-sleeved shirt, and a sweater, prepared for the chill mountain air.

After her cereal and milk and a quick cup of coffee, she grabbed her coat and drove to Thomas's apartment.

The morning was cloudy and cold, too early for traffic. But Nora drove with her full attention on the roadway, the few cars, the street signs, anything to keep her mind off what lay ahead—unwanted entry into the Owen mansion.

Yesterday afternoon on the ride back to Denver she and Thomas had talked about their plan, but they had done so only in general terms. They had not discussed details. This was fine with Nora, because details made it all seem too real, too hard-edged, and she hadn't been certain she was ready to face up to them yet.

When they reached the city, she had invited him to the apartment. She did so on impulse, forgetting that the living room looked like a stockroom in a secondhand store, littered with open boxes filled with clothing. But she didn't want to be alone. Odd, she realized, because for the past eight years she had *lived* alone, just her and the cats, and she had rarely felt the need for company. Or maybe she had simply suppressed it. Had she changed so much in the past week? Or was it because she had never met a man like Thomas, someone with whom she felt so immediately at ease?

The question, though, was moot, at least for the night. Thomas had errands to run, so Nora had driven him home.

She had phoned Goodwill from Annie's apartment and been told that the earliest they could dispatch a truck to her neighborhood was next Tuesday. Then she called her parents. She told them that she'd be staying in Denver at least through the first of next week, but not to worry, everything was under control. Finally she had phoned Hattie at her home and discussed the operation of the shop—and she'd heard her own words echoed back: Everything was under control.

Later, she had gone to bed, trying not to think about what the morning might bring. She slept without nightmares, at least any that she could remember.

At five she had awakened feeling rested and confident.

Now, though, as she pulled up in front of Thomas's apartment building, apprehension tied knots in her stomach. This was real. They were actually going to do it—distract a senile old woman, creep around inside her house, and hope that she didn't have a gun handy or that her giant chauffeur didn't come home unexpectedly and catch them inside.

At least I won't be alone, she thought.

But Thomas wasn't waiting for her. She could see from the car that the building's vestibule was empty. Nervously, she checked her watch. She was five minutes late. Where was he?

For the past few days she had been counting on Thomas's moral support. But now she considered them a team. And today's excursion into the Owen mansion would require more than his encouraging words. She needed his help.

And thankfully, there he was, emerging from the building.

"Sorry I'm late," he said, climbing in the car. "I overslept."

"No problem."

The highway wound between mountain slopes under a cold, dreary sky. Nora stayed in the far left lane and drove as fast as the traffic would allow, sliding by cars and swooshing past semis as if they were standing still. She saw a few white spots dance past the windshield. Snowflakes.

Thomas rode in silence, obviously nervous about what lay ahead. Finally he said, "I should be the one going in the back door."

She glanced at him. "What?"

"I thought about it all last night. I should be the one who sneaks in the back of the house."

"No," Nora said with some irritation. "We're not going to change plans now."

"Look, if something should happen and—"

"Like what? Either we get in or we don't."

"Karl might come home while you're still sneaking through the house," Thomas said. *"That's* what could happen."

"You'll be there to divert him."

"How can I, if I'm in front with Miss Owen and he goes in the back?"

"This was *my* idea," Nora said, so tense she sounded angry. "And we've already agreed who goes where." She didn't want to argue about this, or even think about it—she might lose her courage, change her mind. She just wanted to go in there and get it over with. For Annie. For herself.

But Thomas wasn't ready to let it go. "You'd be better at holding Miss Owen's attention than I would. You've talked to her before. She knows you."

"She's senile," Nora said. "She probably won't even recognize me."

"Still, you'd be better at—"

"I'm going in the back, Thomas," she said, more loudly than she had intended. She drew in a breath and said, "Let's just leave it at that, okay?" She felt his eyes on her.

He was silent for a moment. Finally, he said, "Sure. Whatever you say. Let's talk about the details."

In a way, she wished he would have talked her out of it.

They arrived in Lewiston at seven thirty. The town was quiet, and Main Street was nearly deserted. The shops were all closed, including Berardi's grocery store. Nora parked in front with the motor running, while Thomas got out to read the small sign on the door.

He returned to the car and said, "It opens at eight."

"Time enough for a cup of coffee."

The courtyard held tables but no chairs. The large, colorful umbrellas were closed tight and pointed like fingers at the lowering sky. Sparse snowflakes danced about Nora and Thomas as they pushed through the door into the restaurant.

They sat at a table by the window, which gave them an unobstructed view across the courtyard and up Alpine Street toward the Owen mansion. The cupola showed itself over the tops of distant trees, its painted windows turned toward them like blind eyes.

Celia the waitress came over with menus and a smile. She gave a start, though, when she recognized Nora, and her demeanor chilled at once.

"Just coffee for us, please," Thomas said. Celia hurried away without a word or a smile. Thomas looked after her. "What's her problem?"

"Nothing we can help her with."

They drank their coffee and waited for Karl.

An hour later they saw the black Cadillac glide smoothly down Alpine Street, stop at Main, and turn left. Thomas dropped money on the table, and they walked quickly from the building and through the courtyard to the corner. They watched the Cadillac park at the curb near Berardi's market.

Karl climbed out slowly—a tall, gaunt figure in a dark sweater and black slacks. He walked into the store with long, lethargic strides.

Like a zombie, Nora thought. "Let's go," she said.

They hustled around the corner to the Mustang, then drove up the hill to the Owen house and parked before the towering hedge. At the gateway Thomas put his hand on Nora's arm, stopping her. Occasional flakes fell from a leaden sky.

"Are you sure you want to do this?"

She stared uncertainly at the house. She nodded.

"Because if you're not—"

"I said I was ready, didn't I?" her voice was tight.

Thomas hesitated for moment, studying her face. There was fear in her eyes, to be sure, but mostly what he saw was determination.

"Okay," he said.

Thomas followed Nora through the opening in the hedge. He brushed a snowflake from his eyelashes and watched her cross the yard to his left. She disappeared around the corner of the house. He paused for a moment, then went up the walk to the yawning front porch, quickly reviewing their alternative plans.

First, Nora would wait five minutes to give Miss Owen sufficient time to answer Thomas's persistent ringing. Then she would enter through the back door and search the house for ten minutes—or until she heard Thomas wish Miss Owen a very loud good-bye. At that point she would get the hell out.

If Nora was unable to make it through the back way, she'd hurry around to the front and sneak in the front door, which Thomas would make sure was unlocked. He'd draw Miss Owen into the house, away from the door. Since they didn't know the floor plan, they had no idea if Nora could slip by unseen. But if she could, she would search as much of the house as possible—for what, neither of them was certain—and then let herself out the back.

If all else failed, they would fall back and regroup.

Thomas climbed the steps and crossed the porch, old boards groaning underfoot. He twisted the lever. The bell inside sounded like an alarm. He waited a few moments and rang it again. And again. Then he heard the latch click. The door slowly swung inward, and Miss Owen stood in the gloom, dressed in black, her face and hands pale and insubstantial.

"Yes, what is it?" Her words were as dry and thin as pressed flowers.

"Hello, Miss Owen. My name is Thomas Whitney. I was Annie Honeycut's . . . fiancé."

The old woman studied him through her round, wire-framed bifocals as if he were a traveler from some strange, distant land. "*Whose* fiancé?"

"Annie Honeycut. The young woman who died in a fall here two weeks ago."

"Oh, yes, I remember." Her hand went up to touch the cameo brooch at her throat.

"I wonder if I might come in and ask you some questions."

"Questions?"

"Yes, I understand that you were home the night Miss Honeycut fell. I'd like to talk to you about that. It would mean a lot to me."

"I don't know. . . ."

Thomas said calmly, "I just spoke to Karl at the grocery store, and he said it would be all right."

"Karl said that?"

Thomas forced a smile. "Yes, ma'am. And I promised him I wouldn't stay long."

She studied him, frowning.

"Ten minutes, that's all I ask."

"Well . . ."

"Please."

"Well . . . all right."

She retreated into the gloom.

Thomas went in after her. He wondered if Nora had made it through the back door.

38

Nora tried the back door.

Open.

In a way she wished it had been locked. For all she knew, Miss Owen was waiting for her just inside, a butcher knife in her bony hand. Or maybe something worse was in there, something . . . unnatural.

Like what, evil spirits? Come on, do it.

She licked her dry lips and pushed open the door, wincing when it creaked. She hesitated, then entered the house.

Nora stood just inside the doorway and closed the door behind her. It took a moment for her eyes to adjust to the dim light and take in the room—a large pantry with a floor of blood-red linoleum tiles. A countertop ran waist-high along three walls, and above it were narrow wooden cupboard doors coated with thick white paint. They reached nearly to the high ceiling. Across from her was a doorway leading deeper into the house. The door was closed.

Nora held her breath and strained to hear the voices of Thomas and Miss Owen. But the only sound was her heart bumping frantically against her chest, like a rabbit trying to escape from a trap. She could feel the weight of the house pressing down on her, compressing the air until it was too heavy to breathe.

Don't be ridiculous. This is merely a house, no different from any other.

She wondered, though, if Thomas had talked his way past Miss Owen and made it inside. If he hadn't, he was supposed to give a shout to warn her. But the house was enormous. What if he had yelled and she hadn't heard? Perhaps she should just wait here by the back door—where it was safe—and give him time to walk through the yard and around the house, tap on the door, and tell her to get out fast. Or maybe she should just forget the whole thing and leave now. They could drive to Denver, and she could catch the first plane home, go back to her life and let Annie rest in peace.

Stop it.

She had come here for a reason—Annie. And the secret behind Annie's death lay within this house, she felt certain.

She took a deep breath and let it out, then crossed the room as quietly as possible. The linoleum tiles squeaked and growled underfoot like small, angry animals.

The ornate brass doorknob was cool in her hand, and it rattled softly when she turned it. She pushed the door open a foot. It squealed once, loud enough to wake the dead. Nora held her breath, then peered into the next room. A spacious kitchen with walls papered in a cheerless pattern.

Nora stood unmoving, listening. She thought she heard a brief murmur of voices, but it was quickly gone, and she wondered if she had only imagined it. The house seemed deathly still.

She closed the door, deciding to initiate her search there in the pantry. She began going through the cupboards, starting in one corner and working her way around the room, not even knowing what she was looking for.

What she found were stacks of old dishes, dusty cups and saucers, forgotten pots and pans—and plenty of food. There were scores of cans, jars, and boxes, everything from oatmeal to olives, pickled beets to peaches. Much of it was coated with a patina of dust, as if it had been purchased years ago for people who had long since moved away or died ... or changed their dining habits.

In the cupboards beside the kitchen door she found the baby food.

Karl had unpacked the boxes and placed the jars neatly on the shelves according to content—puréed carrots and peas here, bananas over there. He had stacked the empty boxes in the cupboard beneath the counter. One box had been set aside with the flaps open. Inside were about a dozen small, empty jars. Nora took one out and read the label: BEETS. The jar itself was shiny enough to have been washed. Or licked clean.

She closed the cupboard and thought, *Who eats this stuff, Karl and Miss Owen? Or do they have a baby hidden away?*

She pushed through the door into the kitchen, gritting her teeth when it squealed.

The large room held more counters and cupboards. In the center were four high-backed wooden chairs around a sturdy, square table, its blond wood surface worn smooth by thousands of scrubbings. Against one wall an ancient, ornate gas stove stood on clawed feet. It was large enough for fabled witches to roast children in.

Nora quickly checked the cupboards and then the refrigerator, heavy and squat, dating from the forties. She found standard fare—vegetables, meats, cheeses, rice, coffee, tea. Half-and-half, but no milk. And no formula. Nothing to supplement the jars of baby food.

She had the feeling, though, that there were no babies—only someone with eccentric tastes . . . or no teeth.

She crossed the kitchen to the door and put her ear to the cool, heavily painted wood. Dead silence. She turned the knob and slowly opened the door. Voices. Distant and barely audible, ghostly. She imagined the spirits of Christian and Lucas and Sabrina Owen, moving about the house.

Nora allowed herself a smile. The voices were real, not supernatural. And she wasn't alone with the senile Miss Owen. Thomas was here.

She peeked around the doorjamb. Stretching before her toward the front of the house was a dimly lit hallway.

It was a place she had been before.

Impossible, she thought.

But goose bumps had risen on her arms. And the longer she stared down the long hallway, the more certain she became that she had seen it before. Then it struck her—she had *dreamed* of this place. And more than once. Dreams so frightening they had forced her from sleep, even from her bed, made her switch on every light in Annie's apartment.

The hallway lay before her exactly like the one in her dream, filled with shadows. She was terrified to see an enormous presence halfway down the hall, rising from floor to ceiling, waiting for her. But most frightening of all—and most familiar—was the figure at the far end. It was insubstantial, draped in a diaphanous white gown, suspended above the floor.

Annie.

Nora nearly cried out.

No, this can't be. There are no such things as ghosts.

The urge to turn and run was almost too much to resist. But she forced herself to hold her ground. She peered down the murky hallway, trying to scrutinize the figure at the end. Gradually it began to resolve itself. It wasn't a ghost at all, Nora realized, only the long, lacy curtains covering the window in the front door, faintly illuminated by pale outside light. And the huge, dark presence on the right side of the hallway was merely the paneled rear section of an ascending staircase.

Not the same hallway at all.

But the similarities between her dream-hall and this one seemed too close to ignore. She told herself that it had to be a coincidence. It had to.

Now she noticed doors set in intervals along each side of the hallway. They were all closed, except for the one nearest the front of the house. Faint voices drifted to her from there. Miss Owen and Thomas.

Nora shook herself from her reverie. She had lost track of time, and she had no idea how much longer Thomas could keep Miss Owen occupied. Without hesitation she stepped into the hall, then pushed through the first door on her right.

The room was large and open and gloomy. Old, wood-framed

chairs with faded satin backs and seats were lined along two adjacent walls, facing forward. Crouched in the opposing corner was a grand piano. Its lid was closed and covered with dozens of framed photographs, like small birds on the back of a huge, foraging beast.

Nora stood beside the piano and looked at the photographs without touching them. Wedding photos from another era, the bride and groom heavily dressed and stiffly posed. Family photos depicting a man, woman, and child—unsmiling, staring at the camera as if it were a gun. One photo showed the child, a girl about six years old wearing petticoats, seated on a piano stool that had been cranked up high enough for her to easily reach the keys. Her feet dangled above the floor. Nora smiled. And then she realized that the picture had been taken right where she stood. A great unease settled over her, as if the ghosts of the people in the photographs were watching her.

A board creak overhead.

Nora's head jerked up toward the high, shadowy ceiling. Someone had taken a step in the room directly above. Had Thomas and Miss Owen gone upstairs? No, there had been no other footfalls, no sound of them moving along the hallway and climbing the stairs.

Nora held perfectly still, listening. The room—and the room above—were silent.

It's just the old house settling.

She moved quietly to a set of double doors and pushed through into an adjoining sitting room. There was a small octagonal rosewood table and two matching chairs set up beside an enormous window, covered with a heavy curtain. Against the opposing wall was the largest sofa Nora had ever seen, upholstered in tufted midnight-blue velvet, with an inlaid back rail, elaborately carved feet, and heavy side cushions. The room had probably once felt warm and cozy, a place to take high tea. But now there was a deadness about it, as if no one had been in there for decades.

Nora went through a doorway that opened into the next room. A library, dark and stale. There were books on the walls and a rich, worn carpet underfoot. Heavy old chairs and ottomans were placed here and there, creating solitary thrones, while Tiffany lamps and pewter ashtrays on floor stands stood in attendance.

The door leading into the hallway was partly open. Through it Nora could hear Thomas's voice.

She peeked around the doorjamb and stared across the hall into another room, which she guessed to be the parlor. Thomas sat in a wing chair—Nora could see the top of his head. He was speaking to Miss Owen, who was out of sight. His words were partially muffled: ". . . wonderful town . . . fortunate for you to . . . grand old house . . ."

Quickly Nora retraced her steps back through the rooms until she reached the kitchen doorway. She passed it by, crossed the hallway, and pushed through another door.

This room, she decided, had once been the dining room. The ceiling was adorned with grapes and vines in bas relief. Faded wallpaper was spread above waist-high oak wainscotting, and a large, ornately tiled fireplace was set into one wall. But there were no dining table and chairs. Instead, a high, free-standing wooden screen divided the room into one-third and two-thirds, with a bed on either side.

The smaller division of the room held a narrow bed, a chest of drawers, and a wardrobe. Nora swung open the tall, narrow doors and found men's clothing—pants, shirts, sweaters, all in extra-large sizes. Karl's clothes.

On the other side of the screen was a much larger bed with four posts, a finely carved walnut headboard, and a lacy ruffled bedspread. Miss Owen's bed. There were several wardrobes and a dressing table, all containing the old woman's things. Nora guessed that the furniture had once resided in an upstairs bedroom and been brought down when climbing the stairs became too difficult for Miss Owen. Possibly this was why they had abandoned the second story of the house.

But she had found nothing on the ground floor to explain the baby food—or Annie's death.

So the answer must lie upstairs.

Nora reentered the hallway. The muted voices of Thomas and Miss Owen wafted from the front of the house. She walked quietly toward them, passing along the descending balustrade. Now she turned and stood at the foot of the carpeted staircase and looked up toward the distant, dark landing.

She wondered how much longer Thomas could keep Miss Owen occupied. If he were forced to leave while she was upstairs, she would be trapped. Not that she couldn't get past Miss Owen. But if Karl returned . . .

Nora took a long breath and let it out slowly.

Now or never, she thought.

She started up the stairs.

39

Willy had finished his morning meal, and he was dozing.

Suddenly he sat up in bed, wide awake. There was an intruder in the house. No, not one. Two.

He heaved his naked bulk from the bed and stood on the cold wooden floor, quivering, alert. Whether it was a minuscule change in the house's air temperature or the muffled creak of old wood, he didn't know. But he could sense two strangers below him in the house.

He shuffled from the room, pulling himself along with his

massive right arm. He stood in the dark at the top of the stairs, swiveling his huge head, listening—and *feeling* with every nerve. One intruder was in the rear of the house, sneaking from room to room. The other was in the parlor, talking to Miss Owen.

That voice. It was almost like . . . the hated One.

Willy gripped the newel post hard enough to make it creak.

The man spoke again. Willy strained to catch every inflection, every nuance of his voice. Finally, he decided that this was not the One, only someone who sounded similar. Still, Willy remained tense. Who was he? And who was the other, creeping through the house?

Willy considered going down to find out.

He hesitated, though, for he did not sense imminent danger. He did not sense the One. And he knew beyond a doubt that if the hated One ever entered the house, or even set foot on the grounds outside, he would know it, he would *feel it.*

Then who were the strangers? Friends of Miss Owen? It seemed unlikely, because one of them was sneaking about, searching for something. For him?

Maybe they are spies sent by the One.

Willy heard one of the intruders approach the stairs. He backed away from the landing, unsure of what to do.

Hide.

It was the only safe course of action. At least until he knew who they were. Of course, if they came upstairs and found him . . . Well then, he would have to deal with them.

He shuffled into a room and crouched naked in a corner, his misshapen body so white it showed in the dark.

40

Chief Fellows had just poured his second cup of coffee, and when he turned around he nearly dropped it. Cole Newby stood in the office doorway.

"Morning, Chief." Cole had trimmed his beard, and he had brushed his hair back into a little tail and fastened it with a rubber band. He wore a pair of blue jeans, a green chambray shirt, and a grungy denim jacket that was lightly flecked with snow. The shirt and jeans were clean and smelled faintly of mothballs.

Fellows sputtered, "What the hell are you doing here?" Cole Newby was the last person he expected to see in Lewiston. The last person he *wanted* to see.

Cole smiled easily. "My father asked me the same thing. I told him I was just passing through and thought I'd stop in and say hi to old friends."

Fellows had difficulty regaining his composure. He was thankful, at least, that Griff was making the morning rounds of the town and wasn't here to witness this. The question was who else knew? He set his cup on the desk and sat down.

"You've got to be crazy to come back," he said.

"How so, Chief? I'm a local boy, same as you."

"You're a fucking punk."

"Now, now." Cole turned the visitor's chair to face Fellows's desk.

"Don't get comfortable. You're leaving."

"Hey, I just got here." Cole sat, then slid down until his head rested on the back of the chair. He folded his hands across his flat belly and gave Fellows a smug look. "Besides, we've got a few things to talk about."

Fellows doubted that he had ever felt more hatred toward anyone in his life. It was all he could do to keep from storming around his desk and smashing in the young man's face. Ironically, like it or not, he owed his present financial security to Cole. If Cole hadn't seen Willy outside the Owen mansion on that night five years ago, Fellows would still be scraping by on a small-town cop's wages.

"Your being in town is bad for everybody," Fellows said. "Don't you know that?"

Cole spread his hands. "Can't be helped."

Fellows could feel the anger burning inside him like a smoldering fire. It wouldn't take much of a breeze to burst into flames, perhaps even rage out of control.

"The best thing would be for you to leave," he said. "And I don't just mean this office. I mean Lewiston."

"Sure thing, Chief. Eventually. But first we talk."

Fellows sucked in his breath and felt the heat stirring in his belly. "I mean *now*. I want you out of town today."

Cole smirked. "Or else what?"

Fellows's face darkened. He put his beefy hands flat on the desktop and slowly pushed himself out of his chair. He spoke with forced calm, giving Cole one last chance, hoping he'd take it, knowing that he was right on the edge.

"I mean it, Cole. Get out."

"Don't try to threaten me. I know too much."

Fellows came around the desk.

Cole casually crossed his legs and said, "I had a long talk with my father last night. He told—"

Fellows grabbed him by the throat with one hand and lifted him out of the chair. Cole swung wildly with his fists, but Fellows held him at arm's length, and Cole's blows reached no farther than the chief's shoulder. Fellows walked the smaller man backward and slammed him against the wall. Cole's eyes were bulging and his mouth worked like a fish's. He danced on his toes, tugging madly at Fellows's thick wrist.

"Listen to me, you little bastard," Fellows said, his voice low and mean. "I'm the law in this town. If I locked you up for jaywalking and you committed suicide, say by hanging yourself in your jail cell, nobody around here would question it. You understand what I'm saying? So when I tell you to get out, or to do *anything*, you'd better fucking do it."

Cole's face was turning purple and his eyes bulged. His mouth worked soundlessly.

Fellows held him a moment longer, then let him go and stepped back. Cole dropped to his knees like a supplicant. He pressed both hands to the base of his neck and sucked air in harsh gasps. Fellows watched him with amusement, one hand resting idly on the butt of his holstered revolver.

"You'd best go on home now, Cole, and start packing your things. And maybe have your daddy wash that shirt. You smell like a storage closet."

Cole stood unsteadily, still clutching his throat.

Fellows moved aside to give him a wide path to the door. But to his utter amazement Cole went back to the visitor's chair and sat down. Fellows didn't know whether to knock him out of the chair or jerk him to his feet.

"I know . . . all about you," Cole croaked, rubbing his throat. "You and McOllough and Miss Owen."

Fellows towered over him. "You don't know shit."

Cole grinned weakly. "Come on, Chief. You've been using Willy to make yourself rich."

The fire in Fellows's belly flared, and it must have reddened his face, because Cole raised his arm as if he anticipated a blow. He spoke quickly, his voice strained. "If you lay another hand on me, I swear I'll have the real cops in here, state and federal. I'll tell them everything."

Fellows's hands twitched at his sides, and he strained to keep them away from Cole Newby's throat. Here was his worst night-mare come true, a ghost from the past, returned to haunt him, to ruin him. To ruin them all.

Cole rubbed his neck and swallowed. "And don't think you can just kill me and make it look like a suicide. My father knows I came here, and he'd never let you get away with that."

Fellows drew in a long breath, then let it out slowly. He rolled his shoulders and flexed his fingers, as if he had just put down a great weight. *He's bluffing,* he thought. He said, "You'd never call in the outside cops."

"Don't bet on it."

Fellows laughed once, harsh and loud. "You *are* a dumb shit." He went around his desk and sat down. "You've got more to lose than anybody."

"Not more, Chief. Exactly the same. We're all accessories here." He counted off on his fingers. "You. Me. My father. McOllough. Karl." He spread his hands. "And of course, Willy."

Fellows stared at a point between Cole Newby's eyebrows and thought about how good it would feel to put a bullet there. "Why did you come here, anyway? What the hell do you want?"

Cole shrugged and turned his palms up. "My share of the money."

"*Your* share?" Fellows face spread in a grin. "There is no 'your share.' "

"According to my father, it was supposed to be a three-way split. And that's how it's going to be."

Fellows shook his head in wonder. "I still can't believe he told you all this."

Cole smiled. "Hey, I'm his only son and he was glad to see me. Plus he's been feeling guilty for five years and he needed to get it off his chest. And of course he was drunk, so he proba-bly thought he was making *me* feel guilty by telling me. Like it was all my fault, or something."

"It was your fault."

"That's right," Cole said evenly. "My fault, my risk, and *your* profit. Not exactly fair, would you say?"

Fellows said nothing.

"Well, all that changes as of today," Cole said. "I'm in. I'm an equal partner."

"Just like that, huh?"

"Just like that. Or else I bring in outside cops."

"You said that before."

"And I meant it."

Fellows shook his head. "You don't want to go to prison any more than I do."

"I've *been* in prison, Chief, and I'll tell you a fact, it ain't all that much worse than my life on the outside." He paused. "But I don't think we can say the same for you. See, cons don't take kindly to ex-officers of the law. They see one in the yard and right away they start sharpening their spoon handles. You know what I mean?"

What Fellows knew was that it was no longer a question of *if* he'd blow Cole's brains out, but *when*. He glared at him and demanded, "Just how much do you think you've got coming to you? I mean exactly."

Cole put on a smug look, leaned back in his chair, and opened his mouth to speak. He was interrupted by a squawk from the police radio.

"Unit two to base. Over."

Fellows's glare lingered on Cole's face a moment longer, then he turned his back on him and punched the button on the microphone.

"Go ahead, Griff."

"I'm at the Owen mansion," Griff said. "We've got a serious problem up here."

41

Chief Fellows tightened his grip on the microphone. "What is it?"

"There's a yellow Mustang parked in front of the Owen place," Griff said. "I do believe it belongs to our friend, Miss Nora Honeycut. Over."

"Son of a bitch," Fellows muttered.

"Who's Nora Honeycut?" Cole wanted to know.

Fellows ignored him and spoke into the microphone. "Is she in the car?"

"No, sir."

"Then she's snooping around the grounds," Fellows said, more to himself than to Griff.

"I was about to check, but I thought I'd contact you first."

"Okay, I'm on my way," Fellows said. "Just sit tight till I get there. Out." He set down the microphone.

"Who's Nora Honeycut?"

"*Another* pain in the ass," Fellows said.

Cole grinned. "This must not be your day, Chief."

You don't know the half of it, he thought. A few minutes ago his mind had been working furiously, trying to figure the best way to deal with Cole Newby. But now, compared with Nora Honeycut, Cole seemed almost like an ally.

"This woman could be trouble for everyone involved," he said. "Including you. We'd better hope she hasn't seen anything at the house."

Cole's grin faded. "What are you talking about?"

Fellows squared the hat on his head, then lifted his fleece-lined jacket from the coatrack and slipped it on. He made sure the butt of his revolver hung free.

"I'll tell you later."

"We still haven't discussed the money."

"Later," Fellows said and walked out, wondering how he was going to deal with Honeycut *and* Cole Newby and still keep Griff in the dark. After all, his deputy wasn't completely stupid.

He drove to the Owen house and parked behind Griff's car. The young patrolman was waiting for him by the gateway in the hedge. Snow was spitting down from a bleak sky. A tiny flake touched Griff's eye, making him blink.

"Have you seen her?" Fellows asked.

"No, sir."

"All right, we'll have to assume she's somewhere on the grounds." *And hope to God she's not inside the house.* "You go around that way and check behind every tree and bush. Don't let her slip past you. If you see her, arrest her. And *cuff* her. I'll go the other way and meet you in back."

"Gotcha."

Fellows made his way around the left side of the house, quickly peering behind evergreen trees and juniper bushes. He paused to stare up at the trellis, half expecting to see the woman up there, imitating her sister, trying to look in a window. The vines at the top were broken and brown, peeled away from the trellis like dead skin. His eyes moved to the cupola. He shivered once, then continued around to the rear of the house.

When he saw that Karl's car was gone, he feared the worst. The old man was the house's last line of defense.

Griff appeared at the corner of the house. He walked toward Fellows, shaking his head. "No sign of her. Maybe she's inside."

"There's no maybe about it," Fellows said gravely. "I'll go around to the front, and you stay here in case she tries to slip out the back door." He doubted that the woman would try to run away from him. But if she offered the least bit of resistance, he intended to come down on her hard—and he didn't want Griff there as a witness.

He strode to the front of the house, anger and apprehension boiling in his stomach and sending hot vapors up to his chest. Things were beginning to unravel. An hour ago he had been as calm as a cat in cream. And then in had walked Cole Newby, the *last* person he wanted to see, shooting off his mouth and making demands. And now Nora Honeycut was back in town, inside the *house*, for chrissake. Miss Owen must have let her in. She was too old and senile to be trusted. God knows how she would answer the wrong questions. Worse, what if Honeycut had come in contact with Willy? If so, then it was all over. He might as well shoot everyone inside and burn the house to the ground.

And then what, he thought wryly, *leave the country and change my name? Hide out for the rest of my life?*

A man needed money for something like that. And he had sunk most of his in the ranch in Montana, his "retirement" home. He couldn't just kiss that good-bye. He was too old to start over. He'd have to work this mess out. Somehow.

He mounted the front porch and rang the bell, while the caldron in his gut rolled and steamed.

42

Nora slowly went up the carpeted staircase.

A step groaned underfoot. She stopped and held her breath, listening for the murmur of voices from the front of the house. But it was as quiet as a morgue. Where was Thomas? It was essential that he kept Miss Owen distracted. If he had left the house, then it wasn't safe for her to—

The low drone of Thomas's voice drifted up to her.

Reassured, she continued up the stairs.

As she approached the second floor she smelled a peculiar odor—an earthy, musky, primal scent. She stopped, half a dozen steps below the landing, her chin just above floor-level. She peered through the balusters as if they were a thin line of trees at the edge of a dark forest.

The hallway above her was thick with shadows, empty.

But she had the uneasy feeling that someone—or something—had recently been there, perhaps only moments before, and had moved out of sight.

She hesitated, then climbed the last few steps to the landing. She peered down the murky hallway.

A railing ran along the left side, safeguarding against a fatal plunge to the floor below. There was a single door at the far end and three doors set in the wall on the right. All but one were closed. The door nearest to her hung open like a invitation.

But what dominated the hallway was a set of steps, halfway along, that rose up through the ceiling.

Into the cupola, she thought.

She stood immobile at the head of the stairs, reluctant to release her grip on the newel post, clutching it as tightly as if it were a pier post and she were in danger of being swept out to sea. She strained to hear voices from the floor below. She had no idea when Karl would return home. If he did, Thomas was supposed to give out a warning shout. But what if Karl had slipped past him? Or what if Thomas had left and the senile Miss Owen was now making her way back through the house? Perhaps she should go downstairs and check. Yes, it was best to be safe. Leave now.

Stop it!

She knew that if she left, she might never get another chance to search the house.

She released her hold on the post and moved away from the stairwell. Hesitantly she walked to the first door in the hallway, the open door.

She stopped just outside the doorway and peered into the room. The odor she had detected from the stairs was stronger here, palpable. The room itself was dimly lit and heavy with shadows. There was a bed set against the wall beneath the dark, painted window. The pillow was wadded up and jammed in the corner. The top sheet had been kicked to the floor, and the under-sheet was wrenched and twisted as if by passionate love-making. Or nightmares. Nora wondered if this was the room where Christian Owen had murdered his wives. Or where Miss Owen's mother had killed her father.

Whatever the case, it was obvious that someone slept in the room now. Someone other than Miss Owen or Karl.

They're hiding somebody up here, Nora thought.

And judging by the size and condition of the bed, it wasn't a child. Certainly not a baby requiring puréed food from a jar. Then who was the baby food for?

And what was the cause of this stink?

Nora had never smelled anything like it. She doubted that it could emanate from a human. Whoever slept here must keep a dog. Or some other large animal, something wild.

Maybe it's in one of the other rooms.

Suddenly, Nora wanted to be anywhere else but there. She backed away from the doorway and moved quickly to the top of the stairs. She started down, intent on getting Thomas. Together they could—

Then she heard a sound that chilled her blood. It came from behind her at the top of the stairs. A low-pitched sound, somewhere between a gurgle and a groan.

Inhuman.

Terror surged through her. Afraid to even look back, she clambered down the stairs. When she reached the main floor she was startled to see the broad, uniformed back of a policeman standing in the doorway to the parlor. She turned the other way and ran down the hallway, sprinted through the kitchen and the pantry, and burst out the back door.

Someone grabbed her from behind.

43

Thomas stopped in mid-question when he heard the doorbell.

When he had first sat with Miss Owen in the dimly lit parlor, he asked her about the night Annie had died—had she seen or heard anything? She hadn't. Then, groping for a topic that would hold her interest, he complimented her on the house. She began to reminisce, starting with her earliest memories—and there were plenty of them, since she had been born right here. "Not in the parlor, you understand," she said, "but upstairs in Mamma's bedroom." He listened to endless details of her favorite toys and dresses, her early school days, her first pony ride, and so on. He had wanted to ask her flat out about the cases of baby food, but he was afraid to break the flow. So he followed her through her girlhood into her teens. She mentioned Meg Andrew, and he was asking her about the woman—when the doorbell rang.

"Oh my," Miss Owen said, touching the brooch at her throat. "More visitors. I wonder if Karl will let them in."

"Karl is at the grocery store."

She frowned at him, then smiled. "Yes, of course, I had forgotten." She rose, and so did Thomas. "Won't you excuse me?" She glided past him, trailing the scent of violets.

Thomas stood alone in the gloom. He wondered if it was Nora at the door. He hoped so. He had been uneasy about their little "operation" from the moment Nora had suggested it yesterday, and he would be glad when it was over and they were both out of this house.

Although he'd had trepidations about Nora's plan, he had gone along for several reasons, not the least of which was a feeling of loyalty to Annie.

When he had first heard of Annie's death, he was shocked, of course. It had taken him a while to accept the reality, the finality of it, and when he had, he had been deeply saddened. There was no describing his emotions, though, when Nora had first told him, and later convinced him, of her suspicions that Annie's death had been no accident. He had felt anger and abhorrence at the very idea that someone might have taken her life. And he felt total frustration that the police would not or could not do anything about it. Obviously Nora felt the same way, and she was determined to act. He wanted more than anything to help her. For Annie's sake, of course.

But also for Nora. Maybe more so for her.

He wished they had met under more favorable circumstances. There was something about her. . . . But he couldn't dwell on that. The reason they were together was morbid in the extreme.

And being in this house did nothing to lessen his sense of morbidity. The place was as dark and silent as a mausoleum. He would be glad when he and Nora were finished here.

Miss Owen returned, slightly miffed. "Someone to see *you*," she said.

Thomas was relieved. Now he and Nora could—

The parlor doorway was suddenly filled by a large man in uniform.

"Here he is, Chief Fellows," Miss Owen said. "Thomas Something-or-other."

Fellows perfectly matched Nora's description of him—broad shoulders, heavy gut, western hat and gun, and a fleshy face that could mold itself into genuine expressions as easily as if it were made of clay: sympathy, sincerity, cynicism. Right now it displayed hostility.

"So you're Miss Honeycut's fiancé."

"Yes, sir, that's right." He held out his hand. "My name is Thomas Whitney." He prayed that Nora was out of the house.

Fellows looked at Thomas's hand as if it were diseased. "And *which* Miss Honeycut were you planning to marry, Mr. Whitney? Miss Owen wasn't quite clear on that point."

"I was engaged to Annie Honeycut."

Fellows regarded him with distaste. Then he turned to Miss Owen with a pleasant smile. "Have you two been having a nice chat?"

"Indeed we have." Miss Owen sat and folded her pale, fragile hands in her lap.

"What were you talking about?"

Miss Owen opened her mouth to speak, but Thomas interrupted. "Nothing much," he said quickly. "In fact, I was just leaving."

Fellows held up a hand, as if he were an oversize crossing guard warning Thomas that it would be dangerous to go any farther. He turned to Miss Owen. "What exactly did you tell him, ma'am?"

"Oh, I told him all about my house and how much fun I had here as a child. Why I remember one time when my mother—"

"Yes, yes," Fellows said impatiently. "But is that the *only* thing you discussed? Your childhood?"

Miss Owen put a finger to her lips and looked up at Thomas. "Why yes, I believe it was. Isn't that right?"

"Absolutely," Thomas said. "I'm, ah, researching the history of—"

"Has Mr. Whitney been anywhere in the house except this room?"

"Why no, of course not," Miss Owen said brightly. Then tiny worry lines formed in her wrinkled brow, as if she were remembering something she should never have forgotten. She glanced up anxiously at the ceiling, then looked at Thomas with fear in her eyes. When she spoke, her voice trembled. "You had better get out of this house right now."

"Of course. I'm sorry if I—"

"*Get out!*" she screeched, causing Thomas take a step backward.

"Now don't you worry, Miss Owen," Fellows said calmly. "I'll take care of Mr. Whitney." He scowled at Thomas, then moved out of the doorway and jerked his thumb. "Outside."

Thomas hesitated, then walked past him, down the hallway, and out the front door. As he stepped off the porch Fellows said, "Hold it."

Thomas turned to face him. Icy flakes of snow sprinkled on them from a dead sky. It seemed colder to Thomas than when he and Nora had first arrived. Darker, too. However, there was more light outside the house than inside, enough so that Thomas could clearly see the blotches on Fellows's face and the broken capillaries across his nose.

"Where's the sister?" Fellows asked him flatly.

"Who?"

"Don't play dumb. That's her car out front. Where is she?"

"In Denver. I borrowed the car and—"

Fellows stepped up and punched him hard in the stomach. Thomas doubled over, gasping for air, trying not to vomit, trying to call Fellows a bastard but unable to form the word.

"I *told* that woman not to come back here," Fellows said. "So what does she do? She sends you. Well, I'm taking you in for trespassing and harassment and—"

"You can't . . ." Thomas straightened up, still struggling for breath.

Fellows punched him again, getting his full weight into it, again doubling him over, dropping him to his knees. "That's for resisting arrest." He pulled Thomas to his feet, then forced his hands behind his back and locked them tightly with handcuffs. He shoved him toward the gateway in the hedge.

Thomas could taste the gorge rising in his throat. He fought it back until he could hold it no longer. He lurched over and retched on the lawn. When he was finished, a thread of saliva hung from his lower lip. He spit it out.

"We'll tack on littering," Fellows said, amused.

Thomas's nausea was overridden by anger and fear—anger toward Fellows's brutality, and fear at what might yet happen. Fellows was obviously out of control, and there was no telling what he might do once he had him locked away, out of the sight of any witnesses.

His one hope was Nora. He prayed that she had sneaked out of the house and that she would stay hidden until Fellows took him to jail. Then she could drive into town and phone for Sheriff Parmeter. He'd have to count on Parmeter showing up before Fellows got too violent.

His hopes sank, though, when he stepped through the gateway. There were two police vehicles parked behind the Mustang, not one. Fellows hadn't come alone.

Fellows pushed him toward the first car and yanked open the rear door.

"Inside," he said; then he stared over Thomas's head.

Thomas turned and saw Nora coming through the gateway, ushered by another Lewiston cop. She looked terrified. Perhaps more so than the situation warranted.

She's scared of more than these cops, Thomas thought.

Fellows said, "Well, well, look what we have here."

44

When Nora ran out the back door, she was in a state of full-flight panic, her mind seized by a terrifying image of the thing in the house.

Not that she had actually seen it. But she had heard it—a low, guttural, half-human sound that still echoed in her head. That sound had followed her—*chased* her—down the stairs, through the hallway, and out the back door, while her imagination strained to form an image of what sort of creature could generate such an inhuman utterance.

She had flown out onto the back porch—and a hand had landed heavily on her shoulder, nearly jerking her backward off her feet. She had whirled around, lashing out with closed fists, desperately trying to break free.

But she stopped immediately when she saw who had grabbed her—Griff, the young Lewiston cop. She was safe now, protected. She nearly blurted, "There's something horrible upstairs in the house!"

But Griff had spoken first. "You're under arrest."

And while he snapped handcuffs on her wrists, she understood that this was Fellows's man, not to be trusted. Whatever that thing was upstairs, it was responsible for Annie's death. Fellows knew it. So did Karl and Doc Newby. And, by association, Griff. That's what they were hiding. That's what they feared.

She shuddered at the memory of the creature's "voice." And as Griff led her around the house, she felt relieved at being taken away from there. Still, she knew she had to be very careful about what she said. Because if Griff or Fellows knew that *she* knew, they might drag her back into the house, drag her upstairs . . .

When she stepped through the gateway, there was Fellows. No surprise—it had been his broad back she had glimpsed in the parlor door during her flight down the hallway.

When he saw her, he smiled without amusement.

"Well, well, look what we have here."

Nora's attention, however, was on Thomas. He stood beside Fellows, slouched over and pale. He looked ill. And, oddly, the knees of his pants were wet, as if he had been kneeling on the ground. Thomas stared hard at her and shook his head almost imperceptibly, no. Obviously, he understood that they weren't free to talk. Not that it would make much difference, Nora realized. It would be apparent to Fellows what they had been doing—searching the house. She couldn't let on, though, that she had nearly encountered *something* upstairs. God only knew what it was.

"I caught her coming out the back door," Griff said.

Fellows's look darkened. "So, she was inside, too."

"Yes, sir."

"*Where* exactly?"

"I don't—"

"I was in the kitchen," Nora said to Fellows. "When I heard your voice at the front of the house, I left."

"Ran is more like it," Griff said.

"What were you doing in there?"

"Looking for Thomas."

"She was probably in there trying to steal something," Griff put in.

Fellows shot him a glance to remind him who was in charge and who should just stand there and keep his mouth shut. Then he turned to Nora. "What do you mean you were *looking* for him? You *came* here with him."

"I . . ."

"Get in there," Fellows said with disgust. He motioned toward his vehicle's open rear door. "Both of you."

"We've done nothing wrong," Nora said, trying to sound indignant.

"You and Mr. Whitney are going to jail," Fellows said evenly. "Now get in that car before I throw you in."

Her anger flared and she spoke without thinking, her voice sounding strange in her ears, as if it belonged to someone else—to Annie.

"Don't threaten me, you fat son of a bitch."

Fellows face flushed, and his chest expanded. His hand came up as if he were going to grab her. Thomas stepped quickly between them, his back to Fellows, leaning forward so that his face was close to Nora's.

"It's all right," he said. "He can arrest us, but he can't hurt us." He turned and faced Fellows, who still looked as if he might explode. "He won't hurt us," Thomas said, still addressing Nora, "because the first phone call I make will be to Sheriff Parmeter."

Fellows snorted and jerked his thumb. "Inside."

Nora climbed in, and Thomas followed—awkwardly, because his hands were cuffed behind him. He sat on the edge of the seat.

Nora remembered the last time she had been in this vehicle, alone with Fellows. She had been vulnerable, bullied. And yet she had retained some sense of control. But now she felt powerless—even though she wasn't alone, even though Thomas was with her. And she understood why. She was in the rear seat, not the front. The difference was profound, because there was a heavy mesh screen separating the seats. Before, she had been a passenger. Now she was a prisoner.

Fellows told Griff, "Have the car towed away. Then find Karl and make sure he sees to Miss Owen. I'll take care of these two." He slammed the door and walked around to the driver's side.

Nora quickly leaned close to Thomas and whispered, "Somebody's living upstairs. I saw a bed. Smells bad. Like an animal or—"

Fellows pulled open the door and sat in the front seat, jouncing the car with his weight. He rested his beefy arm on the back of the seat and for a full minute he scrutinized Nora through the wire screen.

Finally he asked, "What did you see in the house?" His tone was indifferent, as if he couldn't care less.

"Nothing," she said, with forced calm. "A kitchen."

Fellows continued to study her face, as if he could read the truth there. She feared that he could.

"What were you looking for in there?"

"I already told you. I was looking for Thomas."

Fellows worked his fist and said, "That's a goddamn lie and you know it."

Thomas said, "Listen, you have no right to—"

"*Shut up!*" Fellows shouted. He glared at Thomas for a moment, daring him to speak. Then he spoke to Nora, his voice as deep and cold as a winter lake. "I *know* why you two came to Lewiston. You think your sister's death was no accident, and you're trying to prove your theory by digging up some *evidence.*" He spat the last word. "What I want to know is this what did you think you'd find in the Owen house?"

Nora nearly said, "Nothing." But that was too obvious a lie, too ridiculous—of course they were looking for *something.* Her mind raced.

"We . . . thought maybe Miss Owen had seen something the night of Annie's death, and we wanted to talk to her alone. So we waited until Karl left the house, and then Thomas rang the bell and asked permission to go in and talk to her. She let him in, and I stayed outside to watch for Karl, to warn Thomas if he returned. Then I saw the police car coming, Griff's car, I suppose, and I rang the doorbell to tell Thomas. But nobody answered."

She was rambling, making it up as she went along, aware that Fellows was watching her closely.

She licked her lips and said, "So I ran around the house trying to find an open window or a door, some way to get in. When I found the back door unlocked, I poked my head in and shouted for Thomas. There was no reply, so I went into the kitchen, and then I heard voices in the front of the house. *Your* voice, it turned out. So I ran out the back door and, well, Griff grabbed me."

Fellows's eyes probed her face, as if searching for a flaw in her story. She had no idea if she had sounded convincing. Probably not. But the question was what was Fellows going to do about it. For the moment, at least, he had them completely in his power, handcuffed and locked in a virtual cage. And the only witness was his man, Griff. Nora could see him sitting in the other police vehicle, talking into a handheld microphone.

Fellows regarded them a moment longer, then turned his back and started the engine.

"Let's see if a night in jail does anything to change your story."

He swung the vehicle in a U-turn and headed into town.

45

Fellows parked in front of the police building.

He felt certain that neither of his two prisoners had seen Willy. If Thomas Whitney had gotten a look at that monster, then he wouldn't have been idly sitting and chatting with Miss Owen. And the old woman, senile or not, would have

screamed bloody murder. As for Nora Honeycut—if she had laid
eyes on Willy, she would have probably gone into shock. She
was frightened, sure, he could read that in her face, and it was
easily explained—she was under arrest. But she wasn't terrified.
At least she didn't show it, and Fellows figured she wasn't strong
enough to hide something like that. One look at Willy could
scare the piss out of a hard-rock miner, much less some woman.

So the question wasn't had they seen Willy, but rather did
they suspect his existence?

They claimed they had merely wanted to question Miss Owen
about the night of Annie Honeycut's death. That was probably
true, as far as it went. But Nora's story about why she had
entered the house through the back door was bullshit, pure and
simple. She had been sneaking around in there looking for something. But what? Or was she just on a fishing expedition?

Whatever, something had to be done about them. He had to
put a stop to their goddamn snooping.

He shut off the engine. Then he leaned over and rummaged
in the glove compartment until he found what was he was looking for—a folding knife with a single blade and a lock-handle.
He palmed it, got out of the vehicle, and slipped the knife in
his pocket. Then he ushered Nora and Thomas into his office.

"Sit down," he told Nora, pointing to the chair before his
desk. He pulled open the side drawer and took out a set of keys.
"This way please, Mr. Whitney."

"Where are you taking me?"

"To a nice, cozy cell, where do you think?"

"I want to use the phone first. It's my right."

"You can make your calls later. Let's go."

"What about me?" Nora said.

Fellows gave her a sympathetic look. "Don't worry you'll get
your turn." He opened a door at the rear of the office, swept his
arm in an exaggerated manner, and said to Thomas, "Shall we?"

Thomas hesitated, then walked into the back room.

Fellows followed him through and shut the door behind them.
The room contained a single cell—little more than a metal cage,
furnished with two cots and nothing else. Fellows unlocked the

barred door and swung it open, leaving the keys dangling from the lock.

"Inside," he said.

Thomas stepped past him, then Fellows said, "Hold it." He removed Thomas's handcuffs and hung them on his own belt.

Thomas rubbed his wrists and turned to face him. He said angrily, "How long do you intend to—"

Fellows shot out one arm, striking Thomas squarely in the chest with the heel of his hand. Thomas stumbled backward and fell to the floor between the cots. He scrambled to his feet.

"You son of a bitch."

"So I've been told," Fellows said. He pulled the knife from his pocket and clicked open the six-inch blade. Then he took out his handkerchief, carefully wiped off the blade and the handle, and tossed the knife at Thomas's feet. It clattered on the concrete floor.

"Pick it up," Fellows said.

Thomas looked from the knife to Fellows's face.

Fellows smiled. "Go ahead, it won't bite. I just need your fingerprints on it."

Thomas took a step backward.

Fellows shrugged. "No matter. I'll just put it in your hand after you're dead." He drew out his revolver and held it casually at his side.

"Here's the official version," he said. "I failed to frisk you because you seemed like a harmless enough guy, but you had that knife hidden on you all the time. When I took off your handcuffs, you attacked me. Stabbed me right in the meaty part of my thigh. By the way, that's going to hurt like hell when I do it to myself. But it'll be worth the pain. You know why?"

Thomas stared at him in silence.

Fellows said, "Because then I get to shoot you in self-defense."

He raised the gun and pointed it at Thomas's chest.

"No." Thomas backed away from Fellows until he was pressed against the concrete wall. He swallowed and said, "You . . . you can't get away with this."

Fellows grinned with one corner of his mouth. "Oh, really?

Think about it. Who's going to say it happened any different? *You* sure won't be around. And even Miss Honeycut will have to believe me when I go hobbling out there to call an ambulance with a knife stuck in my leg."

Thomas licked his lips.

Fellows pulled back the hammer with his thumb, and the cylinder turned and clicked in place. He was pleased to see that Thomas's gaze was fixed on the gun. He knew what the man was staring at—the leaden noses of hollow-point bullets and the deep, black hole of the muzzle.

"Four ounces," Fellows said. "That's all the pressure it takes to pull this trigger."

"No . . . don't."

"Four ounces and you're dead."

Thomas's face had gone white. He was standing so still that Fellows didn't think he was even breathing.

Fellows let him stare at the revolver a little while longer, then he slowly lowered it and eased the hammer down with his thumb. As he stepped into the cell and picked up the knife, he heard Thomas finally let out his breath. He didn't smell anything foul, though, so he knew the man hadn't lost control of his bowels.

I must be losing my touch, he thought. He backed out of the cell and locked it. "Next time, Mr. Whitney," he said. "Next time for certain."

He left the room and closed the door behind him.

46

Nora sat with her hands in her lap and waited for Fellows to return from the back room. She had an irrational impulse to flee from there, to run down the street yelling for help, shouting for someone to call the police.

But she just sat with her hands cuffed together and waited. She guessed what Fellows was doing—locking Thomas up to separate them so he could question her at length about what she had seen in the house. Of course, she would tell him nothing—not that she had been upstairs, or seen the rumpled bed, or smelled the animal stink. Or that she had heard the guttural sound of whoever or *whatever* was hiding there.

Chief Fellows emerged from the back room and shut the door. There was no expression on his face. He walked directly to Nora and showed her a tiny key.

"Let me take those off," he said.

She held out her hands, and he removed the handcuffs. Then he sat behind his desk and began shuffling papers and filling out forms, acting as if she weren't even in the room. She watched him silently—and waited.

A short time later Griff walked in. He was carrying Nora's purse—a little self-consciously, she thought. He gave her a sideways glance and set the purse on Fellows's desk. Fellows sat back, pushed his Stetson hat up with one finger, looked at Griff, and raised his eyebrows in query.

"Karl's home with Miss Owen," Griff said, "and Ed Gunther towed the Mustang to his garage."

Fellows nodded. Then he leaned forward and stared at Nora, his forearms on the desk, hands together, fingers interlocked. "Now then, Miss Honeycut," he said in a surprisingly friendly voice. "Here's the situation. Judge Stevens is the only one who can set your bail, and he's on a fishing trip and won't be back for another two or three days. Which means that if I arrest you and Mr. Whitney I'll have to keep you both locked up in our little jail until then. The problem is we have only one cell, and if I put a man and a woman in there together overnight"—he grinned sheepishly, as if embarrassed.—"people in town would talk." He cleared his throat. "The other problem is the city of Lewiston would have to feed you both for several days and, frankly, we have better things to do with our money, which we don't have much to begin with." He gave her a look that seemed to ask for sympathy. "So I'm going to have to let you both go."

"What?" Griff couldn't believe it.

Fellows held up his hand.

"But, Chief, you can't just—

"Griff, please."

Griff wanted badly to argue, but he knew when to hold his tongue. He sat behind his desk, a disgruntled look on his face.

Fellows turned to Nora. He spoke quietly, still maintaining his friendly tone. "Now don't get me wrong, Miss Honeycut, I'd keep you both locked up if I thought for a second that you weren't reasonable people. What you did over at the Owen house was wrong. More than that, it was illegal. But I know the kind of strain you've been under, your sister dying and all, and sometimes grief makes people do funny things. Believe me, I sympathize with you. I've lost loved ones, too. So I'm letting you and Mr. Whitney go." He paused, staring at her without blinking. "Under one condition. I don't want you to come back to this town. Neither one of you. Ever. Do you understand?"

Nora had no trouble seeing through his good-old-boy act. If

she and Thomas left town now, Fellows would be rid of them, and whatever secrets lay in the Owen house would be safe. But if he arrested them and brought them before a judge, they could voice their suspicions in open court. And that might make life complicated for him.

She nodded. "Yes, I understand you perfectly."

Fellows slapped the desktop with the palm of his hand. "Good. Griff, go get Mr. Whitney, if you would please. And Miss Honeycut, you'd best come over here and dig into your purse. I'm going to have to ask you for some money."

She stood before his desk.

He held up a form printed on yellow paper. "First, there's this ticket for illegal parking. Forty dollars. Then there's a towing charge of sixty-five dollars, plus a charge for impounding your vehicle—one hundred dollars per day." He scribbled numbers on a pad, the tip of his tongue tucked in the corner of his mouth. "Let's see now, if my addition is correct, you owe the city of Lewiston two hundred and five dollars."

Nora withdrew her wallet from the purse and flipped through the bills, knowing that she didn't have anything close to that amount. A twenty, two fives, and three singles. "Do you take credit cards?"

Fellows grinned broadly. "Well, sure. We're not a bunch of hicks up here, you know."

Nora signed the papers and the credit card slip. A moment later Thomas and Griff emerged from the back room. Nora noticed a change in Thomas. When they had arrived here, he seemed indignant, angry. But now he would barely meet her eyes. He looked . . . defeated. Something must have happened back there, either with Fellows or Griff. Something bad.

Fellows pushed himself up out of his chair. "Miss Honeycut, your car is at Gunther's garage, where I took you once before. I'll point the way, in case you've forgotten how to get there."

He ushered them outside. Snow was still falling in scattered icy flakes, and there was a slight dusting of white on the cars parked along the curb. Nora squinted against the cold air and stared across the street. The Owen mansion's cupola towered above buildings and treetops. Nora imagined someone in there, watching them.

Fellows stepped between her and Thomas and pointed up the street—a friendly policeman helping out a couple of tourists. "You go down here to the corner, take a right, and it's a few blocks up. You can't miss it."

They started away, but Fellows stopped them with, "And folks." He gave them a wide, cold smile. "Remember, I don't want to see either of you again."

They turned and walked away. Nora felt Fellows's eyes on her all the way down the block. When they turned the corner, she gave Thomas's hand a squeeze.

"Are you all right?"

"Yes," he said dully.

"Did something happen back there?"

She saw a worm of muscle at the point of his jaw. "Let's wait till we get out of this goddamn town."

They walked hurriedly along the cold, tree-lined street. The tidy Victorian houses, which had once appeared so quaint to Nora, now seemed threatening, pressing in on them from either side, listening to their every word. Watching them.

Nora was thankful that Thomas offered to drive back to Denver. She was physically drained. And cold. And her bruised shoulder ached. She hadn't been aware of the soreness in her arm until she sat in the car, but she guessed that it had been hurting for some time. She had just been too preoccupied to notice.

Thomas drove up the on-ramp and into the stream of highway traffic. Nora worked the heater controls, and soon the fan was pushing forth warm air. She began to feel as if she were awakening from a nightmare, reentering the real world.

She asked Thomas, "What happened between you and Fellows at the jail?"

"First, tell me about the house," he said. "You saw something in there, didn't you?"

"Yes. How did you know?"

He gave her a brief smile. "When you come through the gateway with Griff, you looked scared spitless."

"I was." She hesitated. "Maybe I still am." She told him what she had found in the house—the downstairs rooms and the upstairs bedroom. She described the peculiar odor and the inhuman sound that had chased her down the staircase.

"Inhuman?" Thomas glanced at her, then returned his attention to the roadway, both hands on the steering wheel. "You mean like a dog?"

"No, it wasn't a dog. Or even a wild animal. It was . . . *nearly* human." She had a sudden image of Annie's last photograph—someone crouching far below her in the yard, a squat-looking creature with an overly large head.

"Nearly human," Thomas repeated, frowning. "I know it's spooky inside that house, but we've got to be logical. What you found was evidence of someone living upstairs, and whoever it is—whoever *he* is—is apparently hiding. He's human, all right. And as far as what you heard and smelled—he's either keeping an exotic pet with him, or else he talks funny and stinks. And he probably eats baby food."

Nora felt like laughing. Or screaming.

She said, "And maybe . . . he killed Annie."

Thomas nodded gravely. "I think so. The rest of them are covering it up—Fellows, Karl, Miss Owen, Doc Newby, and who knows who else in town. And Fellows, for one, is prepared to do just about anything to keep the lid on." Thomas described his encounter with Fellows in the jail cell. His voice cracked with rage. And shame, Nora thought. "I felt completely helpless," he said. "I truly believed he was going to shoot me. I would have begged for my life, if I could have gotten the words out. It was more than terrifying. It was . . . humiliating."

"That bastard," Nora said heatedly. "We should go to Parmeter right now and tell him."

Thomas slowly shook his head. "There weren't any witnesses. Fellows was careful about that. It would be my word against his."

Nora wanted to disagree, but she knew that Thomas was right.

"Damn it," she said, "there has to be some way to get Par-meter involved."

"We can't just drag him into town."

They rode for a few miles in silence. Nora said, "Would you say that whoever is hiding in that house was probably there before Annie died?"

"Absolutely. It's possible that she saw him and he killed her to keep her quiet."

"That's what I'm thinking, too. So before Annie showed up, he was a fugitive from the law. The *real* law, I mean, not Fellows. And who-ever or whatever he is, he's certainly not normal. If we can find out anything at all about him—even who he *might* be—then maybe we can get Sheriff Parmeter to search the house with a warrant."

Thomas gave her a doubtful look. "How are we going to do that?"

Nora hesitated. "I don't know, yet. Let's go talk to Meg Andrew."

47

They came out of the mountains, leaving the falling snow behind. The air wasn't as cold down in the flatlands, but it was still chilly, and the sky was clouded over. Thomas drove to Wheat Ridge and parked in the lot of the Crest Manor nursing home.

"Let's hope she's back from the hospital," Nora said.

The receptionist informed them that Meg Andrew had indeed

returned from the hospital and that she was resting quietly in her room.

"However," the receptionist said, "we're only allowing family members to visit her for the next few days."

"That's good," Nora said without hesitation. "Aunt Meg needs her rest. I promise we won't stay long."

As they rode the elevator to the second floor, Thomas said, "Aunt Meg?"

"Hey, she's probably *somebody's* aunt."

There were two beds in the room, but only one was occupied. Meg Andrew was propped up with pillows and staring out the window. Nora knocked lightly on the door frame. The old woman turned to them with wild eyes. Her gray hair was in disarray, and it framed her gaunt, pale face in a ragged halo. She glared at them through dark-framed glasses.

"You're not taking me back to the hospital," she snapped.

"We're not here to—"

"You can both go straight to hell." Her voice was raspy and brittle, and twin spots of color had risen to her cheeks. "They poked me and stuck me with needles and cut me with knives and I'm finished with them. You hear me? I'm not going back." She folded her bare, skinny arms in defiance.

"We're not from the hospital," Nora said gently.

"No?" Her pale eyebrows rose briefly, then quickly plunged into a frown. "Then who the devil are you? *I've* sure never seen you before."

Nora stood at the foot of the bed and introduced herself and Thomas. "We'd like to ask you a few questions."

Meg Andrew aimed one eye at Nora. "How do I know you're not from the hospital? You're not trying to trick me, are you?"

"We're not, I promise."

"Prove it."

Nora began to wonder if this woman were as senile as Miss Owen. Perhaps coming here had been a mistake.

"We just want to ask you about Lewiston," she said.

"Lewiston?" The sharp lines softened in Meg Andrew's face.

"Yes. And about Chastity Owen."

"Chastity," she said with fondness. Her mouth crinkled into a smile. "How *is* Chastity? I haven't seen her in I don't know how long."

"She's well. In fact, we saw her just this morning. She was telling us about her childhood in Lewiston, and she mentioned your name."

"Of *course* she did," Meg Andrew said, her eyes lighting up. "Chastity and I grew up together. We were inseparable, like sisters. Right up until . . ." Her expression clouded and she shook her head.

"Until what?"

"You know. The tragedy."

Nora remembered what Celia the waitress had told her. She nodded and said, "Her father molested her, and her mother killed him for it."

"Lucas Owen was an *evil* man," she said heatedly. "I pray that his soul is roasting in Hell. He ruined that poor girl. She was never the same after what he did to her. Who would be?"

The old woman's eyes were blazing and her face was flushed. Nora read pure hatred in her expression, and she began to have second thoughts about continuing this discussion. It was a moment before she asked quietly, "After Lucas Owen's death, who lived in the—"

"I went to his grave," Meg Andrew said, her voice venomous. "And I *spit* on it."

Nora cleared her throat. "I see."

Thomas said gently, "After his death, who lived in the house besides Mrs. Owen and Chastity?"

The old woman did not answer, but stared intensely into the space between them, obviously lost in her thoughts. Nora and Thomas exchanged a glance.

Nora said, "Miss Andrew? Who lived in the Owen house after Mr. Owen's death?"

She blinked and cocked her head to one side. "Well, who do you suppose. Chastity and her mother. And Karl Gant."

"Karl?"

"He did odd jobs around the house. Tended the grounds, made repairs, sometimes even drove Mr. Owen's car. He wasn't much older than Chastity. A tall, strapping young man." She smiled wistfully. "Is he still there with Chastity? It's been years since I've seen him."

"Yes, he's still living in the house," Nora said.

"Well, bless him."

"Besides Karl, did anyone else ever live there?" Thomas asked.

Meg Andrew wrinkled her pale brow in thought. "No."

"Does Chastity have any relatives who might have moved in with her?"

She shook her head. "None that *I* know about."

"Any friends who—"

"I was the only friend she ever had," Meg Andrew said. "And after her tragedy, she wouldn't even let *me* come to the house. She just sort of hid out from the world."

Nora said, "We think someone is living there now with Miss Owen and Karl."

The old woman glared at Nora as if she had just accused her of lying. But slowly her look softened. "Of course, I wouldn't know, since I haven't been there in years. But I'd be mighty surprised if anyone else lived in that house. Mrs. Owen and Chastity stayed pretty much to themselves after the tragedy, and they hardly ever came into town. Karl ran their errands and such. I can't imagine Chastity letting *anybody* in there now."

"Why did they paint the windows?" Thomas asked.

"The windows?"

"On the upper floor of the house. And the cupola."

"Oh, yes, I remember that now. I don't really know for certain. Some people said that poor Chastity was ashamed to show her face, even to people passing by the house."

Nora shook her head regretfully. "All because her father molested her."

"He didn't just molest her," Meg Andrew snapped. "He *raped* that poor girl."

"He what? I was told that her mother stopped him before—"

Meg Andrew was shaking her head. "That demon got her with child."

"Chastity had a baby?"

"No, thank God. The infant was born dead. Its life would have only added to Chastity's shame."

Nora was thinking of the bedroom upstairs in the house. "Are you sure the baby was stillborn?"

"Well, of course I'm sure. My mother, God rest her soul, was there at the birthing. She assisted Doc Prentiss."

"Was anyone else there?"

"I wouldn't know. But I doubt it, because Mrs. Owen never told anyone about the pregnancy except my mother, and *she* never told a soul but me, not even my *father*." Meg Andrew studied their faces. "Well, don't look at me like I don't know what I'm talking about. If you don't believe me, go ask Chastity. Or Doc Prentiss."

"He's still alive?"

"Of course, he's alive. I get a card from him every Christmas. He lives with his grandson down in Colorado Springs."

48

Nora used a pay phone in the nursing home lobby to call long distance information. Since Meg Andrew did not know the old doctor's phone number or even his first name or the name of his grandson, Nora asked the operator for every listing in Colorado Springs with the name "Prentiss." There were five.

The second person she called told her that the man she was looking for was Steven Prentiss. But the grandson of the former doctor of Lewiston did not answer his phone.

"I'll call again later," Nora told Thomas. "It's possible Dr. Prentiss knows more about the Owen family than Meg Andrew."

"Let's hope so."

They walked out to the car. Thomas held up the key. "Do you want me to drive?"

"I don't even know where we're going," Nora said, and they both laughed.

"How about lunch?" Thomas suggested. "You know, there's nothing like interviewing an old woman after you've been beaten up by a small-town cop to whet your appetite."

Nora laughed again. It felt good, as if she were setting down a weight she had been carrying around for days.

"Sounds great," she said. "I'll buy."

"No, no, it's my treat."

Thomas drove into the heart of the city and parked near the governor's mansion, not far from Annie's apartment. Across the street was a restaurant with a fenced-in courtyard, although it was too chilly for outdoor dinners.

"Two choices," he said. "Over there we can get beautiful, tasty portions with a Continental flair. Or we can walk around the corner for the two B's."

"What's that?"

"Burgers and beer."

She smiled. "Let's walk."

They sat in a high-backed booth and ordered Canadian beer and burgers with everything, fries on the side. The restaurant was quite crowded—all the tables were filled and there was standing-room-only at the bar. Since this was Friday, Nora assumed that many of the customers were getting an early start on the weekend.

"Annie liked this place," Thomas said.

"I can see why. Lots of people. Lots of action."

The waitress brought their beers. Nora took a sip, then wiped a bit of foam from her lip with her fingers.

"How far is it to Colorado Springs?" she asked. "I want to question Dr. Prentiss in person, not over the phone."

"An hour and a half, depending on the weather and the traffic."

"Will you go with me?"

"I was planning to."

She smiled. "Good."

They sipped their beers.

"Although," he said, "I hate to put too much hope in Prentiss helping us."

"Why? According to Meg Andrew, he lived in Lewiston for years. He even knew Miss Owen's mother."

"Exactly my point. The man has to be in his nineties. He may not be as lucid as dear old Meg."

Nora hadn't considered that. But there was nowhere else to go.

The food arrived, and they ate in silence.

Thomas dipped a french fry in a small puddle of ketchup on his plate and chewed it thoughtfully before he said, "You know— and don't take this the wrong way—but it's hard for me to believe that you and Annie are sisters."

"Everybody says that. Of course, I'm ten years older than her. Than she was."

"It's not just your ages," Thomas said. "It's, well, your personalities, temperament, priorities. Everything. Mostly, though, you seem more sure of yourself."

Nora shook her head. "You've got to be kidding."

"No."

"Hey, Annie was the gutsiest person in our family."

"I'm not saying she wasn't. It's just that she seemed ... I don't know." He held up his hands. "What am I talking about here. I only knew her for a few months."

"No, go ahead. Finish what you were saying. Annie seemed what?"

Thomas hesitated. "Frightened."

"Frightened? Of what?"

"I don't know. Herself, maybe."

Nora frowned. She had always thought of Annie as being brave, never fearful. But maybe she had seen only the surface. Maybe that's all she wanted to see.

"Did I say something wrong?"

She had been staring down at the table. "No, I was just remembering a conversation I had with Annie a few years ago. About her scar."

"Her scar?"

"There was a thin, white scar above her right eye. It was mostly hidden by her eyebrow."

"I never noticed it."

"It had faded quite a bit, but it was unmistakable a few Christmases ago when she came home for the holidays. Naturally I asked her about it. She told me she had been injured here in Denver at a rally on Martin Luther King Day. A group of neo-Nazis showed up to disrupt things, and before long there was a near-riot. Annie waded right into the middle of it, snapping pictures as fast as she could. Rocks were flying, and one smashed into her camera, driving it into her face. The whole thing sounded incredibly brave to me—or foolish. I asked her, 'When you went there, didn't you expect a fight?' She said she did, and I asked her why she hadn't simply brought a telephoto lens so she could shoot things from a distance. She said, 'Where's the challenge in that?' "

Nora took a sip of beer and said, "She was bragging, of course, trying to sound brave. But I saw fear in her eyes, something I had never seen before. And it frightened me. I think I realized then, and maybe suppressed it, that Annie took chances *because* they were chances, because they were dangerous and scared her."

"You mean she did it for the thrill?"

"No. For punishment."

"Punishment? I don't understand."

Nora sighed. "For our brother Robert's death." She sipped beer, then set down the glass. "You see, Annie always blamed herself for Robert being killed in the car accident. He had been out buying her a birthday present. It was something she dearly wanted, but my parents thought she was too young, the gift too expensive, and so on. But Robert wanted her to have it, and he drove to Waterloo because he had read about a sale. On the way home he was hit head-on." Nora sighed again. "Of course, we told Annie over and over that there was no connection between Robert's death and her gift. But she believed there was. You can see why."

"Yes."

"And the gift itself seemed to have an affect on her."

"I think I can guess what it was."

"A camera," Nora said.

After lunch they went to Annie's apartment, and Nora dialed the number for Steven Prentiss. Still no answer. She hoped that Steven and his grandfather were simply out of the house, not out of town.

She phoned the flower shop and talked to Hattie. Things were not going smoothly. Laurie had quit, just walked right out after Hattie had scolded her for fooling around and not working hard enough. Then a greenhouse had screwed up an important delivery to them. And Tara had mixed up two orders—wedding bouquets and arrangements for a retirement party.

Hattie was almost too flustered to talk. She knew the operations of the shop as well as Nora—and in some ways better, because she had worked there longer. But she was starting to crumble under the pressure. She was starting to panic.

Nora talked to her for a solid hour, smoothing her ruffled feathers and helping her straighten out the temporary mess. And she promised her that she'd return in a day or two. Although she was beginning to wonder if that were true.

After she hung up she dialed the Prentiss number. Still no answer.

"I'll try again in a little while. If you don't mind waiting."

"Hey, I've got nowhere to go."

"Would you like some coffee? I'm afraid it's freeze-dried."

They sat on the couch and talked about anything but Annie—where they had gone to college (she, Iowa State; he, the University of Colorado), what it was like growing up in their home towns (she, Cedar Falls; he, Tempe, Arizona), and so on—all the while staring at Annie's things laid out on the floor before them in cardboard boxes.

An hour later Nora tried the number again. This time Steven Prentiss answered. She told him—without elaboration, not wanting to into details on the phone—that she was doing research on the recent history of Lewiston and that she would very much like to visit with his grandfather.

"Wait just for a moment." He put down the phone, and Nora heard him walk away. A few minutes later he picked it up and said, "Yes, my grandfather would be happy to talk to you. How does tomorrow sound? Say around two."

"That would be fine."

"Have you got a pencil? I'll tell you how to get here."

After she hung up and told Thomas, he said, "That's great. Why don't we take my car. I can pick you up tomorrow around twelve thirty."

"Good." Nora had had enough driving to last her a month. And now she stifled a yawn. "Sorry."

Thomas grinned and set his cup aside. "I can take a hint. I should be going."

Nora smiled sheepishly. "I'm sorry. I guess those two beers made me sleepy. I'm not used to drinking during the day."

Thomas insisted on calling a taxi, despite Nora's offer to drive him home. He made the call, then told her, "It will be here in five minutes. I'll wait downstairs."

Nora walked him to the door. "Thanks for doing this with me. It makes things easier. You're, well, easy to be around."

He gave her a smile and said, "See you tomorrow."

Then, without thinking, or maybe because it felt like the natural thing to do, Nora leaned up and kissed him on the cheek. She immediately drew back, embarrassed. Thomas reached out and touched her shoulder, then drew her to him. They kissed again, their arms around each other. Finally, Nora turned the side of her face to his chest and he rested his chin on top of her head.

After a few moments he said quietly, "I'd better go. The taxi."

"Yes."

Nora dropped her arms and stepped back. He touched her face with the backs of his fingers.

"I'll see you tomorrow."

She nodded, and locked the door after him.

That night she dreamed of Thomas and her dead brother Robert. Except that Robert was alive. He and Thomas laughed and talked as if they were old college buddies. Nora watched them from across a vast, snowy field. And then Annie was with them, standing between them, her arms around their waists. Nora tried to move toward them, but her feet kept sinking in the snow. They turned and walked away from her. She was desperate to be with them. She called out for them to wait. But a wind had risen, and it blew clouds of snow into her face, making her choke on her words. She lowered her head into the snowstorm and stumbled forward, finally slipping and falling face-down into the snow.

When she got to her feet, Thomas and Robert and Annie were gone. And there was only the snow.

49

Fellows watched Nora Honeycut and Thomas Whitney walk away from him, down the street, and around the corner. Then he went back in the office. Immediately Griff started in on him—Why didn't you file charges? You should've kept them locked up. The judge would've slapped them with heavy fines. And on and on.

Finally, just to get the big, dumb kid off his back, Fellows sent him with the radar gun to monitor cars coming off the freeway ramp.

He could understand Griff's attitude. After all, Griff couldn't see the whole picture. Sure, he could have arrested Honeycut for trespassing and probably for breaking and entering. But the last thing he wanted was her standing up before Judge Stevens and mouthing off about *why* she had entered the Owen house. Stevens had a suspicious nature to begin with, and it wouldn't take much for him to call for an outside investigation. No, he had been right to scare the hell out of Whitney. That guy would never come back. And if he had any brains at all he'd keep the Honeycut woman away, too.

It was just a good thing that Honeycut hadn't stumbled across Willy. There was no telling what that monster might have done. The only thing for certain was that Honeycut and Whitney would have ended up dead.

But that worry was past. Now he could concentrate on Cole. He phoned Cecil McOllough.

"We've got a problem," he told the banker.

"What is it?"

"Cole Newby's back in town."

"*What?* What's he doing here? Have you talked to him?"

"Take it easy," Fellows said. He could picture the man's eyes bulging out of his pinched face. "I've got things under control. But I want you to be ready if he shows up there and—"

"He's coming *here?*"

"I said *if* he shows up," Fellows said. "He may not. But if he does, you tell him nothing."

"Of course I—"

"You tell him I'm running things, and if he's got any questions he can talk to me. Questions about *anything*, do you understand? Especially dollar amounts."

"What does he know?"

"Too much. Doc spilled his guts."

"Oh, Christ," McOllough whispered.

"But Doc doesn't know how much is involved, and neither does Cole. Let's keep it that way, because we may have to pay him something to—"

"Pay him?"

"—To keep him happy for a while. I need time to figure out exactly what to do."

"Pay him? How much?"

"A few thousand ought to do it."

"A few *thousand?*" He paused. "What portion of that are you suggesting I contribute?"

"All of it."

"*All?*"

"And I'm not suggesting, I'm telling you."

"Now wait just a—"

"Unless you'd rather trade places."

McOllough hesitated. "What do you mean?"

"Well, I'll put on a suit and tie and sit on my butt behind a fancy desk, and you can come out here in the field and do the dirty work."

Silence.

"That's what I thought," Fellows said.

When McOllough spoke it was in a small voice. "How can we be sure that Cole won't make trouble after we pay him?"

"We can't. But that's my problem, not yours. So just relax and don't worry. And you tell Cole *nothing*."

Fellows hung up. He poured a cup of coffee, then sat staring at the black, liquid surface, watching rainbow-colored spots spin and swirl.

Getting rid of Cole Newby would be easy, he knew. Hell, he could even lock him in a room with Willy, maybe *scare* him to death. The hard part would be to do anything without making Doc Newby suspicious. If Cole had an "accident" or simply disappeared, Doc would guess what had happened. And the only reason Doc had kept his mouth shut for the past five years was to protect his son. If Cole died, Doc would talk, simple as that. Of course, Doc and Cole could have an accident together.

Now *there* was an idea.

There had been a time when Fellows considered Doc Newby to be his friend. No more. In fact, now that Fellows thought about it, he didn't have any friends—not Doc, certainly not Griff or McOllough or Karl or Miss Owen . . . or Willy. That was okay with him. After a few more payments he'd own the Montana ranch free and clear. He could live up there in peace and quiet, keep some horses, maybe a few head of cattle, and whenever he wanted a woman, it was only an hour's drive to Billings.

He smiled and sipped his coffee, then made a face, bitter. He set it aside and dialed Doc Newby's number. Cole answered.

"Come to my house tonight at ten," Fellows told him. "We'll talk things over. And don't let anyone know you're coming, not even your father. We don't want to make anyone suspicious."

"Don't worry about my father."

Fellows smiled into the receiver. "Oh, I'm not worried."

❉   ❉   ❉

Fellows was on his fourth double bourbon on the rocks when Cole arrived at the house.

"Come on in," he said, holding the door and looking past Cole into the dark street. His police vehicle was parked alone at the curb. "Where's your car?"

"I walked," Cole said. "You wanted this meeting to be a secret, didn't you?" He stood in the middle of the small living room and looked around. "Nice place."

Fellows couldn't tell if he was being serious or sarcastic. He had lived in this compact, one-bedroom house too long to be objective. It was simply home—sagging furniture, worn carpet, and the same dusty pictures that had been on the walls when he had moved in.

"You want something to drink?"

"I could stand a beer."

Fellows freshened his bourbon and brought Cole a cold red-and-white can. The younger man popped the tab, sucked back the rising foam, then sat in the middle of the couch and balanced the can on his knee. Fellows noticed a narrow-bladed knife in a sheath hanging from the young man's belt. He nodded toward it.

"Going camping?"

"That's for protection," Cole said seriously. "In case you get the urge to choke me again."

Fellows laughed softly and shook his head, then lowered his bulk into the easy chair. "So."

"So talk."

"You think I'm going to pay you some money."

"I *know* you are," Cole said emphatically.

"Let me hear again why I should."

"Because if you don't, I'm going straight to the state cops and tell them—"

"Yeah, yeah, and we all go to prison, including you, but you don't mind because you've been there before and I'm supposed to believe that. That's not what I meant. What's your *claim* to the money."

Cole held Fellows's gaze for a moment. Then he shrugged and took a pull on his beer. "You and McOllough have been squeezing it out of Old Miss Owen for the past five years. It was supposed to be a three-way split with my father, but he didn't want any part of it. Well, I do. I'm claiming his share—past and future."

"Past, too, huh?" Fellows sipped his bourbon. "And how am I supposed to do that?"

"That's your problem."

"It's not a problem, it's impossible. There is no 'past share,' as such. It's been spent."

Cole looked around him and laughed. "On what? Interior decoration?"

Fellows gave him a thin smile. "My share is tied up in a small piece of land up in Montana, and McOllough is buying property in Arizona. There's no cash to give you."

"You're lying, Chief. Everyone knows Miss Owen is loaded. So let's just waltz over there and get it from her."

Fellows sipped his bourbon and smacked his lips. "You *are* a dumb fuck."

Cole's face reddened, and he started to come out of his chair.

"Don't you think," Fellows said, "if that old lady had piles of cash lying around her house, me and McOllough would've taken it and be out of this town by now?"

Cole sat rigidly on the edge of the couch.

"Well?"

"I don't know," Cole said tightly.

Fellows shook his head. "I wish I had a dollar for everything you don't know."

Cole stood.

"Sit down."

"Maybe I'll just go have a talk with Miss Owen and see how much money she really does have."

"You stay away from her," Fellows said evenly. "And Willy, too. Or there *will* be trouble." He held Cole's eyes for a moment before he went on. "Listen, we left them with food money, and that's about it. Didn't your daddy tell you all this?"

Cole continued to glare at him.

"Why don't you sit down and I'll explain things to you." When

Cole made no move to sit, Fellows shrugged and said, "All of Miss Owen's money comes from a trust fund that was set up by her grandfather. He put his money into investments—stocks and shares in different companies and whatnot—and none of that money can be touched. It's what they call capital, you understand? He set it up so that the only money his heirs can put their hands on is earnings. Interest, in other words. See how that works? Miss Owen gets a check four times a year and brings it over to the bank, and McOllough leaves her enough to maintain the house and feed herself and Karl and good old Willy, and me and McOllough split the rest. And as you know there isn't much to split."

Cole chewed his lip.

"Your daddy at least told you how much we get, didn't he?" Fellows knew that he hadn't.

Slowly, Cole sat down. "No. You tell me."

"Less than twenty thousand a year, split two ways," Fellows lied. It was easily five times that much.

"Is that *all*?"

Fellows nodded.

"I don't believe it."

"Ask McOllough."

Cole sneered. "I already did. He won't say anything, as if you didn't know."

Fellows waved that aside. "Look, McOllough and I are reasonable men. We both know that you've got us over a barrel. We're prepared to give you a full one-third share. Just under sixty-five hundred a year."

"That ain't shit."

"Hey, it's tax free."

Cole shook his head in disgust.

"Look," Fellows said, "you told me you were on your way to California, and I think you should go. Lot of opportunities out there. And you'll be getting a paycheck from me every three months, sixteen hundred just like clockwork. You know I'll keep paying, because if I don't, you could come right back here and cause me all kinds of grief, am I right?"

Cole frowned. "I suppose."

"Besides, there's no action around here for a young stud like you. California is where you want to be."

"Maybe," Cole said uncertainly.

Fellows slapped the arm of his chair and said, "Good." He pushed himself to his feet. "When you're ready to leave town, let me know and I'll give you what you've got coming." *A bullet in the head*, he thought.

"I'll think it over," Cole said, rising.

"What's to think? You deserve a full share." Fellows led him to the door. "After all," he said, "none of us would be getting any money if you hadn't killed that slut."

50

Early Saturday afternoon Nora and Thomas drove in his dark blue Chevrolet Caprice through a cold, dazzling rain toward Colorado Springs, seventy miles south of Denver.

Nora rode in silence, staring out the window. The only sounds were the wet hiss of the tires and the steady thump of the wiper blades. On their right the misty peaks of the front range moved slowly by, draped in somber green and gray, like an army of giants marching toward certain defeat. To their left, the low, wet hills flattened out into the eastern plains.

Nora could feel a tension in the car, as palpable as the warm air gushing from the heater. Neither of them had made mention of yesterday afternoon, but the words were there, waiting to be said.

When they had held each other in Annie's apartment, when they had kissed, a feeling had passed between them. A feeling of . . . belonging.

She sensed that Thomas had experienced it, too. And at that moment . . . *dear God, he was her dead sister's lover* . . . she had wanted him. When he had spoken, his first word had been "I'd," and she thought—hoped?—that he was about to say, "I'd like to stay." She doubted that she would have said no. And why should she? After all, they were consenting adults. Prepared to consent, anyway. Why couldn't he stay? Why couldn't they spend the night together, the rest of their lives together?

Because of my dead baby sister, she thought.

When Thomas had picked her up today, they had conversed—about the weather, the drive, anything but themselves. They hadn't held each other or kissed. He had touched her arm briefly when she climbed into his car—touched her through her coat sleeve, a firm, gentle touch. But that was all. She knew he was holding back.

And so was she.

But she wondered if Annie were truly the reason.

She had held herself back from men before. In the years following her divorce, she had been asked out by, to her estimate, every eligible bachelor in Cedar Falls—not that there were hordes of them. She had gone out, never letting things get too serious. At first, she told herself, "It's too soon after my divorce." Later, she revised it to, "The flower shop fills all of my time. I can't afford to complicate my life with a man."

Of course, those had been excuses, rationalizations. She had been *afraid* to get involved, afraid of another horrid relationship. Afraid of getting hurt.

And what about now? Was Annie standing between her and Thomas? Or was she simply using her sister as another excuse?

She wondered if she'd ever know.

✿   ✿   ✿

The Prentisses lived northeast of the Colorado Springs sub-
urbs, an area of gently rolling pastureland. The house was a
large, red-brick ranch with a small front lawn and ten acres of
backyard—native ground sectioned off with arrow-straight fence
lines. The rain had let up, and Nora saw a few horses a hundred
yards or so behind the house, tails flicking and heads down,
nibbling tall, wet grass.

They parked in the half-circle gravel drive and walked up to
the front door. It was flanked by large terra-cotta pots brimming
with bright flowers. Thomas rang the bell.

The man who opened the door was in his mid-forties with
dark hair going gray. He wore a plaid flannel shirt, blue jeans,
and boots with pointed toes. A pair of reading glasses was
perched on his nose.

"Yes?"

"Mr. Prentiss? I'm Nora Honeycut, and this is Thomas
Whitney."

"How do you do," he said. "Please come in. My grandfather
is eager to talk to you. He has a lot of fond memories of Lewiston." He held out his arm. "This way, please."

He led them down into a spacious living room with southwest-
ern-style furnishings. A floor-to-ceiling window offered a sweeping view of the mountains.

There was an old man seated in an armchair, and he rose to
greet them. He was less than five feet tall, Nora estimated, with
wavy white hair and black-framed glasses. He wore baggy slacks
and a heavy sweater knit in a colorful zigzag pattern.

The younger Prentiss made the introductions, then left them
alone.

After they had been seated—the old man in his chair and
Nora and Thomas together on a pale green leather couch—Nora
said, "Thank you for seeing us, Dr. Prentiss."

"It's my pleasure. I don't get many visitors." His voice was
strong, and his magnified eyes were clear and bright. "I understand you're writing a story about Lewiston. Do you work for
a magazine?"

"We, ah, we're not writing a story," Nora said.

His thick, white eyebrows rose above his glasses. "You're not?"

"Ah, no, and I'm sorry if I misled your grandson. I didn't want to discuss this matter over the telephone."

Prentiss looked a bit exasperated. "And what 'matter' are you talking about?"

Nora felt guilty about being there under somewhat false pretenses. She had been afraid Prentiss would be unwilling to talk to her, or that he'd be on the verge of senility, like Meg Andrew. Obviously he was neither.

Nora glanced at Thomas, then said, "My sister died a few weeks ago in Lewiston. The circumstances were unusual, even suspicious. We've been to the sheriff, but he's convinced her death was an accident. We hoped you could help us get to the bottom of things."

Prentiss cocked his head. "She died in Lewiston, you say?"

"Yes, on the grounds of the Owen mansion. There's something strange about—"

"The *Owen* mansion?" He looked both surprised and troubled. "Does Chastity Owen still live there?"

"Yes."

Prentiss hesitated. "Are you implying that Chastity Owen is somehow involved in your sister's death?"

"I . . . I don't know." Nora wondered how close Prentiss and Chastity had been. "Perhaps."

Prentiss shifted his gaze to Thomas, then back to Nora. "Well," he said. Then he turned his head toward the doorway and called out, "Steven!"

Nora guessed that she and Thomas were about to be thrown out. The grandson appeared at the doorway, frowning.

"Yes, Grandpa?"

"Steven, would you bring us some coffee." He turned to Nora. "Cream and sugar?"

51

After his grandson had brought them coffee in earthenware mugs, Prentiss asked, "How exactly did your sister die?"

Nora described the details of Annie's death. She explained how Chief Fellows, Karl, and even Dr. Newby seemed to know more than they were telling. She told how Fellows had assaulted first her and then Thomas, and how he had warned them not to return to Lewiston.

"Threatened, is more like it," Thomas said.

Prentiss shook his head. "I don't know this Fellows character, but I'm well acquainted with Karl Gant. I can't say I ever much cared for him. He's a strange bird. Humorless. A little scary, too."

"More than a little," Nora said.

Prentiss looked worried. "Do you think Chastity Owen is in any danger?"

"I don't know," Nora said. She hadn't considered it before, but now she began to wonder if the old woman might be at risk.

"How well do you know Miss Owen?" Thomas asked.

"When I lived in Lewiston I suppose I knew her as well as anybody—which is not very well at all. She was just a teenager, when she . . . became a recluse."

"After her child was stillborn," Nora said.

Prentiss squinted at her. "Who told you that?"

"Meg Andrew."

He hesitated. "What else did she tell you?"

"Just that she and Chastity were best friends," Nora said, "until Chastity's father committed rape and Mrs. Owen killed him for it. After that, Chastity and her mother rarely left the house. They even painted the windows to keep out prying eyes."

Prentiss shook his head sadly. "A bad business all around," he said. "Especially . . ." He shook his head again.

"There's more to it, isn't there?" Nora asked.

Prentiss stared into his mug, then drank some coffee. He looked tentatively from Thomas to Nora. "I've kept their secret all these years," he said. "And I doubt it has anything to do with the death of your sister. But . . ."

"But it might," Nora finished for him.

Prentiss held her gaze for a moment. Then he seemed to sag within his clothes. "I guess there's no harm in telling you now. It's been, let's see, sixty years or more." He sighed. "Something you have to realize is that things were different back then. Attitudes were different."

Prentiss explained how he had moved to Lewiston to begin his medical practice when he was twenty-eight years old. During his first year there he had become acquainted with almost everyone in town, including Mr. and Mrs. Owen and their teenage daughter Chastity. He remembered her as an attractive young girl, bright and outgoing.

That changed dramatically—in fact, the mood of the entire town seemed to change—the night Mrs. Owen shot her husband to death. People were stunned by the murder, and doubly so when they learned that Mr. Owen had tried to rape his own daughter.

Then, three months later, Mrs. Owen came to Prentiss and swore him to secrecy. She confessed that the rape of her daughter had been more than an attempt and that Chastity was pregnant from the incestuous attack.

"She wanted me to perform an abortion," Prentiss said. "And God help me, I was such a good Christian at the time that I refused. I told her I would help with the birth when the time came and tend to the baby as needed. But I would not kill it."

His expression was grim as he explained how he had been called to the Owen house a few weeks later. Chastity was near death. Mrs. Owen and Meg Andrew's mother had tried to end the girl's pregnancy with homemade abortifacients—forcing Chastity to drink one and douche with the other.

"Those two chemical mixtures might as well have been poison and acid," Prentiss said, "for what they did to that poor girl. It was a wonder she lived. And it was a miracle the fetus survived. Or rather, a curse."

Any further attempt to abort the fetus was now out of the question for fear of endangering Chastity's life. Her pregnancy remained a secret shared only by Mrs. Owen, Doc Prentiss, and Meg Andrew's mother. And of course, Karl, the young caretaker. The rest of the town believed that Chastity was bedridden with a nervous disorder afflicting her since the attempted rape. In fact, she was bedridden, and she suffered greatly during the pregnancy.

When the child decided to come into the world, it nearly killed Chastity.

Nora said, "Decided? So the baby wasn't stillborn."

Prentiss slowly shook his head. "If only it had been." He gave a small shudder. "Mrs. Andrew came banging on my door one night around midnight saying that there was an emergency at the Owen house. When I got there Mrs. Owen was frantic and Chastity was screaming in agony. That . . . that *creature* was being born, and it was lodged half in and half out of the poor girl. And I'll tell you, it was the most monstrous thing I had ever seen, before or since. I have no doubt that the gross deformities were due to the noxious chemicals that Mrs. Owen and Mrs. Andrew had used trying to abort the pregnancy."

Prentiss drew in a long breath and let it out slowly before he continued. "Anyway, I gave poor Chastity a shot to ease her pain, then I assisted in the birth. Eventually, it—I mean *he*—came squirming out of her, all misshapen, nothing symmetrical, like a giant maggot. The skull was lumpy and ill-formed, partly devoid of scalp. One shoulder seemed to be growing right out of the head, just below the ear. The left arm was withered and the right one was enormous. The legs were bent and twisted, and one foot had no toes, and ... I swear, at first I thought the creature had three legs, so gigantic was its male member. Well, and the face, my God, like something from a nightmare. One eye huge, the other pale and tiny. No nose to speak of, just holes offset in that mess of flesh, sucking air. The mouth was purple and ragged and croaking."

Prentiss had been speaking in a trancelike monotone. Nora and Thomas watched him in silence.

"Mrs. Andrew took one look at that thing and fainted dead away," Prentiss said. "Chastity's mother could do no more than stand there and stare, and all the while Chastity was screaming in pain and that child-thing was squawking, sounding more like a beast than a baby.

"I'm ashamed to say I was hesitant to even hold it, but I got it cleaned off and wrapped in a blanket. Then I tended to Chastity. When I looked up, Mrs. Owen was carrying the infant from the room. She said to me, 'This thing must die. I'm going to drown it in the bathtub.'

"Before that moment Chastity hadn't laid eyes on the creature. But now she started shouting at her mother, begging her not to kill her baby. I felt torn between those two, but God help me, I was on the mother's side. I believed with all my heart that the best thing for everyone involved, *especially* the baby, was that it should die." He shook his head. "Six months earlier I'd been dead-set against aborting it. Now I was prepared to assist in its murder. Or at least, look the other way while Mrs. Owen did what had to be done. She asked me to leave them alone with the child, and dear Jesus I did, knowing full well what she was going to do.

"Then late the next night Mrs. Owen sent Mrs. Andrew to fetch me. I thought it was to tend to Chastity, but when I arrived at the house the girl seemed okay, completely calmed down. What Mrs. Owen wanted me for was a more physical task—to dig a grave for the baby."

Prentiss stared down at his hands and shook his head. "I dug it right there in the side yard near the hedge."

"Where was Karl during all this?" Thomas asked.

Prentiss looked up. "Karl? He had gone to St. Louis several weeks earlier to visit relatives. He didn't return until after . . . after this business was settled." He heaved a sigh. "As I was saying, I dug the grave. Mrs. Owen handed me down the poor, dead creature, and we covered it up, smoothed off the dirt, and laid the sod back in place so that no sign showed." Prentiss took of his glasses and pinched the bridge of his nose. "I lived in Lewiston for thirty years after that and all the times that I saw Mrs. Owen and Chastity, never once was that baby mentioned. It was as if it had never existed."

"Are you certain the baby died?" Nora asked quietly.

Prentiss put his glasses back on. "Am I *certain?* I *buried* him."

Nora hesitated. "Did you see him, or was he in a box?"

"He was wrapped in a blanket. But I could feel the tiny, misshapen body when I helped Mrs. Owen lay it in the grave."

Nora nodded.

"I've never told anyone about this," Prentiss said. "Not my children or my grandchildren or even my wife, when she was alive. But it's the sort of thing that never leaves you. And I suppose I've always wanted to tell *someone.*" He cleared his throat. "And unless you think any of this is connected with your sister's death, I'd prefer that it not leave this room."

"Of course," Nora said. She felt certain that there was a connection, but she said nothing to Prentiss. She stood and thanked him for his help and hospitality. The old man showed them to the door.

Nora waited until she and Thomas were seated in the car before she said, "That baby wasn't killed."

"What do you mean? Prentiss said—"

"He buried a blanket with something wrapped in it, something he assumed was the child."

Thomas looked at her.

"I think Chastity's baby grew into a man," Nora said. "And he's living upstairs in the Owen house."

52

On the drive back to Denver, the rain began again. Thomas switched on the wipers and said, "How could Prentiss be mistaken about what he buried. I mean, the man is a doctor."

"It was wrapped in a blanket," Nora said. "And he was *expecting* it to be a baby."

"Then what was it?"

"I don't know—a doll filled with sand, a small dead dog. It doesn't matter. Just something wrapped up that was handed to him in the dark while he stood in the bottom of an open grave. Why wouldn't he believe it was the child? He'd have no reason to doubt Mrs. Owen."

Nora could hear the urgency in her own voice. She was convinced that Chastity Owen's son had lived, that it was *him* she heard on the staircase. She wanted Thomas to be certain as well. She needed him to be.

"I think Mrs. Owen had a change of heart about killing the child," she said. "Either because of the effect it might have on Chastity, or simply because the deformed creature was her grandson and she could not help loving him."

"Then why fool Dr. Prentiss into thinking she killed him?"

"To make sure no one ever found out that the baby was alive.

233

By hiding the child, she probably felt that she was protecting it, preventing it from being subjected to ridicule and scorn from the townspeople and morbidly curious outsiders."

"I don't know," Thomas said, shaking his head. "But, okay, let's assume that Miss Owen's son survived and that he's still alive."

"And living upstairs in the house."

"That's what I'm getting at," Thomas said. "How could he be living there and—"

"Hiding."

"All right, hiding. A town that small, how could you hide a person in a house for *sixty years?* I mean, eventually everyone in town would know about him. It would be impossible to keep it a secret."

"It's not impossible," Nora said. "I know something about small towns. Everyone's favorite hobby is trying to pry into everybody else's business. People become experts at hiding their secrets—illicit love affairs, skeletons in the family closet, whatever."

"Still, to hide a *person?*"

"Okay, look at it this way. In all that time Miss Owen's son never once left the house, and no one was ever allowed past the front parlor. Miss Owen and Karl kept him upstairs behind painted windows. And if the townspeople ever caught a glimpse of him or saw anything strange, they wrote it off as the weird, reclusive Miss Owen and her haunted house."

Thomas was silent for a moment, his brow furrowed. "Maybe you're right," he said. "And the baby food would be for him. Although God knows why."

Nora nodded. "That's why Karl sneaks out of town to buy it and dispose of the empty jars. So no one will know."

"Jesus," Thomas said under his breath. "What kind of a monster do they have up there?"

"According to Dr. Prentiss, he's grotesque. But he's a man, not a monster."

"I don't mean physically," Thomas said. "Mentally. He's been locked away for his entire life. Six decades. Who knows what that's done to his mind."

Nora pictured herself in the doorway of the upstairs bedroom. She shuddered. "He's what I smelled up there. And heard . . ." She bit her lip and stared out at the gloomy, wet landscape.

"What is it?"

"I was just remembering. When I came down the stairs, I heard him behind me. I was too scared to even turn around. But now that I think back, the sound I heard wasn't so much threatening as it was . . . pitiful."

"It was threatening, all right. He killed Annie."

Nora shivered. She pulled her coat more closely about her.

"But before he killed her," Thomas said, "Annie caught him on film. He's the blurred, deformed creature crouching in the shadows."

Nora opened her purse and withdrew the photo. The collection of gray and white blotches had never looked quite like a person, she knew, mainly because the head was abnormally large. But if Dr. Prentiss's description were correct, then the photo was an accurate, if out-of-focus representation of Miss Owen's grotesque offspring. He had been hiding in the yard that night, watching Annie, waiting for her to climb down. Although . . .

She frowned and returned the print to her purse. "What was he doing outside?"

"What?"

"If Miss Owen and Karl have been so careful about hiding him, why would they allow him outside the house?"

"Maybe he went out on his own."

"But why? Surely he'd know the danger of being seen."

"Maybe . . . maybe they *let* him out. To get Annie."

"Oh, God." Nora squeezed her eyes closed and pressed her fingers to her temples, trying to force the image from her mind— a hideous creature set loose like a wild animal to kill her sister.

"Fellows and Doc Newby and Karl knew what happened," Thomas said. "They made it look as if she had died from a fall. They're probably being paid off by that rich old lady to protect her son. Every one of them is an accessory to murder." His grip tightened on the wheel. "We've got to convince Sheriff Parmeter of that. We've got to *make* him believe us."

"He won't," Nora said. "Not unless we bring him something concrete."

"Like what," Thomas said with some sarcasm, "Miss Owen's son?"

She turned to him. "Or his photograph."

"But you've already shown him Annie's photo and—"

"I don't mean that one. I mean we go in there and snap a picture of Miss Owen's son and take it to Parmeter."

Thomas shot her a glance. "Are you serious?"

"You're damn right."

Thomas was silent for a moment. "How do you intend to get past Miss Owen and Karl again?"

Nora gave him a weak smile. "I was sort of hoping that you'd take care of Karl."

"You mean knock him down and sit on his chest, while you run upstairs and snap pictures."

"Something like that."

"Terrific."

"Look, if you don't want to help me, I'll—"

"I didn't say that." Thomas looked at her, then stared through the windshield. "There's one other problem."

"Only one?"

"Chief Fellows. If he catches us near that house, there's no telling what he might do."

"I know," Nora said quietly. "We'll have to be careful."

When they arrived in the city, they drove to Thomas's apartment to get his camera—a point-and-shoot model with a built-in flash. He loaded a roll of color film, then snapped a picture of Nora to make sure the battery wasn't dead.

Then they headed west toward Lewiston.

The rain continued—hard little pellets that punched angrily into the windshield. The late afternoon sky hung low over the mountains, as dark as a funeral pall.

53

Cole Newby switched on his headlights and wipers and drove to the Owen mansion.

It wasn't yet nighttime, he decided, more like an unnatural twilight. The streets were deserted. A thin, wet snow had been falling for an hour, and it was beginning to stick.

He parked before the great hedge and shut off the engine, stopping the wipers in mid-stroke. He sat for a moment, listening to the patter of moisture. It had been a long time since he had visited this place. Five years, to be exact. A warm summer's night.

He and Bonnie Connor crept through the hedge, giggling, more than a little drunk. The grounds were spooky enough to sober them up. It wasn't a uniform darkness within the borders of the hedge, but a mosaic of shadows within shadows. And the great house loomed over it all, brooding. Watching.

Cole didn't care who was watching, he was intent on getting into Bonnie Connor's panties.

He had been trying for months to get her in bed, or even in the backseat of his car. She was always encouraging him, it seemed, and then stopping him just when things were heated up. When he was heated up. But she had a way of saying no that promised, "Next time, for sure."

Well, as far as he was concerned, this was the next time, and he was sure. Every beer he had drunk at the party in Denver had been like kerosene thrown on a fire. He felt as if his insides were blazing.

He groped at Bonnie in the deep shadow of a tree. They sank to their knees on the cool, black lawn. They kissed, tongues darting into each other's mouths. He fondled her breasts and pushed her gently onto her back. She resisted. "That's enough for one night," she told him. But it wasn't enough, not for him, not this night.

He overpowered her.

And when it was over, and the horror of it began to envelope him, he heard movement in the shadows. When he looked around he saw a hideous creature bearing down on him, shuffling and grunting, a thing from Hell. He ran for his life.

Now Cole climbed from the car. He turned up the collar of his denim jacket and ducked his head against the steady fall of snow.

All these years, he thought, *Fellows and McOllough have been making money because of what happened. And me getting nothing. Well, that changes tonight.*

He passed through the hedge and followed the walk, keeping his head down, sensing the grounds pressing in from either side. The porch creaked underfoot as he walked across to the front door. His breath billowed before him in miniature clouds. He rang the bell and waited.

No answer.

He rang it again. He knew someone was inside because he could see a pale light sifting through the lacy curtain, a light from deep within the house. He pounded on the door. No way were they keeping him out. They owed him *money.* And regardless of what Chief Fellows had told him, he knew Miss Owen had piles of cash in there.

He raised his fist to pound again.

The door latch clicked. The door swung inward, and there stood Karl, tall and gaunt, dressed in black. His head hung between his shoulders like a vulture's.

"What is it?" he demanded, his voice rumbling.

"Hey, Karl. How're you doing?"

Karl scowled down at him. "Who are you? What do you want?"

Some of Cole's bravado left him. He had hoped the old man would recognize him. He spread his hands and grinned. "Cole Newby, the one and only."

Karl did not change expression. "What do you want here?"

Anger squirmed in Cole's gut like a centipede. "I'll tell you what I want, old man, I want my share of the money. And I don't mean the piss-ass amounts you've been paying Fellows and McOllough. I mean *serious* money."

There. Now *that* was the look he had been expecting. He grinned at the Karl's uneasiness.

"I . . . I don't know what you're talking about."

"Don't give me that. Miss Owen has been making payments to those two for the past five years—ever since Willy killed Bonnie Connor out there in the yard."

Karl swallowed hard. "No one lives here but Miss Owen and myself."

Cole gave him a hard look. "I didn't come here to play games. I know everything, just the same as Fellows and McOllough. You're hiding a murderer upstairs in this house. Now, you either let me in, or I'm going straight to the sheriff in Idaho Springs."

Karl stood motionless for so long that Cole had to blink to separate him from the gloomy background.

Finally Karl said, "We don't have any money to give you."

Cole shivered against the cold. "I'd like to hear that from Miss Owen. Let me in."

"Miss Owen is not well. You had better discuss this with Chief Fellows." He started to shut the door.

Cole sprang forward and slammed his shoulder into the door, barely keeping it open. "Goddamnit!" he shouted through the narrow opening. "Let me in or I'll tell everyone!" He leaned his entire weight against the door but could not budge it. It remained open a few inches, although he had the impression that Karl could slam it shut if he wanted to.

"You might as well let me in," Cole said in what he hoped was a confident tone. "Because I'm not going away."

The truth was, if Karl shut him out he probably would go away. What else could he do, drive his car through the front door? He hadn't counted on angry resistance from the old man (the *large* old man, larger than he remembered). He had figured on dealing only with the crone. She'd be a pushover. And of course, his threat about going to the sheriff in Idaho Springs had been nothing but a bluff. There was no way he—

The door slowly opened. Karl stared down at him for a moment. Then he stepped aside.

Cole grinned. "Much obliged."

He entered the dimly lit hallway, and Karl closed the door behind him. The sound when it clicked shut gave Cole a chill. He wondered if he had blundered into alien territory. He looked around at the old-fashioned wallpaper and carpet runners, at the ancient photographs in oval frames, and he felt like a small boy on his first visit to a museum.

"Wait in here," Karl said. He showed him into a room crowded with furniture from the last century.

Cole was suddenly apprehensive. "Where are you going?" Again, he felt more like a boy than a man, afraid to be left alone in this big, dark house.

Karl said, "I will announce you to Miss Owen."

The tall man turned to leave, and a floorboard groaned overhead. They both heard it, and they both knew what it was. Someone was moving about upstairs, someone heavier than a frail old woman.

Willy, Cole thought. His hand went to the knife on his belt. He stared at the ceiling and tried to reassure himself that Willy was at least sixty years old. No threat. Scary to look at, sure, but still an old man.

He saw Karl watching him, his face partially obscured by shadow. Was he smiling?

"Just wait here," he told Cole. "I won't be a moment."

Cole stood nervously in the center of the room, his hand on the knife hilt. The movement upstairs had ceased, and gradually

Cole began to relax. He knew how he would deal with Miss Owen—hit her with the same threat he had used on Karl. Either she gave him money, or he'd tell the sheriff about Willy. The question was how much money should he demand? Ten thousand? Twenty? He knew the old lady was rich, but he didn't know *how* rich. The one thing he didn't want to do was shortchange himself. Maybe he should play it cool, let her make the first offer and then take things from there.

He just wished she'd get here. Waiting made him nervous. Or maybe it was this house.

Then he heard Karl's voice drift in from the hallway. He faced the doorway, expecting Karl and Miss Owen to appear at any moment. But they did not. Cole stepped into the hall. Empty. He could hear Karl's voice coming from an open door across from him. He moved quietly toward it and peered inside.

The room was furnished much like the one he had just left, and it smelled of musty books. Karl stood with his back to the door, a phone cradled in his giant hand.

"All right, Chief," he said in a low voice and hung up.

Cole said, "You motherfucker." He entered the room, drawing his knife from its sheath.

Then suddenly he stopped dead in his tracks, frozen by a sound that came from the depths of the house.

A scream.

54

Willy saw the One emerge from the gateway in the hedge and enter the grounds.

He was overwhelmed with rage. His vision blurred and a red mist filled his head. Images swarmed before him, and the past came rushing in—a July night, years ago.

From the cupola window he watched the boy and girl enter the yard, ill-lit by a sliver of moon. The night was warm, and the two giggling trespassers wore clothing that exposed their arms and legs. Willy could plainly see their faces. The girl was beautiful, and the sight of her made his heart race. The young couple paused in the shadow of a tree. The boy put his hand on the back of the girl's neck and drew her to him. They kissed.

Willy watched them, transfixed. In years past, Miss Owen had touched her lips to his forehead—but this was not the same. Willy trembled as the couple pressed their mouths together and touched each other with their hands. They sank to their knees, and then lay on the lawn. They were covered in shadow, except for the boy's feet, which jutted into the sharp-edge moonlight, cleanly distinct, disembodied, as if they had been amputated.

Willy's heart pounded heavily as he watched the young couple thrash about in the dark.

Then he heard a sound that made his breath catch in his

throat. It was muffled by the glass and diminished by the distance, but his good ear easily discerned it.

A cry of distress.

The girl crawled into the moonlight. She was naked from the waist down, and her white flesh seemed to glow. The boy leapt from the shadows with a snarl and tackled her to the ground. They fought. The boy was much stronger, and he forced her onto her back and struck her with his fists.

Willy was sickened. And outraged. The girl struggled and cried out. The boy closed his hands around her throat.

Willy could take no more. He clambered out of the cupola and down the stairs to the main floor of the house, with reckless disregard of Miss Owen's primary rule. He lumbered out the back door and around the side of the house.

The boy still had the girl by the throat. But when he saw Willy, he let the girl go and scrambled to his feet. His face was white with terror. "Oh, my God," he said, transfixed by the sight of Willy. "Stay away from me. Stay away!" And then he turned and ran.

Willy chased clumsily after him. By the time he reached the gateway in the hedge, the boy was speeding away in his car. He went back to the girl. He crouched over her and touched her lifeless cheek.

Then Karl came running into the yard. "Oh my God, Willy, what have you done?"

Willy did not have the words nor the tongue to explain. He grunted and motioned with his hands: It wasn't me—it was the other one. But Karl continued to moan, "Oh my God, oh my God," and he pulled at Willy's arm and drew him into the house.

Willy well remembered the commotion that night—the men who had come to the house, the cries of anguish from Miss Owen. She thought *he* had harmed the girl. And in the days and weeks that followed, he had tried to demonstrate to her and Karl that it hadn't been him, but the One who had done that awful thing. But they didn't understand. As the days passed, Willy gave up trying.

And his hatred for the One grew, week by week. Hundreds of weeks. It filled him.

And now the One had returned.

Willy clambered out of the room and down the hallway to the head of the stairs. He paused briefly, still conditioned by a lifetime of commands. Then he heard the voice of the One—*inside the house!* Willy lurched down the stairs, gripping the railing hard enough to make it creak, feeling in his hand the neck of the One.

Before he reached the bottom of the stairs, he saw Miss Owen hurrying along the hallway. She met him at the foot of the staircase, blocking his way.

"No, Willy," she whispered urgently. "Go back. You mustn't come down."

But Willy came forward, blinded by fury. He tried to gently brush her aside. But he was too strong, too filled with rage, and Miss Owen was knocked to the floor.

She screamed in pain, "Willy, my leg! You've broken it!"

Her cries sliced through his anger like a scalpel. He stood, immobilized, torn between the one he loved and the one he hated.

55

Chief Fellows drove through the falling snow to the Owen mansion, his head pounding and his stomach churning.

Earlier that afternoon he had told Griff he was going home and didn't want to be disturbed for anything less than a full-scale riot. He still hadn't figured out exactly how to handle Cole Newby. He needed time alone to think. Drinking helped him think. In fact, after several hours of doing both, he believed he was on the edge of an intricate yet totally workable plan to get rid of Cole without a trace of suspicion. He had been well into a bottle of bourbon and a twelve-pack of beer when the phone started jangling. He had groaned audibly and knocked the receiver off the cradle reaching for it. He retrieved it, swearing under his breath.

"This better be important, Griff."

But it wasn't Griff. It was Karl.

"Cole Newby is here demanding money."

"Son of a *bitch*." Pain had lanced through Fellows's temples. "All right, I'm on my way." He had slammed down the receiver. Then he yanked on his boots, jerked his gun belt around his waist, punched his fists into the sleeves of his jacket, and jammed his hat on his head. He picked up the bottle for one more shot, then cursed and heaved it against the wall in an explosion of brown liquid and glass shards.

Now he drove through the cold, white night with his heavy fists on the steering wheel and his teeth clenched against the pounding in his head. He was halfway to the Owen house before he remembered to turn on his headlights.

He parked behind Cole's junk heap of a car. Then he strode through the thin snow that covered the grounds, crossed the porch, and banged on the door. When it opened, he expected to see Karl standing there. But it was Cole. Fellows sucked in his breath, ready to grab him by the neck and yank him from the doorway.

Cole stopped him with, "Miss Owen's been hurt."

Fellows hesitated, as the roar of blood in his ears began to subside. "What?" He could see that Cole was nervous. He had *better* be, the little bastard. "What happened?"

Cole moved aside to let him in. "That *thing* upstairs knocked her down. Karl's back there with her."

Fellows stepped in, then turned to Cole, his mouth on a level with the younger man's eyes, close enough so that his breath made Cole blink.

"Get your ass home," Fellows growled, "and I'll be by later to talk to you."

"Not until I—"

Fellows grabbed two fistfuls of Cole's jacket, jerked him off his feet, and heaved him out the open door. Cole landed heavily on the porch, sprawling. For a moment he didn't move, the wind knocked out of him. Then he scrambled clumsily to his feet, his face flushed with anger and embarrassment. He reached for his knife.

Fellows said, "I dearly hope you try that." His hand was on the butt of his revolver, and there was an unfamiliar heat behind his eyes.

A loud moan came from within the house—Miss Owen.

Fellows glanced inside, then returned his attention to Cole. The young man slowly straightened up. His hands hung at his sides, closed in fists.

"Go on home," Fellows said, his voice strained. "I'll be by later to talk to you."

Cole glared at him for a moment, showing defiance, then he turned and walked away. Fellows watched him until he had passed through the hedge. He stood on the porch taking deep breaths, trying to calm down. Only after he heard Cole's car start and drive away did he enter the house and close the door behind him.

He walked down the dimly lit hall and found Miss Owen groaning in pain on the floor. Karl was kneeling beside her, cradling her head in his lap.

"What happened?"

Karl told him that Willy had come downstairs, apparently trying to get to Cole. "Please," he said. "Call the doctor."

"Where's Willy?"

"Upstairs. Please. Call now."

Fellows phoned Doc Newby and explained the situation. Newby said he'd be right over, and he asked Fellows to call the hospital in Idaho Springs for an ambulance.

A few minutes later Fellows let Newby in the front door and led him down the hallway. The doctor knelt beside Miss Owen and began a quick examination, speaking to her in a quiet, soothing voice.

Fellows told Karl, "Go upstairs and see that Willy stays put. An ambulance will be here soon."

Newby looked up. "How did this happen?"

"She slipped and fell," Fellows said. Then he called to Karl, halfway up the staircase. "Do you hear that, Karl? She slipped and fell, and that's all there was to it." He looked down at Miss Owen, who moaned and babbled incoherently. "What do you think, Doc?"

"Her hip is broken, that's for certain, and maybe her left wrist, too. Or else it's severely sprained. I'll ride with her to the hospital."

". . . Karl . . ." Miss Owen's voice was weak. ". . . Where's Karl? . . ."

"He's just upstairs," Newby said quietly. "We're taking you to the hospital."

A short time later two paramedics gently lifted Miss Owen onto a gurney and wheeled her outside. Newby followed them out. Karl came downstairs and told Fellows that he was going to drive to the hospital.

"What about Willy?"

"He's very upset," Karl said. "But he knows to stay upstairs."

Karl left by the back door. Fellows went out the front, pulling the door shut, making sure it was locked. He watched the ambulance drive off, illuminating the falling snow in rotating flashes of red and white.

Then he drove to Doc Newby's house, looking for Cole.

But the house was dark, and Cole's car was not in sight.

Fellows swore under his breath. *That boy needs to be taught a hard lesson.*

For the next half hour he cruised the streets of Lewiston, looking for Cole's junker. The town grew dark, and the snowfall increased, apparently the first real storm of the season. Which did nothing to brighten Fellows's mood. He wondered if Cole had left town, or if he had simply hidden his car somewhere.

Fellows gave up searching for the car and began looking for the man himself, walking into every bar and restaurant in town, bringing the snow in with him, feeling the anger build inside him. At least the pounding in his head had subsided to a steady, dull throb. He knew, though, that when he found Cole he'd beat the hell out of him, at the very least, and damn the consequences.

By the time Fellows left the last saloon in town, his anger had grown until he could hardly contain it. He knew he had to calm down and think. *Where the hell was Cole?* He considered going back in the bar for a quick drink, anything to clear his head.

Then he sat bolt-upright in his car.

"Of course," he muttered. "God *damn* him."

He drove to the Owen mansion through steadily falling snow. Doc Newby's van was still there, now wearing a shroud of white. And another car was parked behind it—a dark blue Chevy.

Fellows frowned. A friend of Cole?

He shut off the engine and climbed out. Fat white flakes clung to his coat and touched his face like frigid fingertips. He studied the ground around the Chevy. There was enough snow to read footprints. At first he thought there were four sets. But then he saw that one person had gone back to the car, then returned to the grounds—which meant there were only two people, Cole and someone else. He followed the prints through the towering hedge, across the grounds, and around the side of the house.

The house was dark and silent, but he felt eyes peering down at him from the painted windows. He stopped at the rear corner of the building and held his breath. He heard whispers.

Cole and who else?

Fellows unholstered his revolver and stepped around the corner.

The back porch and the yard were both empty and silent under the falling snow. For a moment Fellows wondered if the alcohol in his veins was affecting his brain, making him hear things. But the footprints in the snow were real enough. They led along the rear of the house and onto the back porch.

Fellows quietly climbed the steps. The back door was ajar, and there were fresh gouges in the wood. Obviously, someone had broken in.

You're a dead man, Cole, he thought and eased open the door.

The room, a pantry, was dark and silent.

Fellows held his gun before him and went in.

56

B y the time Nora and Thomas arrived in Lewiston night had fallen. But the landscape wasn't completely dark. The mountains that cradled the town were swathed in white, and they seemed to effuse a pale, ghastly light.

Snowflakes swirled about them as they drove through mushy streets past snow-veiled houses and lawns. Nora wished she could have changed clothes after they had returned to Denver from Colorado Springs. Her sweater and topcoat were warm enough, but she would have preferred to be wearing jeans and boots rather than a skirt and flat-soled shoes.

They crossed Main Street, dark and nearly deserted. All the shops were closed under the silent fall of snow. The only places that appeared to be open were a few bars and a restaurant two blocks away, their window lights diffused behind shifting curtains of flakes.

Thomas steered up Alpine Street, covered now by a thick, white blanket.

Nora shivered. Not from the cold—the car's heater was blowing warm air—but from apprehension and uncertainty. An hour ago and fifty miles away this had seemed like a good idea. They would enter the mansion, sneak up on Miss Owen's son, and snap his photograph. Evidence for Parmeter. For Annie.

Now, though, it seemed insane.

The man—if man he was—had to be mentally unbalanced from a lifetime of hiding. How would he react?

As they reached the corner of Silver street, Nora nearly told Thomas to stop the car, to turn around and drive back to Denver. But the words wouldn't come. The sight of the Owen mansion seemed to freeze her vocal cords. The great house rose like a specter behind the massive, snow-capped hedge. Ghostly black-and white pines stood in attendance.

When they turned the corner, they were surprised to see a dark van at the edge of the road, near the gateway in the hedge. Thomas parked behind it and shut off the engine. Snowflakes immediately began to cloud the windshield.

"Miss Owen has company."

Nora's fists were in her lap. She fought to control her shivering. "Who do you suppose it is?"

"I have no idea." He opened his door.

"Wait," she said, putting her hand on his arm. "Are we still going inside? I mean, we don't know for sure who else is in there."

Thomas hesitated. "Let's at least take a look."

They passed through the gateway. Snowflakes fell wetly about them, like chilled tears. No lights shone through the curtains, and the porch was as black as a cave. The cupola, crowned with snow, seemed to glare down at Nora, making her clutch the camera as if it were a weapon.

"Let's try the back door," Thomas said quietly.

"But what about the van? Whoever it belongs to must be inside."

"I don't think so. We'd see lights. I don't think anyone's home."

"Except Miss Owen's son."

"Yes, let's hope." He studied her face. "Unless you're having second thoughts."

Nora hesitated. "No. Come on."

They walked around the side of the house. Nora felt a cold wetness on her ankles as the snow fluffed over the tops of her shoes. When they rounded the rear corner of the building, she expected to see Karl's black Cadillac. But the car was gone.

"Maybe they went for a drive."

"Maybe," Nora said doubtfully.

She mounted the steps, leaving inch-deep footprints on the snowy steps. She put her hand on the ice-cold doorknob and rattled it softly.

Locked.

She looked down at Thomas, who stood a step below her. "Now what?" She kept her voice low, as if she feared someone might be just beyond the door, listening.

"Wait here," Thomas said.

"Where are—"

But he turned without an explanation and walked quickly away, disappearing around the corner of the house. Nora stood alone on the cold, open porch as snow sailed down about her. She felt small and vulnerable, pressed between two masses. On one side was the mansion, dark and brooding, daring her to enter. And on the other side was the mountain, rising steeply into the cascading flakes, blending with them, disappearing into lowering sky.

Nora shivered. She brushed snow from the top of her head and cursed her stupidity for not bringing a hat or even a scarf. Her feet were beginning to feel the cold. She stamped them on the snowy porch. But she stopped suddenly, wondering if she could be heard inside the house. If someone were waiting, just beyond the door . . .

A figure appeared at the corner of the building, and Nora caught her breath.

But it was Thomas. He mounted the steps and stood beside her, a heavy screwdriver in his hand.

He hefted it. "What do you think?"

She nodded, clenching her jaws to keep her teeth from chattering. "Do it," she whispered.

Thomas wedged the screwdriver between the frame and the door and leaned into it. There was a soft, dry, cracking sound as the frame gave way around the lock. The door creaked open.

Nora went in with Thomas right behind her. They passed first through the dimly lit pantry and then the kitchen. The old linoleum floor squeaked underfoot. Nora opened the kitchen door a few inches and peered down the hallway. It seemed darker than the last time she had been here, darker even than her dream-hall. A huge, black shadow filled the right side of the hallway and seemed to absorb what little light there was. Although she could not clearly discern it in the dark, she knew what it was. The rear of the staircase.

She turned to Thomas and whispered, "All clear. The stairs are straight ahead."

He nodded.

She started to push open the door, and he stopped her, his hand on her shoulder. "Maybe I should be the one to go up with the camera."

"But we already agreed that—"

"So, we'll change it."

She swallowed and said, "No. You have to stay downstairs in case Karl shows up." He knew that, of course. He was just giving her one last chance to back out. "Let's get it over with."

She pushed through the doorway, and Thomas followed. The first door on their right was closed. The one on their left, though, gaped wide. Nora peeked into the converted dining room, half expecting to see Miss Owen lying in bed—or lying in wait. But the room was empty.

They crept down the darkened hallway. As they approached the staircase, a floorboard creaked overhead.

Thomas stopped and looked up.

"I heard it, too," Nora whispered.

"He's up there."

She nodded stiffly, aware of a pain in her chest, as if her heart had squeezed itself into a fist. She walked quietly beside the descending balustrade to the foot of the stairs. She peered up into the gloom. A short, squat form crouched at the edge of the landing, motionless. Nora nearly cried out. She quickly raised the camera—and then realized that the figure was merely the newel post supporting the top end of the banister.

She glanced over her shoulder at Thomas, embarrassed. But he was looking the other way, facing the front of the house, on guard.

Nora returned her gaze to the top of the staircase and strained to see into the gloom, as thick as the ink cloud of a squid. For a moment she became disoriented and felt as if she were looking not up, but down, trying to pierce the depths of a cold, dark body of water.

She started up the stairs.

Her body was so tense that her joints ached, and her mouth was too dry to swallow. She kept her eyes on the landing above. And as she drew near it, something emerged from the darkness. There had been no movement. Instead, the shadows seemed to coalesce into a solid form. Nora blinked her eyes, certain that they were deceiving her, convinced that her fear was creating an hallucination.

It moved.

Nora saw a pale, twisted creature of inhuman proportions, its head huge and lopsided. It stared down at her with an eye as large as a hen's egg.

A scream caught in her throat. She raised the camera and fired, filling the stairwell with a burst of light. The creature roared, and Nora fled down the stairs.

Thomas stared up anxiously at her. *"Is that him? Did you see him?"*

Nora did not even slow down, grabbing his arm as she flew by, yanking him toward the rear of the house. They were nearly to the kitchen, when the door swung open.

Chief Fellows stood there, a gun in his hand.

57

Fellows had to force himself not to shoot.

He had expected to find Cole and an accomplice rum-
maging through the house, searching for stacks of nonexis-
tent cash. He had been prepared to take them into custody and
pistol-whip them both for "resisting arrest." But when he opened
the door into the darkened hallway, there stood Nora Honeycut
and Thomas Whitney.

For a moment he was stunned. He couldn't believe that these
two had returned. And not just to town, but to the house. He
had warned them and threatened them and knocked them
around. Hadn't he made himself clear? What the hell did he
have to *do?*

Rage bubbled inside him like lava.

"Put your hands up." His voice echoed in the hallway.

"We know what's going on," Thomas said.

"Get them *up!*" Fellows's finger tightened on the trigger.

They raised their hands. Then Fellows saw the look on Nora's
face, and his anger was replaced by a cold, dead feeling inside.
He could see that she was terrified. And it wasn't from something
as mundane as his long-barreled revolver. She threw panicked
glances over her shoulder and down the shadowed hallway.

Fellows peered over her head into the darkness. The hall was

empty now, but obviously she had seen something that had horrified her. Willy. He wondered if that monster had come downstairs or if Nora had gone up. Not that it mattered. She had
seen him. Just like her sister before her. And damned if she
wasn't carrying a *camera*.

"You're both under arrest," he said, a sick feeling in his
stomach.

"You can't—"

"*Shut up!*" He cocked the gun and leveled it at Thomas's
chest. He nearly pulled the trigger. In a way, it would be self-
defense, since these two could put him in prison. If he let them
go, they'd sure as hell run to Parmeter and tell him about Willy.
And Parmeter would be back in town like a shot. He was a
meticulous, stubborn cop, Fellows knew, and this time he
wouldn't stop digging until he uncovered the whole truth. Finding Willy would be just the beginning. Karl was weak, and so
was Newby. McOllough, too. They'd crack under pressure and
talk. Or at least one of them would. That's all it would take. No,
there was no alternative—these two had to die. God *damn* them,
anyway. He hadn't wanted to kill them, hadn't wanted to kill
anybody. Things had gone so smoothly for so many years, he
had assumed it would keep on that way. He should have known
better. He should have gotten out before this, left Lewiston and
the hell with them all. But it was too late for that now. He had
to deal with this situation. He had to *think*.

He stepped back and held the door open with his free hand.
"Let's go." He motioned them through the kitchen doorway with
his gun.

Warily, they moved past him. He noticed that Nora kept glancing back, as if she expected Willy to come charging out of the
darkness. Fellows followed them through the kitchen and the
pantry and out the back door.

The snow was falling heavily now, obscuring the trees and the
hedge. Fellows marched them around the house, through the
thickening blanket of snow.

Thomas spoke over his shoulder. "We know about Miss

Owen's son. We know he's been hiding in the house for the past sixty years."

Fellows said nothing.

Nora glanced back. "I . . . I *saw* him."

Fellows could not help grinning. "Quite a looker, isn't he?"

"You're in serious trouble," Thomas said. "He killed Annie, and you've been covering it up—you and Karl and Doc Newby. Every one of you is an accessory to murder. The best thing for you to do is to turn yourself in to Sheriff Parmeter and—"

"Shut up," he said and pushed Thomas toward the gateway in the hedge. They passed through, and Fellows gave Thomas a shove toward the police vehicle. When they reached it, he said, "Step aside." He kept the gun leveled at Thomas, while he pulled open the rear door. "Get in."

"Where are you taking us?"

"To jail. Where else?"

Nora hesitated, then climbed in the rear seat. Thomas stood by the open door. "We're not going anywhere," he said. "Not until you radio Sheriff Parmeter and have him meet—"

Fellows hit him in the face with the gun, opening a bloody gash across his forehead. Nora screamed. Thomas staggered forward, reaching out drunkenly. Fellows hit him again, this time in the side of the head, getting his weight into it. Thomas dropped to his knees, and Fellows hit him once more on the back of the head. Thomas slumped face down in the snow.

Nora started to come out of the car, her face pale, eyes wide, whether to fight or flee, Fellows wasn't certain. He pointed the gun at her.

"Get back, bitch, or I'll blow your fucking head off."

Her eyes flicked from Fellows to the still form of Thomas sprawled in the snow. Slowly she backed into the car.

"All the way," he said. "Get up against the other door."

She obeyed. Fellows holstered his gun, dragged Thomas to the car, and hefted him head-first into the backseat. He started to shut the door, but one of Thomas's feet blocked it. He kicked it in and slammed the door.

He leaned for a moment against the car to catch his breath. His head was pounding.

Now what?

Obviously, he couldn't take them to jail, not even temporarily. Griff would be there, and once he saw them, they couldn't simply disappear. No, he'd have to deal with them right now, before anyone knew he had them in custody.

Take them somewhere and bury the bodies.

After that he could have Karl help him move their car. They could leave it on some back road, make it look like the two of them went hiking and got lost. They were tourists, city people. It happened all the time. Eventually, of course, their remains would probably be found, and Parmeter would investigate. By then, though, he would be far away.

He walked around the vehicle, brushing snow from the side mirrors and the rear window. He climbed in and looked back through the heavy mesh screen.

Nora cradled Thomas's bloody head and murmured, "Oh my God."

Fellows started the car, then switched on the wipers to clear the windshield.

It seemed to be snowing even harder now.

58

Thomas's head felt heavy on Nora's legs. His hair was wet with snow, sticky with blood. His eyes were closed, and his breathing was rapid and shallow. She shook him gently and whispered his name, but she could not rouse him.

Please, Thomas, please be all right.

She was trembling uncontrollably—not just because of Fellows's violent attack, but because of what she had seen in the house. Miss Owen's son. She had glimpsed him for only a second, crouching at the top of the stairs. But his image was burned into her mind. Enormous. Pale and misshapen. Nearly inhuman. There was no question that he had killed Annie.

But her concern now was for Thomas. She touched his face and spoke his name, but he did not respond. His head was still bleeding. Obviously he needed immediate medical attention.

"You've hurt him badly," she said, not trying to mask her anger. She glared through the mesh screen at the back of Fellows's head—or rather, his hat. "You can't take us to jail now. Thomas needs a hospital."

Fellows said nothing.

"I mean it, damn you, he may be in a coma."

Fellows eased into first gear and started forward.

"Are you listening to me?" Nora said, a shrill note in her voice. "His head is *bleeding.*"

"All right, all right." Fellows sounded exasperated. "There's a blanket under the seat back there. Put it around him. Under his head, too. I don't want blood all over the seat."

Nora leaned forward carefully, cradling Thomas's head, then reached under the seat for the blanket. She unfolded it and spread it over him. He moaned. His eyelids fluttered briefly, then closed.

Fellows made a tight U-turn and drove to the end of the street. He turned left, away from town. He shifted into second gear and began climbing the snowy mountain road that twisted up behind the Owen house. Nora peered through the rear window and watched the town, nearly obscured by falling snow, slowly fall away from them. She turned toward Fellows.

"Where are you taking us?"

Fellows steered with both hands on the wheel, following the road as it snaked up the white face of the mountain.

Nora felt a stab of panic. "Answer me. Where are we going?"

"You'll see," Fellows said.

His tone chilled her. She peered ahead through the wire screen and the windshield. The headlight beams illuminated the falling snow and the white surface of the road, unblemished by tire tracks. She had driven this way a few days ago to visit Betty Connor, and she recalled what lay along the road—occasional driveways leading to isolated houses. And miles and miles of mountainous forest.

"Stop this car and turn around." She tried to make it a command, fighting her rising panic. "Take us back to town."

Fellows glanced at her in the rearview mirror. "Why don't you just sit back and enjoy the ride."

Nora stared at his reflection. He had a cold, flat look in his eyes, impersonal, without emotion. Nothing there but deadly determination. He was taking her and Thomas away from town, away from civilization, driving them deeper into the woods along a seldom-used road.

She felt rigid with fear, nauseated, her chest so constricted she could hardly breath.

He's going to murder us.

"No," she said, as if Fellows could read her mind. "You can't do this. Please."

Fellows glanced at her in the mirror, then returned his attention to the snowy road. It rose steadily, twisting through ghostly black pines, layered in white.

"You can't!" Nora shouted. She grabbed for the handle, prepared to throw open the door and jump from the moving vehicle, dragging Thomas with her. But there was no handle. And no window crank. She was in a cage on wheels, traveling toward her death.

Please, God, this can't be happening.

"If—" She cleared her throat, and tried to speak calmly, willing her voice not to tremble. "If you let us go, if you drive us back to town now and let me take Thomas to the hospital, I swear I won't talk. My sister is dead, and nothing I do will bring her back." She choked down her rising gorge. "It doesn't matter whether she was killed in an accident or . . . murdered by Miss Owen's son. You can all be safe with your secret. And that monster can stay hidden in the house forever."

"Who, Willy?" Fellows grinned at her in the mirror. His face looked ghastly, lit from beneath by the dashboard lights. "Old Willy wouldn't hurt a fly."

"Miss Owen's son?"

"That's right."

"But I *saw* him. He's . . ."

"Oh, he's nasty to look at, all right." Fellows's voice was jovial, as if he were glad to relieve his tension with conversation. "And he's definitely screwed up in the head. Hey, who wouldn't be after spending a lifetime locked away. But he's no killer. Under that ugly exterior is just a scared old man."

"But he killed Annie."

"No."

"He was *there*, in the photograph. He was in the yard when Annie was climbing the trellis."

Fellows gave her a knowing look. The brim of his cowboy hat rimmed his face like an obscene halo.

And suddenly Nora understood. The figure in the blurry photo looked short and squat because of the camera angle. And he didn't have a grossly oversize head—he had been wearing a hat.

"You," she said, barely a whisper. "It was you in Annie's photograph."

Fellows glanced at her, but said nothing.

"*You* killed her."

Fellows drove on in silence.

Until that moment Nora had been terrified of him. Now, though, she felt only an icy hatred. Willy was not the monster. Fellows was.

And then a strange calmness began to settle over her, almost a feeling of peace. She could see the inevitability of the situation, the cold logic of what had happened and what must come. Fellows would kill them. He *must* kill them to save himself. And there was nothing she could do to stop him. Nothing to do but accept it.

"Why did you do it?" Her voice sounded odd, even to her, void of emotion.

Fellows looked at her in the mirror, apparently surprised by her sudden change in attitude. He held her eyes for a moment, then returned his gaze to the road. He shrugged his heavy shoulders and said, "Because she saw Willy."

Anger stirred within Nora, prodding her awake. She wanted to shout at him, to curse him for taking her sister's life . . . for something so *trivial*. But her words came out small and cold, like bits of frost.

"Tell me what happened."

"I told—" Fellows stopped talking to negotiate a snow-slick, hairpin curve. When they were safely around it he said, "I told her to stay away. I *warned* her." He shook his head and snorted in disgust. "But she came back anyway. And it was only by luck that I caught her, only because I'd had trouble sleeping that night."

Fellows explained how he had tossed and turned for hours

before finally getting out of bed at one in the morning. Rather than sit around the house and watch television, he decided to do something useful, so he put on his uniform and walked down Main Street, checking doors. When he was a block from Alpine Street, he saw Annie hurrying across the intersection and up the hill toward the Owen house.

He went after her, madder than hell. She had been warned away twice, and here she was back again.

By the time he reached the house, Annie was not in sight. He searched the grounds, finally spotting her near the top of the trellis. He couldn't believe it. She was hanging up there like a goddamn monkey, trying to peek into one of Willy's windows.

And then she must have seen Willy, because she let out a scream. She jerked backward and fell, grabbing wildly at the vines on the way down, hitting the ground with a solid thump. She lay still. For a moment he thought she had killed herself. But then she moved, staggering to her feet. She turned and saw him. Her face was ghost-white in the moonlight, filled with terror. He knew before she spoke that she had seen too much. "I . . . saw it," she said, trembling, gasping for breath. "Monstrous . . . we must . . . get away . . . tell people."

"So there it was," Fellows said. "She gave me no choice. She was going to *tell* people."

He told her she was under arrest for trespassing. She didn't argue, so desperate was she to get away from the house. He ordered her to turn around so that he could handcuff her hands behind her back. She obeyed, casting about wild glances, as if she expected Willy to come leaping out of the shadows at any moment. He stepped up behind her, and then quickly and efficiently, a man of experience, he put his right hand on her chin, his left hand on the back of her head, and gave a violent twist, snapping her neck. She slumped to the ground, dead.

"I went home and drank myself to sleep," Fellows said sadly. "Karl phoned me at daybreak, and I returned to the house. He was in a panic. He was sure that Willy had killed her. And in the light of day I could see that the position of the body was all wrong. I told Karl I would cover for Willy, and I sent him inside to call the sheriff. Then I rearranged your sister's body to make it look like she had died from the fall."

Nora's fists were clenched so tightly that her nails dug into her palms. She wished she had a weapon—a gun, a knife, anything. She'd kill Fellows right now if she could.

"I know you won't believe this," Fellows said quietly, "but I'm really sorry it happened."

"You *fucker!*" Nora screamed and clawed at the screen, jamming her fingers through, trying to gouge him.

He leaned forward, away from her, and suddenly he was fighting the wheel, trying to steer around a tight, slippery curve. The rear wheels slid in the snow, coming dangerously close to the edge.

Nora prayed that the vehicle would go off the road and plunge down the sheer face of the mountain, if it meant that Fellows would die.

But he regained control of the vehicle. He came to a complete stop, shifted into four-wheel drive, then started forward again. He steered cautiously now, hunched forward, away from the mesh screen.

The road climbed steadily up and around the mountain.

59

Cole Newby had driven halfway to Denver before his anger subsided.

When Chief Fellows had thrown him down on the porch of the Owen house, he'd been ready to kill that fat son of a bitch. He might have, too, if Fellows hadn't been armed. Instead, he had taken off in his car, roared out of town, and vented his rage on the highway, pushing the old junker to its limits, veering in and out of traffic, shouting back at the blaring horns.

Eventually, his rage spent, he had turned around and headed back toward Lewiston, into what had become a driving snowstorm. It didn't slow him down, though, because he was intent on finishing what he had set out to do—get money from Miss Owen. A lot of money. And this time nobody would stop him.

Now he steered down the slippery freeway ramp and drove through the quiet, snowy town. When he turned in front of the Owen house he was surprised to see two vehicles there—and one of them was his father's van.

He swore under his breath. The last thing he wanted were witnesses, especially his father.

He climbed out and stood in the gateway, hands jammed in

his jeans pockets, heavy snow falling around him. The house appeared to be deserted—dark and silent and clothed in white.

He kicked through the ankle-deep snow and mounted the front porch, leaving a white track across the dark wooden boards. He rang the bell, then tried to peek through the curtains. No light shone from inside, and no one answered the door. He tried the knob. Locked.

Shivering in his lightweight jacket, he held the collar closed with one hand and trudged around the house through the deepening snow, as snowflakes gathered on his head and shoulders. He could see faint footprints, but they were almost completely covered, and he couldn't tell whether they were coming or going. He climbed the back steps, prepared to gouge open the lock with his knife. To his surprise, the lock was already broken.

Cautiously he pushed open the door. Warm, dark air oozed out, like blood from a fresh wound. He hesitated for a moment, then stepped into the darkened pantry.

He crept through the kitchen and into the hallway, listening for the slightest sound. But except for the whisper of his shallow breathing and the squeak of the linoleum floor, the house was silent. He decided that they had all taken Miss Owen to the hospital, his father and Karl and Fellows, and that no one was home.

Except for Willy. Cole's hand moved to the knife hilt at his side.

Not a problem, he thought. *One old man, more or less. And since Miss Owen isn't here to give me what I want, I'll just take what I find.*

The only trouble was this was an enormous house with hundreds of places to hide cash and jewels. It could take him days to thoroughly search it. He stood in the darkened hallway and let his eyes move from door to door. Where to begin? Where do most people keep their valuables?

Upstairs in the bedroom, of course.

Cole walked quietly down the shadowy hall. His hand fumbled along the wall, searching in vain for a light switch. He passed by the staircase, then stood at the foot of the stairs and stared up at the darkness above. His mouth had gone dry. And he realized, shamefully, that he was afraid.

He's just an old man, he chided himself.

He rested his hand on the handle of the knife.

When he sees this, he'll know I mean business. He'll stay the hell out of my way.

Still, Cole felt afraid, enough so that he considered leaving the house. And what would be wrong with that? Maybe Fellows was right about Miss Owen not having money in the house. Why not just pack up now and drive to California, as he had originally intended? Fellows would send him money every few months and—

The hell with that.

Slowly, he started up the stairs, licking parched lips, one hand firmly on the knife's hilt.

For the past hour Willy had been moaning and shuffling about and beating at himself with his fist.

He had hurt Miss Owen, and he wished he were dead. He had hurt her so badly that Karl and others had taken her away, and he had felt as if his heart were being ripped from his body. He loved her more than his own life. She had cared for him always. She had fed him, loved him. She had even read to him from her books, wonderful stories about the world outside, a place he could never go. Sometimes she sang to him, the sound so beautiful it made him weep. And now he had hurt her. Broken her bones. If he could somehow sacrifice himself to make her well, he would. He'd even throw himself from the roof of the cupola if it would change things.

Of course, he hadn't meant to harm her. He had wanted to confront the hated One, and his rage had blinded him.

Afterward, he had gone from room to room, wailing, trying to escape his own anguish. Finally he climbed the stairs into the cupola, curled up naked on the cold, wooden floor, and sobbed himself to sleep.

Later, he had awakened to the sound of someone creeping up the lower staircase. Had Karl returned with Miss Owen? So concerned was he about her welfare that he didn't stop to listen or to *feel* who might be coming. Instead he clambered down the stairs from the cupola and shuffled to the head of the staircase.

His great eye pierced the gloom, and he saw a woman on the stairs. Before he could react, he was blinded by a flash of white light so brilliant that it caused him to roar out in pain.

He had staggered backward, purple splotches swimming before his eye. He heard the woman run down the stairs and along the hallway toward the kitchen. There were voices—others had joined her. He felt afraid. But then they left the house. He had climbed back up inside the cupola, wishing that Karl and Miss Owen would return.

And now he heard someone else enter the house.

Willy held his breath and listened as the intruder crept along the hall of the main floor and then slowly climbed the staircase.

Willy pushed himself erect, like a huge, pale sea-creature, roused from slumber by the presence of an enemy. He could sense evil in the house. He shuffled to the head of the stairs that descended from the cupola, pulling himself along with his enormous right arm. The person in the house was not Karl or Miss Owen or the intruder who had come earlier. This was someone else. He could sense who it was. And then he *knew* who it was, knew with every cell in his body. He was so overcome by rage and loathing that he staggered and nearly fell.

He descended the stairs from the cupola, his heart pounding madly in his chest, blood roaring in his ears.

When he reached the bottom of the stairway, he stopped. The upstairs hallway was dimly lit, but his great eye could discern every detail—the faded designs in the wallpaper, the grain in the wood floor. He shivered. Not from the cold, but from excitement. His long wait was about to end.

The hated One emerged from a doorway. He turned and saw Willy.

"*Jesus.*"

The One stared wide-eyed, as if he had come face to face with a mythical beast, something glimpsed long before, perhaps in a nightmare, but not believed, a thing more huge and real than he had ever imagined. He looked desperately about him, seeking escape. But there were only the stairs, and Willy blocked the way.

"All right, take it easy." The One held his arm straight out, palm forward. "I'm not going to hurt you. Just get out of my way and I'll leave."

Willy stood unmoving, sensing the One's fear, savoring it. He shuffled forward, the blood pumping thick and hot through his veins.

"Goddamn it, you stay away from me." The One withdrew a narrow-bladed knife from its sheath and took a step back.

Willy came forward slowly, as patient as a beast stalking weak prey.

"I *mean* it, goddamn it."

The One held the knife before him, as if it were a holy relic, a talisman to ward off evil. He walked backward and glanced nervously from side to side. The railing on his right marked the edge of the abyss. The doorways on his left opened into cave-black rooms. There was no escape. He backed all the way to the end of the hall, a look of panic on his face.

Slowly, though, he changed, like an animal trapped in a corner. He narrowed his eyes and clenched his teeth in a grimace. He crouched, arms low and held before him, the knife in his right hand. Its blade shone dully in the weak light.

"All right, you want it?" he croaked. "Come and get it. *Come on!*"

Willy charged, roaring like a bear, crashing his bulk into the One. The smaller man squirmed and kicked and slashed. Willy ignored the fire-hot steel blade that plunged into him again and again. He clutched the One in his heavy arm and squeezed him like a lover, like an enemy. The One's mouth gaped as the air was forced from his lungs. He kicked and stabbed desperately at Willy.

Suddenly, there was a loud crack, as if a tree branch had snapped under a heavy weight. The knife clattered to the floor. The one collapsed in Willy's grasp.

Willy stood for a few minutes, breathing heavily, his arm wrapped around the lifeless man, as if they were old friends.

Then he hoisted the body over his shoulder and carried it down the stairs. He walked unsteadily, as if he were trudging under a great weight, rather than merely carrying the corpse of a small man. Perhaps the fight had weakened him. He moved ponderously along the dark hallway, then through the kitchen and the pantry and out the back door.

The snow fell, thick and silent.

Willy had never been out in the snow before, and it felt colder than it looked. The flakes touched his naked body in a strange and sensuous way.

He shuffled around the side of the house, plowing through the soft, cold snow. The bushes were laden with it, rounded by it. And the towering pines were more white than green. Willy trudged on, ignoring the bitter chill that crept up his feet and legs. He carried his morbid burden to the front hedge.

He stopped at the gateway, the virtual edge of his world.

The snow settled about him. He stood for a moment, catching his breath, feeling the cold sneak into his bones. Then he summoned up his strength and heaved the One's body into the street. It landed with a muffled sound, an awkward twisting of limbs. Willy stared at it for a time, watching the snow erase its color.

Then he turned and made his way to the back door.

The cold was a painful presence now, not only in his feet and legs, but his shoulders and arms and back. And there was another pain, sharper and deeper, in his chest. He lumbered up the back porch steps. Before going in he paused and looked up at the delicate white flakes falling from the sky. They touched his face gently, like fingers.

He smiled crookedly and entered his house.

As he shuffled through the kitchen he noticed a trail of blood, black in the dim light. His blood. He hoped Miss Owen and Karl wouldn't be angry with him for soiling the floor. He moved, trembling now, down the hallway to the stairs. It was difficult to climb them. Where was his strength?

He collapsed into bed and dragged the sheet around him. He felt so cold, colder than he had ever been.

And tired, so very tired.

60

Nora peered out at the falling snow. The white-hot flash of anger she had felt a few minutes ago had burned itself out. Once again she was filled with a cold hatred of Fellows, for what he had done and for where he was taking her and Thomas. To their deaths.

The windows were beginning to fog, and Fellows switched on the defroster. Nora could see that they had topped the first rise in the mountain. The curves in the road became more gentle, the upward angle more subtle. She saw a mailbox pass by wearing a cap of snow. Beside it a white-shrouded driveway pointed into the darkness between the trees. She tried to remember how far along this road she had driven before reaching Betty Connor's driveway. If she could somehow get away from Fellows and run to the house . . . Betty had a rifle. And a telephone. They could hold Fellows at bay, call the sheriff, and . . .

Nora squeezed her eyes closed and forced back a cry of anguish. She was deluding herself. There was no escape, no way out of this car. Not until Fellows let her out at the point of a gun. She watched him closely. His complete attention was on the road, illuminated by headlight beams that were thick with swirling flakes of snow. The edges of the roadway were indistinct, and beyond them marched a solemn procession of pines, shrouded in white.

271

"You'll never get away with killing us," Nora said.

Fellows said nothing. He seemed to be studying the occasional mailboxes that passed slowly by, counting them.

"Someone will come looking for us," Nora said. "And when they find ... our bodies, they'll know it was you who murdered us."

Fellows glanced at her in the mirror. "Maybe they'll find you, and maybe they won't."

They drove on in silence, as mile after mile of snow-covered landscape passed by.

Finally, Fellows slowed the vehicle to nearly a halt and shifted into first gear. He cranked the wheel and drove off the road, bumping across a shallow, slippery ditch. He steered through a narrow opening in the trees. The headlights briefly illuminated a dead pine tree, killed long ago by a lightening bolt, its trunk split, half of it angling downward like a giant finger, pointing the way.

Fellows drove slowly. Even so, the vehicle was jarred from side to side by deep ruts and large rocks. Nora noticed that Fellows crowded the left side of the trail. To the right, the ground dropped steeply away.

Thomas moaned.

Nora looked down, and she was startled to see him staring back.

"Is he awake?" Fellows asked, taking a quick glance behind him.

Thomas closed his eyes.

"N-no," Nora said. "You've hurt him too badly."

Fellows nodded, fists on the steering wheel, fighting the crude trail. "Just as well," he said quietly.

Thomas looked up at Nora again and held her gaze for a moment. Then he shut his eyes.

Nora sat rigidly, afraid to say a word or even move. Obviously Thomas wanted Fellows to think he was unconscious, probably to surprise him at the right time. But when? And what was she supposed to do?

She fought to clear her mind, to *focus*, now that there was hope, a chance that they could get out of this, that they could live. Together they might surprise Fellows, overpower him. Of course, he still had the gun. They'd have to do it at just the right moment. But *when?* She would just have to stay alert and be ready for whatever happened.

She glanced down at Thomas. His eyes remained closed. Had he lapsed back into unconsciousness?

No. She refused to believe that. He was with her.

And he must know that Fellows wasn't taking them to jail. She wondered if he had heard Fellows confess to Annie's murder. She hoped so. She wanted him to understand exactly who they were dealing with—a murderous psychopath.

Suddenly the vehicle jounced to a stop.

Fellows shut off the engine. A massive silence enveloped them. When he killed the headlights, Nora was surprised that they weren't wrapped in darkness. Instead, she could see for dozens of yards, as if the snowy woods were glowing with an unnatural light.

"End of the line," Fellows said. He climbed out and slammed the door.

Nora noticed that he had left the keys dangling in the ignition, as if he planned not to be away from the vehicle for long. She watched him walk around to the passenger side and open the rear door.

Fellows drew his gun and kicked Thomas in the leg. "Come on, wake up, let's go."

Thomas moaned softly.

"Come *on,*" Fellows said, and he kicked him again.

Thomas moaned, but did not move.

Fellows muttered, "Son of a bitch." He reholstered his revolver, as snow settled on his hat and shoulders. He jerked the blanket from Thomas and tossed it aside. Then he leaned in and grabbed Thomas by the belt and pulled, grunting with the effort. Thomas slid heavily across the seat, his body a dead weight. Fellows looked at Nora. "Lift up his shoulders and push. Let's get this over with."

Nora hesitated. She wanted to shout at Thomas, *Now! While*

he's not holding his gun! Do it now! She glanced down at his face. His eyes were closed, his forehead was caked with blood, and drool lay at the corner of his mouth. Her anxiety turned to dread. Was he really unconscious?

No, I won't let this happen! I won't let myself die!

She put her hands under Thomas's shoulders and pushed. His head lolled to one side. Fellows pulled on Thomas's belt, dragging him toward the door.

Nora focused her mind on one last chance—the moment Thomas fell out of the car, she would scrambled over him and throw herself at Fellows, go for his eyes with her nails, blind him, then run for her life.

But what about Thomas? She couldn't just leave him at Fellows's mercy. Perhaps she should try for Fellow's gun and—

Thomas came alive.

One moment Nora felt his slack shoulder muscles grow tense, and the next moment she felt nothing at all because he had launched himself out of the car at Fellows.

She watched a slow-motion film of the two men staggering away from her. Thomas's head was pressed into Fellows's chest and his arms were wrapped around his waist. Fellows was waving wildly, trying to maintain his balance, his mouth open in an expression of surprise that was almost comical. Then they stumbled and fell and rolled off the trail, hugging each other like two boys playing in the snow.

Nora clambered out of the car. Falling snow swirled about her as she hurried to the edge of the trail where the two men had fallen. The ground sloped steeply down for twenty feet, then rose upward into the trees. The men were at the bottom of the slope, struggling desperately on the snowy ground, locked in a deadly embrace. All around them the white-cloaked trees seemed to glow, illuminating the death-dance with a ghostly light.

Part of Nora's mind screamed, *Run away! Save yourself!*

But she had already started down the slope.

She saw Fellows push himself out of Thomas's grasp, rise to his knees, and draw his gun. Thomas was on him in a moment.

The two men fought for the revolver, four hands wrapped around it. They swung the shiny weapon from side to side, then held it high over their heads, as if they were performing an arcane ritual, making an offering of death to some dreaded god.

The gun fired, flicking out a short, bright, blue-orange tongue of flame.

Nora stopped halfway down the slope, as the gun swung toward her, then toward the ground, four rigid arms pointing it. The gun went off again. Its hard, flat report was immediately followed by a high-pitched whine, as the slug ricocheted into the trees. Another gunshot, this one fired wildly in the air.

Then the weapon was out of sight, hidden somewhere between the two men. Nora clambered down the slope and threw herself onto Fellows's back. She reached around him and clawed at his face, his eyes. The men spun and stumbled, tossing her off. Slamming her to the ground. The gun was still pressed between the two men. As Nora scrambled to her feet, the gun fired again, the sound muffled. And again. Suddenly Fellows broke free, shoving Thomas away from him. He leveled the gun at Thomas's chest and fired as Nora screamed, "NO!"

Thomas clutched his chest and staggered drunkenly to one side. Then he dropped to his knees and fell face-down in the snow. He twitched once, then lay still.

Nora stared in horror, first at Thomas, then at Fellows.

The big man was breathing heavily, his chest heaving under his jacket. His hat lay on the ground beside him, where it had been knocked off during the fight. Nora saw that he was nearly bald. There were parallel gashes that began near the top of his ear and plowed down through his cheek where she had gouged him. His left pants leg was soaked with blood from the thigh to the knee. Nora guessed that one of the wild shots had buried itself in his leg.

Fellows stared at her, his mouth twisted. He raised the gun and pointed it at her.

"So long, bitch," he said and squeezed the trigger.

The gun clicked, empty. Fellows swore. He lunged toward her, then stumbled and cried out, holding his wounded leg.

Nora turned and scrambled up the slope on all fours, her coat flapping about her, the flat soles of her shoes slipping on the snowy ground. Her hands clawed madly at the rocks. One of her fingernails tore, and a flame of pain went up her arm.

She was desperate to reach the trail . . . and the vehicle. Fellows had left the keys in the ignition. If she could get there before he caught her, she'd be free. She could lock the doors from the inside and drive away from there, back up all the way to the road, then head down the mountain and through Lewiston. She wouldn't stop until she reached the sheriff's office in Idaho Springs.

She climbed upward, expecting at any moment that Fellows would grab her by the ankles and drag her down the slope. That thought made her climb all the harder. And still, she hadn't reached the top. Something was wrong.

She risked a glance over her shoulder.

Thirty feet below her she saw Fellows standing near Thomas's body, reloading his revolver. And directly across the gorge, slightly below her and a good twenty feet above Fellows, she saw the police vehicle resting in the snow.

Her heart nearly stopped when she realized what she had done. In her panic, she had gone up the wrong slope.

Now she saw Fellows stoop and retrieve his hat from the ground and put it squarely on his head. He looked up at her. From her point of view he appeared foreshortened and squat— just as he had in Annie's last photograph. Just before he had murdered her. He raised his revolver with both hands. His arms formed a V, pointing directly at her.

She turned and scrabbled up the slope, slipping on the wet ground, losing a shoe, banging her knee painfully on a rock. Then she heard a gunshot, flat and explicit. A chunk of bark exploded from a pine tree just ahead of her. She scrambled to her feet and started to run, slipping again. She threw out a hand to break her fall, landing heavily, wrenching her wrist. She got her feet under her and scuttled up the slope through the silent trees.

She cast one quick look back.

Fellows was climbing after her.

61

Snow sifted down about Nora as she climbed desperately up the slope. She leaned forward, grabbing at tree trunks to pull herself along. The rough bark tore at her hands, and soon they were raw and slick with blood. Her feet were wet and cold from the snow—her right foot, especially. She had lost a shoe, and with each step pine needles and twigs poked painfully through the sole of her pantyhose.

She could hear nothing but her own labored breathing and the muted crunch of dead needles as she slipped and staggered upward. It sounded as if Fellows were crashing through the trees right behind her, but she didn't know if that were real or only her imagination. She was afraid to turn around, afraid she'd see him a few feet away, pointing the gun at her, squeezing the trigger.

How would it feel to be shot? she wondered.

She had watched Thomas stagger and die. It had been over so quickly. Had there been much pain? And what had he felt at the exact moment of death? She had always imagined death to be like falling asleep, quietly drifting away. But perhaps that moment was excruciating, the ultimate agony, as life was ripped from the body.

Stop it!

She forced herself to concentrate on the ground, the trees, and the falling snow. She climbed onward, slipping more often now. Her feet were numb with cold. They would come awake, though, suddenly and briefly, whenever she stubbed her toes on half-buried rocks—the quick, fiery pain almost welcome.

Her legs grew weary from the climb. Her coat tails kept snagging tee limbs holding her back. She felt as if she were in a dream, trying to run hip-deep through ice water. And there was a pain in her side. It had started as a dull ache, but it had grown steadily sharper, an icepick stuck between her ribs.

She struggled on until she could go no farther.

Everything seemed to give out at once—her legs, her arms, her wind. She collapsed on her hands and knees and managed to crawl beneath the high, sheltering branches of a pine tree. She stayed on all fours, her head hanging, her chest and shoulders heaving, gasping for air, not enough air. The blood was pounding at her temples, and she felt as if her head would explode from the pressure. She turned with effort and sat facing downhill, her aching hands and feet flat on the ground, her knees pulled up. She drew in ragged gulps of air, searing her throat and lungs.

At first she could hear nothing but her pounding heart and wheezing breath. But after a few minutes she became aware of sounds around her—the quiet rustle of wet snow falling in the trees and the occasional moan of pine branches shifting under their load.

Nora strained to hear Fellows clambering up the mountain. But there were only the subtle sounds of the woods. She stared downhill, trying to pierce the darkness between the trees. The landscape seemed to glow with its own dull, unearthly light, enabling her to see for fifty or sixty feet. Beyond that the trees and the night converged into deep blackness.

She began to wonder if Fellows had given up the chase.

Perhaps he had been wounded too badly to continue. She recalled the muffled gunshots when he and Thomas had struggled with the gun pressed between them, and she had seen his trouser leg soaked with blood. There was no doubt that he had been struck by a bullet. The question was how badly was he wounded? Was it merely a flesh wound? If it was more serious, if an artery had been severed, then he might bleed to death. She prayed for it.

She held her breath and listened. No sounds but the scarce ticking of tiny, frozen bits of snow.

Perhaps Fellows had given up the chase after all. His wound was serious, and he knew that unless he got to a doctor he would die. Yes. He must have returned to his vehicle and was now driving back to Lewistown, or more likely, to the hospital in Idaho Springs. He had no choice—he had to save himself. He was probably miles from here by now. He certainly wasn't still following her or she would have heard him. It would be impossible to climb this slope and not make a sound. She was *certain*.

She shivered and hugged herself.

She wondered, though, how long she should wait here. If Fellows hadn't yet reached his vehicle and she started down now, she might overtake him. Or perhaps he had been too weak to make it to the car and he was lying somewhere, waiting in ambush. If so, she'd have to outwait him, just stay right here until she could safely assume that he had lost consciousness from his wound. Of course, if she waited too long, the cold would overtake her. Hypothermia. She would die here.

She'd wait a little longer, she decided, and then go down.

She shivered again and squeezed her fists closed, feeling tiny stabs of pain. She opened her hands and saw that her palms were sticky with blood and cross-hatched with pine needles. She began to clumsily pick them off, her fingers numb and stiff from the cold.

Suddenly, she stopped, struck by a new fear—what if she couldn't find her way back down?

Ridiculous. She had come straight up (hadn't she?)—she would go straight down, directly into the ravine where Thomas's body lay. Then she'd climb up to the trail where the vehicle had been and follow it out of the woods to the road. Once on the road, though, she wouldn't try to walk all the way back to Lewiston—it was at least ten miles and she'd never make it in her present condition, cold and exhausted. Besides, Fellows might have alerted Karl or Griff, and they could be waiting for her. No, she'd walk up the first driveway she came to and pound on the house's front door until someone answered. She'd phone the sheriff and—

She heard a noise.

It was faint, but distinct, something more than dripping snow. There it was again. Her heart turned to ice. Someone was struggling up the slope.

She shivered uncontrollably now and stared into the darkness below her. At the limit of her vision she glimpsed a faint, pale form that shifted in and out of sight like a ghost.

The shape took substance.

It was Fellows, of course, lurching up the hillside, head down, breathing noisily. He leaned heavily on his right leg, nearly dragging his left foot behind him. Even from this distance Nora could see that his pants leg was thoroughly soaked with blood.

She was certain he hadn't seen her, because his head was lowered and the brim of his hat covered his face. He trudged toward her. Perhaps if she held perfectly still and made no sound, he would pass by, far to her right or left.

But no, he continued on, one slow step at a time, dead on line with her, watching the ground.

Then she realized that he was tracking her, following her obvious trail through the snow and pine needles. She moved from under the branches and stood, summoning her last bit of strength, ready to run.

Fellows must have heard her movement, because he stopped and looked up. He was a scant thirty feet from her, and there were few trees between them. Their eyes met. He smiled. She expected him to speak, to curse her or command her to surrender. But he said nothing, merely watched her, smiling. His silence made him seem more deadly, less human.

He drew his gun.

Nora turned and ran.

The gun cracked behind her, and she heard (or perhaps imagined) the bullet zipping past her ear and plowing into the trees ahead. She ran, stumbling, her legs leaden, her body quivering and weak with fatigue. Another gunshot. The slug thunked into a tree at her side.

She scuttled up the slope through the snow-laden trees, wondering if they would be the last things she ever saw.

Then she heard Fellows cry out. A moment later there was a muffled crash, as if a tree had been felled. Or a man.

She scrambled on for a few more steps, then fatigue overtook her. She dragged herself up to the next large tree and crouched behind it.

There were no more gunshots and no sounds of Fellows lumbering up the mountain. She peered downslope through the trees. At the edge of darkness she could just make out Fellows's form. He was sitting with his back to her, bent over and holding his leg.

She watched him in silence. He raised his head, as if he were listening for her. She held her breath.

Suddenly he shouted, startling her. *"We're both going to die up here!"* He grunted with pain, then swore, his voice clear and plain in the snowy night air. He raised his head again and shouted, though not so loud this time, "I'm hurt bad! I can't make it to the car! But neither can you! You can't find it without me!"

"I'll find it," Nora said under her breath.

Her must have heard her, because he turned, prone now on the ground, looking up the slope, trying to spot her in the trees. He spoke in a normal tone of voice, knowing she was near. "No you won't. You're lost up here, But together we . . . ahh." He groaned and clutched at his wounded leg. "Listen to me," he said, his voice now gentle and sincere. "We'll both die up here, unless we work together. You can help me walk, and I'll show you the way. I promise I . . . ahh." He groaned again, and when he spoke, there was desperation in his voice. "I promise I won't hurt you. You can have the gun. Look. Here it is."

He threw it toward her, a silver arc in the night air. It thumped to the ground, disappearing in the snow a dozen feet up the slope from him.

"Go ahead, pick it up. It's your insurance. Just help me down to the car. We'll go back to town and I'll turn myself in, anything you want, just don't . . . ahh, God, ahh . . ." He rolled on his side and gripped his leg with both hands. It was a moment before he spoke, his voice ragged with pain. ". . . Just don't leave me here."

Nora stood, pulling herself erect beside an aspen tree. She looked down on Fellows. There was a pleading expression on his face, and he reached out his hand toward her.

"You don't deserve to live," she said quietly. She began walking along the side of the slope, away from him.

"No, *wait.*"

She moved in a wide half-circle, maintaining her distance from Fellows, making her way around him.

"You can't leave me here!" he shouted. "You'll get lost without me!"

She continued on, keeping him to her left, just out of sight. And when she felt she was clear of him, she started down the slope.

"*Wait, goddamn you! You're going the wrong way!*"

And now she hurried down the mountainside, stumbling along as fast as she could, trying not to fall. She heard him cry out once more.

Don't leave me!"

She ignored the plea, feeling neither guilty nor vengeful, thinking now only of saving herself.

She descended through the trees, shivering uncontrollably. Her feet were so numb she could barely feel them beneath her. She angled to her left, head down, squinting through the falling snow, searching for the tracks she and Fellows had left. But except for dark circles of needles and pinecones beneath the evergreens, the ground was uniformly white. She continued down the mountain side, bearing to her left, desperate now to find their tracks, to know she was headed in the right direction.

But after awhile she thought, *I must have missed them. They've been covered by the snow and I walked right over them.*

Now she headed directly downslope, hoping that she hadn't

gone too far off course. Or perhaps she hadn't gone far enough. There was no way to tell. The trees and the ground looked the same no matter which way she turned.

The slope went down and down, seemingly without end. Had she climbed that far?

Maybe Fellows hadn't been lying. Maybe she was going the wrong way. If so, then she would surely die. She could wander for miles, even walk in circles without realizing it, never finding her way out of the woods. And no one would come to her rescue, because no one was looking for her. She'd freeze to death in the dark.

Although that wasn't such a terrible way to die. Hadn't she once heard that before you froze to death, you felt warm and comfortable and then drifted off to sleep? And she was so tired now, maybe the best thing to do was to sit down and rest. Why fight the pain? Just lie down beneath that tree and—

She squeezed her fists, digging her fingernails into her palms, feeling her mind come awake as dull stabs of pain surged up her wrists and arms.

She stumbled on, straight down the slope.

And at last she reached the bottom. She expected to see Thomas's body there, half covered with snow. But it was nowhere in sight. She walked first one way, then the other, looking for the corpse, *needing* it for a reference point. That morbid thought made her cry, and the tears seemed to freeze on her face.

Finally she stopped searching. The area was completely unfamiliar. She was lost. Fellows had been right—they were both going to die in the woods tonight.

But not yet. The opposing slope rose thirty feet above her, and she forced herself to climb it.

When she staggered to the top, she found herself on a faint, snow-covered trail that curved in either direction through the trees. For a moment she had a glimmer of hope that this was the trail Fellows had driven them in on. But his vehicle was not in sight. And there were no footprints or tire tracks.

Still, the trail was at least a chance. But which way should she go—right or left? Left seemed correct, but her sense of direction was confused, her mind so exhausted that she couldn't be certain. Maybe it didn't matter. For all she knew this trail would take her deeper into the woods no matter which direction she chose.

She turned left and started walking. There was nothing else to do. Press on until her strength was completely gone. She walked with short, shuffling steps, afraid to hurry lest she fall and not be able to get back up. Her coat was pulled tightly around her, her hands were jammed into her pockets, and her head was down. She concentrated on putting one foot in front of the other, keeping to the middle of the narrow trail as it wound through the trees.

She rounded a bend in the trail. Something made her look up. Fifty feet from her a large, white mass blocked the way. She stared at it for a full minute before she realized what it was.

Fellows's police vehicle, covered with snow.

She stumbled forward, hurrying now. And as she drew near, she noticed something lying in front of the vehicle—a low boulder or a dead tree. No doubt it was the reason why Fellows had chosen that spot to stop. But as she approached the object, her heart quickened. It wasn't a rock or a tree.

It was Thomas.

62

Nora rushed to Thomas and knelt beside him in the snow. He was curled up on his side, and there was a thin layer of white on his jacket and pants and in his hair. The front of his jacket was soaked with blood where Fellows had shot him. Nora guessed it had taken every bit of his strength to crawl up out of the ravine.

"Thomas," she said and shook him gently. "Please be alive."

She shook him again, but he didn't move. Then she touched his neck, searching for a pulse, but her fingers were too numb to feel. She leaned over and put her ear next to his nose and mouth. He was breathing. Barely.

Then his eyes fluttered open. He moved his mouth, but no words came.

"Hang on," she told him.

She stood on wobbly legs and pulled open the vehicle's rear door. Then she got her hands under Thomas's shoulders and dragged him toward it. For the first time that night she was thankful the ground was covered with snow. It lessened the friction. Otherwise she doubted she would have been able to drag Thomas to the side of the vehicle. She tried to lift him inside. But he was too heavy, too limp.

She shook him. "Come on, Thomas, wake up. You've got to help me. Come on!" She lightly slapped his face. *"Lets go!"*

Slowly, he responded. He worked his legs and helped her get him in a prone position on the rear seat.

Nora slammed the door, then hurried around the back of the vehicle, brushing snow from the rear window. She climbed in the driver's seat, started the engine with a roar, and switched on the lights. Blood was smeared on her coat. Thomas's blood. She ground the gears into reverse, and the vehicle lurched backward.

The trail was too narrow to turn around, so she drove with her body turned to the side, one arm on the seat-back, one hand on the wheel. Her palm was so numb and bloody that it was difficult to grip the wheel. Each time the vehicle dropped into a rut or struck a rock, the steering wheel would momentarily jerk free, and twice she nearly drove over the edge.

At last she reached the head of the trail. She bumped across the roadside ditch, shifted into low, and headed down the mountain. The road was deeply buried in snow, and even though the vehicle was in four-wheel drive, Nora felt it slide into the first curve. She pumped the brakes, got it straightened out, and continued on, crawling around the hairpin turns. She dared not go faster, though, for if she went over the edge, it would be the end of them both.

She wondered if Thomas would survive in any case. He must have lost a lot of blood. She glanced over the seat, saw him lying motionless—not even breathing, for all she knew—then returned her eyes to the white, winding road.

As she came around a tight, right-hand curve she got a glimpse of Lewiston, far below to her left, the streets and yards and rooftops coated with snow, as soft and perfect as whipped cream.

Each curve brought her nearer to the town—and the Owen mansion. It sat on its hilltop, as massive and white as a mausoleum. Except for the lights—tiny, pale, yellow window-squares of lamplight. And outside the house there were other lights, faint and colorful, moving.

At last, she rounded the final curve, shifted into second gear, and accelerated down the hill toward town. As she sped past

Silver Street she saw the source of the moving lights. Several police cars were parked before the towering, black hedge, their roof lights whirling. For a moment she considered stopping so the policemen could radio for an ambulance. But what if they were Fellows's cronies? How could she trust them? So she drove on, knowing she had to get Thomas to a hospital and that she could drive as fast as any ambulance.

She roared through town and sped up the ramp onto the interstate.

The highway had been plowed and sanded, and it was nearly free of snow. Nora swerved in and out of traffic, driving as fast as she could without sideswiping other cars. She didn't slow down until she reached the turnoff for Idaho Springs, then she sped through town and jerked to a halt at the hospital's emergency entrance. She jumped out and began shouting for help.

She stood aside while paramedics rushed Thomas into surgery. A nurse led her to the emergency room, where she was wrapped in warm blankets and her lacerated hands were tended to.

"What happened?" the nurse asked.

"Please," she said, "would you call the sheriff?"

Sheriff Parmeter listened to Nora's story on the drive to Lewiston. Following close behind them was a deputy sheriff's car and a rescue unit.

She had given him a shortened version at the hospital, and he had asked her to show him where to find Fellows. She wanted to stay until Thomas came out of surgery, but there was no telling when that would be. And so she had ridden with Parmeter, a heavy blanket wrapped around her and a container of hot broth held between her bandaged hands.

Parmeter listened in silence, nodding his head at times, as if she were confirming what he already knew. When she was finished, he told her what had happened at the Owen house.

Karl had returned home, found the dead bodies of Cole Newby and Willy Owen, and phoned first the chief of police and then the sheriff. When Parmeter arrived, Griff and Doc Newby were already there. Griff was as stunned as Parmeter, not only by the double killings, but also by the existence—and the sight of—Miss Owen's son.

Parmeter and Griff pressed Karl for details. He stammered, afraid, until Doc Newby stepped in and explained in detail the murders, the blackmail, and the cover-up. Newby seemed relieved to finally be able to tell the truth. And he had been mistaken on only one matter, which Nora cleared up now.

"Miss Owens son didn't kill my sister," she said. "Chief Fellows did."

Parmeter nodded, his mouth grim, as he steered around the hairpin curves that rose above Lewiston. When the road began to straighten out, Nora leaned forward, peering through the windshield. The snowfall seemed to be letting up. After several miles, she pointed.

"Through there."

Parmeter followed tire tracks that led off the snow-covered road and into the trees. He steered carefully along the trail. Nora grew tense, half expecting Fellows to leap into their headlight beams, gun drawn, ready to kill.

But the woods were silent and still.

Parmeter stopped where the tire tracks ended in the snow. Nora showed him the direction she and Fellows had taken, and she gave her best estimate of the distance they had traveled.

Parmeter got out of the car, spoke briefly to the other men, then rejoined Nora. She watched the small group, clad in parkas and boots, head off into the woods. Bright circles of light danced before them like wood sprites. She was thankful that Parmeter kept the motor running and the heater turned on. She dozed, waking briefly when he gently pried the container from her hands.

She awoke again when Parmeter climbed out of the car. The men had returned, bearing a heavy stretcher.

She lowered the window and heard Parmeter say, "How is he?"

One of the men shook his head. "We're too late. It looks like he bled to death."

Somehow, Nora knew that was how they'd find him. But she

hadn't been certain how she would react—sorrow, relief, or righteous joy. To her surprise, she felt nothing at all. It was as if the men had found a pile of litter left behind by careless campers, and now they were hauling it out, leaving the woods feral and uncorrupted.

She pulled the blanket more tightly around her and drifted into a warm, dreamless sleep.

63

N ora spent the next few days in Idaho Springs—living in a motel, eating in cafés, checking on Thomas.

The bullet had pierced his lung and exited through his back. After surgery he was still in critical condition. The doctors weren't certain if he would survive.

Nora phoned her parents Sunday night, saying she would be in Colorado for at least a few more days. "There have been complications," she said. But she could not bring herself to tell them how Annie had died, that their sweet daughter had been murdered simply to preserve a blackmail scheme. She'd have to tell them face-to-face.

On Monday morning she had a long phone conversation with Hattie. The orders were starting to pile up. She helped her organize the workload as best she could, but obviously Hattie needed her there. Or, at least, she needed *someone* there, someone to take charge.

At the hospital the doctor told her that Thomas's condition had improved, and that he was drifting in and out of consciousness. Around noon Thomas awakened briefly while Nora sat at his side. He looked at her. Recognition showed in his face before he closed his eyes.

Later that day Sheriff Parmeter visited the hospital—to check on Thomas's recovery, but also to speak with Nora. He told her that Cecil McOllough was being held in the county jail on charges of blackmail and accessory after-the-fact to the murder of Bonnie Connor. Doc Newby had been granted immunity as the state's witness, the loss of his son being considered punishment enough. And, of course, the official report would state that Chief Fellows had murdered Annie Honeycut.

Then he apologized for what Nora and Thomas had been through. "I feel responsible," he said.

"That's ridiculous."

"No, it's not. I should have dug a little harder after you showed me that photograph."

"That photo was nothing but a bunch of fuzzy blotches," Nora said. "I don't even know how *I* managed to see anything in there.'"

"Maybe because the photographer was your sister."

Nora smiled. "Maybe."

On Tuesday Nora drove to Lewiston to attend the funeral of Willy Owen. Nearly everyone in town was there, and the crowd filled the church. Miss Owen was still in the hospital with a broken hip, so Karl sat alone in the front pew. For the first time since Nora had met him he looked frail.

Willy was buried in the town cemetery beneath a monument of a winged cherub.

On Wednesday morning Nora sat beside Thomas's bed, reading the newspaper. She turned the page and heard him say in a weak voice, "Pass me the sports section."

She put down the paper and smiled at him. "You're awake."

"Sort of. How long have I been out?"

"Three days."

"What?"

"It's Wednesday."

"Jesus." He seemed to notice for the first time that oxygen tubes trailed from his nose, an IV was taped to his arm, and his chest was heavily bandaged. "I remember. Fellows shot me." He looked at her. "But how . . . how did we get away from him?"

"It's a long story. Maybe we should let them know you're awake."

"Okay, but . . ." He raised his hand and she held it. "I'm glad you're here."

"Me, too."

Nora summoned the nurse, who spoke briefly with Thomas, checked his monitors, then allowed him to elevate his bed. After she left, Thomas said, "Pour me some of that water, would you? And then tell me what happened."

Nora described in detail her flight from Fellows after he had shot Thomas and then attempted to shoot her. She explained how she had eventually made it back to the vehicle, helped Thomas inside, then driven like hell down the mountain.

He shook his head. "I don't remember any of that."

"You were out cold."

"This is a bit of an understatement . . . but thank you for saving my life."

She took his hand again. "We saved each other."

He smiled. "Maybe so."

"By the way, Sheriff Parmeter was here to see how you're doing. He feels responsible for what happened."

"He shouldn't. Not really."

"That's what I told him."

"What did he find out?"

"Everything. Doc Newby and Karl told him. Some of it we knew, or at least guessed."

She explained how for sixty years Chastity Owen had hidden

her son from the world—for her sake because of the incestuous birth, and for his sake because of his horrible deformities.

Their secret had remained intact until five years ago, when Cole Newby raped and strangled Bonnie Connor on the grounds of the Owen house. Willy Owen came outside to stop him, but Bonnie was already dead. Cole fled in terror and burst into his father's house, where Newby, Fellows, and McOllough had just finished playing poker. Cole was so shook up that he blurted out what had happened, that he'd killed Bonnie, dear God he hadn't meant to, and that a monstrous creature had come after him.

The men drove immediately to the Owen house, where they found Karl dragging away the girl's body, apparently to hide it or bury it. Karl broke down and begged for mercy. He confessed that Miss Owen had a son, a retarded brute who had killed the girl without knowing what he was doing. He begged the men to spare Willy's life, saying that if anything happened to him, Miss Owen would not survive the shock.

Of course, Fellows, McOllough, and Newby all knew the truth—that Cole had murdered Bonnie—but they seized on Karl's misunderstanding. Doc Newby was horrified by what his son had done, but he truly believed that Cole was at heart a good boy and that he had acted in the heat of passion. In short, he was prepared to lie to save his son from life imprisonment. Fellows and McOllough were willing to lie, too—for money. They began to blackmail Miss Owen, or, as McOllough called it, "engage in a fair exchange." They would keep their silence and Miss Owen would keep her son. Doc Newby refused to take part in the blackmail scheme. But he was forced to keep quiet about it to protect his son. He sent the boy away.

As for Fellows and McOllough, they collected quarterly pay-offs from Miss Owen's trust fund and went about their daily lives as if nothing were wrong. And, in fact, things went smoothly for them for five years.

Then Annie saw Willy, and Fellows murdered her.

"But we got him," Thomas said grimly. "We got that son of a bitch."

Nora nodded. "Yes. Maybe Annie will rest easier."

After a moment Thomas said, "I've wanted to tell you . . . before all this happened . . . that night at Annie's apartment, when I kissed you I . . . well, it had nothing to do with Annie, I mean, that you're Annie's sister. I was attracted to you. I still am."

"I know." She held his hand. "I feel the same way."

They were quiet for a few moments.

Finally, Thomas said, "So, when are you going back to Cedar Falls?"

"Probably tomorrow. It will be difficult. I still have to tell my parents about Annie." She sighed. "And it sounds as if my business is falling into chaos. I need to get things straightened out before I sell it."

"What? You're selling the flower shop?"

She nodded. "I've received a generous offer, one too good to turn down."

"But I thought you loved that business."

"I used to. Lately, though, it has seemed more like a burden, something that's holding me back."

"Holding you back? From what?"

"I don't know. From whatever else there is."

"After you sell, then what?"

"Well, I was planning on moving out of Cedar Falls." She hesitated. "And then sort of playing it by ear."

"Moving where?" He sounded hopeful.

"Here. I mean, Denver. I guess I was thinking that maybe you and I . . ."

He smiled and gently squeezed her hand. "There's no 'maybe' about it. I was thinking the same thing."